A.E. FORTIN

The Magic Fairy Rose

in the Lowland of Scotland

The History of the MacGregors

BOOK 1

THE MAGIC FAIRY ROSE IN THE LOWLAND
OF SCOTLAND BOOK 1
The history of the MacGregors

ISBN (Paperback): 979-8-89672-000-3
ISBN (Ebook): 979-8-89672-001-0

5830 E 2nd St, Ste 7000 #9983
Casper, WY 82609
USA

CONTENTS

CHAPTERS

CHAPTER ONE

Scotland in 17th Century

IT HAS BEEN a long day, there was still horses up in the hills. It was slow going the rain had been coming down. He was fighting with his thought. Michal wasn't home much neither were ye Ronald. How could he straighten out all these thoughts. When could he sleep his thoughts was like the wind it through me one way. Then it change course and went the other way. Ronald ye had taken too much on. We didn't even know what was happening in the Lowlands of Scotland.

It's hard to work when your grieving. The rocks was slippery, mean time the horses fought to keep their balance. How does our father deal with all of this. Ronald told me what he's been doing, our family been in it all the way back to the 16th century. Right now, he wished he could sleep. That's a laugh, sleep what's that, he should eat but his stomach couldn't take anything.

All most home, will have to see if we can find the missing horses. At last home. "Come boy let me get ye bedded down, ye work hard for me today."

Thomas came into the castle, dad was coming up behind me. He got some cheese and bread. He need a two finger of Scotch. It had burn going down, his throat was raw. He hopes he could sleep tonight. All his mind was think about his brothers.

Then he went to the library, may be reading could put him to sleep. Looks like the Hearts are here. Whatever!

Then a book seemed to jump out at him. He wonders what kind of book was, ye have—cigam. That's a funny name. Wait that word is backward, in the mirror it came out to be magic. So, the title is ye have magic, interesting.

As he came out of the library Just before going around to the back of the castle, he had overheard his parents talking with the Hearts. At first, he thought the subject was his sister and William's sister. They would be turning sixteen and able to marry. The two families were making a list of suitors for the two girls. Why did his parents put William on the top of his sister's list.

Then Thomas heard his name. The Hearts had his name on the top of Eleanor's list. She was like a sister to him…, was she. Then why was she always with him. William felt the same way about Catherine…, did he. Then why was his sister always with William. "Damn it. All this is too much to handle. My head hurts from thinking about all of this at the same time. Everything is all mix up together. I must solve one problem at a time. This knew problem has been there for a while now that Catherine was at the age to marry. Of course, Eleanor's parents thought I should court their daughter. The two of us has been together since we were little. How did all of this come about. It was when the girls didn't want their brother to teach them anything. "We're not going to be here."

Thomas was now in a bad mood. He didn't want to go pass them. Back in the rain, he ran around to the door leaning up to the bedrooms. He took two stairs at a time.

There was a storm building outside and in his mind. In his room a flash of lightning went passed his window. He knew he wasn't going to get much sleep tonight. There was too much on his mind. Another flash of lightning lit his room up. He had closed his door and went over to light a candle. Thomas had gotten undress an put a nightshirt on. He walked over to the window to watch the lightning dance over the land. In the darkened window Thomas saw his reflection. A young man of nineteen stood staring at him. How could things have changed this fast. Tonight, everything that has happen nine months ago until now. His family was giving him too much to think about. If it wasn't the lightning it was his thoughts kept him up.

A memory

William came to him ready to strangle his sister. He chuckle when a memory popped up. They were toddlers, even then the girls didn't want their brothers. He had to show Eleanor how to walk. She would step on his feet and the two of us went down. She had landed on top of him.

When they were older William then said. "Eleanor don't listen to me or dad, Jonathan was out of the picture he had a family of his own."

He knew just how William felt, Catherine was doing it to him. It was his brother's that had wash their hands of instructing their little sister anything. They called her their little wild cat, both brothers made sure they were gone a lot. Then the idea of switching sister's he came up with. William jump at the chance to dump his sister on to me. He had loved the idea of Catherine to teach her how to ride. She listens to him Eleanor don't.

Then the question came back to him. What were their parents thinking of. How could he marry his best friend's little sister. She's not little anymore, Eleanor been by his side for a long time. If that is so why is he fighting not to court her. All he came up with was the promise that he will all ways think of her as his sister. Why would he marry his sister. To him that made a lot of sense. But it didn't tell him what his mother saw in his eyes last spring.

$$*\quad*\quad*$$

No, I'm not finish solving the first problem. Then the lightning filled the sky and as quickly the light hit darkness took back the night. I don't understand why both brothers had to leave the Highlands. Okay think a little bit of one problem then go back later and try to solve then.

It was only nine months since the burial of his sister-in-law and nephew. Four men went missing and two of them were his brothers. The other men were Peter his cousin and William's older brother Jonathan. Why did his two brothers have to leave. What made the other men go with him. He knew Ronald blamed himself for the death of his wife and child. He wanted to be with them. That men was going to be watching for him, they had orders. Ronald wouldn't be coming back home alive.

*　*　*

"Damn it stop this." Lightning had danced across the sky breaking into his thoughts. Thomas watched another flash. This time it made a spider web and lit up the land below. This storm there was a battle against night and day. Each time the darkness took over after the lightning hit. Could that be the same with good and evil.

There were just seven hours until sunrise. Thomas needed to get some rest. He went to bed and snuffed out the candle. He turns away from the window to get some sleep. As he closed his eyes and drift off to sleep. His dream turn into a nightmare of Marian's accident. His thoughts wanted to solve this problem. In his dream he could hear the man who found his sister-in-law. Something wasn't right about this man's voice. Those thoughts dance through his mind. It didn't help when he overheard his father. Michael said they killed her because Ronald wouldn't go vote their way. The three men thought this was no accident, the wood was sought into its part way. The man had been playing with his father and brother.

Even Marian said she couldn't stop the horse, something spooked him. That's when the wheel had hit the rock, and the buggy broke away.

It had flipped the buggy over on top of her. That man had asked why she was driving that buggy alone in the first place. The man was trying to make them feel guilty. Thomas thought he was making it as if we had caused the accident.

That had infuriated Michael, he thought that man was part of why Marian had died. He was only giving bits and pieces of what happen. His father had gone and try to explain why everyone was out on rounding up the horses. Now Thomas woke up when the thought of his father trying to defend his family.

He had said Marian was going to stay home. The one who brought her the note said her mother was hurt and calling for her. How would he known that her mother was calling for her. Did he read the note. When Marian went to the barn to get the buggy, it was ready to go. She didn't think nothing was wrong, with no one around. She assuming the same person who had brought the note had hitched up the buggy. Marian was five months pregnant, she climbed aboard and set out for her mother's place.

That Good Samaritan who had found Marian had explained. "Marian's accident was deliberate. He had seen it unfold, something had spooked her horse. The buggy had broken away leaving Marian unable to control the buggy. The wheel hit a boulder flipping the buggy over on top of her. By the time he was able to get the buggy off her, Marian was in labor. How could he not be able to turn that buggy over, he was a big man.

Ronald made it back in time to be in the room when his son was born. He knew his son was going to die. His little lungs wasn't develop enough. He was holding his son when he took his last breath. Ronald knew his wife was not long for this earth. Thomas had no idea how to help his brother. He just ran out of the castle to the bench in the rose garden. What had scared him, that was the question he had.

Thomas knew the moment Marian had passed away. In his dream, he heard that bloodcurdling scream once again. This time it was the thunder. He could hear the rain come pouring down as it hit his window. How could Ronald bear it, he didn't. He knew that the men would be watching for him, he went back there to die.

Thomas thoughts had all most solved that problem. But the first problem came back, what would he do if he took a wife. They wanted the MacGregor's men to die out, if he took a wife and it happened to him, what would he do.

Okay that question came back, what did his mother see in his eyes. He was up then down and now his thoughts drove him out of bed. Once again he lit the candle and went back to the window. In the days following Marian and his nephew's death, he often stood with Ronald. He didn't chastise him from running that day, he didn't have to. Thomas had done it for him, he was still doing it. Why did he run when his brother needed him. He knew it had to be the raw pain, which was in his brother's eyes. That was what had struck him. Thomas couldn't get a grasp on himself. It was too much to see all that rib pain coming from his brother. This man he looked up to him. He had to run he never had to deal with death. When his grandparents died, he was too young to remember. Now not much could scare him, but that night did. He knew he could fight a man. When ye fight with a man that was different. It would be to save someone's life that he cared for. To see the one person, he cared about who he loved die. Because of evil, this man wanted our family name to be wiped out, but why. Thomas had always seen Ronald as a strong, stoic hero. The death of Marian and their baby had devastated his brother. How could he ever hope to deal with such a loss himself.

His eyes

There was that question, what did his mother saw in his eyes. Would that tell him why his name was put on Eleanor's list. He had to try to bring what had happen to her that spring.

His mind tried to block what had happened, he slammed his fist into the wood. "Damn it. I must remember, I can't back down this time. I know mamma wants me to court her but why."

He told himself to think of Eleanor when she was catching two fishes. That day was when the fish were running. She looked sexy, how she try to get him to look at her top. I did… she had change her blouse, it was cut lower than before. That he had enjoyed watching her as she moved around him, I wish her breast would fall out. He never had feelings for her in that way.

The promise he made with his best friend, her brother held him back. What he liked the most her hiking up her skirt, on each leg. But on that time, his little friend took notice of all her goodies.

Thomas chuckle his little friend, wasn't little and that had fix him. He had to go deeper in the water to make him go away. Did he hear her giggle if she had then she knew he liked what he saw. Eleanor caught two fish that she was fixing for them. She had tried to get the fire going with no luck. She knew how to start a fire. Calling him over to her she was setting a trap for him. May be things would have change but didn't have a chance. That's when he heard her scream, one that drove a cold shiver up his back. He was walking out of the water from there he was running as fast as he could. She was in trouble that's when he saw the black bear. He had his dirk out and was stabbing the bear in his back. That bear just slam me with his clause across his chest. Nothing help to get him off her, that big paw with long nails. Hit her back she tried to protect her head and face, she turned to protect her breast. He claw her legs then hit her into the rock. There was so much blood.

This part was a little fuzzy to him. Everything he did seem to go in slow motion. The bear had hit her again across her arm and back, spinning her around. She screamed again, for a moment their eyes met. He saw the fear in her eyes. Her arms came up to block another blow.

He remember screaming at the bear, trying to get him to look his way. He had stabbed the bear, nothing had changed his mind. For a moment, the bear looked at me.

Eleanor try to get away, but he hit her slamming her into the boulder knocking her out. It cut her forehead deeply. There was so much blood coming from her body, fear of losing her went through his mind. Could that be the clue to find out what his mother saw.

Didn't he go a little mad, he remembered not caring what happen to him. All he knew he had to get that damn bear away from her. He had thrust his dirk into the bear side. The bear hit him across his chest, he remember not caring. He had his attention, the bear was moving slower. He had to get to that injury on top of his head. It gave him time to jump on his back, his dirk help him to climb the bears back. This bear wanted to hurt someone, he didn't want the fishes that was hanging in the tree. He wanted revenge for the pain that was on top of his head.

Thomas didn't care about his injuries this bear must die. He didn't care if he die, but she had to live that drove him up the bear's back. That bear swung him from side to side. His claws cut him each time he was in reach. Once at the top the bear bit him, he kicked him to let him go. He had one chance to get his dirk in that spot. He took it and pushed down as far as he could. He had all his strength going to his dirk, still the bear wouldn't die. Now he pulled back on his dirk to open the cut more. He pulled opening it more until he fell and died. Thomas had to get his leg out from under him. He was a live he knew he was hurt. It was all about her she came first.

For a moment he thought a lot of this, that bear should had been dead. Then he thought, magic had been there, that was what kept the bear going. If he had cross over who ever did that to them wanted them dead.

When he open his eyes, he was looking into the darken glass. What he saw was his brother's eyes. No this can't be, those eyes were his. That's what mamma saw in his eyes. She don't want me to miss out, of having a life with Eleanor.

Today he had found out that Duncan wasn't back yet. That mean they have four weeks to wait for him. That is enough time to find out if there is something between them.

He found magic

Unexpectedly he waved his hand. The question he had was is he in love with Eleanor. Thomas felt dizzy he held on to the window cell. He had close his eyes when he open them he saw Eleanor washing herself. She was naked and was very beautiful, those breasts he wanted to touch. She had a nice figure and pussy. Oh, he had gotten it, when his little friend took notice. How could he see her. Then she saw him and went to the corner of her room. Eleanor didn't scream she just looked him over. Thomas didn't know how he got to her room. But he was here with her, did he go back in time for she should have been sleeping.

Could this be his chance to find out if he could be in love with her. He had decided to let her see him. Slowly he took off his nightshirt and let it drop on the floor. She had put her hands to her side and his friend loved what he saw. Thomas notice her nipples, she liked what she saw.

When he took a breath his friend moved. She had gave a little giggle, for her cheeks was pink and she had a big smile on her face. He wonder if she would let him touch and kiss her. He saw her head move, did she hear him. Another nod of her head. Now to go over to her, he went slow just inches from her.

Eleanor took his hand and place it on her breast. Both of his hands cup her breast, her nipple cry to be sucked. He wanted this then he kissed her lips softly his tounge went over her lips. She open and he took her mouth in a hungery kiss. He wanted to touch her pussy and finger fuck her.

He had to know what it would do to the two of them. As he kissed her his hand ran down her leg and over the inside. He found her pussy then her lips, now the opening to her pussy. She wanted this and pushed him inside her heat.

Eleanor held his finger until her body had all the pleasure from what he had done. Thomas push back her hand and started to move inside her. She came again and he was kissing her, every part of her body reacted to him. When she touch his heat, his head went backwards he had sucked in air. She smiled and both hands touch his chest. Her hands went up to his neck and round him. She then kissed him, he reacted to her. By putting his heat between her legs. He took hold of his heat and rubbed over her lips never to go inside her pussy.

Eleanor push him backwards and led him to her bed. She made him sit on her bed then went between his legs. She took hold of his heat and wrapped her mouth around it. He wanted to put a finger in her pussy but went for her nipple. He had a hand on her head, then he spoke. "Don't let him go deep in your mouth he will."

When he came she took his seed and swallow. He got up and made her sit, he laid her back and put her legs on his shoulder. She felt his tounge moving in her pussy. He made her cum and sip on her nectar. He pulled her to him and kissed her.

In his mind, he told her. "I'm going to court ye, I like what I see in ye. I'm going to start clearing my land. Would ye, like to help me. That first week will see how it's goes. I know now we won't keep our hands off each other. I will get ye ready for my heat. Ask mamma for something that will stop ye from getting with my child.

Don't tell your mother, she can't keep a secret. He had to go for if he didn't. She would have his seed in her pussy. He grabbed his nightshirt and put it on. One more kiss and touch of her breast. I'll see ye soon, I didn't realize I was in love with ye. I'm taking care of that promise between your brother and me. The promise had worked, it kept me away from ye. You're not going to those parties unmarried."

Then he wave his hand, and he was in his room. He went back to bed, did it really happen. He had to say yes, the taste of her pussy was still on his lips. He did know how long he would be able to keep away from her body. He wanted to see her again.

Eleanor was on her bed she cried out in her mind. "Thomas, I want ye for my husband. I have felt this way for ye for a while. I don't want no other man's cawk inside me. My pussy and my body, hungers now for ye. Please make me your mate, I love ye."

* * *

Thomas remembered his father took his side. But his mother new what he felt for her. What she had spoken she was right. Mamma believe that they should court the girls before they leave. They're leaving in four weeks, this should give the young men enough time. They're not little boys they are men. Once they cross over. They must stop thinking of them as their little sister or just a little girl. Our son must think of her as a woman. May be they will find out, that they their true loves.

Thomas wanted to be with her. "If he have's magic, I will have to watch myself. I had a taste of her sweetness and the feel of all her toys. She wasn't afraid of me, she knew he wouldn't get her with child then leave her.

He wanted to see if William loved his sister. "William do ye have conflicting feelings for Catherin. Old friend here is a gift. I'll take ye back a bit in time. When my sister was washing herself. Careful old friend it's not a dream what ye touch his her. fine out if ye are in love with Catherin. Good Luck.

"Tomorrow after lunch we must talk, Uncle Donald would like to get started in four weeks. He had sent Duncan ahead to find the first town in which they will stay. It will be enough time to see if Catherin could be the one."

What Ronald did

Thomas closed his eyes, one thing to figure out. "Ronald, I have done what ye asked of me. Uncle Donald and Duncan, William will also be going with me to find ye."

He had waved his hand and thought of his brother talking to Michael. This is what he heard. "Thank ye for coming. Michael ye know how I feel about the death of Marion and my son. I'm not one to take my own life. Ye know I need to go back to the talks. However, those men will be waiting for me, along with the man who order the hit on my wife. I want to get some pay back and send them to be judge by the Lord."

Michael didn't want that. "Ronald I would do anything for ye. Let me fight with ye we can take them down together."

He saw Ronald had taken a breath. "No…! ye are going to have your first child. I want ye to find those other men. Thank ye for taking down the once that killed my wife and son. I'm going to have Thomas to come and find my body. I want to be with my wife and son. I don't want to do this to ye or Thomas. Ye know our sister is of an age to marry. The two of us knows he love's Eleanor. Our brother is a strong man, he may get mad at us. I know he will figure out all of this.

Thank ye for keeping your marriage a secret. That note, told me he would go after your wife if he knew about her. After we buried my wife and son the Lord called to me. I must take down all those evil men. I have asked Jonathan and Peter to come here, it must be this way. I don't want ye in the fight I want ye to only safe my body.

*   *   *

Ronald greeted the men. "Jonathan and Peter thank ye for coming here today. I know what ye are going through. Ye don't like your son seeing ye that way. Ye were about to give your wife another child. I want to know if ye like to go with me, to take more of those men down. Like myself you're not one to take your own life. I must go back to the talks, that evil man wants the MacGregor's name to die out. He's been taking out anyone who would go against him in the talks. I don't know who he is. There has been families, who has been wiped out of the pictures.

"Peter your health is not that good, it been hard to watch your twin courting someone. I ask ye, would ye, join me to take down those men who killed my wife and son. I will leave here in three days. Those men will be waiting for me. I know ye wouldn't take your own life. Us Scotts are proud people we rather, die in battle then weather away.

"Michael, ye know that I'm not coming back. I don't want ye with me. What I want is for ye to save my body. If they come with me save their bodies also. I told ye where there is a safe place. Jonathan and Peter, ye heard me what I said. It's up to the two of ye if ye come or not. If ye do ye know what will happen this is up to ye both.

"I have talked with Thomas. I asked him to come and find me. He will have a lot to think about. If ye come with me Jonathan n your brother will go with Thomas. Peter ye know Duncan will go with them. If ye are going, be here on the third day after today."

*   *   *

Thomas now knows why Jonathan and Peter their cousin was going with him. Aye… they are grate fighters but the two of them can't last for long. He have a feeling this man wouldn't play fair. No…, Jonathan and Peter didn't want to die the way they were going. The men ye were up against, did ye know that they were hired killers.

"He figured out that Peter was taking Michael's place. Ye had asked him to safe your bodies and find these men. He understand now what ye said about Michael. That I don't have to worry about getting married. Did ye stand with our brother when he got married. I hope so.

That is why he was gone a lot, he had gotten married. "Ye sent Hauk to pick up the three bodies. Then he went after that man that started all of this. Ye wanted him to pay for what he had done to your family. Did ye know, I would feel Michael's grief. I can imagine what it was like to watch ye die. Ronald ye were the best fighter around. Ye knew they were coming after ye. If the three of us were together we could have taken them down. Instead ye kept Michael and I away from the three of ye. I had felt something was wrong,

Ronald did ye have to called to Michael. No...! us brothers saw what was happening to ye. I felt the anger from our brother, those men were going to burn ye alive. I remember it was dark that night. Did he have to use his ability to see in the dark to save the bodies. Our brother got to took down the once ye couldn't.

*   *   *

"Damn it! Ye set me up, ye saw my eyes like mamma did. Ye knew our parents would want me to court Elenor. Ye let me think our parents only care about the MacGregor's name. Did the two of ye knew I would go through this courtship. Ronald did ye know about the magic."

Scared

I don't know if I can manage seeing ye dead ones I find your bodies. I wasn't strong enough to help ye when I saw the fear and pain in your eyes. Ye knew I was strong enough because I have gone through it once before. I pray to the Lord that I will be able to help ye now.

"Ronald ye knew, I would be all right. What ye saw in my eyes, I saw in yours. Ye knew they wouldn't live, but Eleanor was a strong woman. Did the two of us talk in our dreams as we healed. I didn't know that Eleanor was always with me. When I ran she follow me. She sat down next to me and patted her lap. She was my salvation. When my arms went around her I couldn't let her go.

The talk with Ronald

Then the lightning had another fight with darkness, it started to down pore. The wind was pushing the rain into the glass. His brother wouldn't let his mind rest. Now he was remembering the talk they had. He had to tell me why he had to leave the Highlands. Thomas had to close his eyes. The day was sunny the earth was wet from the rain the night before. His brother's mind seems to be far away. Could he be thinking of his wife.

Unexpectedly he started talking. "Thomas, I feel so guilty I should have been here. Then they wouldn't have gone after my wife and unborn son. They did a good job setting it up. Michael told me that he had scents that magic was involved. That wagon went right over that big rock. What better way to cut into that bord? Then when she went by him, he could spook the horse. With magic he could make sure the wheel hit that rock. Why did Ronald have to get involve with the government.

Because there are bad men out there trying to take over our country. For many years, the MacGregor's men have been fighting for Scotland's government. My duty was also to my country. Men—women have already paid a big price for their freedom and so have I."

Then Ronald looked off in the distant. "Little brother ye may be the youngest male in this family. There are things that I'm going to put ye through. I want ye to remember ye are a strong fighter. Ye are the best swordsman around the Highlands. Ye can throw a dirk and hit what ye throw it at. Ye could out throw Michael and me. Dad said ye are just like granddad's brother. He was call Eagle-eyes like ye are. Little brother I hope ye will understand this part. I have unfinished business and will be leaving soon. Thomas there are things that I'm asking ye and Michael to do for me.

Please when he comes home our brother will be hurting. I won't be there to help him. Ye two must bond together and be there for each other. Michael don't know how to be the oldest. He will have to learn as he goes. Help him out, you're the key to all of this."

*   *   *

Then Ronald saw a magnificent golden eagle overhead. "Little brother, do ye see that eagle?"

Thomas remember nodding his head yes. "Aye… I enjoy watching those magnificent eagles."

His brother looked at him. "Ye would say those eagles are free to fly were ever they like. When that eagle takes a mate, he don't have to share her with anyone.

He could see the expression on Ronald's face had gone serious. "Ye must know that us Highlanders, at one time couldn't have the one we married first. Grandfather had to go to battle so he could have his woman for himself. Back then the Nobles would take their woman that they had just married to bed first. She had to let the Nobles have her even though to her he was raping her.

"It took us until 1603 to unite the two crowns of Scotland and England. There was a lot of fighting even then. I remember when dad was a part of that. By the very end of the 1690, dad had enough with the fighting, being the oldest I took over for him. I remember stories that dad told us about how granddad lost his brother in one of those battles. Little-brother because of those men we now have the United Kingdom of Great Britain and Northern Ireland.

In this time frame we're trying to form the two countries and give them their governments. Thomas, it took us this long, and here it is 1707. I'm afraid that there will be a fight... even now. Can ye not understand why we are fighting so hard for our freedom. Don't ye remember the stories that our father and grandfather told us as boys. Thomas the MacGregor's has had their hands in how the future of Scotland would be shaped."

Then there was the question that his brother asked him. "What do ye see when ye look out over the horizon."

Through the rain Thomas looked over the land. He remembered that his answer didn't please him. "Ronald, I don't know much about the outside. I know of the land and the beauty around us. I never seen the outside of are family land and the town. The stories dad told us, I didn't understand. Back then I was working hard on my skills. Tell me what ye see.

Thomas remember standing in the garden with his older brother. Ronald's words burned in his memory. He remembers watching his brother looked over the family land. His brother's voice softened, and he spoke. "I see the land of Scotland, to me the land is a virgin. There are parts Scotland that know man hasn't place a mark on her."

Thomas heard the passion and pain pouring through Ronald's voice. He felt ashamed not to know what his brother knew as he watched him surveyed the land. While his brother spoke, He could feel how important this was to him. "We are playing a very serious game, these evil men will try to stop any MacGregor from helping our people.

Ye see the land is the prize. We are fighting to see who will claim her first. Their trying everything to stop us, to force us out. Evil is working very hard to claim the land and people.

We Scots are proud people we are not sheep. They can't lead us around and use us as slaves. But still they try. Ye know many men, women have given their lives. Right now, all over Scotland we have held ourselves back from indulging our rights. We should not relinquish our privilege to have our legal system. We Scots are working to retain our entitlement to have our own Church. We need to teach and give our children the kind of education that we see fit to give. They are trying to wipe out everything we believe in. When ye takeout the history of Scotland, ye can change the people the way they want ye to think."

Thomas wonder how many times history will repeat itself. He has his own land, he can fight to keep what he has. What his brother was telling him that these men will come here if we let them. Now he knew what he must do. When he is away, he will learn what his brother is telling him. Any stories and old person tells him he will listen to them. He will see what is out there. Thomas has the ones that will go with him. He has everything is in motion.

Getting to know Eleanor again

It's time for him to court Eleanor. The rain had stopped, soon it will be sunrise. There was still a lot to think about. Last night when I went to Eleanor, I was think about all her tops. She wanted me to see what she had, that her breast were big that he could touch. Even back then, I wanted to touch them. It was nice to hold them in my hands. I liked when she started to touch me. It feels like a dream, but her sweetness of her flower was on my lips.

When us two boys, switch sisters. When would we realize, we taught them everything we knew and like. She knew I wouldn't hurt her. When she kissed me back she knew how to get my blood boiling. My little friend took notice, he was ready to do his part. It was hard to rain him in. When he shut down my brain. The only thing that kept him under control. was the fear of getting her with my child. He couldn't take what he had seen back then again. She knew his brother eyes scare him. Stell she came after him.

Thomas went back to bed, he snuffs out the candle and laid on his back. He closed his eyes and thought of Eleanor, what was it when he ran from the castle. She came after him and he remembers not being afraid to show her how he was feeling. No, he must go back farther. Last year the two of them was always together. There were things about her what were they. He had noticed her breast were bigger. Aye… I like that very much. Then he remembers the promise to William to always call her his little sister. That had killed a lot of feelings about Eleanor. I must take that out of the picture. What else did he like about her, she was wearing her hair down for him. Sometimes he would help her down from her horse. She always made sure that he could smell her hair. The scent was of roses even her skin had that scent, and it was soft to the touch. He found out that he liked to hold her around her waist.

All right I must keep going. At the riverside when they were fishing. Eleanor always got right in the water with him. Now he could see her hike up her skirt. She had long legs that looked to be strong. His thoughts were going where he never let himself go. If she were on her back, what would happen if she grabbed him around the waist with those legs.

That did it, that thoughts he had kept at bay has popped up—literally. He had gotten out of bed and walked over to the window. But why did he stop thinking any farther. What did he feel when he thought that way. Thomas looked down at himself his friend was growing. He remember going into the cool water that day, so she didn't see him. After his friend was gone to sleep. I'm just going over everything. "Damn it… go to sleep, I need to tell my parents my decision.

He knew what happened to the bear, that part he has already gone over. What did he feel when he looked at her body. There was so much blood when he ran to her. His thoughts were please don't die.

Then he told himself stop thinking do what ye know. He ripped his sleeve off his arm so he could clean her up. One of the pans he use to get water to see how bad the wound was. He knew it was bad, with the other sleeve he made a bandage. Then he went to make something to carry her in. He use the rest of his shirt to tie the branches together. Carefully he laid her on the cot he made. Thomas dragged that cot for a long time.

How far was he away from the castle, it was over three miles. That part didn't madder to him.

When he got home his brothers tried to take her in. He remembered yelling at them. "Stop right there. I'll bring her into the castle. Michael get Grana she really hurt."

Then he saw his mother. He rambled his words out what his mother needed to know. "She was attack by a bear, the cuts are deep mamma. What room do ye want me to lay her in.

She had told me to take her to the room across from me. All that time his brother and father walked behind him. At last, he got her to the bed. "Mamma don't worry about me. Just take care of Eleanor. I don't know what I would do without her in my life."

They had come full circle, now to find out could they make it as husband and wife.

*   *   *

Thomas knew he couldn't sleep, it was sunrise. After getting dressed he took the candle and made his way down the hallway to the back door. Ones outside he made his way to the rose garden. By the light of the candle, he saw shadows coming toward him. It was a mouse running for his life. He didn't stop just kept running past Thomas. The other shadow was their barn cat. He was trailing just three leaps behind the mouse.

He walked to the bench in his mother's rose garden, where he would watch the sunrise. The light from the sun had slowly taken over the night. The ghostly shadows of the night were being chased back. It was dreamy to watch the sunlight push back the darkness. In the fields when the light hit, a small herd of large red deer was lurking in the shadows of the night.

The grief of losing three family members was heavy on his mind. Thomas knew Ronald would never hunt these majestic creatures again. "Would that also be Michael's fate. No… Michael would give Ronald his promise, to find those other men that is in volve with these killers. At first, he was so angry with Michael, but thinking about all of this.

Ronald must have had this plan out. What he didn't know was they would come after his wife and unborn child. That's why Michael kept his wife out of the picture. Ronald put a lot on both of our shoulders. Why was I feeling, Michael left me with all of this. Because I haven't cross over to man hood. Didn't Ronald tell me he will make me grow up faster. A tear rolled down his cheek. Quickly He brushed it away. "I'm not a baby to give into tears like this, not again. Am I not going to take Eleanor for my wife. I want more of her and her sweet toys."

*　*　*

Thomas thought he would look back to see if he missed anything of what Ronald had said. That day he had turned and faced me. It must have shown in Thomas's expression. That he didn't understand what he was talking about. He spoke, "I see that this history lesson is boring to ye. Little brother. Damn it," Thomas remember he had made a fist, "I can't call ye that anymore. After we leave ye will be going over this of what ye must do. Brother, I know ye will figure everything out. Ones ye do that ye will be stepping into man hood."

Then Ronald stopped and bent his head down. "I can't call ye little brother anymore. Thomas ye will all ways be Michael and my little brother. What I'm about to ask ye to do for me, will change every part of your life. Everything granddad, dad, and I have done is for our people. Somehow, I know ye will add your part to it also. We wouldn't have our history to tell our children. Thomas it will even affect your children. One day ye will tell them of what their grandfather and their uncle did for them. Scot's dream of issuing our banknotes. We may or may not get that right. All of this is necessary for the growth of Scotland. "Thomas one day soon ye will understand what I'm telling ye. There will come a time when ye will look over the horizon and be able to see the whole picture. It is not just the land… it is the people who live and work in Scotland. That is why I must go. This way the death of my wife and only son will not be in vain. Do ye understand a little of what I say to ye Thomas."

CHAPTER TWO

Eleanor being with him

TIME HAD SLIPPED away from him. He had his hands over his eyes remembering those days with Ronald. The sun was fully out now. Thomas felt a gentle hand on his head. He knew that touch was Eleanor as she brushed his hair. He didn't think but just act. His arms went around her waist pulling her closer to him. His cheek pressed under her breast as he held her.

He must tell his parents he will court her. Every part of his body wanted her, I want her for my wife. To have time to get to know each other's body. "Eleanor did something happen in your bedroom."

She smiled and came down to kiss him. Thomas brought her to set on his lap. "Do you know how much I want to make love to ye. I'm so tired my little brane wants me to take ye now. I can't let him, those men will come here after ye. I all most lost ye once I can't lose ye. Then he thought I will touch her. I want to bine her to him, he took her mouth in a hungery kiss. His hand went to her pussy and inside her wet lips. He moved in her until she came. "You're mine I did this to tell ye I will marry ye."

Thomas wanted this and put his finger in his mouth. "It wasn't a dream, I was with ye last night. I want ye to have mamma get ye on something, to stop ye from getting pregnant. I want to mate with ye and give ye my seed. I want to play with my toys. I don't want to sleep by myself anymore."

Eleanor touch his face and ran a finger over his lips. "I would have waited for ye. I'm glad I'm going to be your wife. Last night when I saw ye, I thought it was a dream. When ye let me see your body, I wanted to touch ye. I wanted those strong arms to hold me. Your hands my breast hunger to be touch. The pleasure ye gave me, I wanted more. But ye stopped and your friend wanted my pussy. I want to know what it was like to do what I had done. Then ye took your tongue to my pussy, my body tried to get away. But my bottom had no place to go.

"That day the bear attack me, I saw what ye did for me. I knew ye liked what ye saw. Off and on I open my eyes that bear tour into your skin. Ye pulled me to your home, all that time I called to ye. I thought I was going to lose ye. Ye took so long to wake up."

She was so tender with him, her hand felt so good. He knew if she kept doing this he would go to sleep. "Thomas last night ye was trying to figure out what Ronald want ye to do for him."

"Eleanor all a long I taught ye to speak your mind to me. I showed ye a lot of things, I like and don't like. I was so please that ye didn't scream when I showed ye my body. I like when ye took my hand and place it were ye wanted me.

*　　*　　*

"My love we are going to be lovers. What I need to tell ye, why your brother went with my brother. He had called for Michael to tell him he wants him to come with him. But not to fight with him. I heard what he told Jonathan and Peter. He told them the men that killed his wife, Michael took care of them. But the men who had my wife killed. He will be waiting for Ronald, ye know that your brother was dying a slow death. The same with Peter. All three men wouldn't take their own life it's not the Scottish way. They would rather die in battle them wither away. Michael is to save the bodies and take them to a safe place. Everything has been done up to this point. My job will is to find them and learn about Scotland. There is a lot I do not know. I'm asking my parents for two years. If I can come to ye I will. Uncle Donald is going to take us around the Highlands. Your job will be to pretend you're not married. I'm going to have mamma go with ye. I have a bad feeling something is going to happen. Ye must play the game. I can't have anything happen to ye. I wouldn't be able to live without ye."

Eleanor knew this was hard to tell her this. "I had a bad feeling when he said goodbye to each of us. My mother is so mean she didn't believe his wife was pregnant. His best friend been helping him out. He was enjoying making love to her just trying to get her pregnant. She wanted another baby, he gave her one. He asked his best friend to watch over her and the ranch. He knew she would turn to him.

"I forgot that William got up he said he was going to court Catherin. It's like he knew ye was going to court me. Mamma said to have us over here. William told her no. If we do this it will be over Thomas home. Ye hounded Jonathan everyone knew before he even asked her."

With a wave of his hand all the things that need to be done was done. I want ye to go get some clothes with William also. I will not have us go through that. Your mother can't keep a secret. I will ask my parents if we could court ye here at the castle. Soon I will start touching ye, ye been having lessons with mamma."

Eleanor enjoyed sitting on his lap. "Yes, my mother hasn't been teaching me nothing. The test I fail, I want out of that house."

Thomas liked her in his arms, she giggled because his little friend was close to her pussy. "Honey I'm sorry he has a mind of his own. He tries to shut down the brain I think with. I was so happy ye took control of him."

She touch his face, and he looked at her. "I can feel him my pussy tingling, being this close makes, me want ye."

Thomas knew how to please her, he need something to hind them. A wave of his hand there was a bubble around them. Another wave his finger got a little bigger around. "Here take care of my little friend."

Thomas got her moving over his heat. He went for her pussy. In his mind he heard Thomas they will see us. He told her. No, I took care of that. I'm going to get ye ready for me.

When she came his finger got bigger. One of her hands held his heat the other grabbed his kilt. Her body came each time he got bigger. One last time he made it bigger, this time he came with her. He wave his hand she was clean. He went for his finger to take her sweetness. Then he clean himself up.

He kissed her." Ye do know I'm bonded to ye. Ye are also bonded to me. I will not let ye go to these parties without my seed inside ye... Damn it, I want ye for my wife. I hunger to be one with ye. Ye already knew what I want, how to take care of me. Now ye show me as my wife ye know sex is a big part of the marriage. A man who enjoy making love to ye, when his little friend want's her he will go for her. Please if ye don't get enough pleasure tell me right off. It too easy to go wham bam thank ye. He kissed her, "Wow..., when I crossed over, I knew right off ye was mind and I'm yours."

*　　*　　*

They stood up then he saw the eagle. He heard the cry of a golden eagle, he was flying overhead. In his mind he called to Ronald. "Are ye free now. Did ye send me this eagle to tell me it's over with, are ye save." The feeling that came back to him it's not all over with. The bodies was safe.

He bent his head then spoke. "Eleanor when Ronald was still here, he gave me this talk. No... it was more of a lesson. I didn't understand why the entire talk was about Scotland, I know now. At the time there was an eagle overhead. Now there is another eagle, I think I will take it as a sign. That our brothers are dead. They knew what was going to happen when they went back.

"From the time they had left I've haven't been able to sleep. The dreams shown me of men fighting, it was dark and rainy that night. Ronald and the others had died on that night. There was this group of men who will stop them any way they can. Our cousin Peter went with them, he is the same age as Michael. If Peter were not a McKinnon, I would believe he was Michael's twin brother. I don't understand why those two went along until now. Ronald said he had plans for Michael. He wants him to find those men and take them down. Michael is the best shot around the Highlands.

It's hard to believe that their gone. The three knew this was the way they wanted to die. Sickness robs their body a little bit at a time. One moment they feel fine, then it hits ye hard and takes a little more of yourself. They knew what they were walking into. Evil was there and while they took down the evil men. A demon was laughing at them. He couldn't get his way, for a brother saved their bodies.

What better way to die, than in a fight of their choosing? There were things that Ronald said that didn't make sense to me. He said that Michael had found his sweet love and fallen in love with her. I believe that our parents don't know about this. Ronald said they were going to make sure that Michael stayed out of this skirmish.

"Eleanor, if I'm right. Michael will be taking over where Ronald left off. These evil men must die. He could have told Michael he must come after them, only after a few hours had passed. This would make sure their bodies would be buried in a safe place, until I come after them. Every time I saw them talking, I went over to listen. After their bodies are safe. Michael will be going after the men who gave the orders for their deaths.

"I wonder if three brothers could feel each other's pain. That night Michael was afraid for Ronald. If he was able to see the battle, he knew right off when to go. As he rode down the road rage felled him. Evil thinks nothing of the people. That night evil almost die.

He knew Ronald didn't want to have his life saved. He had to take down those evil men. When he got to Ronald, I saw a big fire. Michael stop them from burning Ronald alive. That was the anger I felt, he was shooting his arrows as fast as he could. Michael had taken down the men that Ronald couldn't. I'm so tired of these nightmares, I haven't gotten much sleep. I sorry I just can't stop talking."

*   *   *

Eleanor stayed quiet and let him talk. She try not to cry. Didn't she see her brother get stabbed in the back. She knew that he was having a hard time also. It was hard not to cry, tears came rolling down. Then he heard sniffling and looked at his bride to be. "Eleanor come here honey, let me hold ye."

She try hard not to make a scene. She about ran into his arms. He pulled her close to him. As he brushed her hair with his hand. The tears rolled down his shirt, "I'm sorry honey, I guess we both had watch them die. It was hard for Michael I saw him hold Ronald, he was the last man standing. I hate this, but we will get through this."

She had remember how cold her mother was. "I tried to tell mamma, she just brush me off. No kind of emotion for the loss of her oldest. My sister-in-low after he left she went to her mother's place."

Thomas then kissed her. "I'll send ye home have your brother bring your horse to the breeding pen."

She was so worried about him, she wanted to help. "This is nice how about ye go over by the tree, ye can close ye eyes for a little while."

Thomas sat on his heels and looked at this young woman. He thought, how in hell does Eleanor always know when I need her the most. "Ye are getting your clothes dirty from the wet soil."

She gave him a little giggle, quickly she had a comeback. "Thomas ye know that is why they call them work clothes."

He just looked at her and shook his head. He couldn't stop himself from yawning. He had to rub his eyes to stay awake. "Eleanor ye know the story about these rose bushes. Ye also know how my mother's garden got so big. It is my turn to bring her a rose bush home. I'm so tired I can't stop thinking or talking."

Eleanor took his hand and led him to the tree. She sat down on the ground and pat her lap. "Thomas come here and put your head right here, I'll brush your hair."

It hit him hard, all his strength was gone. "Eleanor I shouldn't do this."

But he laid down and put his head on her lap. "If anyone say different I will tell them I'm going to be Thomas bride."

She just wants me to rest. "My love ye can't say anything like that. The people that will know is my parents and your father. I think I will ask Donald to marry us four. Ye smell so good, I know when ye can sleep with me. I will feel so good, I will be at last hold because ye are with me.

"I don't know who will kill that evil man. Damn that man! He had Marian killed. If they know about me. They could kill my bride to be. Her mother can't know she will blab to everyone. I don't want to think about that bear. Oh… that man he must be a demon he hurt that bear. That's why I couldn't kill him right off."

*   *   *

Thomas hand went under her skirt. He felt her warm leg. "When I marry her and take her clothes off I'll have her wrap her legs around me. Then she can put my heat inside her, I will move in her as her back to the wall."

Thomas thought his finger was big but not as big as his heat. He moved to the inner part of her leg. Then up to her pussy, she's wet for me. That's good I want that pussy, I got to get her ready for my heat. Got to move between those wet lips. There I'm in, I feel her pussy bone. I got to open it more, there I can slide in and out. A little more to widen her for me. I want to feel me pumping her pussy. Eleanor had come. He had just let his finger stay there. I smell pussy, huh.

Thomas woke up, he looked around and notice where his hand was, and finger was. Right then he pulled his hand out. He saw how big his finger was and put in his mouth. He shook his head and looked at her face. "Why didn't ye stop me."

She smile at him. "Ye was asleep, all ye want is to be one with me. Would ye wake me up if I had your heat in my mouth. I was getting ye to cum."

He kissed her and made love to her mouth. "Did I at less give ye pleasure."

Her eyes were dreamy, "Do ye know a man could drown in your eyes and be happy doing so."

I know that promise to William will have to go, it keeps me in check. I never really looked at her face closely, I did last night. I love her long golden-brown hair when she lets it down. She always smells of roses and her skin is so soft. Aye… her breast is bigger now. I like touching them. To look into those bluest green eyes and let her be witch me. Her lips are the shape of a heart, it says her name. Her kiss is like honey. Her flower is sweet, and I enjoyed sipping on her nectar. Wow… when I crossed over, I slipped into her arms and claimed her as his mate.

*　*　*

Now he was looking into her eyes. "Woman ye have brought me to my knees. I can't think of ye as my little sister. Not when I had your nectar, and my finger was in your pussy. Ye are mine I will have ye. I will take your virginity and give ye my seed. Ye will have my name and know you're my wife. When if I still have magic I will try to come to ye. Some time it may be a dream. Ye will know I had given ye my seed. Don't go off what mamma gave ye. For what would drew me back, it ye and your pussy.

"I like calling ye my love. Ye will live here in the castle. Ye will help mamma with her people that she has. If your mother can't have feelings for her patience. Mamma and Grana will that them away.

Eleanor went into his arms she felt safe. "I want ye to tell me what ye dream of. I think once we are one. Together are dreams will tell us what to do. I know that ye heard me last night. At times call to me and I will answer ye. We must make that strong. If ye need help I will come to ye.

Then Thomas pulled her away from him. He took her hand and kiss the back of it. The rose scent was there. Her skin was so soft. "Ye said that ye have to go now." He had found that he watched a tear run down her cheek. Then he was catching the tear with his finger. Suddenly he had put it into his mouth. Something like that is private between to lovers. That is what a man does when he courts a woman."

For a long time, the two of them held hands. "Thomas, I know how your brother felt about this place. When I look at these mountains, I love how it makes me feel. Mother Nature knows how to take care of her children every night. Can ye see how she tucked her children into bed? She carefully placed the clouds under the tops of the mountains… This is the way I would tuck my children, into bed each night."

Thomas knew she was talking about their children. "Honey went I'm back after a year our play time will become making a baby. Ye do know we can have twins. If that happens if we want more will plan the next one.

*　*　*

He kissed her lips. "Ye got to go I must talk with my parents. I want ye away from your mother. That is sad to say. But when William say that

I will not let my sister go through that. When the two of ye are ready. Call to me and I will bring ye here to me and my sister.

Surveying the land, he could see the swimming hole where he and his brothers swam. This was the land their family fought and died for… They chose to live here on this land. Who wouldn't love to wake up to all this beauty? Did one of his relations before him, ever come out here in the morning as he does? Here one could feel the warmth of the sun the moment the rays hit the earth. One could even enjoy the rich green grass after it rains. Strong feelings came over him and he spoke aloud. "I must find my brothers. One way or another I will bring them home where they belong." This was his oldest brother's last wish, it shall be done.

CHAPTER THREE

Talking to William

THOMAS WAS WALKING to the barn to feed the horses when William rode up. "Hay Thomas can we talk?"

He turn toured his friend. William was just getting off his horse. "Sure, what's on your mind."

Thomas had gotten the oats out and was feeding the horses in the barn. "Ye look like ye didn't get any sleep."

Thomas gave a chuckle. "So ye saw your sister."

William picked up some hay to put out for the horses in the barn. "Aye… she said that ye been having a lot on your mind. So ye know about us courting each other sisters."

Thomas looked at his best friend. "Aye… Are you worried about this?"

With that done, he headed to fill their water up and put hay in the pens. "William will ye… just say what's on your mind. "Eleanor told ye the truth. I haven't slept all night. Out with it."

William had put the hay out for Thomas. "Let me say this. Catherine been making me forget that she is to be my little sister. I've had it I want to give in to how I'm feeling. Thomas, I can't pretend anymore. Ye have a beautiful sister. I want to find out if she is the one for me. That promise we have for our sisters is getting in the way."

This time Thomas laughed. "Ye are right about that. I was up thinking about my brother's. Also, why my mother thinks I'm in love with Eleanor."

William had just closed the gate to the pen. "What did ye come up with?"

Thomas had gotten some of the cold water and poured it over his head. "Damn it that's cold. I better find a place to set. That sleeping wall is coming up fast. Put it this way, don't get bent out of shape. There is a book that has a word backwards. What it says is ye have magic. Will I do and I was thinking of Eleanor. My body went to her room, she was naked. William damn it."

He waved his hand and sat him down without touching him. "Do ye want me to send ye home. So ye don't believe me."

He snapped his fingers William was in his bedroom. Thomas then brought him back. "Now do ye believe me."

William looked at his friend. "Ye haven't lied to me. So that will explain how I got into Catherin's room. I thought I heard you're voice. I do have a lot of feelings for her. It was as if she knew. Just like ye said. I let her see me, she had let me touch her. She took care of what I needed. For my friend want me to have her right then. Thomas, I want this, after a week I'm hoping we can marry."

He had his eyes close. When he open them he spoke. "I want the same no one will have her virginity but myself. I will give her my seed the day I say I do. That is putting it bluntly, now will ye help me get into the castle. We must tell them we will court them. We will teach them all the trick's men will try to pull on them. As we do those tricks.

"One thing the girls can't tell anyone. They must play the game looking for a mate. That goes for us also. We got to play looking for a mate, that mad man will kill them. I can't lose her, I almost lost her from that bear who attacked her. This could be their way out but if he has magic. That man could have done it and hurt that bear. The things I did to that bear didn't stop him. Something kept the bear going.

"It's time we must get the ball going. William hang on we are going into the castle. I have no energy to clime those steps."

William and Thomas was inside the castle. "Dad and mamma where are ye. Us boys must talk to ye."

They came from the kitchen his mother and father had two plates of food with them. "Come on let us eat, Catherin's on her way to get Eleanor. Son sit before ye fall on your face."

He had his eyes close. "Eat now ye have burn through all your energy."

Thomas started to eat he tried to get the food down. "I feel better, William and I want to teach the girls what a suitor my do. What I'm trying to say is we want to marry them. We like to do this at the end of this coming week. Mamma, we can't afford to get them pregnant. Could ye put them on something to stop that from happening. Right now, there still developing, and we have a lot to learn.

"Things has happen that promise don't worked anymore. We both took apart things that the girls have been doing. William and I don't need that promise. Why I say that. Ye see it's stop working. When are little friend took notice of them. I found out that little friend can take over my mind, William also found that out. We have found out that we have special women. They knew what to do when that happen. The girls are not compromised, but they are bond to us as we are to them. When did that happen, I would have to say last night.

"It started when I got this book. The name of the book is very strange. Have ye see ye have—cigam. If ye look in a mirror it would read ye have magic. I was up for two days, all these thoughts ran together. After I read that title everything was broken down and the problems was being solved. I was able to find out things. What I took a part was the question what ye mamma saw in my eyes. It was also tied to my brother, that's why I ran out of the castle.

"When I saw my eyes I thought of Eleanor. She been there all this time. For some reason I wave my hand. I found myself in her bedroom. She was naked and as I took in her beauty. My little friend liked what he saw. It wasn't fair to her that she couldn't see my body. That is just what I did. I notice her nipples was hard. She liked what she saw. In my mind I asked if I could touch her. She nodded aye…that is why I said we are bonded to each other.

"When I was back in my room. I gave William a gift to see if his feeling for Catherin was love. He had done what I had did. Our women took care of our little friends. What also helped us was the fear of the man taking their life from us.

"By now ye must know we want to marry them this at the end of the week. We need something to stop them from getting with our child. There not ready for a child, and we must grow up more. But they will not go to these parties unmarried. I'm hoping that ye can help us. Their gift to us is their virginity. Their gift to them is our seed and name. I know it right to the point. We also like to stay here the four of us. This part is hard to say, William had told his mother how he felt. For the two of their sake, I must request that the two of them stay here. No diss respect to his mother. But she can't keep a secret. William knows that she will hound them. Like she did to his brother. If his mother find out she may say something to the wrong person. That evil man will come after them. It will only take one person to put them in danger.

"I want my bride to be, to take care of us. Cooking are meals washing are clothes. We want them to have a taste being a wife. Then when we marry adding us to the mix. William do ye think I covered everything."

William nodded yes, Daniel was doing a good job not giving it away. His mother told them, "It will take two weeks to get into the system."

William looked at Thomas. Both boys was hoping for more time to make love to them.

His father scratched his head. "Let see the girls will need a dress. Ye boy's new kilts, a cake food and someone to marry them. Donald do ye think ye could marry them."

He came out and looked at the boys. "I think I could do that for them."

The boys had their mouth open. "We will need Theseus to give Eleanor away. Do ye think ye could do that."

Thomas felt he been had. A big smile on the boys that the men wanted to help. "We have plans in motion for ye two. The girls have been on what I made them for a week. Son I knew that the girl's would try something. You two were coming on glue. I can see that book help ye both."

William took a breath. "Sir my I have your permission to marry Catherin."

Daniel smiled. "My boy ye had permission to marry a while ago."

Theseus looked at Thomas. "When ye took that bear down by yourself. I saw my little girl stay by your side until ye open your eyes and look at her. She was yours and she was going to make ye hers."

The two girls walked in with clothes. "Thomas why are ye still up. Come on it time ye get some sleep."

They watch as he got up and looked at her. "Eleanor do ye think ye like to marry me the end of this week."

She touch his face. "Ye what took ye so long to know ye loved me as I loved ye."

He had to think about it. "That bear and the promise to think of ye as my sister. Thank heavens you're not my sister. For I couldn't marry at the end of this week."

Thomas felt the wall as he went down on one knee. "I'm all right I think I going to lay down for a while."

Eleanor had and arm around him when Thomas wave his hand to go to his room. She was along for the ride. He had landed on his bed she still had her clothes with her. Walking into her room she put her clothes down and went to kiss him. He had pulled her next to him. "Just for a while." Thomas was out and nothing was going to wake him.

*   *   *

After some sleep Thomas got up. Eleanor had gotten up before him, had felt her but he needed more sleep. He had to go the back way, coming around the core he saw William and his horse. Thomas laughed, William had put little foot in with his sister horse. He heard him yelling "No…ye can't have her."

Thomas came down to where William was. "He's been with her for a while. It just fitting, Catherin horse Buttercup can have a baby, leave him. He had her many times, she may be with a baby."

Then they heard Catherine's horse whinny. "She will let him know if she had enough with him. I'm going to let Midnight mate with Sunshine. I'll take him to the other reading pen. Willian don't watch when Catherine with ye. It can stir the juice in us."

William shook his head. "Ye can say that again. Thomas thank ye I didn't know how to get us to this point. The four of us have been going down this path. Do ye think the girl knew what they wanted."

Thomas thought about that. "Do ye remember all the little things. They like watching us practicing doing are sword play. I know they watch us washing are self. Snowball fight, the girls had a good arm on their self. I know Eleanor was always there for me. I'm glade the blinders are off I enjoyed the job with her. Your sister is beautiful, I have but one thing to stop me from having her. Is that evil man. After we marry I will enjoy having her as my wife.

"William I'm going to put up a bubble that only saw the landscape. This way ye can work on your land with the Catherin. The ye can get my sister ready for ye."

William was proud to have Catherin as his bride to be. "Thomas you're a good friend, we work good together ye always know what to do. Do ye think we will have to fight."

Thomas was quite. "I've been thinking about that. My brother had told Michael where to take the bodies. That evil man wanted all the bodies burned. They won't let them come to the Highlands. Even with my magic it won't help to get them here. We must learn everything about Scotland. My magic will help us when the girls may need us. I will find out as I go. One thing read that word and have my sister also read it. Who knows we may have magic. But we must do things for are self."

William then thought. "I don't want to go to their where mamma it. I wish I had something I could call for what I need."

Then Thomas thought of something to do just that. He wave his hand, and a bag pop up.

"Here think of what ye won't then take it out of the bag."

William was happy about that. "I like to go and check on Sunshine, could ye send me there."

Thomas did something better. He had Midnight across the river and Sunshine with him. "That's even better."

*　　*　　*

Franceam had been in the attic to get the dresses down. Brinia was coming over to see what they can do. The girls will have their fitting tonight. She was remembering what Donald had said. Ronald had asked Thomas to come and find their bodies. I know he wanted his brother to know about Scotland and their people. What hurts he had Michal kill the men who killed his wife. He knew he was going to lose them both. He had to get there to say goodbye to them. Ronald ye gave your brothers a lot to do and think. Don't make him kill that evil man.

Thomas now has magic. "She knew his side of the family had magic. When the time comes could Thomas pull the boys fathers to them.

"Franceam had heard that Thomas didn't have to take a wife. It's been taken care of. If this is true my boy is married. Ronald found out that man wanted all MacGregors dead."

He saved is brother and his wife. Did he get her with child. My two youngest boys, Michael he had to save the bodies. Thomas will bring the body's home, now my two youngest is going to get married. She hope we will have children in the castle again.

"Brinia I hope she will be all right. Now that Peter is gone, I hope Damian can go on. He knew it was hard for Peter to watch his twin kiss a girl."

Daniel had gone looking for his wife. "There ye are. Did ye find the dresses."

Franceam always enjoy when her husband puts his arms around her. "Have I told ye I love ye.

She look at her man and touch his face. "Aye, it was just this morning. I love ye also. I hope these dresses will work for the girls."

Daniel looked at his wife. He kissed his wife and held her for a bit. "I think everything will be just find. William put his horse next to Buttercup he found out the hard way she was in heat. Little-foot jump in the pen and went to please her.

"Thomas pulled Sunshine from William's home. Then put Midnight with her. The four horses fits the four of them. It's sad that William didn't want to go home. He know that he's hurting his father. Thomas told me Eleanor went to her to tell her about her dream. That her brother is dead. She just shrug her off, he said Jonathan wife went home to have her baby. I thank she will be under ye for help. All are boys are kind and strong. I know it hurt Michael that Ronald didn't want him there. Thomas had seen the battle that went on. He said that the evil man wanted Ronald through into the fire. He took down the two that had him. Michael try to get the last ones. One of them had magic."

She tried not to cry but give him a smile. "I'm glad that I knew something was going to happen. It's good that he wants her to play the game of looking for a husband. But her mother she is in the worse way. She is driving everyone away from her."

Daniel kissed his wife. "I think I'll go see the boys, there had grown up a lot. He went down the stairs when a strong feeling of being helpless, he looked to the heavens for help. "Dad I wish ye were here, have I gave them enough to be able to manage everything that they must do. I feel, my wife is right that we have lost our oldest son.

"Dad why do I feel, Ronald is staying here on earth for a little while. He has plans for his two brothers. I had to let him go to finish what he had to do. Dad it's not over with. There are things in the works that my last two sons are involved with. Keep them safe dad if ye can. I know he is going to be in danger once he fines his brother. There is going to be a fight. Thomas has magic, could he be able to bring us to them. If ye can help him out, it's been hard here we lost five people. Please no more, our youngest is wants his best friend little sister. She knows all what he like this one will do anything with him. My little girl she landed the one she wants. It seem like her brother had a hand in it. This was their fate not knowing the boys was show the girls everything they like."

Daniel saw the boys laying on the grass. "It's going to be a quiet night for us men. We be eating soon. Your brides is cooking. Both are good cooks."

Daniel saw in the two boy's eyes the strain of being up all night. He wished that these boys didn't have to go through this like he did. Son last night did ye find out what Ronald was going to do."

Thomas thought about what to tell his father. "Aye…, Ronald had a plan to have Michael take down all those evil killers. That storm made me feel all of this will be finish in the Highlands by the three of us. Dad I could see things in the storm. Not only that he said the Lord want him to bring all those men to be judge.

"Peter going to die in battle. But he will take Michael's place. My brother is married, and he is going to have a baby. That's why Ronald sent him home to be with his wife. He had a dream or vision when to go check on them. Ronald had him take the bodies to place were the men can't get to them. He was smart, between the four of them. They would make sure they had questions for the ones that tries to take them from their resting place. They are near a church, but my magic can't show me yet.

"That evil man had planned all this. Even when to tell Ronald what was to happen to his wife. That's why Michael was able to get him here in time. Ronald was on his way back to the Highlands. They had told him that his wife was going to die with his child."

Daniel could see that Thomas had figured out everything that had happen. "Dad when Ronald asked Peter and Jonathan to go with him. He had given them a different destiny. Peter along with Jonathan a way to die as men in battle. As we know they were dying a slow death. We know the talks are getting out of hand. Jonathan had gone with Ronald off and on before.

"Whoever put out this order wanted all the MacGregor men to die. Jonathan was worried about William, he knew that he would go with me. Peter had freed Michael's to go undercover, so he could become Hawk. This way he could move around the countryside. Everyone would think nothing of it. Michael MacGregor was dead. Now he can go after the man who gave the orders for his family's death. I know the three took many of those hire killers with them. All three were the best fighters in the Highlands. Ronald was the strongest the last one to die. Eleanor saw a man that stab her brother in the back. That got her upset."

*   *   *

Daniel saw his son had drawn out everything from his mind. It was as if he was in Ronald's head. He could see that it made sense to even him. "Ye mother said the same thing to me." Daniel could see the pain in his son's eyes. His son has the gift of sight. His gift is stronger than his mother's. What Thomas said his son believes it to be true and he is dead serious about it. "Dad that was ruff I told ye what we had done. Then to see her father, I could feel William wanted to crawl under the table."

Then William spoke up. "Thomas I'm right here. I can hear ye."

Then the three of them had a good laugh. The two girls came out. "Are ye three hungery. We have it all ready for ye."

Daniel got up and head in. William took Catherin into his arms. All he wanted is a kiss before heading in. "Will see ye in there."

Thomas pull Eleanor into his arms. "Will ye come with me tomorrow. I like to get some trees cut down for the barn. Bring clothes if we get wet, or we can go naked. I have my finger to give ye pleasure. But it's not for long, ye will have me inside ye. When I say I do."

He kissed her deeply. "Thomas ye knows how to get me hot. I love ye."

He touch her face. He thought she shouldn't know about all of this. "Honey I'm glad thing with us happen. I'm proud of ye, learning to be a midwife. I think mamma going to try to keep the two of ye busy. That's what I'm going to do. There is things that I want to learn myself. We better get in there to eat. I hear ye are going to have your fitting for your dress."

Eleanor took his hand and the two walk back into the castle. William spoke. "Hay ye two we thought ye got lost. Your dad had an idea, we can be three brothers. I don't know what Duncan will say."

Eleanor had brought out there food. "Did I miss something."

Thomas got up and pulled out her chair. She smiled at her man. "Just we were talking about using Donald McKinnon name."

After everyone had ate. The girls clear the table. "Mamma if ye need anything for the dresses let me know. I want them two of them to be happy."

She thought time has gone so fast my babies are all grown up. I have wonderful boys. "I will if we need any material I will let ye know."

Donald and Malinda had come over the men was in the library. "So ye got that book from here. Wow, have ye read anything inside."

Thomas had called for the book. "Dad ye read that word have ye tried to do anything."

He thought about it. What would I like to do. "I'll do something simple."

He had wave his hand and the women got a rose. "I don't think it worked."

Then Thomas got out the locket. When Daniel saw the locket, he smiled at his son. "Son that was given to me by your grandmother. It was her promise for marriage. It seems each time someone goes to war. It's given to the one we love. Only three times has this locket been pass down. You're the third one. I like that ye put a rose on it. What are ye going to ask from her."

Thomas has been thinking about this for a while. "I'm thinking of putting my hair in the locket. I will ask her to give me a small braid of her hair for her promise to me. I'm going to have her go to these parties. At all costs, her mother can't find out. I want it to be a gift to each other."

Damiel got out the Scotch and poured some drink for them. "A toast two our boys. Donald would ye let the boys use your last name."

Donald looked at them. "Aye..., I have watch them become strong men. They are my boys in my heart. I'll be proud to call them my sons."

Thomas thought. "Then we have two dads' for right now. So, dad what history will ye show us."

Donald thought about that. "We have many castles that we can see. A lot has fallen but it's a reminder of what the land and peoples had gone through."

William looked at them. "As Thomas talk about what Ronald told him. I'm in the same boat as he is. I know nothing about Scotland. Sometime dad and Jonathan talk about what was happening in the talks. It will be good to see all those castles."

Thomas then thought about what Ronald had said. "I've gone over everything Ronald told me. The one thing that stock. He said if we don't have history of what happened in the past then they can tell us anything.

It all most as if we are being controlled, we will believe anything they say. Not knowing history Ronald said it will repeat. Ye know there is not much I know about fighting for this land. I know of my uncle's and Ronald death and that he died for what they believes in. Dad ye kept them safe until they were my age. My brothers know what it costs to be free.

Now I like to have a little history of ye and mamma. How about mamma's favorite rose bush and that big bucks head. Could that have been the start when ye spread your wings."

Daniel watched his son turn from his little boy into a strong young man. Where did the time go. He thought. He had to close his eyes and take a deep breath. He thought it had not been that long ago that he was Thomas's age.

Thomas wanted to know his father and mother much better. "Dad is this how ye felt when my brother and I spread our wings to fly."

The rose and buck

Then there was a calming feeling that came over him and his body relaxed. When Daniel opened his eyes, he gave his son a big smile. "I never told your brothers this story. Because they never asked these questions of me." He looked at his son with a devilish smile and spoke. "Your mother is going to have my head.

Donald laughed. I will tell ye this, she had sized every man that came across her path. Your father got under her skin. We had lost our father in one of the battles. That's when our mother got sick. My sister decided to get out of the lowland of Scotland. Your father told my sister that he lived in the highlands. We sent out to find a MacGregor the man that found us was your uncle. My sister then spoke. "There are two of ye."

"I will tell ye this, that took the wind from our uncle sails. He liked her also. So ye are looking for my twin he is up helping our father. Who is this young lad. That was the start were I found my love. My sister stayed with the MacGregor's, and I help with my wife family. They had lost her father at the time. They need a man to help with the ranch."

"Aye…, my brother he fell for your mother. Now back to the story. At the time I was eighteen a year younger then ye two. I was hunting the red deer for the clan. Ye asked if that buck's head is about your mother and me. Aye… Ye are right. Ye will agree that buck was the biggest we have seen in a while. I had chased him all over until he came across your mother. At the time I didn't think she was a lassie but a lad. Your mother was wearing clothes that a lad would wear. A woolen hat to cover her reddish-brown hair. Which would have told any man she was a lass. If that buck didn't leap over her and knock her to the ground."

Daniel stopped the story, he remembered that arrow could have killed her. Thomas saw in his father's eyes that arrow had come that close to his mother. "To make a long story short after I shot the buck.

"I had to chase him down, I brought him back to where I had left your mother. She was a feisty one still trying to get that rose bush out of the ground. On the way back, my anger built. I could have killed him. I told myself I would thrash him. A twelve-year-old lad shouldn't be out by himself. Then what I thought was a lad became a lassie. I saw red curls sticking out of her hat.

"I had to teach her a lesson. To show her what could happen to a lass when she is by herself. After setting down the buck. I walked over to her and told her, I thought ye were a lad. Don't yet know that soldiers could have raped ye. In their eyes that wouldn't be wrong by their King's law."

"She just laughed at me, she spoke. "Don't be silly I could get away before that happened. She was wrong. I walked right over to her and took her into my arms. She was of the age of fifteen. I kissed her and put into that kiss all the anger I felt. I had her down on the ground before she knew it. My hand went under her shirt, there was something wrapped around her breast. This was to make her look like a lad. That didn't stop me from getting to what I wanted. At first, she was fighting me, I told myself I was trying to teach her a lesson. In doing so it backfired, that lesson was for me also.

"I found that I had gotten lost in that kiss, there was a hunger for more. I took my tongue and brushed over her lips, it happened so fast when her lips parted. I deepened the kiss, your mother was responding to my touch. Then I heard a moan. I didn't know which one of us had done that. What I found out about her, she could light my body on fire.

"I must have done the same to her. It was to the point my finger went where I shouldn't have gone. The feel of my finger in her heat, I wouldn't have stopped if I didn't hear something coming near us. That was the only thing that brought me back to earth.

"The two of us didn't speak of it. I helped her dig up that rose bush. After that day, no other lass could compare to her. Her lips were the taste of honey, I wanted her that day. I couldn't forget the reaction my body taken when I touched her. When she was sixteen, she came to find me. That is another story."

Daniel notice Thomas and William was listening carefully. It looked to be that he wished the story had gone on. "Wow, one thing led to another. So ye and my mother found a home and a mate."

Daniel smile he didn't want to go into any more parts of the story. "Son I saw that the foundation of your home is about finished. Has Eleanor been helping ye at times?"

Thomas nod his head yes. "Aye…, I enjoy working with Eleanor we laugh and just enjoy each other. She know what I need even before I do."

CHAPTER FOUR

Stories

DANIEL GOT NUDGE by Donald. After the story was done the two boys were trying not to nod off. "Old friend, we have gone through a lot. My boy watching his brother choose the young woman he wanted. He had to do something about it. As your twin had done. I hope that the next twins can have a life with soon one."

His father looked at him. "Ye are right about that. These boys need to go to bed."

Thomas had hear his father. In his mine he thought William upstairs and change and put to bed. Then he waved his hand and William was in bed.

"Donald, I tried to make sure my sons were strong fighters. These men your brothers had gone up against were higher killers. Ones he find their brother's body, and the other family members of the three families. If ye need us make sure ye send word. They have two years to see Scotland, until they are twenty-one.

"They must learn what ye can about the land of Scotland. Seek out what your brother was talking to ye about. Talk to the people who work the land. Send word home to let your mother know ye are all right. Ye can even write to Eleanor to tell her about what ye saw. Thomas if ye don't find your brothers in this time frame, ye must come home." Where's William?"

He had heard all what his father had said. "I sent him to bed. We wants to work on our land. Thank ye for the stories. I like to see Eleanor before I go to sleep. Thank ye dads that was wonderful to hear. Things are not too different now then in your time."

Thomas left to say good night to his bride. He had nock at the bedroom door. "Mamma I like to say good night to Eleanor."

He had heard just a minute. What he saw was his sister and his bride a sleep on the bed. "I had sent William to bed he was out."

The two women saw his magic. When his sister was changed and sent to bed. Now his bride, first he said good night to his aunt then his mother. "I want to thank ye for helping us. It means a lot to the four of us. Come on honey."

Thomas picked her up and her arms went around is nick. He climbed the stairs with his bride. Donald and his wife said good night to him and his mother and father. Good night and snap his fingers and they were home. With horse and buggy.

Thomas had snapped his finger and Eleanor was change and the bed turn down. He kissed her as he put her in bed and covered her up. Thomas then snaped his fingers and he was change and in bed.

*   *   *

The next day after they had lunch. Thomas and his father rode together to the breeding pen. Eleanor was coming after her lessen. It was too hot to cut down the trees. The four was meeting up to go riding.

Daniel was watching his son ride. His son made him think of his own brother. He knew what Thomas was feeling about Ronald. His wife was right that their son would find out and answer his questions. He was very proud of his boys. All three sons had wide shoulders and was tall like him. Each time when one of his sons hurt… he hurt right along with them.

When the two of them rode up to the breeding pen. They could see Midnight was doing some courting of his own. There was a lot of kissing. They move around together as one. After the courtship he will mate with Sunshine. He will stay with her until she had enough of him.

The breeding pen was near a small river. This river had tall sides, it had run near the holding pen. There was only two ways across the river. A bridge to cross by and there was the way to jump over the river. His father came along with his son. He needed to check on the other horses on top of the hill. Ronald had given his two brothers his horses. Daniel thought they will have their hands full when the horses give birth.

"Son! I'm glad that I gave ye one of Thunder's horses that he sired. Being half Andalusian and Quarter horse. Midnight is a strong and fast horse. Ye two match quite well together. You're a strong man when ye fight ye move quickly. Ye both are handsome and look good together. Sunshine is a strong runner she can jump over a long way. She is a beautiful Palomino Colored Quarter horse. When Eleanor is on Sunshine. They look good together, both lassies complement each other. "Thunder's father had saved my life many times with his bravery. He got me out of places when he was hurt himself. I believe that Eleanor's Palomino. Along with your horse will make a strong fast and beautiful horse. Remember my horse was a twin. Sunshine may have twins. It would be nice if ye had a black and a Palomino Quarter horse with Andalusian crosses."

Thomas was looking at Midnight. His mind was far away, it's been hard not to push himself onto her. I must tell her stop me if I going to fast at her. "Aye… they well make a beautiful colt together. Dad ye said twins. My sister has Midnight's twin. Wow! Come to think about it. Don't twins run in are family also?"

Daniel laughed to see his son's face. "Aye… Ye or your sister could have twins. I don't think William and Catherin knows this."

Then Thomas laughed. "I think the four of us will do just find. The two of us had the same idea as the other. We both gave each other the same talk about not hurting our sister's. I know that he is a strong fighter.

As young boys we did some roughhousing together. For are ability we are match quite will together. Now for the girls that is another story. The two of them when they fight watch out. I showed both girls how to take care of themselves. William and I will have our hands full if are temper flairs up. Both girls has a temper themselves."

Daniel laughed. "Aye… Those two girls will have ye doing things like your mother has me doing. Son, remember what we talked about. I see Eleanor."

*　　*　　*

At 1:00 his father and Thomas was waiting for Eleanor. He was watching the two horses; he was thinking of Eleanor when they were younger. She always made him feel good even as children. Even their horses were starting a family. Off in the distant he saw her coming towards them. Thomas and his father watched her ride closer. She was riding fast, the sunlight was shining on her golden-brown hair. Eleanor had left her hair down for him, she looked so beautiful today. He watch her hair as it bounced from side to side. She had dress up for him, it was a green riding dress. His mind took in that Eleanor wasn't going to take the bridge. He watch as she bypass it, his mind went into a panic.

"Damn it…, what is she going to do, she's not on Sunshine. No… she can't do this to me. Does she not have a brain in that pretty-little head." Daniel heard his son swear in Gaelic. He watched his son slam his fist down on the fence. "What does she think she is doing? Does she not know that she could kill herself? Can't she see she is not a child anymore? I didn't teach her to jump a horse for fun. It was to have a way to escape danger. Damn it…! What is she thinking about?"

Thomas watched her as fear filled him. The memory of the bear attacking her was fresh in his mind. He could lose her this time if she missed the jump. He thought, will I watch her die if she miss that jump? "No!" He watched as the horse left the side of the ridge. He notice she didn't realize what she was doing. There wasn't a thought that the horse could throw her. It could stop before she had to jump the river.

Daniel watched his son hold his breath, as she leaped over the river. When she landed, he let the breath go? "Thomas don't be too angry with her. Eleanor is still young."

He turned quickly to look at his father. There was no anger in his son's eyes. Only fear for Eleanor's life. He placed a hand on his son's shoulder. "Thomas, I'm going to look at the other horses. Ye two must come to and understanding about that. Ye are going to be married soon. Things that scare ye let her know. As her what worries her, remember ye must talk to make a marriage work.

*   *   *

Eleanor realized at the last minute she wasn't on Sunshine. Her thoughts ran through her mind. "What was she doing? She was so happy to go see Thomas. Before she knew it, she was at the edge of the riverbank flying over the river. She realized she had no idea if this horse would be able to make the jump. What would Thomas say? She had told him she wouldn't jump over anything unless to save her life."

Eleanor could hear someone screaming. She heard. "Eleanor don't jump the river." Fear closed in on her. She knew right then why Thomas was screaming at her. Her horse could miss the jump or stop not making the jump. She could die hitting her head breaking her neck. This wasn't her horse, Sunshine; she knew her horse could jump over this. "Lord help me to get over this river. I don't want to lose the chance to become Thomas's wife."

In a blink of an eye, she was landing on the other side of the river. Eleanor watched Thomas as he stormed over to her. When he looked at her, she saw a mix up of emotions in his eyes. She watched him grabbed her horse's bridle. As he pulled the horse to the fence and tied him up. Thomas went quickly over to her and grabbed her around the waist. He pulled her down to him, as he grab her shoulders and gave her a little shake. She watched his eyes closely, Eleanor could see there wasn't any anger in his eyes. She saw the fear that he might have lost her. There was something else in his eyes, with her hands were around his waist. She bit the inside of her lip, not to start crying,

*　*　*

Eleanor watched his face closely as she let him have his say. "Do ye not have any sense in that pretty head of yours? Eleanor you're becoming a beautiful woman. A woman that I'm going to marry. Do ye not know that scared me. I almost lost ye last year."

He pulled her into him, she felt his heartbeat faster. He had his face buried into her neck. When his breathing slowed, he looked at her. Then pulled her into him for a long kiss. "I love ye, the two of us finally found out we love each other. Will talk about what scares us. Honey ye must be aware of your surroundings. When ye are not, a men can kidnap ye, he can do things to ye. As ye know when I come home I will need an heir to carry my name on. But we have my brother also. Don't put yourself in danger. Your brother and I wouldn't be around to help ye if ye get hurt. I don't know how long I will have my magic. Please don't make me ride home as my brother did. It will tear me apart."

Thomas pulled her into him and buried his face into her neck. Her hands went to softly rub his back. He felt a calming feeling that came over him. There in her arms he breathe in her scent. "Eleanor please don't do this to me again. I almost lost ye to that damn bear."

The scent of sweet roses was on her skin, she felt so soft to him. When he lifted his head up, she had stayed in his arms. Eleanor didn't give him any protest she just watched his eyes.

She could see his eyes was on her lips. Gently he lifted her chin, with a soft touch of his lips on hers. Thomas felt her hands go around his back. With his tongue softly moving over her lips. Her mind demanded to taste the forbidden fruit again. His strong arms held her tightly against him. Eleanor gave Thomas as much as he gave her. He found that he wanted more, the moment her lips opened everything changed for her and him. She want him to touch her to get her ready for him. After tomorrow it will be six days left. Honey we will have to play the game of fining a mate. I must keep ye safe."

Thomas love touching her. His hand moved over her cheek to the back of her neck. He drew her into him for another kiss. His arms held her against him as his tongue made love to her mouth. This time when he looked at her, she had bewitch him.

"That damn bear rob me of finding out ye must be mine. A thought came to me just now. If we was on this page as we are now. That man could have killed ye and my brother's wife.

Ye and I will play the game of looking for a mate. I will give ye a locket with some of my hair inside. I would like a small braid of your hair. I'll keep it in my sporran, this will be for when we marriage.

"Your mother and mine are taking ye and my sister to your mother's, cousin's home. Ye will be in the Lowland of Scotland. There ye will be meeting other men. They will try to kiss ye, I think ye know what ye want. For myself and your brother there is so much we must learn about Scotland. I want to know what my brother was talking about. Besides, I need to grow up more to be able to manage ye and our children. Woman ye know how to bring me to my knees."

*　*　*

Eleanor gave a little giggle. She knows he would take good care of her. As he talked to her there was those butterflies in her stomach but farther down. "Thomas ye have always been honest with me. My mother lately she hasn't told me much. Right now, I have butterflies in my stomach but farther down. My body want ye to bring out the pleasure. I'll take care of your little friend.

She smiled at him and through her arms around his neck. Eleanor pulled him down to her mouth. When they came up from that kiss. She saw hunger in his eyes, he had closed them quickly. Thomas worked to get control over his friend. "Eleanor, ye have showed me ye want me. Honey sex is new to us, we must watch out we don't push each other to the point I get ye with my child, we have six days left. Then again if I take ye to fast it will hurt ye. But it goes away fast, so they say."

Thomas stopped her he had kissed the underpart of her hand. Then he kissed her lips again. "It is said that most women know their own hearts."

She was enjoying kissing him. "Aye... may be my brother won't want to go riding."

Who knows but tomorrow I'm going to work on my land to clear a spot for the barn. I would like to know if ye would like to come along. If ye do bring some clothes to swim in. It's going to be another hot day. We will need food also."

Eleanor was looking at his lips. Then she answered him. "I would love to go with ye. I will bring that magic bag with me. The two of us must tell each other what we like and not like."

*   *   *

He was feeling different each time he kissed her, he wanted more of this. "Aye... to have someone who would love me, the way my mother loves my father. If my father wants to take my mother to the barn and make love to her, she will go. There have been times that my mother threw her arms around my father's neck and kissed him.

"I enjoy those feelings, I just don't want to mess this up. Ye been around my family for a long time. There was times my father picked my mother up. He would bring her to their bedroom, eye know that sex is a big part of their marriage. They do a lot of kissing and touching each other.

I've heard ye been cooking, I do love good food. I'm strong because of it. I like the meal that ye fixed. I know that the two of ye worked together.

Eleanor found that she wanted to kiss him again. "Thomas could ye tell me why your tounge ran a cross my lips?"

Thomas thought she knew how to make him feel different. Eleanor was able to bring out the woman that he don't know about. He must find out as much as he can. He found that when he kissed her, she made it easy for him to take it to the next step. "Eleanor ye know that answer, when ye parted your lips for me. Ye told me I could deepen that kiss."

She looked at Thomas. Did she know everything about him? No… because he is thinking of me as a woman. His kiss made me feel different inside. It made her do things that she never would have done. "When we get back to the castle, I'll make ye something to eat."

*   *   *

At the table Thomas and his father took a bite of their food. "Wow this is good." Thomas was really pleased with her cooking. His mother was very proud of her student.

After she help with the cleanup. Thomas took her for a walk. As they walked, they hell hands. They had check on the things Thomas would need tomorrow. Then Eleanor tried to help put things on the wagon. "Honey leave it, it's too heavy for ye. Your body is still changing, and I like the changes."

After that was done, they walked to the rose garden. He walked pass the bench to the part where no one could see them. Thomas pulled her into him, "I thought that I knew everything about ye. I didn't think ye could surprise me like ye have. That food was good. Ye even put a spin on what my mother has always made."

Eleanor was please he like what she fixed everyone. She had notice that the butterflies were back. There was powerful feelings running through her. She wanted him to kiss her. The feelings of his arms around her she wanted to get closer to him. "Thomas your stirring up those butterflies."

Her hands went under his shirt, how she loved his body. Then her top was down, and he sucked her nipple. She had pushed into his heat she went under his kilt and took hold of him.

He looked at her, in her eyes he saw what she wanted. He held his finger up and it got bigger. This time longer, he pulled up her skirt and parted her legs. He went slow and her heat push into his hand. Now his heat was on her leg, and she had her hand on top. She wanted to say something, and he took her mouth. Just a bit thicker, and a hair longer. She came hard, he kept moving in her again. Until they both had another climax, it had drove them over the edge. It wasn't enough for him. Thomas made his finger the size of his heat around. He cleaned himself and her leg up. He was just there not passed just before her virginity. "Damn it five more days and I can have her. She try to give him skin on skin. She was having trouble also. She wanted more of him. She wanted him inside her not his finger.

He backed out quickly and wave his hand. He had to walk away and got a hold of his self. What was happening to his bride to be. He told himself that he was going to fast with her and himself. Remember she was his little sister for a long time. Things have changed she not my sister. I had scared her moving too fast for her. We still have time, I need to work on our land. If I slow down she can get used to me. He had to take a breath, I can see she's trying to be a woman, but the young girl will keep coming back off and on.

Until she tells herself she is a woman. I must tell her what I'm doing. Not just doing it and making her to indoor it. Like I did. He walked up to her. "Honey I'm sorry what I did to ye. I like those pleasure I give ye and ye give me. I want to much all at ones. Will ye forgive me."

Thomas was watching her closely. He slowly came up behind her putting his arms around her waist. She was relax, slowly he started to kiss her neck until she was relaxed more.

Eleanor had stopped moving her hands and started to relax her body. "I think I know what is happening to the two of us."

Then he went over to the bench to get the blanket to lay down on. She was watching him as he try to open the blanket up for them. Eleanor went to help him, and it was now ready for them. The blanket was on a hill side so they could look at the stars. "I'm sorry I was upset with ye. It scared me that ye could do that to me."

The two of them sat on the blanket. "Thomas I'm sorry about that. I didn't know I was about to do that to ye. My body just reacted to your kisses."

Thomas laid back and pulled her down to the blanket. He pointed to the stars in the sky. "We can't do anything here tonight. Ye can lay on my arm if ye like."

Eleanor moved closer to him. He wasn't mad at her, so her body let her enjoy what he was talking about. Now she turn into him her hand went on his chest, his arm pulled her closer to him. Thomas knew she had fallen asleep in his arms.

*   *   *

Upstairs in his room his mother and father watched the two of them. Thomas's dad asked, "honey should I go down there to break them up?"

She looked at her husband. "Know let them be. Thomas is finding out there is a lot more to Eleanor. He must find out things about her. So, the two of them could solve it together. All we can do is be here if they need us. Right now, I know he try to get her ready for him. But it made him want her more, time is going to slow and too fast.

"The four of them must play the game when their away from each other. They been on the stuff that will help the girls not to get with child. They must get through this week. Then they will get what they have been waiting for."

"I can see Thomas is going to sleep. Their starting to relax with each other. Now ye can tell them it's time to come in. Don't be surprised if he carries her upstairs. He must get over what happen to her with that bear. It's just part of healing they will do just fine as man wife."

Daniel found out that she knew more about the two of them. "Honey do ye think Bridget told her daughter about her feelings she may have."

Now she was in her husband's arms. "Honey Bridget is going through something she don't understand ye. She can help others but not herself for now. Right now, she can't help her daughter. She is pushing her away from her. She is too proud to ask for help. I'm going to have to help her when it comes to a head. The boys will be putting Bridget in her place. If her daughter don't do it first. If she knows that Thomas will back her, she will do it soon."

*　　*　　*

In the garden Thomas's father went over to his son. He had tap him on the shoulder. "Son it's time ye two come in."

Thomas opened his eyes and smiled. He looked over at Eleanor and gave her a kiss on her forehead. "It's all right, I needed ye to lift your head so I can stand to pick ye up."

Eleanor's eyes lazily opened. "I can walk Thomas."

He just smiled. "I know ye can. Just let me have this tonight. Put your arms around my neck. That's it hang on to me."

Eleanor nuzzled into his neck. His father thought his wife knows their son. Daniel picked up the blanket and brought it upstairs with him.

Thomas laid her on the bed and gave her a kiss. Her eyes open and she sat up. "Get some rest for tomorrow we have things to do. Good night. With a wave of his hand, she was change, and so was he."

*　　*　　*

The next day Eleanor made breakfast. She had brought lunch for them and packed clothes into what they could change. Thomas had the wagon ready with two horses to help them. He had also brought a sled that Eleanor could place tree branches on. So, she could take them to the pile.

As the day progressed, Thomas had already made great strides taking out three of the five stumps. Eleanor kept a close eye on Thomas, she was making sure he had plenty of water to drink. Each time she would bring him water she would gently touch his face, as if secretly saying, "I love ye." Of course, Thomas always took notice of this affection. At times she would run a hand down his arm. One time she laid a kiss on his lips and walked off. A while later Thomas couldn't see Eleanor. He walked over to the hill and saw her by the water. He made his way down the hill he could see she had her blouse off. She was pouring water over her arms, chest, and face. Thomas took off his sporran then his boots. He went down to her and picked her up and carried her into the water. He had a bad feeling their parents was coming down here. He made sure her blouse was not see through.

All I do know is I would give my life for her, didn't I do that with the bear. I'm finding this is happening more often. I can't wait to see her or have her in my arms. I love being with her, walking holding hands. I love to kiss her, I wish I could slow down but I can't. I like when she laid on my shoulder. The two of us fell asleep, it felt right to do that.

He was hot in more ways, than one. He took them both under the cool water. Then she had splashed him. Her legs was kicking the water, and he took her under again. When they came up he took her and kissed her. He wasn't going to start anything. That last time it was too much for her and him. They walked out of the water holding hands. He took down the two smallest trees, the big one is going to be the hard one to take down.

*　*　*

It was time to have lunch, Eleanor had the blanket and food out. She had laid it near the water the food was ready for them to eat. Now she went to get him, and saw his shirt was off. She likes to see him that way. Eleanor wonder if he was going to get bigger in his chest. She went behind him and put her arms around him. She loved to feel his arms and chest. Now she kiss his back, and he brought her to the front of him. We got to eat honey your making those butterflies come back. "Can I get a kiss?"

Then she turn toward him. His shirt was back on him. "Thomas there is something that's making me jumpy, for her hands were twisting.

He grabbed her hands and pulled her to him. She looked into his eyes, he saw the little girl in them. "Eleanor you're not a little girl anymore. Ye wasn't afraid of my body when I came to ye."

She blinked and blinked again. "No, she thought I'm not a little girl and I want to touch his chest. She stepped into his arms her hands laid on his chest. He pulled her into him his mouth took her into a deep kiss. "I like this a lot, I don't want to do anything wrong. Is this all right to run my hands over your chest."

He gave a little laugh. "Honey what were ye thinking about."

What my mother would say. "She makes me so jumpy in her eyes, I do everything wrong.

They were standing in place. His hands were still around her waist. It's been quiet I like this. Thomas ye have strong arms, I like you're chest. Her hands moved over and around. I'm sorry I don't know why I've been having those spells."

He brought her into him and kissed her. "I can feel my mother is near here. I don't want her around me."

Thomas knew if she feels her around. Her mother is around. He put his shirt back on.

She looked at him and smiled. "Thomas ye can keep your shirt off. But keep it nearby if your parents come to check on us."

He gave her a smile. "You're not worried about my parents. It's just your mother, William is the same way. I was happy that he told her off."

He smiled at her. "Honey when ye say things like that. I find it don't take long, for it to happen."

Thomas had his shirt on, while they ate the food. She was so beautiful even in her work clothes. After they ate, he laid back on the blanket. Eleanor was putting any food left away. She went over to him and gave him a kiss. His arms went around her pulling her on to him. Then he turn her over and slip his hand under her blouse.

He took her mouth in a hungry kiss. "Thomas those butterflies are back."

He looked into her eyes. "I want to touch ye, if ye don't want me to do this tell me now."

She touch his face, her hand went around his neck. "Do ye like what ye see."

He looked into those bewitching eyes of hers. He nodded his head yes. "Aye… can I play with one of these lushest breasts of yours."

His hand was under her blouse. He didn't go any farther until she said it was okay. "Thomas we have slow down a lot. That one time I mess up everything."

Eleanor held his hand there, for she knew right then. She poured cold water on him.

The day was getting closer. "We are going to be married soon. Do ye want me for your mate."

Eleanor looked at him. "Thomas we been together for a long time. I'm looking at ye different. I never had these feelings for ye like this. All I know is these butterflies are getting stronger. Ye can play with them for now. Thomas, I'm scared to lose ye. I don't want anyone else but ye."

He looked at her. Eleanor had crossed over to a woman. She knew what she wanted. Then he looked at her lips she had ran her tounge over them. He found he was breathing hard when he went for her lips. The hunger was back, and he was going for her breast. He kissed her neck all the way down to her breast. Quickly he pulled her blouse up to one of them. Both hands held her breast as his thumb played with her nipple.

She had her eyes closed, the feeling was making other parts of her body feel different. Now he was sucking her nipple. She cried out. "Thomas why is it making my pussy ache. It's starting to hurt."

His head popped up. His little friend was taking notice. Oh my god what was he doing. He better stop and think about this. One last kiss, her hands showed him she wanted to keep going. Then he pulled her blouse down and stood up. "Ye are right I must think more on this. Ye did nothing wrong. I love what was happening to us. Let's both of us think on this. Make sure ye have your wedding gift to me for tonight. I must get that last tree down. Are ye all right?"

Thomas helped her to her feet. She through her arms around his neck. Then kissed him deeply. Before he could take over, she pulled away from him. She gave him a big smile and taken up the blanket, food and brought it to the wagon. He watch her walk away from him. His thoughts told him, no this is not over with. It didn't take much to light him on fire. He walked back to that tree. It was down before the next thought came up.

Thomas smiled when he remembered that he also lit her on fire. For a moment, they got scared. Now would he like to take it to the next level? Aye… she is everything I want in a wife. If she likes what I'm doing to her. I hope I did the right choice, to marry her now. Aye…, we will be away from each other. Her body will be older and stronger. I e older and much wiser, to manage this beautiful woman. When we are away from each other. We must play the game, somehow, I must keep her safe.

*　*　*

That night the two of them took a walk to the rose garden. As they walked the atmosphere was set for lovers as twilight was upon them.

There in the garden, they gave each other their gift for marriage. Thomas took out the locket he had promised Eleanor. The locket held some of his hair. He got down on one knee and spoke. "Eleanor will ye become my wife?"

She nodded her head yes. And answered "Aye…"

Then he got to his feet and spoke. "With this locket, ye is my gift of marriage. Then he placed the locket around her neck and gave her a kiss.

It was Eleanor's turn. Inside her skirt pocket, she pulled out a small braid. Then spoke, "With this braid, I give ye this gift of marriage to ye. Thomas watched a tear roll down her cheek, as she placed the braid in his sporran. He just stared at the tear until he took his finger and scooped it up. He made her cry, he spoke. "Why are ye crying? What did I do wrong?"

Eleanor try to stop the tears. She touched his face and spoke. "Ye have done nothing wrong my love. I'm afraid of losing ye. I'm scared I won't be enough of a woman for ye.

"My love ye are going to try and find our brothers. Those evil men would be watching for someone to do just that. Thomas our time together is going too fast. Ye won't be safe out there. Here at home, I know I will be safe. If something happens, I don't know if I will be strong enough to deal with your death. Another woman I can fight. I can't fight death…! How can I fight for ye-if ye are dead? Plcase, Thomas, ye must come home alive. If not for me, do it for your mother, father, and your sister."

Thomas saw another tear rolling down her cheek. He took his lips and scooped the tear up. "There now I don't want any more crying." Gently he kissed her. Then brushed her hair out of her eyes. "Now let me see that pretty smile of yours. Ye know that I can't stand to see tears in your eyes. I know ye are scared for me. Ye know why your brother and I are doing this, we must. How could I become a man if I'm too scared to leave the Highlands? I need to see what my brother and father and my grandfather saw. I don't know what they are fighting for. I will come back when I do. I don't think there will be any woman better then ye. When I say I do. I will make sure ye only think of me in your pussy.

Thomas walked over to his mother's favorite rose bush and cut a rose for Eleanor. "Ye are so beautiful in the moonlight. It would be easy to let myself go. Dad was right when he said sex would get in the way. I know I love ye, I fought for ye. I was scared to lose ye. I don't know if I cried as I clean ye up. I didn't care about my cuts how deep they could be. Your blouse was coming down one cut was so close to your breast. I wished I could take those cuts from ye that day.

"To tell the truth I don't know much about love. I guest sex makes it hard to know what love is. Almost losing ye told me there is no one that could take your place. No one that I enjoy doing things with. No one that could cook as good as ye can at this age. Your beautiful and I know every part of your body will get better."

*　　*　　*

That night after the two of them went to bed. He was thinking back when Eleanor and he took herbs to Grana. He had brought Catherin with him. William and she was going riding that day. I had met up with him and Eleanor.

The four of us had been doing that for a long time. "Good morning ye two, it's been nice today. Mamma wants me to take Grana more herbs. Ye two have a nice ride this morning."

Thomas remember how pretty she looked that day. "Thank ye for coming with me. It had worked out Catherin was going for a ride also."

Eleanor always try to be with him whenever she could. "I was happy to do so, mamma was in one of her moods. I just didn't want to be with her."

Thomas started riding again when a vision hit him hard, he couldn't see the land anymore. In his mind he saw Eleanor with a baby boy. He was laying down in bed with them. Thomas had his mouth around her nipple sucking on it. He saw their child pull on his mother's nipple. She had bopped her husband when their child did that.

Eleanor had heard him say. "My god what just happen?"

She was watching him when he had stopped. His eyes had a surprised look in them. She heard his voice in her mind. "Thomas did ye have a vision just now?"

He had just shook his head no and kept riding.

*   *   *

Then he remember another time. Eleanor walked down the hill. She saw Thomas watching her. Daniel was walking up the hill at the same time. "Eleanor, have I told ye that ye look beautiful this morning."

She had her eyes on Thomas and had to stop and focus what Daniel had said. "Thank ye for saying that. It's always nice to hear."

When she reach Thomas, he took her hand and kissed the back of it. In his mind he spoke. "I would love to take ye in my arms to kiss ye. Ye are so beautiful this morning."

Eleanor remembered what his mother talked about. "I love being in your arms. When we get away from here will ye kiss me?"

When the two of them were in between the horses. He took her into his arms and kissed her. Then he helped her to get on to her horse and went to get on his. They wave to his parents.

Eleanor's memory

She was remembering the day she became a woman. Thomas was the one to see that she had blood on her skirt. She remembered she was so scared not knowing what was happening to her. Thomas told her. "It's all right, that she didn't hurt herself, that she has just became a woman." At the time she was eleven years old, that day he took her into his arms. Now she understood why his touch felt so good. His hand was warm to the touch as he rubbed her back. Thomas has been the one who always told her what she need to know. Why didn't her mother tell her? Everything she needed was in her saddlebags. Her mother had done that for her.

CHAPTER FIVE

A Gift of Marriage

THOMAS WAS LOOKING back on how the four of them grew up. He remember trying to teach Catherin how to ride her horse. She just didn't like listening to him. One day William came over to speak with Thomas. "Thomas are ye having trouble teaching Catherine."

At the time he was feeding the horses. "William Catherine just don't want me or my brothers to teach her how to ride. We have given up on her, now how's the teaching going with Eleanor."

William just looked at him. "Thomas even my father tried to teach her. She just lost interest in what he was showing her."

He turned and looked at is best friend. Thomas when the four of us are together Catherine listens to me. Do ye remember when we were having a snowball fight. Eleanor always wanted to be with ye. How about we try to teach each other sister. If ye can teach her how to ride a horse. Then we will make a pack to trade sisters, then we will have two sisters each. Thomas told William that's if we can teach them how to ride. He enjoyed teaching Eleanor, she was a lot of fun to be with.

Sometimes the girls played with their dolls. As William and him use their toy swords as they pretend fighting. At the pond, the boys would throw rocks into the water to see how far they could throw. As they got older both boys were shone how to throw a knife. Thomas had a good arm for throwing. He always hit what he threw at.

As time went on the four of them started to pair off. It never came to them that they were heading to a stronger relationship. Thomas and William always call Eleanor and Catherin their little sister. Both boys had two sisters. For a long time, that's how they hid their feelings. They would think the girls were their sisters when they weren't.

Things were changing for the four of them. Thomas never thought he was heading down the path of marriage. It took the death of his older brother's wife and son. His mother had seen something in his eyes the day the bear attacked Eleanor. He found out that he had to court Eleanor before he leaves the Highlands. Three days ago, he had to find out about the questions he had. Now he knows why his mother said he must court her.

In his mind he told himself to be careful. Now that his feelings has come to the surface, he don't want to get her with their child. There was strong feelings when he ran his hand up her leg and over to her heat. He never thought that he would enjoy what he did. It wasn't just him, Eleanor was wet he had given her a little pleasure. We have four weeks to find out if we are in love. I can't let anyone know that she's promised to me. I must fine Ronald's body with the other two. I couldn't believe her kiss lit him on fire. Why did it take him so long to find out all this? Because a promise I hold strong, a man who keeps his word ye can trust him.

*   *   *

Eleanor looked into his eyes. Then she spoke. "Thomas in my heart I know ye are in love with me. Are ye having trouble knowing what kind of love it is? I'm not supposed to know about sex with a man until I'm married. Why can ye not show me a little of lovemaking. We are going to marry. Unless ye don't want me."

Thomas thought he wasn't strong enough. "Eleanor am I the type of man that goes and change his mind. Didn't I say we are going to marry."

She knew she made a mistake in what she said. "Thomas I'm sorry, I know I have ye. But I'm scared that ye may think I'm trapping ye."

To stop him from talking, she threw her arms around his neck and kissed him. "I know what my mother would say. My love it's not her life and I don't care. I just need to feel your hands touching me. I know if I said stop, ye would stop no matter what it would cost ye."

Eleanor saw the surprised look on his face. She had thought, that may be she had gone too far. Could he be thinking the same way as she does. "Thomas I'm sorry. I don't know what I was thinking of. I must have gotten too much sun today."

A smile came over his face. "Aye, we both got too much sun. When we marry, no one will know. I will still have to leave. I must keep ye safe somehow, we can have a celebration, Michal will also be home. Eleanor do ye trust me?"

She had touched his face. She ran a finger over his lips. "I know we must be careful. Thomas from the age of eight years old. Ye have shown me how to ride a horse and saddle my horse. Then ye went and showed me at the age of ten how to jump my horse over things. This is a way to save my life. Ye were also the one who showed me how to climb a tree. Ye had taught me how to take care of these roses. Without knowing ye showed me what ye like and don't like. Why can't ye show me what it feels like to be touch by ye? Thomas, I like when ye put your arms around me. Ye can't tell me ye don't like when I brush your hair, or when I let ye lay your head on my lap.

"Thomas a young man who's not my brother. Fought a bear to keep me safe, ye didn't try to scare it off or to get me out of the way. My love I saw your eyes that day. Ye thought the bear killed me. I was afraid for ye, I didn't understand until I saw your brother's eyes. I remembered what your eyes looked like. Ye didn't care if ye lived or die. Ye can't tell me that ye don't love me."

Thomas took her hand, and they walked a bit. He knew she was right. "Eleanor when did ye get so smart, ye saw my eyes. That day after as I healed, I used my pain to block everything that happen to ye out of my mind. It hurt too much, your right that day I couldn't see myself without ye. I didn't die that day, I prayed that ye were still alive. Eleanor this is all new to me. With ye, I've jumped into this pool of sex with a beautiful woman who can light me on fire. That first kiss took the wall I had up down so fast I couldn't think. Then my friend who thought ye were my sister. He was the one to tell me, she's not your sister wakeup. Now that I'm older and so is she my little friend took notice of her. I'm finding since I've cross over, I want more of this. Will see if ye like what I'm going to do to ye. Honey if ye don't like making love with me, our marriage won't work. It's better we find out now then later."

He had his body against the wall, her arms went around his neck. "My love I've always trusted ye, I don't know if I can trust myself. From last year to now, I've been trying to make this happen. When ye kissed me the hunger for ye came out. I moved to fast the first time. My body is doing things, I don't know anything about. I scared myself the other day. I was afraid my mother would yell at us."

Thomas kept kissing her neck. Slowly he turned her putting her back to the wall. "Honey if ye don't like what I'm going to do. Ye know ye can tell me to stop."

Eleanor felt relax now, he took her mouth in a deep kiss. She didn't even know she was against the wall. As she found herself going under his shirt. Thomas followed her lead, as his hand went under her blouse. Her lips parted and she found herself moving with his tounge. When he felt her breast, her head went back to the wall. He like kissing her neck, as his hand found a warm breast. Thomas found her nipple, he rub his thumb over it and made it a hard nub. He wanted her nipple between his lips. With his tongue he will tease and suckle her nipple. He would see if she reacted to his touch. He lifted her blouse to get to that nipple.

She had moved her leg closer to his heat. "Thomas why is those butterflies starting to hurt."

He had found that she was rubbing his heat. Her body was begging for release. "Eleanor we could marry right now. But we still must wait for the medicine to work. I can't get ye pregnant ye."

Her eyes opened to look into his eyes, she had seen the hunger in them. Eleanor knew it was also in her eyes. "No, I'm not ready for ye. Ye said that if ye came into me now. It will hurt me."

He knew that day she got scared. She don't know that her pussy is wide enough for my heat. She had found her courage to start making love with me. I will let her lead me to where she wants me to go.

"It's time to get me ready for ye." She pulled her skirt up then his kilt. On her leg she had placed his heat. "I will touch your friend, could ye make those butterflies stop. I will make sure your friend stays on my leg. Please teach me how to please ye and I will tell ye what I like."

Her hand laid on top of his heat. Thomas hand was feeling curly hair as he moved down a little more. He had slid a finger over a piece of skin, her body had jumped. He had found that piece of skin was her little man in the boat. Just past that skin he felt two wet lips. "Thomas those feelings are getting even stronger."

He looked into her eyes she wanted this to happen. The time we got scared was over. I will teach her and explain things to her. "My brother Ronald called this finger fucking. Honey ye know about this place, when ye take three fingers there. Then ye will be ready for me. What ye have on your leg will go where I'm going now. Tell me if ye want my finger to go there?"

Eleanor showed him as she pushed one of his fingers inside. Thomas took her mouth and made love to her with his tounge. Then he felt her body stiffen as she came, her hand grabbed his hand holding him there. "Eleanor are ye all right?"

He knew he could make his finger bigger. The first time he went to fast. Her mother told her nothing. I won't make the same mistake I will teach her as we teach each other what we like.

He had felt her other hand dig into his bottom. She didn't answer him until the feelings had washed over her. The pleasure was so strong she didn't want it to stop. "Aye… that was wonderful."

Thomas smiled at her. "Good… hang on to me for I'm going to give ye more of this. This time I will come with ye. When she came again, he pulled away from her. It didn't take much to bring him over the top.

When they had cleaned and fix themselves up, they walked over to lay on the hillside. She was laying on his arm. Thomas had lifted himself up to look at her. "Did ye enjoy what I did to ye."

Eleanor looked into his eyes. She ran a finger over his lips. "Thomas at first, I never thought my body would ever feel something as wonderful as that. I know that's where a baby would come out, I remember all of that. What I want to know, did ye enjoy how it made ye feel. We have gone through a lot together. Could ye see going on with what we had just done. I do enjoy those feelings, I would want to keep going. Until my girlfriend could take three fingers. Thomas ye know what I had said about this. Would ye want to come inside me with your friend. Ye know in your heart I've always been meant for ye. I know ye gave me you're gift of marriage. I enjoy your kisses how ye make my bodied sing to ye. If ye don't want this, please let me go now."

Thomas looked at her he was surprised of that question. He knew he had to answer, "Could he let her go?" After finding out that he loved to kiss her. The way she makes him feel, to the point that his friend took notice. She was his best friend over her brother. He enjoyed being with ye on that job we had done. We were good teammates. Her body and the way she looks. Her kisses lights him on fire. Then Thomas was kissing her again, in his mind he cried out. "No, I can't let another man have ye. She is mind and when she is ready for me. We will marry."

Eleanor now was surprised she heard him in her mind. "Thomas, I love ye, do to me what ye want to do. I've been yours for a long time."

When the kiss ended, they didn't say anything about what each other heard. Thomas got to his feed and pulled her up to him. He scooped her up into his arms. "Eleanor when did my mother say I could have ye?"

She looked at him and spoke, "Your mother said the end of this week. That's three days away."

Thomas kissed her lips. "Then we have some work to get ye ready for me. I can't let another man have ye. He knew she was ready for him. He thought it's his little friend that is the problem. I do want to enjoy her pussy. Eleanor going to have to get me hot three time. I must clean him good, before I come inside her. I didn't know that sex will give ye a hunger for more. For a young man and woman can be pulled into that hunger. Some men can't control his little friend. He wants her pussy. They forget he has two brains. The little one is very strong, he can shut down the big brain.

*   *   *

The next day Eleanor made breakfast. She had brought a lunch for them and packed clothes. Thomas had the wagon ready with two horses to help them. He had a sled already at the land. Eleanor could get more rocks for the fireplace.

The day was hotter then yesterday. The stumps were out, and the land was leveled. Eleanor kept a close eye on her man. She was doing what she always did. It was time for him to drink some water and rest. They were out of the sun away from other people's eyes. When she kissed him, Thomas pull her down on top of him. He role her over to deepen the kiss. Eleanor could see it in his eyes. In her mind she cried out. "Thomas touch me." When he broke the kiss. His eyes went to her face. He found he was breathing hard and so was she. Did he hear her in his mind? Last night it wasn't a dream. My parents can also hear each other at times. Little by little things has showed him she is his mate. "I thought so. Woman ye make me hunger for ye. I like this blouse now let's bring it down more. When she touched his face, he took her hand and kiss his way down her arm. He laid kisses all the way down to her breast. Thomas looked at Eleanor, her hand moved her blouse down. "Your breast are beautiful." His hand had cupped one of them as his thumb rubbed her nipple hard. He was watching what it was doing to her. When it was hard, he came down to suckle on the nipple. He heard her again. "Thomas give me more?.

He had broken away from what he was doing. "Woman what are ye doing to me. I wouldn't get anything done. Let me get the walls done so I can put a floor and door for the seller. Then it will be our time. You're not mind yet." He went quickly back to work. As he worked, he thought. "Why did I run from her?" Because he likes what he was doing. Thomas found his little brain was hungry for her. He didn't know if he could control him. "Ye not going to make me take her. I know ye wants to join with Eleanor's friend. I can't get her with my child. Ye got to wait. Right now, your too strong for me. I'll find a way to control ye." Thomas knew once he joined with her. He will want her as much as he could get. We must wait until the end of this week.

*　*　*

Eleanor sat up she could hear his thoughts, and he could hear hers. She took a deep breath. He was the one who started the kissing. "My love I like the fourplay. After lunch will see what we can get into. Don't worry about your friend."

Eleanor smile as he worked harder to make their seller deeper. He was going after the soil as he did with the stumps. She realize he had a battle going on with his friend. This was going to be her job to take care of his friend. His job was to make her girlfriend ready. Eleanor went back to what she was doing.

She smiled with the thoughts that the next time. Thomas touched her girlfriend it will get her closer to becoming his wife. She must help him keep control over his friend. She don't want him to take her until the end of the week. Eleanor knew he would worry about her when he's gone. She had notice it didn't take much to get him hot. She found that she was talking to herself but aloud. It was lunch time the sun was very hot today. She had brought food that wouldn't be heavy on their stomach. She had place everything down by the water. Before she went to get him, she would cool her body down.

*　*　*

Thomas looked around the two of them has gotten a lot done. If they have a cool day, he will burn the stumps. Now he couldn't see Eleanor, where was she? As he looked around, he saw a lot of rocks for the fireplace. His stomach was telling him he was hungry. She must have set up down by the water. There she was sitting on the rock her feet in the water and her blouse was off. She had put her hair in a ponytail. He could see those breast of hers. Thomas thought. "I'm not even touching her breast, and I can feel my body wants her. My friend now that he found out, her girlfriend wasn't his sister. I'm finding it's hard to control him. Thoughts came to his mind. "That he could slip inside her it would only hurt a bit. "Damn it! No… I'm not going to let ye have her. He wished she take off her skirt. Ye can't touch her. He can't get to that point. It's not about ye little friend. Stop it…"

Eleanor knew his little brain was fighting for control over his body. She knew once they married, anytime his friend wanted her. Thomas would let him have her girlfriend. It was cute calling their heat his friend or girlfriend. Sometimes he called his heat his little brain. Right now, she must help him with his friend. Slowly she took off her skirt so he could see all of her.

She could feel his eyes moving over her body. When she unbutton her skirt, she gave him a show as she wiggle out of it. She heard him say. "What a beautiful bottom she has. She would hold my heat or place him on her leg. He needs to feel the movement over skin to get him to come. Then he could give his love some pleasure."

In the water Eleanor turn just a bit so he could see what she was doing. With her hands she cupped some water to pour it over her breasts. She ran her hand down to her heat. Her body wanted those feeling back, she need to come. Her mind told her to place a finger inside her. With the knowledge that Thomas was watching her, it made her body react. From the corner of her eye, she saw that Thomas had something in his hand. Could that be his little brain? For what she saw it looked to be big. She knew that somehow that would fit inside her. Didn't she see where the baby came out of. Now she wanted to be touch by Thomas. Quickly she got out of the water and put a towel around her body.

Thomas finished what he was doing. He took care of his friend, he didn't realize that Eleanor heard him. His little brain had taken over when he saw her cum he then came. Now that his mind was clear, Thomas saw Eleanor was frustrated. It wasn't his hand or finger to make her come. Thomas thought he didn't know much about sex either. With his mind clear, he took his shirt off and his boots and ran into the water. The cold water had helped his friend go down. As he came out of the water, Eleanor brought him a towel to dry him off with. She looked into his eyes, she found that she would do anything for him, and she did.

She had watched Thomas go into the water. She was enjoying his bare chest, she had forgot that she had only a towel around her body. Her mind was only on his chest, she was remembering when his finger went inside her heat. Her man was strong, but his touch was gentle. She took a deep breath when he came out of the water. She thought why was her hand shaking when she handed the towel to him?

Thomas was watching her, she had helped him to take care of his friend. As he looked into her eyes. There was a different kind of look in them. Now he knew what it was. She had a hunger to be touch by him. Eleanor tried to hied her feelings. He could see the battle in her eyes. She wasn't strong enough to control them by herself. Not yet. He knew that he had a bit of time before his friend would wake up.

At first, he let her dry his back and chest for him. "Honey I know what ye need from me. How about ye leave these towels here. I'm going to give ye some pleasure."

Then he scoop her up into his arms. Her arms went around his neck. All she knew she wanted to belong to him. Then he spoke. "If my friend wakes up take care of him."

Eleanor nodded her head yes, her mind felt as if in a daze. Thomas smiled and placed her against the rock. the water was knee deep. He looked into her eyes, these eyes have been bewitching him. When he can have her for his wife, he will take her here in this spot but not yet. He told his friend that this was for Eleanor not him.

Thomas looked over her body. Her breasts were getting bigger, he knew they would be even bigger when he gets home. She had presented her breast to him, and his mouth took her nipple and suckle on it. His hand laid on the back of her head when he took her mouth in a hungry kiss. He was learning quickly what got her hot. As he suck on her nipple his hand went to her heat. He didn't stop until his finger slip inside her. His tounge made love to her mouth, as his finger brought her up and over. There was an explosion inside her, he found that she was very wet. Eleanor held on to his hand. This time it was a strong climax, he made her body come again. She was so wet he tried to push another finger inside. He moved her leg apart more as he gently pushed his finger into her.

He had forgotten he has magic. As he suck on her nipple her hips were grinding on his finger. With his middle finger he push as far in as he could. After she came, he did something he didn't understand. Why did his finger go into his mouth? All he knew she was sweet to the taste. Her pussy was a flower, and he taste her nectar. He put his arms around her back, as he kissed her lips. He let his body go backwards, bringing them into the water and under. He could see her eyes were dreamy when they came up. She wrapped her arms around his neck. "That was wonderful. I love ye Thomas. Thank ye for giving this pleasure to me.

His body was on shore she was sitting on him. "When your mine, I will let my friend do this to ye. I've heard from my brothers. This is one of the deepest ways to get my friend deeper inside ye.

Thomas felt they went back in time, he had forgot that he has magic. When she had his finger in her he made it bigger, his finger was the size of his heat. I wanted to have ye honey, could ye make him come again.

He had her laying down on top of him, she took his friend. As he moved his finger in her as he sip on her nectar. She was ready for him. That bubble went up. He didn't want to take her virginity on their wedding day. He want it now. "Honey make sure all the cum is out of him. I will wash him. I want to join with ye now. Ye can say no. But I thought on our wedding day, we could enjoy the sex once your maiden head is gone."

She wanted him and he is giving himself to her. He knows he will have to marry her. "Thomas this is your idea. I'm not trying to trap ye."

As she looked into his eyes she said. Aye…,"

He laid her down quickly, he didn't know how much time he had with his little friend. Ones she was on the blanket, he had kneeled between her legs. She was so wet, and he knew she wasn't going to feel him take her. Now he was just inside the door of her pussy. "Hang on now and he was inside her. He kissed her neck he was going to come out of her. Then he felt her take hold of him. She saw his eyes she took hold of him again. Now he moved and her body moved with him. She came and he brought her up again. He came out of her quickly and finish the job, she got him to cum four times. She checked to make sure he was safe. Then she kissed him, they went in the water were she wrapped her legs around him. She had slip him back inside her. "Eleanor what are ye doing."

She had smiled and her hand went down to feel him inside her. She got him to lay on the sand. Eleanor wanted to feel him go deep inside. She had sat up to fast and felt him go deep. Her eyes closed. "Honey put your hand there and lift yourself off me."

She did just what he had said. "Did ye find out what ye wanted to know."

She was so happy now, she was a woman, his woman. "I like making love with ye. Tomorrow we must make the food. See if my dress fits and Catherin does also. After we eat ye can't see us girls. We will have to take and wash up. It's going to be cool ye can burn the stamps at William's place. Bring all of ours there with your magic. Ye can use your magic to get the wood hotter. Then both lands will be cleared."

His mind was only on her. He knew it would have taken them months to get where they were now. But he wanted this foreplay to get her ready for him. He didn't like to go this fast with her. "We better get dress. I heard dad say they were going to check on the horses today."

The two of them were drying each other off. "Honey would ye, like some food now?"

Thomas smiled as he looked over the woman he was going to marry. "Aye… working and making love to ye, has made me very hungry."

*　　*　　*

It had been a cool morning, now that it was past noon it was getting hotter. At the pond, the trees made it cooler there was shade from the sun. They were eating their food when they heard two horses riding up.

He stood up he had his shirt back on. It was his mother and father. "Thomas where are ye."

He told Eleanor it was his father and mother taking a ride together. "Dad where over here by the pond having lunch."

He saw that they had seen how much work they have done. Eleanor made sure that she looked all together again.

The two riders rode up. "I see ye have a lot of work done, I don't want the two of ye to overdo it today. It's getting hotter to do any work out."

Thomas smiled, he was thankful that he didn't get caught with what the two of them had done. "We won't Dad. I have the wood for my barn now. There is just a few more things to do. I need to mark out the barn. Then we will call-it-a- day."

Thomas watched his father and mother ride away. He went back to Eleanor, she had put all the food away. "Honey did that scare ye to see my father and mother."

He had seen her take a deep breath. "Aye… What else do we have to do today?"

Thomas was setting on the blanket, he moved himself closer to Eleanor. He wanted to kiss her a bit more, his feelings for her was getting stronger. He found that he like touching and kissing her. Slowly he laid her down on the blanket as the kiss deepened.

His hand had her breast her arms were around his neck. "Please no more wile your parents are this close to us. Thomas stop it I said no more right now please."

She was so beautiful he had focused his mind on her. Eleanor's eyes were closed when he came back to her mouth. Then she pushed him away from her.

He notice that he had brought out those feelings again inside her. She was hot for him again, it didn't take her long for those feelings to come out. Good to know, then he thought he heard some horses again. He had picked Eleanor up into his arms, his lips were on hers. He was walking into the water slowly with her in his arms. His lips took her into a deep kiss, she didn't know what was happening. That's how his parent saw them. They watched their son take them under the water. His parents laughed when Eleanor broke away from him. When he came back up, she had pushed him back under the water. They heard Eleanor say. That wasn't fair, ye use your kissing to get me wet. They watch them for a bit as Thomas came up and grabbed her around her waist. Then he kissed her again.

Franceam was pleased that their son had found out he had feelings for Eleanor. He had enjoyed kissing her, and still was playful with her. She knew her son was doing a lot more then kissing her. "Honey let's go home it's too hot out. I got a lot to do for their wedding. Tomorrow the girls are going to help with the food. Will see if their dresses fit better."

I know Thomas like to burn the stumps in the morning. The afternoon ye can take them to town. It's a good time to get them things for their trip."

*   *   *

Eleanor liked what he had called her. "So, I'm his Angel."

He came over to her now. "Angel it's too hot let's go and rest for a bit. Then we will head home. Tonight, we can bring one more horse to Midnight. This will be the start of our horses. Did ye know that Sunshine could have twins."

She looked at him. "Twins that is what Catherine said. That she has Midnight's twin."

Eleanor smiled then she spoke. "Wait didn't your mother's say that there is twins in your family."

Thomas laughed and spoke, "Aye…" Then he kissed her. "We will do just find if we do have twins."

*   *   *

When the two of them came back from working on their home. Eleanor went quickly to clean up, Catherin was also getting ready. The two girl's work quickly to make a nice meal. At the table Daniel told them that. "Tomorrow us three will meet Theseus. Where going into town to get some supplies for your trip. While the men are doing that. The women will pick up supplies from Grana."

Thomas looked at his father. "Dad I had plans to bring one more horse to Midnight."

Franceam smiled at her husband. "Thomas ye and Eleanor can go and take care of that after your done eating. Your father will help me in the kitchen. Also, the girls are going to help me Tomorrow. Ye men can get a new kilt for the boys. Have ye forgotten we are going to have two weddings."

Franceam almost laugh the look her husband gave her. "Be careful son remember Midnight is a twin. Don't overdo it with these horses. The same with ye William. One or all could have twins. We will have are hands full."

Thomas nodded his head. "I think Midnight can manage it."

His mother looked at him. "Aye…, I wasn't talking about him. I was talking about the once that was going to help the females that will be giving birth."

Then it hit him. It also hit William. Two of them hit there forehead. Oh boy I understand now. We have a horse from Ronald, Jonathan, and Peter. He wanted Michael to have a good amount of the horses. His home also goes to him."

After they took their dishes to the kitchen. Thomas and Eleanor went to pick a female for Midnight. He looked at the females. "Witch one of these females do ye think Sunshine would let him have?"

Eleanor picked out one that she had her eyes on. I like this one. I'm hoping Sunshine will have a male. When ye come home if she give us a male. By the time are son is old enough to ride. Ye will have him train."

With the horse picked out they headed to the breeding pen. Thomas open the gate to let in the other horse. It was Sunshine who went to look the horse over. Thomas and Eleanor watched for a while, they found out that was a bad idea. The two of them felt the rush of heat between them. He spoke "I never thought I would have these feelings for ye. Come on before we can't stop what we would be doing."

Thomas went to place her on her horse. Instead of doing that he took her into his arms and kissed her deeply. This time he was able to touch her. His blood was running hot for her. It was getting late they had to leave now. He was finding he was getting stronger to say no to his friend.

The next day the men got dress they had to meet Theseus at the halfway point. At breakfast Daniel gave Thomas some money to buy what he would need for his trip. "Use some of it to buy ye lunch. Get that kilt of ye wedding. Tell them you're taking a trip. Don't say anything more about it."

Thomas smiled at his father. "Dad I have magic, he showed his father their new kilts and a knew shirt also, we have everything.

Thomas and William went to the barn, to get the horses ready for them to ride. Franceam gave Thomas some herbs to bring Grana. "This is so she can make some more medicines up. Eleanor after Thomas leaves, ye will be the first one to learn how to make these medicines. Ye will stay with Grana for two weeks. She will show ye how to grow these herbs. Catherin ones she come back then it will be your turn. How are ye getting along with the boys.

Franceam saw Eleanor's and Catherin cheeks was getting pink. She smile at her future daughter in law and her daughter. "I'm glad that he found out that he love's ye. The other night I saw ye my daughter I know that I could teach ye how to make the medicines. It will be good for ye after Thomas and William is on their trip. I didn't think my two sons would let ye go to the parties unmarried. I saw ye two likes to kiss ye. Our men they enjoy making love with the one they love. I think ye both are like myself. Ye like his kisses and his touch."

CHAPTER SIX

Their Wedding Day

HE FIREPLACE WAS where the four of them was going to be married. The girl's clean as the cake was brought down to the basement. It was much colder of place to keep their food cold. There was a special room made for nothing could get at it. Food was made for tomorrow the girls got wash up. Their hair was wash and braided. They had their bouquets made, everything was going to plan.

When the men got back they had to go to the library. Thamas saw where they to be married. He had made it with flowers and other pretty things for his sister and his bride to be.

Donald and Malinda was helping, was time to eat. Malinda and Franceam brought two plates out for the men. She went back and got the other plate. The women ate in the kitchen they had told the girls to look where they were going to be married. Eleanor knew that Thomas had done it for them. In her mind she told him, "Honey I love it thank ye, your sister also loves it."

The next morning Malinda and Franceam gave them breakfast, quickly all the men eat and went to feed the horses. Last night Thomas and William went to choose where they would sleep. Thomas found the room he liked. Everything was clean the bed made and firewood in the fireplace. Flowers and wine and Scotch was place for them.

William was a room down from them. Thomas did the same thing to their room.

Time was getting closer. Thomas had a bad feeling he went to look in the water. With a wave of his hand. He saw Bridget was planning to take her horse for a ride.

With a wave of his hand, he pointed to the heavens, please make it rain. To stop Bridget. It started to come down. Thomas went back to see what she was doing. She had turn around and went back in the house.

The women went past the window and saw that it was raining. Thomas heard Eleanor say, it's raining out. Then she heard Thomas say, "I had to make it rain, to stop Bridget from coming here to the castle."

Then Franceam looked at her daughter and Eleanor. "Oh, it's raining out we had sun, now it's raining." Eleanor smiled she didn't care. "The Lord let it rain to stop my mother for coming here."

Malinda and Franceam took the girls hand and led them to Franceam's bedroom. The women then show the girls the wedding dresses. Both girls were overwhelmed. After they got into the dresses, they looked at each other. Eleanor went over to Franceam, "Thank ye for all of this. Ye has always been a mother to me. Sis ye are the best, I love ye as if ye were my sister, soon to be my sister-in-law."

Catherine smile and nodded her head. Tears filled her eyes. "I love ye too." She went into her mother's arms. "Thank ye for being the best mamma around. Out of sadness came joy. I just found out that my mother always had my back."

The wedding dresses came from Franceam's mother-in-law that was for Eleanor. Catherine had her mother's wedding dress on. The two women had made them look just like knew. There was two bouquets of flowers for them.

*   *   *

In the den the three men got the two young men dress in their best clothes. It was time for Daniel and Theseus to bring their daughters to the young men. Donald was the one to marry them.

At the bedroom door when they knocked, and the door was opened. Both men felt like crying. Theseus looked at his little girl. "Thomas will make ye a good husband. Ye are so beautiful daughter. I wished it didn't have to be this way."

Eleanor wasn't going to let this spoil their wedding day. The rain was their cover, that no one would know what was happening. "Dad I'm glad ye are here to give me away."

He took her into his arms and lay a kiss on her cheek and another one from her mother.

Daniel looked at his little girl. "Ye look so much like your mother when we got married. Now I'm going to give ye to the young man who help ye to grow up. William was always yours as Thomas was always Eleanor's. I knew the four of ye always took care of each other."

*　　*　　*

Then Theseus open the door. That was when Franceam started to play the piano. Donald brought out Thomas and William. The young men were in full dress, a sheath of plaid with down there back a big emblem to hold it in place. The music told Theseus it was time to take his daughter to the man she will marry.

Thomas eyes were locked on Eleanor. There was flowers in her hair with ribbons going down to the end of her hair. She heard him say in her mind. "My beautiful angel, I'm the luckiest man around." When Thomas saw her, right then he knew this was right. He never saw a more beautiful woman before. He couldn't believe all this time he had kept her away from him. No more she will become his. Once he comes back home. He will have her as often as she lets him. When the time is right, she will give him a son. I still have a lot to learn. Tonight, we will enjoy each other when we become one and I will give her my seed. William was so proud of his sister. He watched Thomas eyes as his sister came up to him.

*   *   *

Then the music started over again. When he saw Catherine and her father coming down to him. He knew what Thomas felt. She had taken his breath away. He couldn't believe he thought of her as his sister. "No more he thought, she will be his wife. Tonight, they will become as one."

Thomas took his eyes away from Eleanor. He had to watch his sister come down with their father. There was so much pride in his eyes for them.

Theseus stood by his son, as the two of them watch Catherin come down the walkway. Then Daniel went and stand by Thomas.

*   *   *

Daniel could see his son focus was on his bride. He knew the feeling as his wife had walked down to her husband side. When Eleanor was next to Thomas, he had taken the locket out. Eleanor had her braid in hand.

Donald had two ribbons with him. He spoke, we will end this together. Thomas ye will speak first. Then William will speak. Eleanor ye will go after William then Catherine. Ones ye four said your promises to each other. Then I will wrap these ribbons around your hands, ones ye have the ribbon I will say some words. Thomas ye start first.

*   *   *

Then they started. "I Thomas MacGregor take ye Eleanor Heart to be my wife. To have and hole through sickness and health until death do, we part." Thomas took the chain and wrapped it around her right hand to her arm.

Then William spoke. "I William Heart take ye Catherine MacGregor to be my wife. To have and hole through sickness and health until death do, we part." William took the chain and wrapped it around her right hand to her arm.

Then Eleanor spoke. "I Eleanor Heart take ye Thomas MacGregor to be my husband. To have and hole through sickness and health until death do, we part. Eleanor took her braid and wrapped it around his right hand to his arm.

Then Catherine spoke. "I Catherine MacGregor take ye William Heart to be my husband. To have and hole through sickness and health until death do, we part. Catherine took her braid and wrapped it around his right hand to his arm.

Donald took the ribbon and wrapped it over their promise to each other. With all four of them had their ribbon around their promise. He spoke. "Here in front of God and the people who loves them. I declare them to be husband—wife. What the Lord brought together let know man break them apart. Ye may kiss your brides."

Thomas took the locket and put it around her neck. Eleanor then put her braid into his sporran. "Ye are now my wife forever. I love ye so much honey." Thomas drew Eleanor into his arms and kissed her deeply.

William took the locket and put it around her neck. Catherine then put her braid into his sporran. "Ye are now my wife forever. I love ye so much honey." William drew Catherine into his arms and kissed her deeply.

"We have here Mr. & Mrs. MacGregor also Mr. & Mrs. Heart."

*　　*　　*

His mother went over to the piano and started to play. They dance to the music after that they had their meal. Eleanor went to change her dress, she had given the dress back to Franceam.

Thomas's mother had placed the wedding dresses in the box and put it away for her. "Eleanor this is now your dress. I had my mother's when I married Daniel. My mother-in-law said that there will be a time when one of your sons will marry. The young woman will need a dress to marry him in."

Catherine had her mother's dress. The two girls had tears in their eyes. Eleanor let Catherine to go out first. She needed them to be first this time. The two hugged and she watch her friend to got to her brother.

*   *   *

That's when Franceam took her into her arms. "Are ye scared for what is to come."

Then she looked at Franceam. "No! For a long time, Thomas and I have been going down this path. Little by little Thomas found out he like holding me. He told me that list had scared him. He had to look back when the bear attacked me. Franceam, I saw what he had to do. That bear went mad I think Thomas had gone a little mad also. I knew then if we survive that day, I was going to make him my husband. The only thing stopping him was the promise to my brother. I knew once he let that go, nothing would stop him from finding out if he loved me.

"Aye… Sex had jumped in the moment we had kissed. We both had gotten hit with it hard. Thomas had to find a way to control his friend. The first time he try to touch me. His friend tried to take over. He had run from me. At first, I thought I did something wrong. When I was by the pond, I was trying to cool my body down. Thomas came looking for me. That's when I found out that I could hear his thoughts. That's when I gave him a show and he took care of his friend. I know a lot now about sex. It's always been Thomas to teach me about my body. When I started, he told me it was all right? Today ye have become a woman. My mother told me nothing about my body. It's been Thomas who told me what to expect. I think when we were talking about being away from each other. It scared him when I told him. What if another woman got ye hot enough that your friend takes over? I won't stop ye from going. If it happens with another woman, she will stop ye and make ye marry her. Where will that leave me?"

Franceam smiled at Eleanor. "Well played… he knew ye had made up your mind. It had force him to think if he should take the chance. I believe that on his twenty first birthday my brother is taking him and William to learn how to please a woman. When he comes home, I have a bad feeling he's going to have to fight. That man is not going to let him bring his family home with them."

Eleanor looked at her mother-in-law. "I believe your right about that. Right now, I don't want to think about that. There will be plenty of time to think then. I want to enjoy my husband."

*　　*　　*

Daniel was talking to his son. When the door open Thomas got up from his chair. The sun was going down. His father laid a hand on his son shoulder. "It's time for the two of ye to go upstairs."

Thomas walked over to his wife. He took her into his arms and kissed her. Daniel had some wine for the two of them to drink. They thanked both of their parents for what they have done for them. Then he took Eleanor's hand and walked up the stairs. His parents watched them go up. Eleanor didn't have any nerves, she knew what was going to happen.

*　　*　　*

She was a little giggly. Thomas turn to her he brought her into his arms. "Are ye worried about anything?"

Eleanor enjoy having his arms around her. "No… it felt funny knowing that your parents was watching us heading to our bedroom. This will be our first time sleeping with each other."

At the end of the hallway, he stopped at the doorway and opened the door. Before she could go in, he scooped her off her feet. He had caried her over the threshold, and with his foot he pushed the door close. The back room was all set up for them, there was a fire going in the fireplace. On the little table was a pitcher of water if they need it. They even had a bottle of wine and some food to eat. Beautiful flowers were also on the table. With her arms around his neck. She drew him to her mouth and kissed him.

When the kiss ended, she spoke. "Thomas let me undress ye, I would like to touch your body. Ye have had your fun touching me, it's my turn to enjoy ye." Before he could protest, she had his shirt off. Then she was working on his kilt next, it was taken off him quickly. He was setting on the bed, she had parted his legs, as she kneel between them. Eleanor had his friend in her hand. She was telling Thomas about the sack below his friend. "It has two jewels inside. I see your friend is waking up. I didn't know that the sack filles up also, good to know. He wanted to take over, but she had started to move her hand over his friend. Thomas eyes went wide when her mouth went around his friend. He had his hand on the back of her head, all he could do was watch her take control. What a rush for him, when his body arch, and his friend came. When she was done Thomas help her to her feet.

*   *   *

Thomas had her undress quickly and on the bed under him. "I didn't think ye would do that. I'm glad ye did, for now I'm going to enjoy ye. Your girlfriend and mind will become as one. Let's see if she is a wake. He sucked on her nipple until Eleanor said. "She's up."

Thomas was on one elbow his friend in hand. As he moved between her friend's lips. He was going to play with her a bit more. He had found that his friend was ready to play again. At the door to her girlfriend his friend knocked. Her lips was wet and so was he. When her lips open, his friend came inside. Eleanor felt the thickness within her, her girlfriend felt him twitching. It was her girlfriend who took hold of him. Thomas took her mouth in a hungry kiss. She was watching his eyes.

*   *   *

Right then she saw the hunger when his friend took over. The feeling of his friend moving quickly inside her. She felt the power of his strokes, as her body stiffen until she came. Thomas didn't let her rest as he brought her back up. She had felt his body stiffen, his friend was pumping his seed deep inside her. Thomas drop on top of her, he kissed her neck as he felt little quakes moving over his friend. Then he turn her over on top of him. "I love ye so much. I couldn't let anyone take ye from me. Thank ye for doing that for me."

Eleanor went to sit up she knew that she had to go slow. Now she wanted to know how it feels when he cum in this position she moved over getting them both hot. "He told her sit up straight. She watch when her man came. His climax was strong and powerful it was wonderful.

Thomas pulled her down to him, "What a day my sweet Angel. I like my toys do ye mine having me more than ones."

In our bedroom or on are land, I will take as much as ye let me have your pussy. I will put a bubble around us and your brother. How about we go to sleep. Let him have her until he comes out on his own.

"What a feeling to have him go deeper within me. I love taking hold of your friend like this. Thomas the feeling when ye came inside me, I want more of this. Honey I want ye to make love to me as often as ye like."

Thomas looked at her his hands around her waist. "Are ye saying ye want my friend inside ye like this?"

She looked at Thomas and spoke. "Aye… I need to come again."

Thomas looked at his wife and pulled her down to him. He turn her over and started to move, until she came again. She had to work hard to come. Her body was relaxed now, as he turned her over on top of him.

"Honey let's get clean up." Once they were back in bed, he pulled her into him and fell asleep.

* * *

The next day the two of them went riding. His mother had made a picnic lunch for them. The two of them rode side by side. He had turn off at a place where they could be alone together. When he got off his horse Thomas told Eleanor to stay there. He brought a blanket with him and laid it out for them with their picnic basket. He led the horses inside so they wouldn't be seen. Thomas walked over to her and placed his hands around her waist. She was riding sidesaddle her body was facing him. For just a minute he laid his head on her lap. He felt Eleanor's hands run through his hair. Softly she moved her hand over his face. Then he looked up at her.

Thomas put his head back on her lap. "Honey right now I can't get enough of ye. I want to bring ye with me. I know I can't, it wouldn't be safe for ye. I want to touch ye to feel every part of your body."

She knew what he wanted to do to her. It was imposable to do right now. Thomas lift her dress up to her heat. "Let's see what ye think of my lips kissing my way to your heat." Thomas started at her knees. He moved her legs apart and started to kiss the under part of her thigh. Eleanor's hands was on his head. She had her eyes close. Those butterflies were back when his lips was near her friend. Her hands pulled his head harder against that spot. Thomas had to pull away from her. "So ye like that? When I get home, we will enjoy each other like this. After we have a year together then we can try for are child."

She looked at her man and spoke. "I wish ye could come to me at night. To make love to me so we could sleep in each other's arms. I love to be touch by ye, what ye are doing is making me want ye."

Thomas smiled at her. He took and pulled her to him. With his hands, on her bottom and her dress up. He took her off her horse. Eleanor laughed and giggle of how she looked. Slowly he let her down along with her skirt going to the ground. He put that skirt a side and went for her top and took it off. Laying her down he came down on top of her. Thomas looked at his wife and spoke. "Ye no me to well, my love. I'm thankful ye are just as hungry for me as I'm for ye. I wish I didn't have to go. Right now, I want ye as many times as I can have ye."

He was enjoying her breast making her want to touch him. She was pulling at his top trying to get it off him. Now he was laughing as she got him to work, with her. To help her out he took off his kilt."

Eleanor went for his friend. "Will ye tell me, why a man would try to ride his wife like his horse ride the female. Is that why he gets behind her?"

Thomas looked at her. "For a horse it the only way. Honey everything, we do is the first time for me and ye. We can try it out if ye like."

After they got dress, they laid on the blanket. "One thing about that way. When your head is on the ground, I can go deeper inside ye."

She was laying on his arm with one arm over his chest. "For myself, your friend went deeper inside his girlfriend. I wish that the days wouldn't go by so fast."

Now Eleanor was looking at Thomas. He pulled her to him and kissed her deeply. She had a tear rolling down her cheek. Thomas had gone and kissed it away. "I don't know what is worse having ye now or waiting until I get home."

Eleanor cup his face with her hands. "I know what you're saying. Remember when you're with another woman. Don't think of me when your eyes are close it would be easy to think she was me."

Thomas smiled and spoke. "I'm glad we married now. Honey ye know me to well. It's good to know that. That's why I want to know your body. When I dream of ye. I want to think we're making love to each other. Now ye know what my lips feel like. The butterflies is telling ye somethings happening to your friend. The inner part of your thigh is sensitive. For myself when I touch your breast, and my friend tries to take over. I'm glad we are married. I'm getting more control over my friend.

Thomas loved holding her in his arms. "Ye know the way I have ye right now. I like this a lot. You're a beautiful woman. It took a long time to see what I had right here. Honey this is all new to us. Ye have been there when I need ye. I love the food ye cook for me and the way ye take care of me. Even when we weren't married."

Eleanor made shore she moved over his mouth with her nipple. "Everything I can to ye. When ye come home to me. I will have my fun driving ye to want me." Then she told him open your mouth. Don't bite me. His arms was still over his head. Then he felt something soft moving over his face and lips. She had given him something to drive her a little crazy also. His tounge lick then suck on her nipple. "Aye… those butterflies are back. Thomas, I need ye again. Every time I think of ye away from me. Makes me want ye friend inside of his girlfriend. Thomas, we just found each other. Soon ye will be taken away from me."

He had taken his shirt off. He pulled her to him it was time to please her. He had laid her down on her back. "Thomas your kilt has to come off and my skirt also."

They got to their feet. He made quick work of his kilt. Eleanor didn't drop her skirt yet. She had turned away from him. "Thomas, I'm glad you're my husband. I don't want any other man to touch me. I almost wish ye would give me a child. I'm scared ye may come back to me dead. If we didn't marry and ye brought a woman home. I can fight to try to win ye back. I can't fight to bring ye back from the dead. Now that we have made love, this is all I would have left. If something happen to ye. Oh Thomas!" She was crying now.

He came up to her and put his arms around her waist. He pulled her into him and kissed her neck. "Honey do ye want to try for a child now?"

Eleanor had gone quiet she closed her eyes. She saw a baby boy not knowing his daddy. "No… I'm still too young to have one now. I would like to have a baby when I'm twenty. I want to enjoy ye when ye get home."

Thomas turn her and drop her skirt and the shield for her friend. He came inside her friend. He took hold of her bottom and lifted her legs around his waist. There was a rock he took her over to and laid her on. As he moved inside her. "I will be back, I'm not going to give ye our child yet. I want to see your body grow with are child inside ye. I don't see anything of my death. Honey I wasn't going to say anything until I was home. I had a vision of ye and are child. Ye were feeding our baby boy. I was lying next to ye. I had taken your nipple and started to suck on your breaths. Our child didn't like that, so he pulled your nipple and ye bop me."

She lift herself up and looked at him. Now she started to laugh. What a wonderful feeling it gave her. Then she spoke. "Is this when ye stared off in the distant? Ye had a big smile on your face."

He nodded his head. "I love when ye laugh. It's a sweet sound, I even like it more when I'm inside ye. Ye can ask me anything right now."

Then he stopped moving. Even when she had taken hold of him. "I still must leave. There are things I must see. I want to know why the men of my family fought so hard for Scotland. I've heard there are skills I can learn and bring back here to the Highlands."

Thomas ran his hand up to her breast. He started playing with her nipple making it hard. He knew his wife feared losing him in a battle. She is using sex to chaste these feelings away. "So be it." As he worked to get her to come her body had relaxed after she came. He clean them up and the two of them got dress.

It was time to have some food. How things have change for the two of them once he crossed over. As he ate, he realized the two of them was meant to be together. After eating he drew her to him. He loved kissing her those sweet lips was meant to be kissed by him.

Thomas helped Eleanor to pick things up. Wow, he thought. I used to tease her when she had to do something. With everything picked up he pulled her into him. He loved to kiss her, for a bit he held her in his arms. What will it be like when he gets home? He knew that she will be studying to become a midwife. He knew mama would make her learn how to make medicine with Grana.

*　　*　　*

When Grana met his mother, she had put her to work teaching her to become a midwife. At the time there was no healer in the Highlands. Daniel's mother had taken Franceam in after her mother died. Her brother was taken in by Grana's brother. His wife had died after childbirth, he was looking for a husband for his daughter. When Donald saw Malinda, he fell in love with her. Grana brother had died in battle. As the war went on. The three men Daniel Theseus and Donald became good friends. For a long time, Grana took care of his daughter Malinda and her daughter Bridget.

Grana had move to the Highlands to help her brother. She had lost her husband in the war. At the time the Highlands wasn't affected. In time men were pulled from the Highlands. Then women and younger men had to take care of their homes and farms. In the Spring the three men had chosen their mate. It was hard on Daniel when he lost his twin to the war. Both men fell in love with Franceam. His brother knew that she loved Daniel. When the knife came at his brothers back, he took it for him. Franceam felt the grief that Daniel had felt. She knew that he lost his twin.

Then Thomas remember his father was a twin. "Honey do ye know when ye conceive our child ye may have twins?"

Eleanor was haft asleep when she heard the words 'twins. She lift herself up and looked at him. "Don't tell me there is twins with your horse and ye. Wow! Ye better come home. I will need help with our children then."

He looked at her and ran a hand over her stomach. Your built to have children. Your tall and your breast will be able to feed two babies. I'll be home to watch ye get bigger with our two children. Most of all

I will enjoy making our children with ye. They say a woman will know when she conceive a child. When I'm home will ye tell me if ye did?"

Eleanor was in his arms when she pulled away from him. "Aye… I will tell ye if I'm with child. Right now, I like sex too much to become pregnant right now. I want ye here to feel what I feel. To be with me when our child or children is born to us. Will ye do that for me."

Thomas smiled he got to his feet and pulled her up. "Aye… That I will do. I must lay with ye and our child so ye can bop me on the head."

He liked when she turns red. Thomas pulled her to him and kissed Eleanor. We both Then he brought her to her horse and lifted her onto the saddle. "Let's go get the females and bring them to the castle. I don't think that Midnight will let Sunshine out of his sight."

A thought came to him. He has magic I wonder if she could feel him inside her. Just think of her pussy got him hard. With a wave of his hand, he pictured his heat inside her pussy. He moved inside his wife. She had to grab the saddle horn as he got her to come. Her heart was beating fast. "Thomas!"

He rode up to her and show her it was him. "I didn't know if it would work. On the days ye can't sleep I will send ye my little friend to ye. What I feel ye will also feel."

*　*　*

At the breeding pin Thomas looked at the other females. "Honey I wish I could help ye with the birthing of these colts. Ye may have your hands full. If Midnight is like my father's horse. Then all three of them will have twins. I made sure that the female could carry twins. That will make us ten horses. Honey can ye ride the other way so ye can help me with these two." When they got there, they had seen that there was another horse was added to the others.

Donald had brought Midnight another female. He was watching Sunshine look over that female. She had made that female put her head on her back. While Midnight went right to work. The scent of this female made him horny. It was as if Sunshine told her, she would let my man mate with ye. When her tail went up Midnight enjoyed her. When she came, he mounted her? Eleanor watch as she remember what Thomas had done to her.

Donald had gone over to the two of them. "Ye two look good together. How is the honeymoon going?"

Thomas looked at his bride. "I wish it wouldn't stop. I like to thank ye dad for helping us four."

Donald smile at the two of them. "Think nothing of it. Remember not to tell Duncan when he gets back. Sunshine loves her mate. When I brought that one in the pen. Sunshine came over to the new female. The female stopped prancing. Sunshine moved around her then she called Midnight over."

Thomas smiled and spoke. "She was his first female; they grew up together. We saw that each time he had mated with one of them. She made him drink some water. Then she backed away from them. Midnight went to see if she was ready to be mated with. Eleanor saw when he licked the female. He whinnied and licked her again then he mounted her. Donald smiled he had saw Eleanor looked at Thomas. Then she understood it was part of mating for the male kingdom. When Midnight was done, Sunshine came over to him and led him to the water. She was his first.

Donald headed back on his horse. "Eleanor so ye are going to be a midwife. Ye may have to help with these four females. Thomas remember your horse was a twin. Catherin has the other twin. There will be other males to mate with your females. This horse came from Peter. He had given a horse to ye all. William got one also."

Thomas walked over to him. "Thank ye dad."

He smiled at Thomas. "Ye remembered that's good my boy. Ye two take care I will see ye later."

One's Midnight was done Thomas went for the other two females. With the other two horses he gave Eleanor one. He took the other horse, and they headed out to the castle. When they came back for the other three. Thomas spoke. "We can let her stay with Sunshine and Midnight. It had taken them a while to get the other two in the other pen. When they came back Midnight was licking her again. She wanted him as she kept her tail out of his way. After he's done, we will take them back with us. We can leave the three together for tonight. Thomas brought out the blanket. The two of them laid down to wait for him to get done. Eleanor was laying on his shoulder with one arm laying on his chest. Thomas had his arm under her arm holding on to her. He was on his back with his eyes closed. He woke up when he heard horses coming over the bridge. "Eleanor, we have company." She quickly woke up. They were smart to hide from anyone sight. It was Thomas's parents that rode over to see them.

Daniel saw that there was another horse and Thunder was mating with her. "Hello anyone here?"

Thomas stood up and wave at his parents. "Dad we are over here. Uncle brought over this horse. This horse came from Peter."

Daniel and his wife came over to them. Then his mother spoke up. "He came over to tell us Duncan will be late coming back. The note didn't say why he was going to be late. My brother is doing what the three of us did. He asked me if he could give Midnight one of Peter's horses. Before they left, he had left this letter to me. He wanted to give Thomas a horse of his. Everything that belong to Peter was given to the people he loved. Even William got one of his horses."

*　*　*

Eleanor and Thomas was on their land. The two was resting before going back to work. That's when William and Catherine came to warn them. It was time to eat, between the two girls they had enough food. The four of them didn't eat much. William spoke. "What can we do?"

Thomas looked at Eleanor. "All we can do is go on with are plans. They had the horses out of sight. Then they heard two horses riding up. The four of them quickly got out of sight.

Bridget and Theseus was looking for their children. "There not here either. My cousin wanted me there as soon as I can get there. She needs help with everything. I have a recipe to get my hormones balance again. I thought I was too young for that. I'm sorry doing that to ye four. Right now, I understand, when your hormones are out of balance nothing make sense. Ye four are under the care of the MacGregor's.

*   *   *

Thomas motion to stay here. Eleanor spoke, "I'm going with ye, she is my mother."

He just shook his head no. Thomas walked out to talk with them. "Hello Mr. & Mrs. Heart."

Eleanor watched her mother. "I see they don't want to talk with me."

Thomas shook his head. "No that's not it. I want to tell ye something. Things have been hard for the four of us. I thought to tell ye when ye talk about my sister and I, could ye use the name McKinnon. Ye, see they came after all my brothers. They don't know about me or my sister. But they knew about my sister-in-law, that she could be having a boy. I'm taking the last name McKinnon to try to find my brother's. William and I want to learn about Scotland. There are things I like to learn more on woodworking and how to make swords.

"Ye will not know about what the four of us decide. For many years, the two girls have been our sister's. No matter what we decide on, we must play the game to find a spouse. It will only take one person to say my daughter married a MacGregor or my son married a MacGregor. This man kills who ever could get in his way. Our four lives are in your hands. If anyone ask about the MacGregor ye do not know them. Please he is in the lowland of Scotland.

"Ronald couldn't live without his wife and son. He knew they were going to come after them. He wanted to kill as many hire killers as possible before he died. Have a safe trip to your cousin's place. Be aware of who is around ye. This man kills people like they are bugs. I had a dream that he tried to burn my brother alive. Please call William and Catherine and me McKinnon. I'm going to ask my mother to use her maiden's name. That is how dangerous this is. Thank ye for listening to me. Have a nice ride home."

CHAPTER SEVEN

Trouble with his mother-in-Law

ON MONDAY, THE two of them went back to Thomas's land. He had to get the root cellar dug out more. Once that was done, he had to put a floor on top. He will have to place a door next to keep out the animals. They were having another hot day.

Before they left to go to their land, Eleanor's mother and father came over. She found out that her mother didn't leave yet. She had to wait until one of the hired hands to come back from seeing his parents. Her brother and Catherine left right at sunrise to their land.

As Eleanor was walking down the path, her mother was heading up. Not even saying a greeting to her daughter, she started in on her. "Did Thomas asked ye to marry him. Eleanor shook her head no. Then her mother got upset with her. She was trying to go past her mother. Bridget had yelled at her daughter. "Eleanor ye will face me and answer my question. Now what is he waiting for? Why are ye helping him with his place when you're not going to be his wife?"

Eleanor could feel the anger building up inside her. "I have had enough of this, just leave me alone mother. Don't ye think Thomas and my brother has enough to think about. Ye were to be heading to your cousin's place. That big talk about using that drink was a lie, mother ye have been heartless to us. William is going to fine our older brother, we all know that the men they gone up against was higher killers. They may have to fight to get them into the Highlands. Leave me alone mother, I have nothing more to talk to you about."

Eleanor thought that everything was all right. That her mother was on her way to her cousin's place. She thought that she was taking what Thomas's mother gave her. "Ye lied to all of us. Catherine and I will be working with Franceam. I'm not coming home with ye."

Franceam heard what was happening. She yell to get Eleanor inside the castle. "Eleanor could ye come in here, I have something for ye and Thomas."

She looked at her mother and spoke. "Leave Thomas and William alone. Don't push me mother, I will find a way to stay away from ye. Ye better have Grana or the doctor in the city check ye out. Lately ye been hateful to us all."

Eleanor turned and went into the castle. She heard her mother yelling for her to come back here. That she will not speak to her that way. Franceam was waiting for Eleanor with open arms. She ran right into her arms. "I'm sorry that's not like me, I don't know why she lie to us. I must write this down so when I get her age, I will know what to do."

Franceam just brushed her hair. "Here some cookies go out the side door. I'll take care of your mother."

She gave her a kiss on the cheek and went out the side door quickly. Thomas saw her coming down the hill. "Eleanor why are ye running? It's too hot out to do that."

Then he saw his mother talking, but Eleanor's mother was yelling. "I see your mother is here. I thought that she would be gone by now. Did she give ye a hard time about me marrying ye?"

Eleanor got on top of the wagon. She didn't say anything to him about what happened. "Your mom gave us cookies for lunch. Are we ready to go?"

Thomas looked at his wife, this had upset her a lot. He looked toured the hill, their fathers were going up the hill. There was two ways to get to his land. The short way and the long way, he took the long way. This way they didn't have to go by his parents. Once they were in the cover of the trees, he stopped the wagon. "Ye come here and sit on my lap."

She wanted to fight about it. All he did was put his hands around her waist and lift her to him. There wasn't anything sexy about it. Thomas had one arm holding her on his lap. "Stop fighting me. I know she gave ye a hard time. It's going to be all right honey."

Eleanor try to pull away from him. All he did was just hold her in place. He knew it was going to come to a head. Once she started to fight with her mother in her mind. He didn't like this way to make her cry. It had upset her too much to let it slide. Then he felt her body relax a bit, she buried her face into his neck. Thomas picked up the rains and headed to their land. He could feel the deep sobs as the tears rolled down his neck.

That was all right with him. Eleanor spoke. "Why does she do this to us? She is a hard person lately to live with. She is going through midlife, mama is at that age. I hope your mother can help her, someone needs to before another person hurts her. Honey I'm sorry for what I did, thank ye for loving me as ye do. He was at his land when he stopped. She took his mouth into a hungry kiss. Then she got up.

Thomas got down from the wagon then lifted her off. She looked into his eyes. When he drew her into his arms and kissed her? "I'm going to miss kissing ye. Honey I love ye so much." This time he deepen the kiss. His hand moved over her breast. "If I keep going, I will be making love to ye."

He had taken off his shirt and through it into the wagon. "Thomas what do ye have in mind for me to do today."

Eleanor loved to see his shirt off. He had led the horses over to where the house was to be. "Honey ye can do what ye like. I'm going to get the root cellar dug out more. I think it will be a good place to go if it's a bad storm."

Eleanor went over to tell him she was sorry. She also wanted a kiss from him. They were now in the third week, it was going too fast for her. Thomas had just got the tools out. She had come up behind him and put her arms around his waist. She had kissed the back of his neck. "Do ye like this honey?"

Thomas had stopped what he was doing. She had moved her hands over his shoulders and down his arms as she held him close to her. "I'm sorry for the way I acted." Then he brought her to the front of him. "There is nothing to be sorry about, I got ye to sit on my lap so I could hold ye." He gave her another kiss. "How about ye look for those herbs ye were talking about. The dirt I will be taking out will be good soil for your garden."

*   *   *

Eleanor gave him another kiss. "That's a good idea my love. Thomas ye said ye must go into town tomorrow. I could drop off the herbs to Grana. That's if ye want the town people to see me with ye."

Thomas saw the worry look on her face. "Eleanor ye are my best friend. Besides my mother is training ye to be a midwife. Ye had to bring these herbs into town for Grana. They all know ye are like a sister to me." Then he laughed. "Never again will ye be my sister." He took another kiss and head to dig out more soil.

Eleanor smiled at Thomas. Then she went off to get something from the wagon. There was string to tie the herbs up. She made shore their food was out of the sun. With the string in hand, she went off to fine the herbs. She found a good size bed of them. As she started to pick some of them and tied them up to dry. She found there was enough for Grana and Franceam.

* * *

Then she started to clean the garden up. Right in the middle of her garden was this big rock. She had dug around it, the more she dug the bigger it got. As she was doing that the sun had moved over her.

Eleanor had forgot to get water for her and Thomas. The more she dug the madder she got. "Ye are just like my mother. I don't want ye in my garden, now she was yelling at it. The rock had become her mother.

Thomas could hear her voice now. He had notice Eleanor hadn't brought him any water. That meant she hasn't had any water herself. He poured two cups of water from their well. One of them he drank the other he brought over to Eleanor. "What are ye doing to yourself? Here drink this, it's too hot for ye not to be drinking any water. Can't ye see the sun is right over ye?"

Eleanor looked to be sweating too much. "I'm fine, I don't need any water leave me be." She didn't realize who was talking to her. Her face and the back of her neck was getting red. That rock became her mother, now she was yelling.

Thomas knew she didn't know who he was. "Damn-it woman ye need this water ye don't know who I am. Drink this water right this minute. Eleanor, please drink the water ye need it."

She had grabbed the cup from him and drank the water down. "There are ye satisfied mother? Can I go back to work?"

The heat was too much for her, the sun was right over the garden. He had to get her down to the water. Thomas notice it was all about her mother, to Eleanor she was this rock. He had taken her hand and tried to make her come with him. "Eleanor why are ye fighting me? Ye need to cool off your body. Stop it… That rock is not your mother. Damn-it leave that rock alone." Thomas had to get that rock out of her garden.

Eleanor didn't say anything, the tears were trying to start. She had tried to pick up a rock that was too big for her. In a deep voice he bellowed. "Damn-it woman ye are going to hurt yourself. Eleanor don't lift that rock." He had seen her jump. Thomas picked her up and set her a side. He picked the rock up as if it was no big deal. Then through it into another rock breaking it into smaller pieces.

Then he went over to her lifting her up to her feet. "Honey ye didn't do anything wrong. Ye were trying to keep your promise to me. Ye know that your mother can't keep a secret, that's why ye didn't tell her. Eleanor that rock isn't your mother. Ye have gotten too much sun today."

*   *   *

She was still trying to cry but the tears wouldn't come. Her head started to hurt, her face and neck felt hot. She didn't even see that he took care of that rock. She was trying to clear her mind. What did he mean the rock wasn't her mother? At the time Eleanor didn't realize Thomas through her over his shoulder and headed down to the pond.

He had her in his arms but wouldn't let him carry her that way. So, he through her over his shoulder. "Put me down right now."

Eleanor's feet was now kicking Thomas in the stomach. "No ye need to get your body cool down. Stop kicking me. Damn it all. Will ye stop yelling at your mother she is not here. Ye are yelling at a rock that was in your garden. Ye had too much sun honey."

He had moved her over so she couldn't kick him in the stomach. "No, put me down I need to tell her off." Now she pulled his kilt up and tried to spank his bottom. "Put me down right now."

Thomas had it and yelled in his mind. "Eleanor ye are my wife, your mother is not here. Stop what ye are doing right now."

At the pond he was trying to take off her shoes. She didn't know what to think of hearing a man's voice in her head. She found that thinking made her head hurt more. He had laid her on the grass with her legs over his lap. She had sat up to try stopping him from taking her shoes off. Thomas took off his boots and sporran.

Eleanor had wiggle out of his arms and was heading back to that rock. Before she could get up the hill, he grab her around the waist. Quickly he spun her around and put her back on his shoulders. Then ran into the deepest part of the pond. There he dropped her into the water, she came up sputtering. Thomas grab her around her waist pulling her to him. She try to pull away from him. "Ye did nothing wrong." He then kissed her. "Stop fighting me. Honey your mother try to get ye to say I was going to marry ye. Your mother don't know that ye are my wife. Eleanor ye did nothing wrong. Ye did what I asked of ye. Ye been yelling at a rock not your mother."

*　　*　　*

She tried to understand what he had said. Thomas brought her over to the rock and sat her down on his lap. Her skirt was up around her waist. He moved cool water over her legs, holding her in place he laid her head in the water. Even her blouse was up he moved the water over her stomach and breast. Eleanor legs was parted she didn't have anything under her skirt.

He kept the water moving over her body. She had stopped fighting him. "How do ye feel now?"

She had her eyes close as cool water moved over her heat. "Much better. I can feel your friend under me."

She try to set up. "Don't worry about my friend. How's your head? Is it still hurting ye?"

Thomas pulled her up to his arms. He had pulled down her clothing as she rested her head in his arm. "Thank ye for saving me from the sun. Ye said I was yelling at a rock that I called my mother. If my head didn't hurt, I would laugh about that."

He had brushed the hair away from her face. "Ye were mad at the rock, it was too heavy for ye. Somehow ye thought it was your mother.

Please don't pick up any big rocks. You're not a man and ye could hurt yourself, to the point that we wouldn't be able to have children. Honey ye scared me that sun did a number on ye. I know your mother can get under your skin, don't let her."

Eleanor looked at her husband. "Have I told ye I love ye. That I can't live without ye. Do ye think we can lay in the water together? I need to be one with ye. His girlfriend needs just to be joined with him.

*　　*　　*

Thomas had pick her up and laid in the water with her on top of him. She had buried her face into his neck. Tears came rolling down her cheeks. "Why does momma do this to me? I would love to tell her. She would tell the hold world because she can't keep a secret."

Eleanor moved her hand over his chest. "I'm sorry for what I did."

He let her do what she wanted, this time it wasn't about sex. It was just the need to be one with each other. He had thought they had fallen asleep for a bit.

Then Thomas heard horses, "Honey, we have company." The two of them went into the water, she had to get the dirt out of her hair and so did he. Quickly they climbed the hill. They saw Thomas's parents and hers. In her mind she cried out. "No… I can't do this again."

All he could do was grab her hand. "It's going to be all right honey." Thomas had to stop and face her. He could feel she wanted to run. He had brushed her hair from her face. "I will be there by your side my love. If it gets out of hand, I will speak to your mother."

*　　*　　*

On top of the hill their father's saw what was happening. As their wives looked around. Theseus shook his head. "Daniel my little girl don't want to talk to her mother. Our sons must keep the ones they love safe.

Bridget been after our son and daughter. William didn't want to be there with Catherin. He didn't want to put her through that. "What am I going to do? She won't see her mother. She even lied to Franceam, about taking the stuff she gave her."

Thomas got Eleanor moving up the hill. They came over to their fathers. Then said together. "Hello dad. What brings ye up here?"

*   *   *

Off in the distant Eleanor saw her mother coming torte them. "We been checking out William's home that he's building. Now we came here to see how ye were doing. Thomas ye two have done a lot together. The same with William and Catherin. That's a good size root cellar, ye can almost stand up right." Theseus saw his daughter she didn't want to be near her mother. "Daughter did ye get to much sun today?" She nodded and looked at Thomas.

He held onto her hand. "Let me go please Thomas." Eleanor try to wiggle her fingers out of his grip. She heard in her mind "No."

Daniel saw what his son was trying to do. He looked at his son and shook his head. Thomas spoke. "Eleanor how about ye get those herbs for your mother and mine. She found a good size bed of herbs. Go ahead and get them."

Thomas watched her go to her garden. Then her father spoke. "Has it been that hard to be around her mother?"

He looked to Daniel. His father nodded his head to speak his mind. "That run in she had with her mother this morning. It had stayed with her until she had too much sun. I wasn't paying attention to how hot it was getting. I wanted to get the root cellar done. Eleanor always made shore we would drink enough water and rest. I found her yelling at a rock that she couldn't get out. She was yelling as if it was her mother. I knew she had gotten too much sun. It was hard to get her to drink the water I brought her. She didn't look right to me. I wasn't going to fight with her on getting her to the pond. I took care of that damn rock. Then I grab her and put her on my shoulder and took her to the water. Where I drop her into the deepest part of the pond."

Thomas heard Eleanor in his mind crying for help. Not saying anything to his father he ran to her side.

Theseus saw that his wife and Franceam was heading over to his daughter. "Daniel did it look like he heard my daughter in his mind?"

Daniel was watching his son. "We better get over there before my son tells your wife off. To answer ye aye… that he did."

In Thomas mind he cried to Eleanor. "Honey I will take care of your mother. Stop fighting with her now." Eleanor head turned toward Thomas. She went right into his arms. "It's all right."

Thomas smiled at his mother. "Hello momma." Then his eyes changed when he looked at Bridget. The tone he had was with authority. "Good day to ye Mrs. Heart. Please do not treat your daughter like that. If ye have a problem with me. Come to me. Eleanor said ye keep trying to find out if I was going to marry her. My parents know I will not marry now. I will not tell anyone but her if there is a promise between us. Do ye remember that my sister-in-law and her son was killed?"

Bridget nodded yes… Thomas went on talking. "Your son hasn't told ye either has he?" She shook her head no. "Eleanor and I know are own minds. I don't think I'm old enough to take care of a wife and child yet. William and I need to fine our brothers. I like to find out what my brother was talking about Scotland. I can't trust anyone with this knowledge of who I will marry. My sister and Eleanor need to play the game of looking for a husband. If they find out about William and me. They could try to kill Catherin and Eleanor. Besides when I marry. I want to be here to watch our baby grow inside my wife stomach. I couldn't do what my brother had done.

"Mrs. Heart no disrespect to ye self, I have heard that ye can't keep a secret. I need to speak from the heart. Ye tell the secret and ye could get Catherin and Eleanor killed. We had talked about this the last time ye were here. What would ye think your son would do? Better yet what do ye think I would do if they killed both girls? Remember I had jumped on a bear to save Eleanor. At that moment I didn't care what happen to me. If the one I love is killed, like my sister and Eleanor. Remember she was ones my sister also. I tell ye this I don't know what I would do to that person. For my life would be over, ye see when I love someone it's with all my heart. That person who told our secret, will I don't know what William and I would do."

Thomas still had Eleanor in his arms. After his say he told Eleanor in his mind. To give both mothers their herbs. Eleanor looked up at him and spoke. "Thank ye honey."

She went over and gave the herbs to her mother. Then went to Franceam and give her some of the herbs also. "Franceam my mother needs your help. Please could ye give her a checkup for us. She has been very hateful to her family. I know my mother would like another child. Now that my oldest brother is gone from this earth. She has even lied to ye about taking what ye gave her, this is not like her.

Franceam nodded. She smiled at her son and at her daughter in law. "I have notice this also. Thank ye for the herbs. I will mix up what Grana had showed me when I was having a problem myself. Come with me Bridget. This must end now, ye need something to help ye how ye been feeling."

Daniel was pleased with his son. He wouldn't let her mother walk all over is wife. It was sad that Bridget was mixed up. The two women left not saying anything to their husbands. His father looked at his son and his son's bride. Another family will start once his son gets home. "Thomas have ye ate ye?"

He was talking with Eleanor about getting them some food. "No! I had to get her body cool off first for us to be able to eat."

Both men smiled. "All right ye two eat and we will get started on the floor. Besides your mother is checking Bridget out. We're not going to get in the middle of that."

Theseus looked at Thomas and smiled. "My boy my family thanks ye. Don't ye think that was a little harsh what ye said?"

Thomas took a bit of his sandwich and thought about what he said. "No, I don't think so. If she told someone about us. Let say both girls were killed. Do ye think ye could stop the two of us. Better yet could ye stop yourself?

Then he heard Eleanor's voice in his mind. "Honey do ye know what ye would do if that happen?"

Thomas looked at the one he loves. "That's just it. I don't know what I would do. It just gave your mother and father something to think about."

His father came over to him. "Son when will ye burn that big pile ye have?"

Thomas looked at the pile. He was thinking as he ate. It was good that Eleanor made him four sandwiches. He had notice that he's been very hungry. "I think this weekend. I would like to have it done before I leave. I will have just three days and one week after would."

Then the two men looked at each other. "Thomas how about ye help Eleanor with her garden. After that is done pick a place to burn that pile. We will get the floor done. Tomorrow William and ye can go to town to get what ye may need for your home. Then on the weekend we will have a big get together."

Thomas looked at Eleanor. "What ye think honey?"

He saw her nod her head yes. "All right that sound's good. I have some money to get what I may need. Ronald gave me and Michael some money. Some of the money is to get the wood cut. He told me how much I would need." With the last sandwich gone. He said all right let's get this done. Honey I'll bring ye the dirt to ye and ye can place it were ye need it."

Eleanor made sure the three men had water. After the garden was done. Then she helped her man with all the brush. This time she made sure that she drank some water. Before it was 4:00 they were heading back to the castle. She had made herself a good size herb garden. She must find out from Grana how she can get some of the herbs transplanted.

*   *   *

On the weekend they had to burn two big bonfires. On Saturday they burn all that Thomas had. Then on Sunday they burned William's pile. Thomas thought he could have brought the wood to them. But it was nice to have a day sleeping outside with his wife. For the two days they laid outside. They enjoyed the outdoors with the family. The two young men laid next to their women. Eleanor laid on her husband's arm. The young women were in between their men, they were keeping them safe. Their father's had fun with the fire, their wife stayed at home. When the fire was at its lowest.

Thomas and Eleanor had check on the horses. Midnight had a small harem. He would be the father of eight or four young colts. Sunshine was his one and only. She made sure that he ate and drank. Midnight made her eat with him. It was getting closer for Thomas had to leave. But Duncan still haven't come back yet.

He had asked his mother if she could make Eleanor a small birthday dinner.

At the pond he enjoy making love to Eleanor. He had made sure she had enough pleasure before he came. "I love ye so much. Be careful at those parties, a man would do anything to get a woman like yourself. I believe that we will be close to where our paths will cross. I will call to ye. Please tell me if ye are with child. Don't lie to me about that, could ye do that for me?" Eleanor made love to his mouth. In her mind she told him she will tell him one way or another.

That night they taken a walk to the rose garden. As they walked, the atmosphere was set for lovers. Twilight was upon them the moon was coming out. When Thomas took Eleanor into his arms. He notice a tear roll down her cheek. He just stared at the tear. Until he took his finger and scooped it up. He had made the one he loves cry. "Why are ye crying?"

She had watch him take that tear. "Thomas our time together is going so fast. I'm scared for ye. I'm safe here at home but ye are going where it's not safe."

Thomas took a finger and left her chin. "Have ye forgotten that they killed my brother's wife and child. Why do ye think we can't tell anyone about us being married. Ye are going to have to be on guard. Watch out when a man take ye down from a horse. Don't leave your glass that your drinking. Someone could put something in it. Don't be a lone with a man he could rape ye, then make ye marry him."

Eleanor had bent her head down. "I'm sorry honey. I'm just scared for ye. I don't know if I'm strong enough if something happens to ye. If it was a woman, I can fight that. I can't fight death! How can I fight for ye if ye are dead? Please Thomas ye must come home alive. If not for me, do it for your mother and father and your sister."

Thomas knew this was going to be the hardest on both. "There now... I don't want any more crying. When we leave no one will be looking for us. I think when it starts is when we find the graves sights."

Gently he brushed the last of the tears away. "Now let me see that pretty smile of yours. Ye know that I can't stand to see tears in your eyes. I know ye are scared for me. Ye know why your brother and I are doing this. We must! How could I become a man if I'm too scared to leave the Highlands? I need to see what my brother's and father and my grandfather saw. I don't know what they are fighting for. I will come back. After a year of making love with ye. If ye let me I will have ye more than ones in a daytime."

* * *

Thomas walked over to his mother's favorite rose bush. He needed to cut a rose for Eleanor. "Honey ye are so beautiful in the moonlight. I think I have told ye that every night. I love kissing and making love with ye. When you're in my arms I feel hole. After we make love, and I clean up. Ye let me come back inside ye and we go to sleep as one. I will miss that, all that I can do is dream of ye as I sleep. Even before we went down this path, I didn't know what was happening to me. Being a young woman ye still have the power to bring me to my knees. Now that ye know what I like, I can't stop ye. Just being in my arms, he wants to make love to your girlfriend."

Eleanor was looking into his eyes. "Thomas from the day ye took me under your wing. I had fallen in love with ye. As I got older, and I watched ye turn into this handsome man. I knew ye were more than a friend. That day the bear came after me. I saw what ye did to save me. I knew then that I would do anything for ye. I had promise myself to make ye my husband. Honey please don't make me a widow. We haven't had enough time to be spouses. I want to have children with ye. To watch our children, grow up and have children of their own."

Thomas took her in his arms and kissed her deeply. "I will do my best not to make ye a widow. Ye do know that is in the Lords hands. Remember I will be home to watch our child grow inside ye. I must be there to have our child pull your nipple. So ye can bopped me, no more crying." Thomas took her hand and brought her to the spot where no one could see them. "I want ye right here and now."

He took her breast it was time to let her girlfriend know he wanted her. After would they laid on the grass to look at the stars?"

Eleanor gazed into the heavens. She had sat down on the grass with Thomas. Together they laid back on the hillside. So much has happened these past three weeks. Hear it was the last week together. "It's so beautiful out here tonight."

Thomas slipped his arm under her neck. "I'm glad ye are mine. The time when I was teaching ye different ways to make love to ye. I knew then I didn't want another man to have ye. What more would I want in a woman? Ye know me to well. Your still young and ye can bring me to my knees even now."

Thomas pulled her closer to him. He then kissed her. They laid back on the grass and the two watched stars together. Eleanor could hear the frogs and the crickets singing. It was making her eyes feel very heavy. She had turned into Thomas and close her eyes. Eleanor felt so good in the crease of his arm. She is everything I want and need. He had to tell himself it's time to go to bed. I would love to stay here just like this. Before he got up, he remember the feeling of having her in his arms. When he sleeps under the stars, he will remember what it was like here in the Highlands.

Thomas try to slip out from her embrace. "Honey I'm sorry I fell asleep."

The moonlight shine down on her face making it into a heavenly glow. "I have ye my love. Put your arms around my neck. It's time to go to our bedroom. There we will sleep naked. If ye wake up and ye want me. I will be already for ye."

Eleanor was having a hard time to stay awake. "Thomas I'm too heavy. I can walk it's."

He smiled thinking of a time when she will be carrying their child. "No ye are not that heavy. The rock was heavier than ye. Put your arms around my neck. That's it." Eleanor kissed him and lay her head on his shoulder. He wave his hand, and they were in their room.

*   *   *

The next day he could feel the day slipping away from them. The sun was hot they went to their land. They rode side by side. He could picture taking her off that horse to kiss her. She already had a way to bring him to his knees, I can't get enough of her he thought. When he gets home all he would want to do was being one with her. She has wonderful toys to play with. In two years, his toys will be bigger.

At his land they rode over to a big tree near the pond. There was a big rock on the other side of the tree. He had gotten off his horse and went over to help her. When he took her off, he made sure he slid her down his body. "Honey I wish ye didn't have to go to those parties. Ye do know what they will do to make ye marry them. Some men would slide your body down his. That's if ye have an outfit that wouldn't bring your dress up. Other men would bring ye down and pull ye close to him for a kiss." He then pulled her into him. His hand went around her waist making her arms to go around his neck. That kiss lasted much longer than he thought. "I think ye have a good idea what I'm talking about."

Thomas felt his need to have her again. He loved the way she kissed him. He wish that the time weren't going so fast. He had to stop himself from kissing her again.

Every part of his body what's her too much. "Honey if I keep kissing ye. Ye know ye would be on the ground and I would be on top of ye. My friend would take over and he would have his girlfriend again."

She looked at her man. Eleanor knew if she wanted him now. It wouldn't take much to push him over the edge. "Honey do me a favor don't think of me when ye are in another woman's arms. Some women if they wanted to make sure ye became theirs. She would subdue ye to make ye marry her. Ye will have to remember that your mine."

Wow he thought. She's trying to make sure he watch out for another woman. She young now, but she is very wise. When I come home, we will know a lot more than we do now. Heaven help us.

I don't think I will be able to keep my hands off her. "Here my love take the basket down, I'll take care of the horses."

Eleanor had put the basket down. With his back to her she put her arms around him. She pulled him to her and kissed the back of his neck. Her hands went to his shoulders and gave him a little rub. Then she picked up the basket and headed down the hill. Thomas turned and watched her go down. Do I really want her to go to these parties? She must do it, what if they know of him? They may be watching her. All I can do is give her all the information that a man might try. At the same time, she is teaching me what another woman would try. I will also have to watch myself around other women.

Eleanor had everything ready for lunch when he came down the hill. Thomas laid down on the blanket. She made their date one that he wouldn't forget. It was nice when she fed him little things she made. She so beautiful and can she cook. I love kissing and making love to her. As she fed him, he watched her lips. Thomas wanted to get a hole of her again.

Then Eleanor asked him a question. "Thomas why did ye stop me from moving that rock yesterday?"

He had brushed a piece of hair from her eyes. "Eleanor if it is more than your own weight. Ye could hurt your chance to have a baby. Honey it could pulled a muscle in your stomach. I've heard momma say that story of a woman had done just that."

Eleanor was just enjoying being here with him. "I know a bit about what ye are talking about. Could ye show me where I could hurt myself. Please!"

Thomas fell right into her trap. He went closer to her. Ye could hurt yourself here. Were your baby will be. It could stop ye from having children if it's bad enough."

When he looked into her eyes, they had bewitched him. He fell into her trap, he didn't mind this kind of trap. His hand went to the back of her neck. He wanted to kiss her again and to make love to her. Now he drew her to him as her arms went around his neck. When he went to lay her down, he found the two of them was rolling down the hill. She had broken away when she felt her self-falling. The two of them were laughing as they came to a stop. Eleanor was on her back she was breathing hard. Her hair was fanout one leg was up and her dress was halfway down her leg. Thomas had roll to a stop next to her, he also was out of breath. Then he turn to her lifting himself up on one elbow. His eyes moved over her body, the sun light was on her hair. He saw the love for him in her eyes, they were a beautiful bluest green. Her lips were a sweet rosy red.

His hand went to touch her face as his finger move over her lips. Thomas came down to kiss those lips. His hand was moving over her breast as he made his way down her leg. He wanted to taste her sweetness as his hand move to her heat. Quickly he went down her leg to fine her sweet lips. He had to have one more tase. He felt these soft wet lips as his finger went between them. His tongue made love to her mouth as his finger moved in and out of her heat. When he felt her heat was good and wet. He slowly took his hand away from her. She watched him put his finger in his mouth. His eyes closed as he enjoyed what he had done. "It's good that I'm leaving."

Eleanor lifted herself up on one elbow to look at him. "Why did ye say that?"

Thomas looked at Eleanor and knew this wasn't a little girl but a woman. He found he wanted to be inside her again. Time was about up for them. He brought her down to kiss her again. "I can't get enough of ye. I want to make love to ye in the water. Let me help ye with your dress."

With a wave of his hand, they were naked. Once everything was off her he came inside her. He made love to her until she came. Then he pick her up and brought her to the rock. With her legs apart he spoke. "I couldn't do this before. I want to do this to ye. Will ye let me have ye this way?"

Eleanor didn't have the heart to deny him anything. She nodded her head yes. Thomas took her place she hadn't been before. Once she came, he let his friend have his girlfriend. Before he could come, he took her sweetness. Then he pushed his friend back inside her. As he felt her nails on his bottom. She had come again, and he had joined her. With her legs around his waist and he was still inside her. Thomas dip them in the water, she was laying on top of him. "Honey ye know I'm going to leave."

Thomas then kissed her. "Ye have learn to bewitch me. When ye go to these parties. Be careful my love when ye look into a man's eyes. For ye have the power to bewitch him. A man would do anything to have a woman like yourself. Honey I know that ye don't want to go to these parties.

"I must see why Ronald fought so hard to try to save Scotland. We all know that they have been killed. I must find where they are buried. All this time with ye I fear someone will find out that you're my wife. We are playing a danger-rest game, I just wish that it were over with. I can't wait until I can have ye again."

Eleanor loved to be one with him. To feel his hands running over her body and have his friend inside her pussy. Thomas didn't know why he married her now. Then he remember when he kissed her the first time. He found that he wanted her. Once he touch her body, he knew he had to become one with her. On the shore she laid on top of him. She was one with him the days were flying by. Not much time left to be able to do this.

*   *   *

The next day she fix everyone something to eat. When she brought his food, he took her hand and kissed it. Quickly she when back to get her food. His mother saw her and took her into her arms. "My child ye know he must leave the Highlands. I know that he's fearful for your life. Those men that did those things to my son and his wife. He believes that they would come after ye, just do as he ask of ye. I know my daughter feels the same way as ye do. "Eleanor ye know if ye try to keep him he won't be happy, and I think ye know this. When my man went to war, I wasn't going to marry him yet. Like ye he wanted to have me. He was afraid someone would make me marry them. There was three of us who had to wait for are men to come home. I prayed that he would come back to me alive. I had our first son a year later. We all have our trials to see how strong our love is for each other. This is your trial. Ye are going to be a midwife, dive yourself into your work. Learn what ye need to know and be ready when he comes home."

There was a tear in Eleanor's eyes. "I will. It's hard to let go."

Franceam gave her a kiss on her forehead. "My dear these feelings ye will come to know quite well. Each time ye will have to let one of your children go."

She gave Eleanor a hug. "Franceam I'm sorry I was thinking only of myself. Ye must let go of your last son. I pray Michael comes home with his family. I had a dream that Ronald sent Michael to kill the other men. With what Ronald had told Thomas. He believes that Michael was told not to bring his wife home. Michael is not using his true name. Ronald made sure that he told know one that he was a MacGregor."

Franceam brushed her hair with her fingers. "Eleanor, I know my son loves ye a lot. He asked ye to play the game that ye are looking for a husband. Before he leaves tell him. When he kiss another lass don't be thinking of ye. Keep it under your clothes. Ye mother knows of this locket. When ye see Grana ask her to put a spell on it. That no one will remember what it was for. I will have "Thomas has magic. If anyone sees it I will tell them it was a birthday gift. I know not to tell them from who."

CHAPTER EIGHT

Time to leave the one he loves

UP STARES ELEANOR stood in the doorway. In her mind she thought, I'm finding it hard to let my man go. She was watching him looking for his old shirts. She knew right where they were. His old shirts were with her, his scent was on them. "Honey what are ye looking for."

Thomas looked up and saw his wife in the doorway. The sun was coming in through the window. It was putting a heavenly glow around her. How am I going to leave Eleanor? He must leave the Highlands, there was no other way to see Scotland. It was time to grow-up and find his brothers. There was so many questions that need to be answered. These four and half weeks he had grown up a lot. It wasn't enough to be able to become a father. He must find his brothers and bring them home. "Ye look so beautiful in the sunlight. Ye stand there and I want to have ye again. I'm finding it's harder to get on my horse and ride away from ye." He took her by the hand and led her to the back room. With the door close he put her back against the wall. "What am I going to do without ye? I love ye so much." They found themselves on the bed, now they were as one. Quickly he got up. Damn it, honey ye must help me, ye know I must leave. I can't be making love to ye every time I look at ye."

Eleanor knew that she had to be strong for him. She love making love with him. "I know where your shirts are. I made ye new ones there much bigger. Ye have one of your old shirts on, I will sleep with it tonight. Before taking off his shirt she rubbed him all over. Then took the shirt off him and led him to her old bedroom. On the chair was five new shirts, she had handed one to him. Eleanor loved to look at his chest. "I have all your old shirts, here is one of the shirts I made for ye. I will be wearing your old shirts at night-time."

Thomas took it and breathed in the scent of roses. He put it down and went over to give her a kiss. "I will be back my love; we both have things to do." Thomas went and picked one of the shirts up. Ye did a beautiful job on this shirt, so that was what ye were doing."

She smile seeing he like what she had made him. "It may be a little big on your shoulders, but ye have wider shoulders now. I've been notic-ing your shirts are getting tight on ye. I made some soap up and I wash your shirts in that soap."

Eleanor enjoy looking at his chest. She ran her hands over his arms and back to his chest. "Thomas do ye think when ye come home, we will go after each other like we have been?"

After he had his new shirt on, he walked over to her. "I hope so, right now, it's new and we both know that I'm going to leave soon. On top of it we are young, I do know that I found I can't get enough of ye. Off and on I will send my little friend to ye."

Thomas took her into his arms that is how she saw them. Franceam wished that her son didn't have to go. She saw that he had on one of his knew shirts. "Son how does the shirt fit?"

He and Eleanor broke away from each other. "They fit quite well I didn't think my shoulders had gotten that big. I'm lucky that my wife noticed."

Franceam smiled at them. "Aye… She notice a lot about ye son." His mother saw the pride in Eleanor's face. "I just came up to tell ye that William and Catherine is back."

Eleanor's face change quickly, their time had run out. Quickly she went for the four shirts. "Honey ye can talk with your mother, I will put these shirts in your bag."

Thomas watched her go out of the room. He knew that she wanted to cry. "Momma I hate what this is doing to her. Please keep her busy as much as ye can. I know I will be bringing her with me, she washed the shirts in the soap she made. I will have that scent of roses for some time. It's her way to make sure I don't forget her. I know uncle has plans to show us the Highlands.

"Momma I like to thank ye for giving her that medicine. It would have been hard to not make love to her." The two of them watched Eleanor put things in his bag. He notice there was many notes being place inside. "Momma this has been going on since we were younger. Ones I stop thinking she was my sister. When I kissed her, I couldn't stop? Thank ye for making me see she was for me. I'm glad I took her for my wife. I know I'm not the only one going through this. William feels the same way as I do. Him and Catherine has been going down that road like we have. When we dropped the promise to think of them as our sister. There was no going back, all William and I told each other. Ye hurt my sister, and I will come after ye. Take care of Eleanor and Catherine. Mamma I know it hurts ye also. I'm your baby. I will be home with my brother. Take care of dad, time will go by fast."

Franceam gave her son a hug. "Don't worry son, she will be staying with us. I will send her to Grana over the weekend, she will be learning more on how to make the medicine. Catherine will stay here also, I will send her to Grana every other week. I don't know if Eleanor will go home to visit. Time will show us what is going to happen. Son be careful out there, we will all miss ye four. As ye know I will be going with them to Bridget's cousin's place. Don't worry about Eleanor and Catherine. I'm hoping what I gave Bridget will help her. Eleanor has enough to manage, without her mother giving her a hard time."

*   *   *

In Thomas room she made sure she had her back to them. She didn't want Thomas to see her crying. Eleanor knew that she couldn't hide, what she was doing. She got all the things he needed put in his bag. She took time to wipe her eyes. His mother saw the movement to her face. She knew what was happening to Eleanor. She remember how hard it was when her man left the Highlands. "Thomas it's hard for her right now. I know how she feels. I'm glad that ye gave her that locket for the wedding. That was a nice touch putting on that rose. Did ye put a spell on it so her mother wouldn't remember."

Thomas went over to his mother and put his arms around her. He needed that hug from his mother. Not only he cross over to chews a wife. But he also cross over to become a man. "I'm sorry I didn't ask ye first. Momma that was your locket for your wedding day from dad. Aye…, the spell is on it."

His mother held on to her son, where has the time gone. "Aye…! We told everyone that it was her birthday gift. I had been taken in by his parents, they did what we did for ye."

In her son's arms. She could feel that his built was a lot like his father's. "Momma was that locket also my grandmother's locket. I found it upstairs in that big trunk."

Franceam remember seeing her mother-in-law giving her son a hug. She had lost one of her sons in the war. "Aye… she had given it to your dad before he left. It was in the garden there was a few roses out there. Your father got down on one knee. He ask me to marry him when he gets back home. He knew I would be waiting for him to come home."

Thomas could feel it brought memory's back to his mother. "Only the ones who was at the wedding knows what it's for. She can tell everyone that it's a birthday gift. Momma I like to thank ye. I had heard what ye said that night. That storm made me look over everything. If I didn't, I would never have the chance to cross over. I don't think we would be happy with another person. When I kissed her, Eleanor knew what she wanted even at this age. She is quite a woman, to be able to set my blood on fire. Now I must become the man she will need once we start our family."

His mother touched his face my little boy he had stayed young-at-heart. She still can remember holding him in her arms. Where has the time gone, "Aye… I was going to give the locket to ye. Ye had beaten me to it. I know ye love Eleanor very much. Ye are your father's son, like ye father he knew he couldn't wait to have me." She could see that her son wanted to say something about that. "Don't say anything let me finish. Once ye had kissed Eleanor ye had to have more of her. Ye didn't think I would know something like this. Thomas ye are so much like your father. Ye look a lot like him, even your built is just like your father's. I believe ye love the way your father does. I knew once ye got the idea, of Eleanor being your sister out of your head. Ye would find out that ye love her more than a friend but a lover.

"Being as your father son, once ye cross over the hunger to touch her would come out. Your father asked Grana to give me something that I wouldn't get with his child. He wanted to be home to help me rase ye four. I told Eleanor and Catherine to ask ye to put a spell on their lockets. That no one will take it for their promise to each other. Ye both have each other scent for a little while. She will need your scent to get to sleep these next few days."

Thomas knew his mother was crying. That is what mothers do when their son leaves the nest. "Mamma have I told ye I love ye. Thank ye for saying what ye did. Ye knew I heard ye talking, that I would take everything a part to find out why ye said that."

Franceam kissed her son's cheek. As the two walked into his old bedroom. She had said a little prayer that her son would come home safe.

"Thomas my boy I'll take these things down for ye. Your father will put it on Midnight. Do ye like the shirts that ye are waring?"

She saw the pride in his eyes, Franceam went on to say. "Eleanor had asked me a while ago how she could make ye some shirts." Thomas looked at his wife. "I love them, I don't feel like I'm going to rip them."

Franceam smile knowing he was very proud of his wife. "Eleanor and I made soap together. I saw her washing the shirts in that soap. I had told her that I had done that to my husband when he went to war. There's are two pieces of that's soap in your bag, it will keep the clothes smelling good. This will let ye know she's with ye. She also made some soap that ye could wash with.

"Thomas your father is also saddling Sunshine, she could say her goodbye to Midnight."

Franceam was trying not to cry. It's hard for his mother to let her last son go. "Thank ye Mamma. I'll bring Ronald home, don't worry I will make sure I come home alive. Mamma in my heart I really don't want Eleanor going to those parties. I know she must, for that evil man won't find out she is married to a MacGregor."

His mother then put her arms around her son. She gave him one last kiss on his cheek. Franceam lay her head on his shoulder and thought my boy is a man now. "Son come home whole and alive. I like to see ye have a family of your own. That's all I want from ye and Michael."

Thomas looked into his mother's eyes. "Mamma Michael is married. Ronald knew things was happening. The only thing he didn't know they would go after his wife. When I come home Michael will be also coming home. I believe he will have a family with him. If I know my brother, he will have someone to tell him the bodies are heading home."

Franceam could see that her son's gifts had started. That storm push him into his inner sight. "Son how do ye know this?"

He smiled at is mother, "I'm my mother's son, it was what Ronald and ye said. Michael is his father son, when he loves a woman, he would make her his. Dad said sex gets in the way, I found out that he was right."

Then he heard a deep laugh. "Thank ye son for that, ye be careful. Those men don't care who they hurt."

He nodded his head then he saw Eleanor. "Ye can say your goodbyes up here. There will be too many people around."

His mother looked into Eleanor's eye's. "Go say goodbye to your man up here, make it a good one."

Eleanor nodded her head. Once Franceam was heading downstairs. She ran into Thomas's open arms, he could feel she wanted to cry. He knew that he had to go, all he could do was make this kiss one he won't forget. "Honey ye know I must do this. I can't let William and Duncan go by themselves. I don't want a baby when we are still teenagers. The age of twenty will be a good age for ye, your body is still changing. Ye are going to be a healer that takes a while to learn and a midwife."

When he looked into her eyes, he pulled her to the far wall. "I can't keep my hands off ye." Thomas took a deep breath. "I want your sweetness one last time."

He move her into him, his lips were soft over hers. Then his tounge brush over her lips, until his tounge pushed inside. When he deepen the kiss, the need to touch her came in strong. She was up against the wall as his tounge made love to her mouth. He could feel her hands moving over his body, her nails dug into his back. One last time he thought, he felt her hand moving toward his heat. "No, my love not this time. This is what ye need, I need to take your sweetness with me." He felt her nails dig into him, the kiss was hot and deep until she came.

Thomas had step away from her and closed his eyes. He first breathe in her scent and slowly tase her sweetness. "You're not fully develop yet. Honey the only thing stopping me is the knowledge of what they did to my sister-in-law. Woman if I didn't have that ye would bring me to my knees. We both must grow up a little more, I know when I come home. Your beautiful body will drive me crazy, every day I can see the difference in ye. Your breast and hips are firmer since we been married. I believe the first time we are alone I will have ye."

Eleanor giggled. "That will be find with me. Honey I will do as ye ask of me. I don't want to look at any other man, I have found what I want right here. I love the way ye make love to me. I think your right if ye stay here any longer, your little friend will make love to me again. I would get ye to make love to me. Please hold me let me feel these strong arms around me. Kiss me again!"

Thomas was finding it hard to let her go. In his mind he said. "When ye are here in my bed. Due to yourself of what I have just done. Ye can think of me kissing ye, send it to me in your dreams. Then again I will send ye my friend." The two of them walked to the window to see what was happening down in the yard. "Thank ye for the new shirts."

Eleanor looked at her husband in his new shirt. "This shirt fits ye much better. Tonight, I will sleep in your old shirt. Honey call to me in your dream. May be somehow, we could come together at night. I will miss the times when we were one together." She laid her head on his shoulder. They had moved away from the window. When she lift her head, she touched his face. In her mind she spoke. "I love you so much. Be careful out there, come back to me alive."

*　*　*

Thomas nodded his head yes; he was looking at her lips. As his finger was tracing those lips of hers. He was trying to put it in his memory of what they looked like. "Honey are ye done talking?"

Eleanor looked at him. "Aye… What do ye have in mind."

She had pulled him into her, this kiss must last them until he gets home. "Just this."

He had pulled her into another deep kiss. She felt his hands cup her breast. In his mind he said. "I can't get enough of ye. Tonight, dream of me making love to ye. Think of the first time I came inside ye. Your finger will help ye come, this will help ye go to sleep afterward. Make sure the door is close when ye do this. I will be with ye in my dreams. It's time to go my love, I think your brother's coming up the stairs with my sister."

Eleanor heard two people coming up the stairs, then they heard a voice. "Can we come in?"

Thomas answered, "Aye…" He had kept Eleanor in his arms. Quickly she wiped a tear from her cheek.

Catherin came in first, she went right to her brother. "We thought that we would say are goodbyes here."

Thomas looked at his sister. He step away from Eleanor so he could take his sister into his arms. She looked just as sad as Eleanor. "Were going to be all right. William and I will keep a close eye on each other. Now are ye all right sis?"

Eleanor went right to her brother, she gave him a big hug. William spoke. "Sis do ye think you're going to be all right?"

Eleanor laid her head on her brother shoulder. She found that he was built a lot like her man. "Aye… I guess so. I don't like to say goodbye to both of ye. Ones we get into are study's our minds will be full. It will be the nights that will be hard on us. That's when we will have time to think. Watch over him will ye?"

Her brother was looking at Catherin. He knew that it been different these three four and half a weekday. Eleanor saw that his eyes was on Catherin. "William, I will watch over her, I guess the four of us must have each other's back. I have a question to ask ye. Have the two of ye talk to each other in your mind yet?"

William thought a bit. "No, I haven't yet?"

She smiled at her brother then spoke to Thomas. "Honey get Catherine to talk to William in her mind. They have what we have, it would be nice if they could."

Thomas looked at his wife. "All right."

William's eyes went wide. "Sis I heard her."

Eleanor laughed. "It's about time, use it when we are close to ye. Can she hear ye?"

The four of them had given each other a hug. One last time they kissed their mate goodbye. Then the four of them headed downstairs. Eleanor told herself she wouldn't cry in front of Thomas. Right now, their men will be safe. The danger will be when they find the bodies. Eleanor and Catherin didn't want to go to these parties. Their men asked them to do this for them. They had to make sure, no one would think they weren't promise to a MacGregor. This was going to be hard for them, they were always together.

*　　*　　*

Outside Eleanor went over to Midnight. She rubbed his nose and gave him half and apple. Then she spoke, "I will take care of Sunshine and your baby. Please take care of Thomas for me, ye both come home safe." Then she gave Midnight a kiss on his nose.

Thomas had the other half of the apple. "Here Sunshine ye will be eating for at least two. I will take care of Midnight for ye." Eleanor came over to Thomas. He took Eleanor by the hand and brought her over to Sunshine. Then he lift her onto her back. In her mind she heard Thomas say that he loved her. She had said it back to him, then he took her hand and kiss the back of it. She nodded her head.

Then she saw her mother. "Thomas why is my mother here? I thought that she was going to go ahead and help her cousin."

William and Catherine came beside them. William spoke. "Why is mamma here? She was going to go ahead of ye girls."

Then their father came up to them. "Your mother wanted to see her son off. She been good taking the medicine. Sometimes I must make sure she took it."

*　　*　　*

The mothers were riding with their husband on horseback. The men led with their wife by their side. Duncan and his brothers were next. The two couples were next.

Franceam looked at Bridget, she was very upset with her. "Bridget said a pretty locket with a rose on it. That was a nice birthday gift was it from Thomas or Catherin."

Bridget looked at her best friend. What the four has done now they have to wait. That was a nice birthday gift from him, I love the rose on it. That is Eleanor's favorite flower. It made her a nice birthday gift, she is one of his best friends."

Quickly she change the subject. "I all most have Eleanor's dresses done for the trip. Malinda do ye think ye could manage Franceam and my patients? On myside there is not much. No one is going to have a baby or had a baby. How about your side Franceam?"

Franceam had to go with Bridget and the girls, just to keep the girls safe and friend in line. "The same. I must check on the babies that have been born. There is just two of them."

Malinda knew that Franceam had to do this. "All right I will do it. Ye can show me where to go. I hope Duncan can find a wife this time?"

*   *   *

Thomas and William couldn't just leave the girls, they had to stop for a bit. They took Eleanor and Catherin by the hand and went by a tree. Thomas watch Eleanor's eyes fight to not cry. He had seen one tear roll down her cheek. With his lips he took it away from her. Without missing a beat, he pulled Eleanor into his arms. There he kissed her deeply. All the kisses he give her was to last him for two years. When he pulled back. He wish he could stay with her. "Ye are my Angel, my mind wants to stay here with ye. I know I can't do that. They will be watching ye and my sister. If you're not playing the game. Then they will know ye are waiting for me. Be careful a man would do anything to have a woman like ye. Ye will know what there up to. Take care of yourself my sweet Angel. I know there is no other women like ye."

She wiped her cheeks from the tears. "My love I will do as ye ask of me. I don't like playing this game. There is no other man that could hold a candle to ye. As ye told me. Ye also must be careful a woman would love to have ye for their husband. Don't be alone with them, they could say ye rape them. Then ye will have to tell them ye are married."

Thomas looked at the woman he married. "I've been worried about just ye... I didn't think about anything else. I know I never thought of a woman doing just that. When ye are on your trip call to me." Now in a whisper he said. "Let me know if ye are all right, and not with our baby. When I talk to any woman, I will make sure they can't trap me."

He took her by the hand and led her back to Sunshine. With his hands around her waist, he place her back on Sunshine. As both men got back on their horses. Ones again he heard her in his mind. "I love ye Thomas. Be careful, come back to me."

Thomas thought she has been his soulmate all this time. He heard her call to him. "I love ye too. We will be all right. This will make us stronger my Angel."

*   *   *

Eleanor found herself crying, as she clean the bedroom they had share together. That night she slept in Thomas old room. As the days went by, she found that she wasn't pregnant with their baby. The medicine had worked. Outside the castle she would call to Thomas. "Honey we didn't make a baby together this time. I sure miss ye, I love ye Thomas."

Today she was cleaning the roses. At his mother's favorite rose bush, she heard her man. "I hear ye my love. When I'm home and our place is done. Then we can try for a baby. Don't cry my love remember that I love ye. I miss making love with ye. Honey were moving again to another castle."

*   *   *

On every other Friday's Eleanor head to Grana's place before dark. She was able to stay away from her mother for a while, until it was getting closer to leave the Highlands. She had to keep busy for the days to go by fast.

Then it was June, this month was going by fast. It was already her birthday, her mother and father came to the castle with Eleanor's dresses. In one week, it will be Catherine's birthday. The next week they will be heading down to her mother's cousin. Now her mother wanted her to try on her dresses so she could see how they fit. When Eleanor did, she found the dresses were cut to low in the front. "No... no I will not wear these dresses this way. What are ye trying to make me look like? Franceam is there anything ye can do to make it less in the front. I feel like my girls will fall out, I should have made these dress's myself."

Catherine looked at her friend, she could see that she wanted to cry on her birthday. She had lace left over from her dress's. "Eleanor it's your birthday I have just the thing to make it look more respectable. Heaven for bed if ye had bent over your lady's would fall out."

Eleanor went to her friend and put her arms around her. In a whisper she spoke. "Thank ye. Why is she trying to make me look cheap?"

Catherin looked at her friend. "She made those dresses before, she was taking that medicine your mother gave her. Eleanor ye breast are bigger now. She forgot that ye body have been changing. But we can fix it. I like to talk with ye as we fix these dresses."

Eleanor didn't know what she wanted to talk about. "Could ye tell me what ye like to know? I will tell ye this before ye ask me about Thomas. He told my mother that no one will know if I'm promise to him, Catherin that goes for ye also. We will talk after my mother and father is gone."

She nodded her head. "No. it's about the barn. Your father and mine wants to know how big of a barn Thomas would like to have. We can talk about it after they leave."

* * *

Thomas felt that he should make a journel of his trip. This way he could show Eleanor everything he had done.

Places he went in the Highlands

Thomas wrote… We've been away from home two months and three weeks. Eleanor was right these girls would love to get me alone. I've been missing her a lot, none of these women could do as my love could. Some of the women never rode a horse or cook before. Uncle Donald told us stories about the castles and what had happened to them. I've learned a lot about the old castles when they were destroyed. There has been some that has been restored, those we have seen. Other's uncle told us about them.

Earconic Tower is a 16th-century house. Located at the hamlet of Hollows, 2.3 km north of Canobie, in Dumfries.

Isoptera Castle is on the grounds of the estate of Isoptera in Morven. The castle is in ruined on the west coast of Scotland. It stands at the seaward end of a promontory which extends to the South…

Kierra Castle it's dating from the 16th century. The castle was destroyed back then. All the insides and the top is gone. It still stands on a rocky promontory jutting out into Loch Assynt in Sutherland, Scotland.

Armadale Castle is a ruined country house in Armadale, Skye, former home of the MacDonald's.

Belone Castle is in ruin. There is hope it will be restored in the future.

Nagina Castle from the embellishments of the nobility who inherited the castle down the centuries. Right through to the dark days of near dilapidation and bankruptcy.

Evric Castle, also known as Castle Erieau. In Scottish Gaelic, is a ruined 14th-century tower house, located at the south-west of the island of Benbecula.

Borve Castle, Sutherland was destroyed. It was from the force the Clan Mackay assembled under John Mor Mackay. They engaged in battle with the Clan Sutherland, known as the Battle of Garbharry

Braal Castle is located by the River Thurso north of the village of Halkirk, in Caithness, northern Scotland. The ruined castle, which dates to the mid-14th century.

Brahan Castle was situated 3.5 miles south-west of Dingwall, in Easter Ross, Scotland. The castle belonged to the Earls of Seaforth, chiefs of the Clan Mackenzie.

Brims Ness is a promontory. The castle on it had three stories and a garret. There was a square stair-wing with a watchtower on top. They had replaced it with a pitched roof.

The Highlands waterfalls

The waterfalls in the Highlands that we have seen. The spectacular waterfall known variously Steal Waterfall. They have called this waterfall by many names. It also Steal Bàn or Steal Falls. Is situated in Glen Nevis near Fort William Highland Scotland. Steal Falls is a beautiful waterfall, as ye watch it tumbling down over many rocks throughout 120 miles. It end up at a wide-open scenic valley backed by tall mountains of the Nevis Gorge. William and I went up part way.

Uncle wanted us to be back before dark. Up there high in the mountains I thought of Eleanor. She had called to me that day. She told me that she wasn't pregnant with our baby, that the medicine worked.

It was around her birthday she was cleaning the rose garden. At the time I was high up in the mountains. I was glad I married her then.

Inchree waterfalls we took a forestry walk combines to other waterfalls. We walked an ancient military road through the village of Inchree. The next waterfalls was Gamache, it was tumbling down a steep narrow cleft in a remote corner of the Highlands. These Falls of Gamache can only be reached on foot. It's a 6-hour hike there and back. Like always William and I had walk it part way. When we got back uncle told us about the time him and our fathers walked it all the way up there.

*   *   *

We were told that we will be leaving next week. The waterfalls were beautiful to see up close. What I also saw was the people in the Highland were having it quite hard. William and I helped them as much as we could when we went hunting. I got them enough food to last them for a while. It's sad that life is so hard for our people. When I help this sheep farmer, I found that I didn't like sheep they have a bad smell. When they are eating the grass, they also take the root. At least I know how to shear the sheep. We spent two months in the Highland's.

*   *   *

Before we got on the road to the fishing village. That's when uncle turned to head back home. He had a lot to do at home before the next part of our trip. He said that he missed his bed and his wife. I told him that I know what he is talking about. But I didn't tell him around Duncan, something was different about him. It was time for uncle to head home, William and I handed him the letters to give Eleanor and Catherine. With the letter, I gave this rock that I had found. It had many beautiful colors in it, so I shined it up for her. I even gave a little sheep fur to show her what I did.

I wrote Eleanor that I have never thought there was so many castles left in ruins. Many were on a hill side looking over the water. There were mountains all around in places. These mountains looked over many valleys. Sometimes we went off the path to camp near a waterfall. Many of these waterfalls that I have seen took your breath away. I thought of Eleanor in that water with me.

After we said goodbye to Uncle Donald. That's when Duncan took us to Aberdeen, it is an old fishing village. This village is at the end of the harbor. He found out this area had a settlement. It went as far back as the Medieval times. One of the oldest men in the village told us all about his home. Two of the squares of Fish Town was known as "Footdee." The old man told us it originally contained twenty-eight single stories of houses. He couldn't imagine all those people in those houses.

* * *

Then we had crossed over to Edinburgh. As I rode up the hill, Eleanor and my sister and mamma was nearby. We were nearby a church it was called St Clément's Church. Duncan didn't take us down the street, we took a path that we could see Edinburgh. The path led the three of us high on a hilltop.

William and Thomas had stopped to look at the church, while Duncan kept riding on. "William can ye feel when Catherine is nearby?"

He had stopped his horse; it was as if he had sense something. "Aye, Catherine is very near here. Are ye telling me ye sense Eleanor also?"

He smiled at William now he was looking around. "I know there here, why don't ye try to call to Catherine. I'll do the same."

While we looked at the church the two of us called to are loved ones. "Eleanor can ye hear me my love."

* * *

It was a long ride to Berwick-upon-tweed. Eleanor didn't have her heart into this. She was going just to ease her husband's mind. She couldn't have him worried about her. May be not now. Only when they find the bodies of their brothers. He will have to have a clear mind to be able to fight those men. Eleanor knew Thomas could sense if she was nervous about something.

It would take all her strength not to blow up on her mother. Every place her mother would talk about some of the history of the towns they bent through. She knew a lot about Scotland, thanks to her older brother. The only thing she wanted to hear was her man's voice.

Eleanor was hoping to hear Thomas's voice today, she knew he was some where's around here. Then she heard his voice. Both girls turn their head and saw two men on top of the hill. She notice Eleanor saw them also. Franceam notice her daughter was looking on the hillside, then she knew her son was up there. Bridget was looking at the church. Franceam has notice that her mind hasn't been the same since she hit midlife.

At last Eleanor heard Thomas's voice. "Eleanor my love can ye hear me?"

Quickly she looked up and saw two men on a hillside. She had seen from the corner of her eye. Catherin also had looked over where Eleanor was looking. Then Catherin heard William's voice. She wanted to yell to him to come down the hill. "William, my love I miss ye."

It looked as if Eleanor was talking to her brother. "Thomas my love." She had cried out in her mind. "I miss ye, I wish we were home together. I've had enough of going to these parties. These men can't hold a candle to ye. Honey when can we be together again."

Thomas nudged William and pointed to the carriage near the church. He had nodded his head. "I hear ye it's been the same here. I know how many months we have left, and that's 22 months. Keep playing the game, I'm glad mamma went with ye. Tell them I love them. I've seen so much; I understand now what my brother was talking about. Honey I had heard ye when I was high on one of these mountains."

Eleanor could see them on the hill. "So ye know that I'm not carrying our baby. I love ye so much. Stay safe for me. Honey I don't want to be here. I miss making love to ye and sleeping beside ye."

Thomas could almost see her in his mind. "I know honey. Somehow, I've been feeling your frustration, it must be with your mother.

Honey ye know that it must be this way. Happy Birthday my Angel. Bye for now I love ye. I got to go before we lose Duncan."

She watched them -ride off. "Bye! I love ye, ye are my life, my husband. I'll see ye in my dreams."

Franceam had look out the window where the girls were looking. She had seen the men on horseback. Even her daughter must have heard William's voice. When the girls looked back there was a tear in their eyes.

Thomas took off running after Duncan. "William isn't Duncan supposed to be teaching us about the Lowland of Scotland?"

The two of them had to ride hard to catch up with him. "I've been wondering why he's been in a big hurry, there is a lot to learn here. William if it was us now that we are married. I know that I would be riding hard to get home to my wife."

William started to laugh. "We three could be married."

Right then they saw Duncan's horse. He had stopped at the pub to get some food and drink.

William and Thomas went inside. Thomas spoke. "Two Scotch and could I have two bowls with a pint of ale for are horses. Can we also order two specials, ye can bring it over to that man at that table, he's are brother? After they gave their horses ale to drink, they came back in. Then the food was brought out to the boys. Duncan spoke. "I will have the same as they have. What were ye two doing with those bowls and the ale?"

The two men started eating right off. "The food was good, tell the cook thank ye for a good home cook meal."

CHAPTER NINE

To Berwick-upon-tweed

ELEANOR AND CATHERIN was heading to Berwick-upon-tweed outside of Edinburgh. This place was on the outskirts of Scotland and England. Her mother was taking her to her cousin's home. There was to be a coming out party for the three girls. Both girls and her cousin's daughter were now sixteen. One day Eleanor had asked Franceam if she could hear her husband. She had told her that only soulmates could hear their mates. Eleanor had remembered when the bear had attack her. That was when she had started to hear Thomas. They were healing in their beds, off and on she heard his thoughts calling to her.

It was her mother that cut into her thoughts. She quickly looked at Franceam her head motion to the hill. Catherin also saw that her mother knew who the men were. The three women was now smiling they had seen the same thing. Bridget had miss seeing her son. She had no idea that Catherin could hear her son. It was Franceam who spoke up. "Bridget leave the girls alone."

Bridget didn't understand what was going on. All she could think of was drilling her daughter on the history of Scotland. "Eleanor needs to know these things. She been daydreaming too much. It wouldn't hurt Catherin to know this also."

Franceam had enough with Bridget. "Bridget, I have had enough with the way ye are acting. Have ye taken the herbs that I mix up for ye?"

Bridget looked at her friend then bent her head. "Not for two days. It's in my bag.

Then Catherin spoke up. "Bridget, we know about the history of the Holy Trinity Church. One day Jonathan and Ronald told us about the church when it was started in 1650. Our brothers told us all about the church when it was built and when it was finished in 1652. They told us that it was a rare example of a church built and founded on law. It was united by the understanding and agreement of the people. This was for the common good of the people. I don't think these young men want their wife to know much history. They need a wife to have children with. To cook and clean for him and take care of their children. At the last party, one of the men heard a woman talking about government. He said that a woman shouldn't talk about things like that. I need a woman to keep quiet and just look pretty. I heard the woman that was giving the party say. She asked him to leave her home."

*   *   *

Both men looked after the carriage as they rode away. Thomas and William gave a look to each other. They knew how the other felt. All they could do was ride hard to catch up with Duncan.

Thomas's mind was just on Eleanor. When he heard her voice, for just a moment. He could see Eleanor the moment he became one with her. What he had seen in the countryside of the women. He was glad that he had married her. Even when she was mad at him, he found that he loved her even more. Each time he called to Eleanor in his mind she was able to hear him. Their thoughts were getting stronger.

William knew Catherin and her mother was with his sister and mother. He knew that the two of them hungered to be with the one they loved. Both men didn't say anything about their women. It's not their time yet to be with them. They must play the game in looking for a wife.

Once they caught up with Duncan. At the pub as they drank and ate. Willian spoke. "Duncan what's up? Why are we riding so hard? It's as if ye have found a mate. Ye are lucky that we know about the Holy Trinity Church."

Duncan didn't say anything to them at first. Then he spoke. "There is a lot of ground we must cover, before we can bed down for the night. Ye have a place to live for a month. This time ye can work and learn that skill of woodworking. The town has many women there your age. There is two men that needs help, each man does different things."

Thomas looked a head there was something bothering Eleanor. He could feel it coming from her. The closer she gets to Berwick-upon-tweed the feelings got stronger. He called to her. "Honey are ye all right?"

She was trying to figure out why she was having this feeling of trouble up a head. "I'm fine my love. I have these feelings were going into some trouble."

Then a little voice whisper to Thomas. Ones the two of ye are back together. This trip Eleanor has taken she will have the key to what is to come. "Honey I don't know what is happening to us. All I know is, be a where of what is happening there at the place ye are going to. It will be the key to what is to come ones where back together."

Eleanor closed her eyes. "I will be careful, ye do the same. We are the keys to all of this. Don't forget to put this in your journal. That way we won't forget it."

Something was going to happen where Eleanor and his sister will be. "I won't forget. Keep an eye on my sister. Let my mother know that trouble is coming your way. My feelings is telling me this. It could be the key to who had killed Ronald and his family?"

William was watching Thomas, the two of them had a close bond. As they rode down the road. William had notice he was staring out in space. "Thomas what is going on. Were ye talking to my sister?"

After Thomas said his goodbyes to Eleanor. He looked at his friend. "Eleanor felt there was trouble up ahead. I could feel something was troubling her. So, I called to her. Don't let me forget to write it in my journal tonight.

*   *   *

They arrived at her mother's cousin's place. When they got to the door Bridget cousin opened the door. "Bridget it's good to see ye. Something has happened to my daughter. It was nine months ago she came up missing. I was going to call this party off. But thought different because of my son. He needs to fine him a wife. I thought to asked ye if he could go with ye to the other parties."

The man who drove the carriage, started to bring their bags in. "Bridget ye can stay but your friend and the girls can stay with my son. I'm not ready to have guess to sleep over tonight."

Then her son came out of one of the rooms. "Mamma everything is set up for tonight. I'm going home to get ready for the party." Quickly his mother asked if her cousin friend and the two girls could stay at his place. "Yes, I would love to have them."

Then his mother asked. "If they could bring Bridget's bags in."

Then she turn to her friend. "Franceam would that be all right with ye?"

Franceam looked at the girls and they nodded yes. "That will be just fine with us."

Then Bridget introduce her to her cousin. The bags for Bridget was already in the house. Mikkel had his horse brought to him. He led them to his home that wasn't that far away. On the way there Eleanor told Franceam that she had a bad feeling that trouble was coming.

*   *   *

Eleanor was looking over the people on the dance floor. This party was different than the others. Every young woman looked beautiful in her dress. There were so many men that the women could choose from. How could a woman choose just one man out of all these men? An idea came to her. If she weren't married, how would she choose a man? Then Eleanor started to take in each man's shape and structure of his body. She found something in each one that she didn't like. One man was too short, too fat, too old, too pushy, and too shy, too scary. Does each man here really look that bad to her? Could it only mean that they don't measure up to Thomas?

Every man Eleanor met wasn't like her man. Many men had asked her to dance. They had asked her if she would live around here. She told them no. She was here because of her mother wanted her to meet her cousin. We are to bring her children with us to the other parties. She looked at the men—women pairing up. Why was she here? Her mother brought her here to find a husband. Eleanor had to pretend she was looking for a man to marry. She was married to a wonderful man. If there wasn't any danger for her, she wouldn't be here.

Now she was looking around at the group of men. She had seen there was an Englishman in the group. This Englishman stood out from the Scots in the way he was dress. As she watched him, she could see he was looking only at the women with blond hair. He was a tall man with blond hair of his own. She had to admit that he was handsome. What did Thomas tell her? To look into the man's eyes, watch how he carries himself. It will tell ye what kind of man he is. Then she notice that he walked not of a young man but much older. More of the age of her father. She felt there was something very wrong with this man.

Why is an Englishman here among us Scotsman? Then she felt a shiver go up her back the closer he came to her. She could feel all her senses go on high alert. There was something about his looks. No... that's not it. It's the way he looked at the women that made her skin crawl. He was looking at the blond hair women the way a wolf would look at sheep. This wolf was going for his next victim. A victim for what? He's not looking for a wife. How would she know that? As they had gotten closer to this place, she knew danger was around here. Could he be the danger she had felt? Eleanor remember what Thomas had told her. "There is one-way ye can tell what kind of man he is. Ye must look into the eyes of the man. That is the key to find out what kind of man he is." This kept going over and over in her mind. At first, she only saw how he looked at the women. His smile wasn't playful, as he made his way over toured the women.

What his eyes was doing was hunting. Could that be why it was making her defenses go up…aye. There is much more to him than being a wolf. Eleanor wasn't blond but he was making his way over to her. This had scared her a lot. She felt like she did when the bear came after her. That bear was hurt and dying. This man felt like he was evil. She could feel it bouncing off him. When he looked at her, she saw his eyes. It was confirming what she saw and felt. His face may be younger. When she looked at his eyes they were from an older man. When he looked at Eleanor, she knew she was in trouble. He had seen that she was afraid of him, none of the other women feared him.

Eleanor had to get away from that Englishman. She couldn't go over to her mother for safety. Her mother would just make her dance with him. Franceam was talking with some of the other women. How could she get away? She needed someone to block him from wanting to come over to her. From out of nowhere a young man she knew.

Kain McNulty had made is way over to her. Eleanor never thought of him as husband material. She had known him from the time he bought a horse from her father. Kain was older than Thomas was. If she had to compare him to Thomas. She would say he was tall like her man, looking at his chest it was much smaller. He wasn't as handsome as Thomas. She knew he was a kind man, and this was just what she needed.

Quickly Eleanor closed the distance between them. "Hello Kain. I didn't know ye were going to be here."

She had seen Kain was all dress up. "Hello Eleanor. It's a nice night for dancing. Would ye care to dance with me?"

Eleanor smiled at him and nodded her head yes. She spoke. "I would love too."

Kain led her onto the dance floor. "Eleanor ye surprised me when I saw ye here. I thought ye would already be spoken for."

Eleanor saw that Englishman coming closer to them. She was afraid he would ask Kain if he could cut in.

"Kain could ye get me away from that Englishman. He scares me to high heaven. I have a bad feeling about that man."

Kain took her hand. "Ye are, let us take a walk in the garden." Eleanor nodded her head, and the two of them went through the doors leading out to the garden. "Now tell me why that man scares ye?"

Eleanor looked toward the door. "Have ye seen how he looks at the women with blond hair?"

Kain shook his head. "No, I was looking at ye. Ye look so beautiful tonight."

Eleanor blushed and spoke. "Thank ye. Tell me Kain. Did ye know that I was going to be here?"

Kain couldn't keep his eyes off her. "Aye… I knew that ye were, your father told me. He said I would find ye here at his wife's cousin's home. He even gave me their address. Along with a note to get me into the house. Tell me how Thomas let ye get away?"

Eleanor looked at him trying not to give her secret away. Then she spoke. "Did ye only come here just to ask me that question?"

Kain held Eleanor's hands. "No, I need to find out something else before I could find myself a wife."

She looked at him. "Kain, what did ye have to find out?"

Kain pulled her into his arms. "Just this," he bent his head and softly kissed her lips. His arms drew her into him. Eleanor knew what he was doing when his tongue brushed over her lips. Her thoughts told her she must play the game.

When Kain had deepened the kiss. He knew he didn't have a chance with Eleanor. Slowly Kain pulled back. "Ye are here but ye don't want to be. He wanted ye to be sure that he's the only one."

She smiled and then said. "Aye."

Kain gave a small smile. "All right, since ye are already taken will ye help me find a wife?"

Eleanor quickly put a finger over his lips. "Please don't say that too loud. I tell ye I do know a young lass. She is a year older than I. We are going to a party where she lives. She will be at that party. Would ye care to meet her? Her mother died and she has been helping her father with the horses."

Kain gave her a big smile. "Aye… That sounds wonderful. May be we can get my mother down here to meet her father."

That made Eleanor happy. "That would be a lovely idea. Shall we go back inside?"

Kain took her hand, and they went back inside. "Aye… thank ye for that kiss." Then he whispered. "Thomas is a lucky man."

She smiled and wished she were with Thomas. "Could we dance together one more time?"

Kain held the door open for her. "Aye… then I will get ye something to drink."

* * *

When Eleanor and Kain came back into the ballroom. She saw a man was talking to her mother's cousin. Then the three women left with that man. Catherin had come over to them. "Eleanor that trouble ye had sensed on are trip. We are going to find out what it is."

She nodded her head yes, Eleanor knew that something had happen. She had a feeling that Englishmen had something to do with it. "I don't know but I'm going to find out."

Quickly the three of them followed her. The man had taken the three women out of the ballroom. They followed them with Kain and Catherin right behind her. Before anyone could close the door the three of them slipped inside. They went over to Franceam, she had placed a finger over her lips and motion tore the man to listened.

The man had a sad face. The news they got wasn't good. "I'm sorry to have to tell ye this. We have found your daughter. Ye have said your daughter has been missing for ten and a half months. Could she have run away because she was with child?"

Eleanor wondered why would they ask if Elizabeth was with child? She had her answer when Elizabeth's mother stamp her foot. "No…! My daughter didn't know any man. Her driver had taken her to the dress shop. She was there for her fittings, the dresses were for her coming out party. This was going to be her first season. The day she gone missing, her driver told me he had to move for a delivery wagon. The dressmaker told him she had left and went up the road that was the last time anyone saw her."

Eleanor never was able to meet Elizabeth. She knew she was around her age with blond hair. She was getting a bad feeling about all of this. Even though Elizabeth wasn't home her mother took them to introduce them to her friends.

When the constable spoke. "Mum we have found your daughter. I'm sorry she was dead when we got to her, your daughter's neck was slit. The baby who is a little girl, she was on the mother stomach. The child was just born may be a half an hour ago. The mother's body was still warm her baby was still attached to her, mum your grandchild is alive. We have a lead a woman that saw a fine buggy. She told us it was an English stile buggy. There was a seal on it she had remembered that she saw it once before. It was eleven months ago. She had never seen it again until tonight."

Eleanor went over to her mother's cousin. "I have a quick question to ask. If there was an Englishman invited to the party." She quickly told her. "No there was no Englishman."

Eleanor went over to the constable quickly. "Sir, tonight there was an Englishman here at the party. He seem to just appear out of no where's. I was enjoying watching the couples dancing. When I saw this Englishman walking around all the girls with blond hair. He man appear young with blond hair himself. The way he walked was more like and older man or a man that was injured. I found it strange that he only looked at the women with blond hair. As I watched him it seem like he cercal around these young women. It made me think of a wolf in what they would do. A wolf would cercal them to pick his next victim. This man wasn't looking for a wife. All the men out there was being playful or talking to the women, not him. This man cercal around them, he was sizing them up.

"He must have felt me watching what he was doing. When he had turned toured me, his eyes seem to look through me. That man scared me to hi-heavens. When I saw his eyes, they were of an older looking man? They were black as coaled, my instinct told me this man is evil, get away from him."

Then Eleanor's cousin cried out. "No, it can't be. I just thought Elizabeth was mistaken. She told me when she came out of the dress shop. This tall Englishman bump into her, she thought it was on purpose. He had blond hair, and his eyes were black. It had scared Elizabeth to the point that she wanted to scream. Her driver came over to her before he could push her into his buggy. He was very pushy to fine out her name. He said his name was Albert Huascaran. As they went home, she thought she was being followed. She said that every time she went to the dress shop, she thought he was there.

Eleanor's mother was standing near her cousin. "Daughter ye must be mistaken I didn't see any Englishmen at this party."

Then Franceam went over to Eleanor. "Bridget that is enough there was an Englishmen here tonight. Are ye going to tell me that I was seeing things. I was keeping an eye on Catherine and Eleanor. I had notice that Eleanor was watching this man. He stood out for he wasn't dress like the other men, but dress as an Englishmen. To me he walked as an old man, his eyes were black. Eleanor head was move quickly to see if she could get away from him. Now my daughter and Eleanor are learning to be a healer and a midwife. I teach them to be aware of the person. The eyes will tell ye a lot, just looking at that man told me he was evil."

*   *   *

The constable had taken notes. "Thank ye Miss. Mum do ye remember how many women is here tonight?"

She looked at Bridget. "There is twelve girls and twelve boys. That was with my daughter and son."

Then the constable told one of his men to see how many women was on the dance floor. "I like to thank ye Eleanor for this information. This will help with are case. I'm sorry to tell ye this that she wasn't the first lass to be taken. Please make shore all these women get home safely."

*   *   *

In the hall they heard a baby crying. Then they heard Mikkel come running down the hall. "Dad Catelyn is missing. One of the girls said a man called Albert took her into the garden. I went out there to see if they were still in the garden. Dad there gone he was the only Englishmen at the party."

The library door open and the constable came out. He told his men "To put a call out for a black English buggy, with a seal on it halfway showing. There is a missing girl she has blond hair. She is with a tall man also with blond hair."

Mikkel was looking at the baby girl. "Dad who's this baby girl belong to?" In the back of Mikkel's mind he thought it was Elizabeth's child. All he said. "My sister is dead, and this is her child. Dad, am I right? Please tell me that I'm wrong."

His father looked at is son. "I wish I could. Son, how did you know?"

Mikkel look at his father then took the child into his arms. At that moment, the child stop crying. "Last night I had a dream of my sister. She told me to take care of her child that she won't be able to. Because she didn't have a son, he will kill me once he sees the baby. I got to see her she looks like an Angel to me. I love you Mikkel. Please get married and have more children of your own. Caerleon told me that it is time for you to marry. Raze this child as if she came from Caerleon."

Mikkel's mother and father looked at him and the baby. "All right son you were very close to your sister. Son could you take care of the party now. Bridget, could you check over the baby. Mikkel everything that was for your child is upstairs. We will take care of the baby until you come back home with a wife. Right now, we will make sure that your sister will have a place to be put to rest."

Franceam came over to Bridget. "I have my bag with me, it's in with my coat. How about we go and check the baby out together."

Bridget's cousin went over to her. "Thank you. My husband and I must take care of our daughters' body."

The constable walked over to the women. "Mum you can take your time. Your daughter needs to be checked over, to see if there is any clues left on her. Only then, will she be place in your hands so she can be put to rest."

Then Bridget saw Kain. "Hello Kain."

Kain was standing near Eleanor. "Hello mum, it's good to see ye again. I'm so sorry for your cousins lost. Eleanor's going to help me find a wife."

Bridget smile at Kain. She had an idea. "Then ye can go with them to the next party. Franceam could ye take over for me. Our driver knows where to go next. I will take care of this sweet baby. We will bring the child to Franceam home within a month."

CHAPTER TEN

The Place they will live and work

ABOUT 159 MILES away from Edinburgh, is Paisley it is north of Gleniffer. Duncan had a place for Thomas to live and work. Lee McDee, he had a small shop where he works with wood. He also made toys for the children. There was one young man that he was teaching woodworking. Thomas was to stay with him for a month. Duncan and Thomas got off his horse he had dropped off William a mile down the road.

Duncan walked in first and greeted Mr. McDee. "Hello Mr. McDee, I have brought ye my brother Thomas. Our father thought it was time for my two brothers to see Scotland. He would like them to learn other skills besides raising horses."

The man walked over to Thomas as the young man in the back looked on. "Will now. Ye are a tall and looks to be very strong. I bet ye can take care of ye self?"

Duncan step in and spoke up. "My brother is the best sored fighter in the Highland games."

Thomas gave him a punch in the arm. "Duncan thank ye for the praise. I'm here to learn woodworking. Not to show off my fighting skills. Duncan is it not time ye get going. I know that ye been wanting not to be with us. Have Ye been courting a lass? Better yet have ye married her. If that is so it's been a long time ye haven't been with her."

Duncan looked at Thomas. "I see ye are all set here. Ye know where William is staying. I'll be back in a month. Thank ye Mr. McDee. I'll be off now good luck Thomas see ye in a month."

Thomas watch Duncan ride off. He knew that what he had said got to Duncan. Then he laughed, "I hit a nerve with what I had said. I hope he has found a lass to marry. It will be good to have children around mamma and dad."

The old man smile at Thomas. "I like ye to meet Jimmy. He will show ye were ye can keep your horse. Jimmy, live not too far away from us. There is a room and a bed in the back of the barn. Ye can eat with us if ye like. We have a stream to get some water to wash up, or ye can just jump in. We also have a pump to just get drinking water. Get your horse settle in, if ye like to wash up before we eat go ahead."

Jimmy looked to be around seventeen. He was tall for his age as Thomas looked at Jimmy and thought.

He needed to do some work outs to get stronger. "Hello Thomas, it's nice to meet ye. Is this your horse?"

Thomas smile as he took Midnight's rains and led him to the barn. "I've had this horse since I was ten years old. My sister has Midnight's twin. Will my boy ye get to sleep in a barn for a month."

Jimmy look on as he took care of Thunder. "May I ask how ye got so strong?"

Thomas took off Midnight's saddle and put it aside. Then he got out his brush and started to brush him down. "Will doing this and cleaning off my land. I'm at the age to choose a wife. But before I do that, I need to see Scotland. I have seen so much beauty around the Highlands.

"As ye know my brother brought me here so I can learn other things. I'm good with my hands as my brother had said. My uncle who was killed in battle was very good with wood. That's why my brother looked for a place from which I could learn. Soon my brothers and cousin will be having a family of their own. I would like to make toys for the children and other things."

Jimmy looked at him as he worked on his horse. Right now, he must use his father's horse to get to work. "Thomas I've been saving my money to get a horse for myself. Could ye help me choose a horse and train him?"

Thomas saw that he was looking for someone to get started on growing up. "I will be happy to help ye. I was wondering if ye have a big brother?"

Jimmy looked at Thomas and shook his head no. "I have a big sister she is at the age to merry. The man she likes is not ready to marry yet. To me he is just a play-boy she hasn't seen him with other women. There is another young man who would like to marry her. He went to the Highlands to raze cattle. Now he has land and a home. This is her second season, our father wants her to marry this year. If she don't find someone, he will make her marry who he choose for her.

"Tomorrow after work I can show ye around. That man I told ye about he wanted to spend some time with me. Would ye come with me tomorrow after work? He don't have much time left here in the Lowlands. I don't know what to tell him. Besides, I must buy myself a horse. My father would like to have his horse back."

Thomas looked at his new friend. It's time to share what he knows. It will be some good practice for when I have my own children, he thought. "All right Jimmy, what is your friends name?"

Jimmy was so please to hear he would go with him. "His name is Dave. He's nineteen soon he will be twenty. When he left two years ago, he looked like me. But now he looks a lot like ye. I was hoping when I bring my horse home, the two of ye could come with me. My sister hasn't seen him yet. When he came to the house only my father was home. She was gone to one of the parties her and her girlfriends went to. Dave spoke to my father. He had asked her hand in marriage.

"Mr. McDee didn't tell ye that he has a daughter. She is fifteen I'm a year and a half older than she is. I was hoping to marry her when I turn twenty. Dave got his land from his uncle. He is giving him four of his pregnant cows when he takes a wife."

Thomas felt this young man needs a big brother. He must not be close to his father. He just listen to his life story. "All right Jimmy ye better get back to work. I'm going to wash up I had a long day."

Jimmy seem devastated. He didn't realize he told Thomas everything he was thinking. "I'm sorry Thomas. Your right I better get back to work I'll see ye tomorrow. Thank ye."

Thomas smile at him running back to the shop. Now that Midnight was bedded down for the night. He had taken some clean clothes out with him to the pond. He had gotten behind a bush and got naked. When he got into the water. The hold day had been washed away. He felt relax for the first time since he saw Eleanor. It was getting dark out when he heard Mr. McDee call to him for supper. "Thomas it's all right I put some food in your room. Take your time getting out of the water. That was a long trip ye had taken."

Thomas knew that he should get out of the water. He quickly washed up and dried himself off. He even wash his shirt so he could keep a few shirts clean. In his room there was food on a table. It's been a while since he had home cook meals. It was a good thing they gave him a lot, for he was hungry. The food was good, but it wasn't as good as Eleanor's cooking. Then there was a knock at his door. It was Mr. McDee. He had two glasses of Scotch with him. "I thought ye like a glass of Scotch to take any aches away."

Thomas nodded his head yes. "I would enjoy some scotch to end a good meal. It was a long ride here. Some of the trails was rough going."

He watched Thomas take a good drink of his scotch. He had let the Scotch burn its way down his throat. "That is just what I needed to end the day out. After I had worked on my land cleaning some trees out. My dad would always bring out the scotch."

Mr. McDee watched the young man. He wanted to see what kind of man he was. "Your brother said that ye are looking also for a wife. Do ye know what ye want in a woman?"

Thomas had an idea what was going on. He had seen what other fathers was doing. He wanted to see if the scotch would loosen his tongue. Thomas knew how to drink, his father had shown his son the right way to drink scotch. "Aye… That I do. The woman I marry must love me. She must be able to cook and take care of all my needs. I don't want a young girl like fourteen or just turn fifteen. She must know how to ride a horse and be able to work by my side. If I had a bad day, I don't want her to cower at my feet. She should be able to say how she feels. I'm not the kind of a man to hit my wife or any woman." Thomas took another drink of his scotch. "I will not let a woman trap me into marriage. I know that ye have a daughter. I will make sure that door is locked. I'm here to learn and to look around to see what's out there. There is a few lasses I have seen that I'm thinking about. Does that help ye sir?"

Mr. McDee looked at Thomas. He had seen how he took care of his horse. Even his clothes were clean. He was a man that take care of his things. "Thank ye for this information my boy. Tomorrow will see what ye can do with wood. Get some rest we start work at 8:00, breakfast will be at 6:00. This should give ye time to feed your horse."

Thomas down the last of his scotch, he handed the glass and plate back to him. "Thank ye for the Scotch and the food. I will see ye in the morning." He followed him out so he could check on his horse. As he went back to his room, he could feel Eleanor was upset. He got undress and got into bed, it felt so good to sleep in a bed. Now why is his wife upset?

Thomas closed his eyes as he cleared his mind. "Honey can ye hear me my love?"

*   *   *

After all the couples were safely on their way home. In her room she felt Thomas calling to her. As she got undress and climbed into bed. She cleared her mind and called back to her husband. "Honey I'm here. So ye felt me being upset. Wow! We're getting closer, even though where so far away from each other."

Thomas could feel her almost next to him. "Eleanor why are ye upset honey?"

In her mind she knew he was in bed, she could almost feel him with her. "I wish I were with ye, so ye could make me feel better. I never thought sex could help a person to feel better. Tonight, they found my cousin dead. She had a child with her, it was her child. On top of that and Englishmen was at the party. He was looking at all the women with blond hair like himself. It was scary the way he looked at the women. He was circling them like a wolf would. Honey I saw his eyes. Those eyes were evil. He saw me looking at him and found I feared him. Kain McNulty saved me from him. He asked me to dance."

Thomas thought of Eleanor being the key to what is happening was coming true. "Do ye know that man's name?"

Eleanor was please that he wasn't afraid that Kain wanted her. Then she felt he knew something like this was going to happen. "His name was Albert Huascaran. Elizabeth had told her mother about him. Her mother thought she was mistaken his attention. Honey she wasn't the first girl to come up missing. There are many women killed and left with a child on them. I have this feeling that ye knew something was going to happen."

Thomas took in all the information. He would ask Jimmy if there were any missing women with blond hair. "I wish I were with ye. I remember Kain, I knew he liked ye. Your right about me knowing something was going to happen. It was after we saw ye. A little voice told me that ye were going to have the key to all of this."

Eleanor then knew why he married her when he did. "Honey did ye know that Kain would come looking for me. Is that why ye married me then?"

Thomas found he all most laughed. "Ye could say that. Besides, I wanted ye. Ye could get me so hot for ye. I knew one way or another I was going to have ye. Honey when I'm home. I will make love to ye as much as ye let me."

Eleanor remembered something. "Honey there is one more thing I just remembered. This man took another girl right under are nose. He has magic of some kind. Also, he has an English stile black buggy with his seal half showing. When the three of ye are back together, let everyone know about this. I'm going to be helping Kain and my cousin Mikkel find a wife. Mikkel is going to raise his sister's child. Honey I must try to get some sleep. We will be leaving in the morning. On the way home there is another party to go to. I wish we could make love, I could use ye right now. I love ye honey."

Thomas thought he knew how to help her. With a wave of his hand, he felt her pussy. "Honey can ye feel my heat moving inside ye pussy. Are ye still on what momma made ye."

Eleanor could feel his body on her. She felt his heat moving in her. "Aye…, Thomas." She felt his hands running over her breast. As he drove her up the butterflies were stronger. She could feel his lips on hers then she came. Then she felt is heat cum inside her.

Thomas had taken the covers off him. As he felt himself cum. "Honey I know I came but my seed isn't here. Did I give ye my seed."

She quickly took a breath after she came. "Aye… that it did. Thank ye for that. I thought I could feel ye moving inside me. Aye…, ye gave me your seed."

Thomas smiled that helped both of us he thought. With a wave of his hand, she was clean. But he didn't clean himself yet. He took his finger and ran it down his heat. Then he put it in his mouth, he had tasted her sweetness. "I like the idea that we can do this. I have all my notes, and I will put this in it also. So, I can still have ye, my friend is very happy. Night my love be careful."

*　*　*

The next morning a police officer came over to Mikkel's home. The officer told us that Suellen was the young woman taken. She was the friend of Katie. At the time the Englishman took grate care looking over her. He didn't like the man hovering over her. He saw the Englishman heading over to her. Mike saw how he was acting to all the blond hair women. The Englishman waited until he was getting Katie and him something to drink. Mike had quickly gone back to her side. He told the man she is taken. The man was trying to get her to go outside into the garden. He didn't seem so happy about her saying no to him. Nor was he happy seeing Mike was back. He asked Suellen who just came back from the pouter room. He had led her onto the dance floor then dance her right through the doors to the garden. That was the last time we saw her. Everyone told the officer once they realize Suellen was gone and so was the Englishman. To them it was as if they vanished with magic.

*   *   *

Franceam had taken her group to another party. Kain and Mikkel came a long they were looking for a wife. Mikkel's father told them to watch over the women. At their next stop just before the Highlands. Eleanor saw another man who was doing the same thing. When he saw Eleanor, he disappeared. Mikkel and Kain stayed close to the three women.

Eleanor went and introduced Kain to Annaly. She had met Annaly when her father came to buy a horse. The two young ladies had enjoyed each other's company. Annaly had brought a friend with her. She introduce them too Jane.

*   *   *

Mikkel seem to be drawn to Jane. "May I ask why you are here?"

Jane was a shy woman with long blond hair. At first, she didn't talk much. When Mikkel started to talk with her, she started to open-up to him. "Ye see my husband died when a tree he was cutting down had fallen on him. That was two years ago. It was Annaly who said that was enough morning for Bill. It had happened just after are honeymoon. We didn't see much of each other, I'm looking for a husband. I went back home but when my father died. My stepmother didn't want me back in the house. She had married a young man. She was afraid I would take her husband."

Mikkel was watching Jane as she talk to him. She made him feel like he knew her for a long time. "May I ask how old ye are?"

Jane smiled but he could see she wanted to be shy again. She had answered his question. "I'm eighteen. It was and arrange marriage by my father. To tell the truth he had sold me to him. I had just turned fifteen."

*   *   *

The two couples hit it off. Kain had sent word to his mother to come to the party. Annaly had her father with her. When his mother arrive, she didn't have any dresses for the party. Franceam had let her use one of her dresses. Once Mary was clean up, she came downstairs to meet Annaly's father. When the two parents met, they had been taken by each other. Kain had fallen in love with Annaly. The next two days after getting to know her. He had taken her hand and asked her to become his wife. She had said yes. In three months, they will be married. Their parents also hit it off. It was a good day for them. The women smiled at the two couples.

*   *   *

While that was going on. Mikkel and Jane went outside to talk. It was a beautiful day out. He had to tell Jane about his sister and her baby. Then he told her about his wife. "My wife died in childbirth. It was my sister who talked me into looking for a wife."

Jane was saddened when she heard that. "I'm so sorry for your lost Mikkel."

He thought she might be the one for him. "How about we go with Franceam to her home. I know my parents will be coming to bring Eleanor's mother home. We can ride back with them. Would you like to get married in two months? By that time, we both should know if we would want to marry."

Jane was surprised that he asked her to marry him. "Mikkel our you shore that ye want to marry me?"

She is surprised that he asked her now. Then he felt that she was scared about something. Why would she hold back that secret about herself? "Jane I'm falling for you. Franceam's home is in the Highlands, she told me we could go home with them. Why are you acting as if you have a secret about yourself?"

Mikkel watched her close her eyes. "I do have a secret. Mikkel my marriage had never been consummated. I'm still a virgin, he never even kissed me. I been scared that someone would think I knew how to make love. I don't even know how to kiss. I would love to marry you. It would be good to make your sisters child as our own. I hope you will want more children."

Mikkel gave her a big smile. "Jane, would you like to go for a walk. I think it's time to get to know each other a bit."

They headed toward the woods. Jane started to tell him about her husband. "Ye must understand he was an old man. I didn't share a bed with Bill. He only kept me to be able to show me off. I don't know anything about making love. I have never been touched by a man. I was sold to him for my father's det. All he did on are honeymoon was to show me off."

When Mikkel took her into his arms. He wanted to see how much she did know. At first, she is scared. Jane didn't know what to do. "Don't be afraid I will never hurt you. I want you to let go. You're going to become my wife. Tell me have you seen anyone kissing?"

She was trying not to be afraid. She had no idea what was going to happen. "I saw a man had taken her into his arms. He had pulled her close to him. This man had put his lips to hers, then he did something else. That kiss had deepened but how would that happen?"

Mikkel knew now he could show her what he likes. She want this as much as he does. "Jane you and I are young. I want children and I need a son. Most of all I want to be loved as I love her. Let us try this kiss. I will slowly place my lips on yours. Then I will take my tounge and run it over your lips. This is to ask you to open, to let my tounge make love to your mouth. Just open a bit so I could move in and out of your mouth. If you let me, I will pull you into me. Let your hands do what it would like to my body. We will see if we can light a fire in both of us. Don't be afraid of me taking you now. If this goes how I think it will. My hand may go after some skin. You may do the same. In a marriage love making is the biggest part of their life together. Do you want this to happen?"

Jane thought she would never be touch by a man. "Yes, Mikkel show me a little of love making. I want to learn how to please you."

He made a point to slowly lay his lips on hers. With loving care his tongue moved over her lips. When she open her lips to him. He had pulled her closer to him as his tongue moved in and out of her mouth. Her hands pulled out his shirt and moved over his back. Mikkel kissed his way down her neck. She wanted him bad as her hand pulled his kilt up to touch his bottom. He had found out she had bottled all her feelings up. Now that she had permission to touch him. Jane went headfirst into love making. It took all his willpower to pull away from her. If she had gotten to his heat. They would have to marry right now. "You are hungry to be loved. If I didn't stop, I would have you now. My wife was a wonderful lover, her passion wasn't as strong as yours." Jane is down hearted. "I'm sorry. Did I do something wrong?"

Mikkel frame her face with his hands then kissed her lips. "No... You did everything right if we were married. Honey were not married yet. I've done some dating now and then. None of the women could light my passion in me. You had turn on the heat that I haven't felt in a long time."

Jane was fussing with her hands. He notice that she was going to shut down on him. "Stop it, don't you dare shut down on me." He took a finger and lift her chin up, so they were eye to eye. Mikkel had to take a breath of air. So… he could be able to do what he was thinking. "You wanted to be touch in all those sweet places that a man would touch. Am I right about this?"

Right then she looked at him. "Yes, you are right about that. I would even take if you went all the way with me. For a long time, all I had to do was reed love stories. I hunger to be touch by a man. To be shown what was making those butterfly's way down near my womanhood. I don't even know what will go there. My mother died before she could tell me about those things. I was very young when Bill married me. If you don't want to make love to me. Could you show me different things? In lest you have changed your mind about marrying me. I will understand if you take back the promise. Every time someone said he would marry me. He change his mind, I was too much for the men to start over. They want a woman that knew how to make love."

Mikkel ran a hand through his hair. "Damn it…" He didn't know what to do. It was as if his wife said. "Don't give me that. Are you going to show her or have her now?" All he could do is look to the heavens. Then he turn and took her hand. He brought her deeper into the woods. They found many rocks one rock had a tree growing out of it. He had taken her under the tree. "So, you like to be shown what will be going into your womanhood. First thing I want you to know, you were able to get me hot enough to take you. Do you see this bump here on my kilt?"

Now he had her attention. "What is that? It wasn't there before."

Mikkel laughed he couldn't help himself. She had the power to bring him to his knees. He place himself against the rock. Then took her hand under his kilt. When she took hold of him his eyes close. She was running her fingers over his heat. Now she had lifted his kilt to look at it. "Is this what will be going into me?" He nodded his head yes. "Mikkel you are big and hard; your skin is soft to the touch. Did I do this to you?" He nodded his head yes.

Mikkel was enjoying her touch. His mind cried out. My Lord I want to have her now, please help me to show her things. I want to marry her first. I'm not a young man of eighteen anymore. I should be stronger than this. When he looked down at her she was looking at his case of jewels. "Come here." He helped Jane up and place her against the rock. "My turn to touch you, I'm going to show you how it will feel when a baby suck on your nipple. Honey I'm not a baby and when a man does it. It will wake up your womanhood. I will also take care of those butterflies with my finger. You will know how it feels to cum."

*   *   *

It was three days later the plans that Jimmy, and Thomas had was change. Now they were at work Thomas was enjoying working on a table set.

Jimmy couldn't look to buy a horse or to have his friend Dave over to see his sister. Dave had to go somewhere else to find a wife.

Mr. McDee came over to see how Thomas was doing. Then the door open and in came Dave. "Mr. McDee how have Ye been?"

He had come over to the young man. "Well now how are ye Dave? Ye are looking good. Farm work has been good for ye."

Dave had notice there was a new man in the shop. At the time Thomas had his back to him. Mr. McDee had called over Thomas to them. When Dave saw Thomas, he almost gave away who he really was. Quickly Thomas spoke up. "Hello Dave, it's good to see ye. Dave had bought one of my father's horses."

Then Jimmy came out of the back room. He had heard that Dave knew Thomas. "Dave your back did ye find what ye were looking for?"

Dave smile at Jimmy. "There was one young lass that I might see if we could be a match. That's if your sister won't have me."

Mr. McDee looked at the young men. "All right how about ye clean up. Then ye can go and do whatever ye like."

*　*　*

The three men then headed down to Jimmy's home. He had to get his money; he wanted his sister to see Dave. When he went into the house his sister had seen the two men on horseback. She went outside to meet the two good looking men. "Hello gentlemen. How are ye? I'm Jimmy's sister Malena."

Thomas was talking to Dave. If ye looked like Jimmy does. She may not know who ye are. "Hear is your chance to see if she would marry ye. How about ye span some time with her. Use another name like John."

Malena walked over to the two men. "What brings to handsome men to my door. Is there anything I can help ye with?"

Thomas went over to Dave. "No not for myself, I'm helping your brother. Now my friend has been looking for a wife. Your brother and I have been learning to work with wood. This is John, we know each other from the Highlands. Jimmy said that he had a sister that he could meet."

While Thomas was speaking Malena was looking John over. "So ye are looking for a wife."

Dave was please to find that she didn't remember him, he played a long. "Malena are ye old enough to marry? Ye look to young for me."

When Jimmy came outside Malena yelled. "Jimmy tell John that I'm old enough to marry. He thinks I'm too young to be anyone's wife."

Jimmy smiled and knew his sister didn't remember him. "John my sister is older than I am. Sis why don't ye go riding with us. I believe mamma will let you take her horse."

Then his father came out and Jimmy went over to his father. "Dad this is the man I told ye about. His friend John is looking for a wife. Malena would like to go riding with us. Would that be all right to use mamma's horse?"

Jimmy's father smiled at him. But he played a long he had recognized Dave right off. He walk over to Thomas first. "My boy works with ye, there is more to ye that meets the eye. The same with John here, so ye like to court my daughter. That will be fine with me, ye look to be able to take care of yourself and my daughter."

Then his wife came over to her husband. Before she could say anything, her husband spoke up. "Dear this young man would like to court Malena. I like for ye to me John, do ye think we can have these two find men over to eat?"

His wife just looked at him and then she knew who he was. "Aye… that will be find with me. Ye must be Thomas, how do ye like working with wood?"

Thomas knew Jimmy's mother knew who John was. "I've been enjoying working with wood. The places around Scotland have a let of old structures. I told my brother that I like to learn woodworking the other skills is working with iron and steel, to take back to the highlands with me."

She looked at Thomas. "Are ye looking for a wife also?"

Thomas had to think what to tell her. "I have my eyes open. There is one lass that I have in mind. But she is in the highlands. I had met her on the way here. When I head home, I will see if she would be the one for me."

Jimmy came with the other horse for his sister. His sister had gone and change her clothes to go riding with them. When Dave saw her, he was please how she looked. Her dress was cut low in the front. She had her hair fixed up. Dave walked over to her and kissed the back of her hand. "May I help ye on to your horse?"

She smiled and nodded her head. When he pick her up and place her on her horse. She had looked into his eyes, then she knew who he was from her past. This Dave she like to get to know. "Thank ye. Ye are a strong man I like that." She had touched his face as she looked deeply into his eyes. One's she was on her horse the four of them took off riding.

Down the road the two of them had decided to break away from Thomas and Jimmy.

Dave and Malena stopped by a small pond. When he put his hands around her waist and lift her off her horse. Malena spoke. "I've always loved ye when I was younger. Ye knew how to bring out the butterflies in my heat. I couldn't go with ye at the time. I had to grow up a bit more. Besides, I must see if someone could make me feel like ye did. Ye are stronger now Dave. I like the red in your hair it makes ye very handsome."

He knew she had remembered who he was. "Aye… Ye have turn into a beautiful woman. Malena, I came back to ask ye to marry me. I've missed ye so much."

She was still in his arms he had pulled her into him. He had let her feel the different in his body. "Dave are ye going to kiss me."

He bent his head and deepened the kiss. She found she wanted him to touch her again. Malena tried to push his hand to her breast. "Hold on for one minute." Dave step backwards and got down on one knee. "Malena will ye marry me."

She looked at him. "Aye…! I love your lips ye kiss different than before. When do ye like to get married?"

He looked at her. "Right now. I want to make ye mind, I have a license to marry ye right now. I know who could marry us." Dave was kissing her down her neck, he had her up against a tree. "I want ye to become my wife, don't try to play games with me. Do ye want me for your husband Malena."

Her hands was all over his back and under his kilt. "Dave I will marry ye, let's go before I have ye now. I'm old enough to marry without my parents' permission."

* * *

Eleanor and Catherin was ready to go home. They had help pair up the men-women. For two days they sometime caught the three couples kissing. It was time to head back to the Highlands. Jane had all her things with her. She said her goodbyes to Annaly and Kain. Everyone thank the three women for helping them fine their mate.

At the castle Jane and Mikkel went riding every day. When she was ready for him, they found someone to married them. That day at the castle Mikkel had told them not to wait for them. He had gotten a room for the night. Now he was able to see her hold body. It took all his willpower not to just take her. The first time it was all about Jane. He needed her to enjoy making love with him. It took all his willpower to make sure she was wet enough for him. He didn't want to hurt her when he came inside her. After they made love, she fell asleep in his arms.

That morning Jane found she wanted him again. She started to play with his heat. It didn't take much to wake it up. Jane wanted to see if she could do this, it was also to see if it would hurt her. He was a wake, but she had to find out things for herself.

She had straddled him and lowered herself on to him. It felt different, he went deeper inside her. "Relax let your body take me inside ye." Slowly she started to move. "Honey ye got it, let me help you move inside ye." Jane knew what to do now as she grind herself on him until she came. Mikkel pulled her down to him. "Good morning my love. Did ye like the way I woke ye up?"

His lips took her in a deep kiss. "I love it, I'm so glad I found ye. Do ye like what I'm doing to ye now."

He was on top of her now. Her body couldn't get enough of him. "Aye… I hope I can have time to enjoy this with ye."

Mikkel laughed. "I hope so, for I will have ye as much as ye let me. Ye have a lush's body, I'm going to make ye come until ye can't do it anymore. I don't know how much time before ye are with our child. Until then I will enjoy give ye my seed as much as ye want it, just like now."

* * *

When Catherin and Eleanor got to the castle. There was two letters waiting for them. Both girls ran to their rooms. Eleanor close her door she didn't want to be disturbed. Daniel had told them Donald will be leaving in October. He will be helping the boys find a place to stay for the winter. He had said he will take any letters back with him. Quickly she opened the letter from Thomas. She had read that he missed her and wish he were with her right now. "I can't believe we could talk that long in our minds."

Thomas had told her when he sleeps, he fines he's making love to her. Every place I go your there with me. Eleanor I'm glad we married when we did. The places he went the girls are nothing like ye. I can understand that they wanted to get away from where they live. Now I'm understanding why Ronald fought so hard. Then he said I'm glad ye told me about your cousin. I've been hearing throughout these towns, there has been many women taken. I don't know what is happening in this little town. There was two girls came up missing. Be careful I have a bad feeling about all this.

Eleanor took out paper and started to write. She had told him more about what had happened to her cousin. This part about this English-man and what she had felt. That man had disappeared as if by magic. He had taken one of the girls with blond hair. I had told the officer about him. Someone saw a black buggy they say it was the style of the English buggies. Then they saw my cousin dead her neck was cut. She had a baby girl on her stomach still a tach to her.

Eleanor went on to say. "Thomas, I'm glad we married I wish ye were here with me. I would have jump ye and made love to ye. Even if we didn't marry. I still haven't found anyone that could hold a candle to ye. Do ye remember me telling ye that Kain had saved me from that Englishman. Honey that Englishman knew I was afraid of him. Most of all he knew I saw the evil in him. I have a feeling that he is the key to what happen to our brother's. He has magic. At the party he tried to cover up what I saw. Now and then I've seen him in my dreams. At first,

I feared him. Somehow ye always come to me and make him go away.
Honey there is something about him. At times, his face keeps changing.
Be careful this man has other men with him."

*   *   *

Thomas wrote down that he hadn't seen Duncan yet. The last time
William and he was together was just last week. They have only three
days left until the end of the month. William was going to come here to
go hunting and to look at the maps with him. They were going to leave
after work. It was very early in the morning when William showed up.
Thomas was in the back doing some training with his sord.

For a bit he watched Thomas go through the motions. Then he
spoke. "Would Ye like to have a workout? I have my sord with me. In
fact, I have all my things with me."

Thomas knew something was up. "You're here early, I thought ye
would come here after work."

William looked at him. Then spoke, "I thought that I better get
going. His daughter was trying her best to get me to marry her. I try to
tell her, there is someone else I'm in love with. She thought that she could
push my hand in marrying her. Her father my boss had followed her to
the barn. When she said I will tell my father ye had your way with me.
That did it, I told her I'm not going to marry ye. Didn't ye hear me, I'm
in love with someone else. Ye are too young for me. Why are ye doing
this? Don't tell me you and that boy I saw, what was is name Neil. Did he
get ye with child, is that why ye are doing this to me. Don't tell me Neil
won't marry ye, will he."

Then she started to scream and ripped her dress. "Ye will have to
marry me now."

Then we heard her father bellow. When she turned, her father was
standing looking at her.

Thomas shook his head. "So, what happen?"

William looked at his oldest friend. "Her father told me that he was sorry for the way his daughter acted. He gave me some money and said that I better leave today. He wished that I did like his daughter. That I was a good worker and would make his daughter a good husband.

After I gathered my things, I heard yelling. When I was a long way from their place, I met Neil. I rode up to him and spoke. "Ye got Anny with child didn't ye." He went to get onto his horse, I had seen he was going to run away. I jump off my horse and knocked him out, she don't have a brother that would do what I did for her. Those two are too young to get married. I had placed him on his horse and took him back to her. I knocked at the door and heard Anny crying. I had walked in with Neil and drop him on the floor. I told Anny, "I don't think of ye as a wife for me. You're like a little sister to me, I saw Neil he was going to run away. I leave him with ye and your father and mother." Then I turn to her father, "Aye… Ye could kill him, but I say to ye. Make him marry her. Teach him your trade so he can take care of her and the baby. The boy is scared he didn't know what to do. He's not a bad lad, looking at his hands he works hard. Ye can see that his father had beat him, then he threw him out. He told Anny to get me to marry her."

By that time Neil was a wake, I had cut the ropes from his hands and feet. Neil spoke. "Sir I love your daughter, I had told my father about what happen. What William had told ye is right of what had happened with my father. I have nothing to give her and the baby. My father through me out, please tell me what to do sir. I will do as ye say."

Then her father told his wife to get a ribbon. Right there in front of me and his wife he married her to him. He told Neil ye will live here with us. Ye will save your money to buy land and build a house for the three of ye."

William looked at his old friend. "Damn it I miss Catherine. I want to go back to the highlands. Don't worry old friend I'm just venting. There was a girl that lived around were I was. She came up missing, they said that black buggy was around. This man do ye think he's a part of what happen to our brother and cousin?"

Thomas knew that they were being watched. "Aye… I don't think Duncan will be coming here. We will have to find another place for the winter. I wrote to tell dad that he should come here next spring. We will go looking around ourselves."

Then William knew they had company. He saw Mr. McDee and Jimmy. "So ye need a place for the winter. William were ye working with wood or did ye do some iron work?"

William nodded his head. "I was working with wood, just filling orders and making tables and chairs along with other things."

Then Mr. McDee spoke. "I will have ye work, with Jimmy. While Thomas and I, do some witling some animal toys for the children. I have a list of people to make their children some toys?"

Thomas slapped William on the back. "I told ye that we would find a place. Aye… we would love it. On Saturday we will do some hunting for ye. Could William do some work for ye now?"

Mr. McDee went and spoke. First, we eat then we can work. William, I want ye to make a bed for yourself. There is a small potbelly stove up in the barn. Jimmy can help ye to bring it down."

At the same time, the two men said. "Thank ye sir."

His wife saw that there was two more men outside. She told her daughter to put more meat and eggs on the fire. Then her husband came in and spoke. "Dear we have two more men to feed. Ye remember William and Jimmy is one of the family. After work Thomas and William is going hunting. They're going to stay with us for the winter."

CHAPTER ELEVEN

The vision that Lizzy and Thomas had

AT THE TABLE Lizzy smile at Jimmy, her eyes were mostly on him. Then her father spoke. "Jimmy ye have been with me for a while. What is your plans after the five years are up?"

Jimmy wet his lips. "My plans are to build myself a home and a shop like ye have. I like the set up ye have here. My uncle is giving me some land. There is a need for someone to help build homes up there. It's about six miles from Loch Ness. I have my eyes on someone very special to me. When she turns sixteen, I would like to ask her to marry me." While Jimmy was talking his eyes were on Lizzy.

She was looking very shy. "When she is of age, I would like to court your daughter Mr. McDee."

He was looking at Jimmy. Mr. McDee didn't give away that he was pleased with Jimmy. "My boy ye have a good head on your shoulders. Ye have been working very hard to learn these skills.

"Ye do know it's up to Lizzy if she would want to be courted by ye. Now for these young men. They have someone that is waiting for them.

Then again, the women could be married to them now. Thomas didn't stop eating and William follow suit of what Thomas was doing. These men with us has a secret. I believe that they must do something before they can go home."

As her father talked Lizzy felt funny. It was Jimmy that realize something was wrong. He had gotten up quickly to catch her. "Lizzy what's wrong?"

Her eyes closed then open. Lizzy looked at Thomas and William. "There is an evil man working his way down through the towns. He has many evil men with him. He is taking all the blond hair women. Your brothers fought his men. One of your brothers tried to stop him in the government. This evil man had his men kill his wife and unborn child. Ye two men are trying to find where the bodies were taken. Don't worry your other brother is in the town ye seek. Your women will be safe. Thomas, your mate will have your powers after ye receive the gifts from the magic roses." Then she passed out and Jimmy took her to the couch.

*   *   *

In Thomas mind he heard Ronald's voice. "Hay little brother. After Lizzy is sixteen, Marcos will be coming down this way. He can't touch her, she has gifts that will tell the truth of what he is up to. She will know him when she sees him. Ye are right that ye will have to fight.

"This man is using Albert's face, before long he has a plan to take over his body. When the ice is frozen, he will try to kill her. The spell he will use Eleanor will know how to break it. Duncan is married, our bodies are near her father's grave. Teach Jimmy how to get stronger. Show him how to throw a knife. Be careful little brother."

Thomas place a hand on the table. He had closed his eyes when the voice of his brother called to him. He had found they had taken Lizzy to the couch.

Only William stayed with Thomas. "All right out with it. Ye also had a vision. What happen or what did they say?"

Thomas took a drink of coffee. "This man Marcos knows about Lizzy's gifts. She is not the only one he is using. He will be coming after her. I have a feeling she will walk out onto the ice and fall through. We will be close to the water, hopefully we will hear her.

"We must get Jimmy stronger. He will be needing to be much stronger than he is. I was right Duncan is married. Our brothers are near his wife's father's grave. This winter we will need a boat to save her. Marcos does have magic, this confirms what Eleanor told me. Also, he has a plan to take over Albert's body. How he is going to do this it's a mystery to us."

William looked at Thomas. "Can ye talk to Eleanor from here?"

Thomas just looked at him. "We will talk later."

*   *   *

That night when Thomas went to the barn, he started his letter. He thought to tell her about what he has seen before jumping into bad news.

"Honey I never thought that Scotland had so many beautiful places. I got to see Plockton is a village in the Loch Ness, west ross area of the Scottish Highlands. Dundee is a coastal city on Firth of Tay estuary in eastern Scotland. Thurso is a town and former burgh on the north coast of the Highland council area of Scotland.

"I made some friends here. Dave lives in the Highlands he was the one that bought a horse from us. He came from the Lowland of Scotland. Jimmy is who I work with in the shop. Dave wanted to marry Jimmy's sister. At the time she didn't want him, but when he came back after two years. She didn't know who he was at the time. I told him to use another name like John. It worked when they could be alone with each other, she remembered him. They got married that day. I think Duncan may be married also. Before he left us, he had found two job each for us. I like working with wood an iron. These two things I know how to do. When the two years are up. I should be quite good at these jobs. This month is all most up.

"Honey I didn't want to just jump into bad news. When we was eating something had happen. I've been told that there will be a magic rose that will help us. We haven't seen Duncan, the family he stayed with her father just died. I know that Duncan married her. For her father is buried next to our brothers. Ronald called to me he told me about all of this. Tell dad not to come here until spring. We will be staying here at Mr. McDee's place. He asked William and I to help him to make toys for the children.

"Right now, ask Grana to teach ye how to counteract black magic. Honey that man Marcos uses black magic, ye will need it to counteract his spell's. I believe ye will have to know these things. Be careful my love. Mr. McDee's daughter had a vision. He knows she can see things in the future. It's getting harder to take girls with blond hair. When we travel, we will spread the word about the blond hair women.

"Honey this is my last letter to ye. The next three months we are going to look around are self. In March tell dad to come to Mr. McDee's place. I had Dave make him a map. We been enjoying looking around at different places. Every time we see young women with blond hair, we tell their fathers to be weir of a black buggy. We did this for three months. At time's we had a feeling that men was looking for women for this evil man. For on are way back some of the fathers told us that buggy they had seen.

"Soon this year will be over. I'm going to stay with Mr. McDee this winter as ye know. There is also a blacksmith that I will be helping at times. Before we left William, and I went hunting we got food for them. What we got will help a lot of people out. I had told Mr. McDee if Duncan came here to tell him where all set for the winter. We will be back when the first snow falls. William and I did some hunting for some people.

"We found work that we been learning. Three months went by fast. When we got back at Mr. McDee's place. The water was starting to freeze, I talked to Jimmy about Lizzy. I told him that evil man will try to end Lizzy's life. Now that she is sixteen, he's been courting her. She don't know about that evil man coming after her. At times I've seen Jimmy's friend poked his head up after being with Lizzy.

I told him ways to help him. He had said that he wants to marry her now. That he was going to be leaving in the summer to build his home. What I found out that he won't be far from Dave and his wife. They have a baby on the way. I heard ye had check out her and the baby.

"I wish that Marcos leave Lizzy alone. Today we had made a small boat. My feelings of him coming for her is getting stronger. The last two nights I've been hearing things in the night. He is trying to set the spell to kill her. Honey I must give this letter to Dave so he can give it to ye. I love ye Thomas."

*   *   *

It was raining hard out there was lightning in the sky. Thomas heard a voice in the wind it was a man's voice, and he was speaking latten. He couldn't sleep he felt trouble was coming their way. Then he heard it, Thomas was talking with Eleanor that night. She told him about a sleeping spell. "William, I hear Marcos he is calling to Lizzy." Thomas couldn't wake William up, in his mind he called to his wife. "Honey hear me, Marcos is trying to kill Lizzy. Hear the words that I hear."

She was awake she had known that trouble was heading toward her man.

As another lightning hit the sky. He could see the water from there window his love had answered him. When their minds was as one, she could hear the words from Marcos. "I hear the words, he is trying to put ye and the others in a deep sleep."

Then she gave her husband the words to wake William. Then another lightning hit the ice. Thomas knew that was the place were Lizzy would fall through. William was brought out of the spell, the two men was running to the river. They were calling to Lizzy to wake her up.

Thomas knew if she stayed asleep, she would go to the bottom of the river and die. Now he spoke the words Eleanor had given him, it had broken Marcos's spell.

When she fell through the ice it had woken her. Now the two men worked to get the boat over to her. They had a rope tied to the tree to help them pull them back. Jimmy had just ridden into the yard. He saw what was happening and went to get her father and mother. He found that he couldn't wake them up. He grabbed a blanket to wrap Lizzy in. Now he ran to the edge of the shoreline. Thomas called to him. "Jimmy stay there we will get her out of the water."

Lizzy try to pull herself on to the ice. It was getting too hard for her to do so. Every part of her body was slowing down, the cold was getting to her.

Jimmy had an idea to help them, he ran to get his horse. When he went home tonight, he left his horse saddled. He also heard the whispers in the wind. At last, they got to her Thomas had to pull her into the boat. While William used his weight to keep the boat from pulling Thomas into the water.

On the shore Jimmy had the rope tied to the horn of the saddle. Thomas used all his strength to pull her into the boat. Lizzy may be a small woman, she was already dead weight. Her wet clothes had added weight to her. They heard Jimmy yelled to them, "Do ye have her?"

He had heard them call back, "Hang on ye are going for a ride. He had gotten on his horse and pulled them quickly to safety. Jimmy had a bad feeling if he didn't get them off that spot, he was going to lose them all.

William got the blanket and put it around Lizzy. Jimmy took her from Thomas, he had brought Lizzy to the living room and laid her on the couch. Both men went to get the fire going. While Jimmy helped Lizzy out of her wet clothes.

When he was up stares earlier, he had brought her something warm to wear. "Thomas what can I give her to help her to get warm."

He had turn to see she was wrapped up in another blanket. "She needs a drink of Scotch, do ye know where the bottle is kept?"

Jimmy got up and went to get the glasses and the Scotch. He had a cup for Lizzy an got something to get the Scotch hot for her. After the men drank their Scotch William went to put Jimmy's horse in the barn. Thomas went to the back room to wake her parents up. At the open-door Thomas spoke the spell to counteract the black magic. Once that was done, he then knocked on the door. "Mr. McDee, could I speak to ye in the other room?"

He had looked at Thomas. At first, he felt as if he was coming out from a thick fog. Once his mind was clear he got up. He turn to his wife. "Honey are ye all right?"

His wife nodded her head yes. Then he followed Thomas into the other room. "What is going on here. Why are ye in my house?"

Thomas was at the table pouring him a drink of Scotch. "Here ye will need this. Tonight, about which man William and I was talking. He tried to kill your daughter. Your daughter is fine sir. Jimmy and I heard the whispers in the night. William and ye was put under a sleeping spell.

"It was the day before we left for three months. We were here at this table having breakfast. When we were all together your daughter had a vision. She spoke about William and me, what she told ye is true. I can't tell ye how I knew that man was going to do something to Lizzy. If it weren't for Jimmy riding here Lizzy, William and I would be dead. Once I had pull Lizzy from the river. The rope we had tied to the tree he had place it on the horn of his saddle. Jimmy pulled us to safety just before the lightning hit that spot."

Mr. McDee looked at Thomas. At first, he didn't understand what Thomas was talking about. Then it hit him between the eyes. "Are ye telling me my daughter went into the ice-cold water?"

Thomas took another sip of his Scotch. He had nodded yes. "Aye… that is just what I had said."

Mr. McDee jumped to his feet. "Where's my daughter? Who took off her wet clothes? Do I need to get my wife up?"

It's been a long night Thomas thought. "Sit down sir. Your daughter has been taken care of. Jimmy her husband to be took care of her. He is with her now. There is one thing he like for ye to do for him. When everyone is up, he would like ye to marry them. He don't want to be that far away from her ever again."

Mr. McDee went and through back his Scotch. "Jimmy wants to marry my daughter. Is he in bed with her now?"

Thomas shook his head no. "Come with me sir. The two of them are next to the fire. He took off his shirt because it was wet. He has her in his arms. Sir he carried her in. When she saw him, she went right into his arms? William and I got a fire going. He went right to work getting her warm. He got her a dry night gown and something to dry her hair. Jimmy went for the Scotch and warm it up for Lizzy. He made her drink some of it. What she didn't finish he did. Then he got two blankets one he laid it on the rug and the other one over her. She begged him to lay down with her. She was scared that it was going to happen again."

Mr. McDee went to get him a night shirt. Then he went into the room, he saw the two of them in each other's arms. He bent down and tapped Jimmy on the shoulder. "My boy will ye get up for a bet."

He had him a night shirt to put on. "Hang up your kilt so it will dry. Thomas is there a fire going in my daughters' room?"

Thomas looked at Mr. McDee. "Aye… I had built a fire before I waked ye."

Jimmy came out of the other room. "It's time for ye to take your wife to be to her room. I will let ye lay with her there. We will have a ribbon ceremony in the morning. After that ye may make her yours. Not until then."

Thomas left them and went to get some sleep. He had thought, as he gets closer to his brothers resting place. He has found out that things were happening a lot more. This man didn't like us telling people about him and his buggy. If he has black magic, we will be in trouble. I wonder about these magic roses that Lizzy talked about. I guess we will find out about them soon enough.

*   *   *

Thomas sent a letter back with Dave. He was visiting his father-in-law. Here it is another year had gone by. Ones it is at the end of this month I will be nineteen. As he read the letter from Eleanor. He found that he missed her very much. He thought that she had wrote a letter every day to him. William also got a letter from Catherine.

I've been finding when sleeping the dreams of my love is getting stronger. Before I got this letter, one of the nights. I had a dream of Eleanor it was the time she had seen that man. Somehow, I had the same dream as she did. She had written about it in this letter to me. Eleanor was right about those eyes of his, they were pure evil. On that night William had told me when he had heard me. I was talking to ye telling ye that I was the one holding ye. My love wasn't one to get scared easily. She didn't like dreams that came from an evil man. At times Thomas would have Eleanor's dreams, each time it felt there was magic involve.

The vision Lizzy had told me about a magic rose. As I write this part, I been finding the dreams have been giving me bits and pieces. The last dream had place us in a pub. This man had sent uncle a note. It was one of Marcos men. He is to tell us a story on what happen to our brothers. Lizzy's vision spoke of Duncan that he knows of this place. He also knows where our brothers has been laid to rest. It's right next to his father-in-law's grave. I have a feeling that he wasn't supposed to find the grave without all of us.

The places William and I have seen, our homeland is beautiful. Each day we rode through the towns there was always something new to see. I understand why Ronald fought so hard for Scotland. One thing I know is I miss my home. I have no hunger to live any place else then the Highlands. Scotland has many beautiful lassies that I have seen. One thing I know is none of them could hold a candle to my wife.

As I read Eleanor's books of letters to me. I'm finding her going back to this man Huascaran. She has a feeling that he will be coming to the highlands. Once uncle gets here, I have a feeling we be heading to some place near Karnal. The name of this small town was given by Cumbria Mandark. There is a place that is fence in that Mr. McDee told us about. I'm hoping Duncan will show up around the time uncle comes here in May. I want to be home before August. We have our home to build and get everything started for wintertime.

The three months we went on our own. I was glad we told the people about this evil man. There has been sightings of him and his buggy. There hasn't been any blond hair women taken. Right now, there is just seven months left. As we ride through the towns, we will be warning the people about Marcos. I have a feeling that we will be fighting Marcos in the highlands.

When we have are brother's Marcos will have his men fight us. I will wait to see what the roses will do for us. Could that be why we must find the magic roses a long with our brothers.

I know that dad gave us two years. I find one year was enough for me. Aye… it would take us the two years to see everything. Then again, I think it would be a lot longer to really see Scotland.

I'm glad that Eleanor stayed with my parents. Mamma was right when I was home that I needed to court Eleanor. It's been hard to be away from her right now.

There has been time he felt his dreams were real, he was waking-up with his bed wet. Thomas found that he was dreaming of the times they made love. She was so beautiful, and her breast were bigger. The shirts she made him was getting small on him. He had to buy himself new once.

After his birthday, the months went fast. He was glad that they were staying at Mr. McDee's place. The snow was deep at times, one day we couldn't open the door. There was no way to get out or see out of the window. I had to use my magic to clear the snow. Jimmy had to clear the shop. I had clear the roof and the pipe for are hear. Mr. McDee's had some wood that we could make toys with. I liked witling small toys.

*   *   *

The month of May finely came around. It was good of Dave to show dad where we were. Lizzy had another vision, this time she told us to head to Karnal. Once Dave and Donald was here the three men headed out. Duncan didn't show up yet, but William and I knew which way to go. We had ridden through three of the towns. Dad took us to a pub for food and drink. We had found out about a place that had a fence around the church yard, it was in Karnal.

That night we made camp, who showed up but Duncan. Ye should have seen his face when Donald spoke. "Will now, it's about time ye check on your brothers. I hear ye, ye better be married for your sake. It's a good thing that your brothers could take care of them self's."

He was sitting on his horse with his mouth open. Then he stared at Thomas and William. "How in hell did ye know I'm married?"

William and Thomas just laugh, Thomas spoke. "Get off your horse and bed him down. We have food and drink. Ye can tell us all about your wife. There are many questions we must ask ye."

After he was done, he came over and sat down next to Thomas. He had given Duncan some food. "This is nothing like my wife's cooking."

William just looked at him and spoke. "If ye don't like it. Then ye can fix something else for yourself."

Donald gave his son a look that he wasn't please with him. "Son that is no way to come to a camp, ye know better than that. These young men don't need this kind of talk. Be thankful for the food ye got."

Duncan didn't say a word until he was done eating, he had looked at William and his father. "I'm sorry to speak that way. The last time I was with Thomas and ye. I like to say. Aye... ye were right about me being married. I think Ronald must had led me to that place. Thomas before ye say anything ye are right. I had met her on my way back. Why is it ye know a lot more about all of this?"

Thomas took a drink of his Scotch. "I've been having visions, I believe there coming from Ronald. Also, the people we were staying with Lizzy also had some visions."

Duncan looked at them. "Ye are talking about little Lizzy."

Thomas smiled and nodded his head. "Lizzy is married to Jimmy, a lot had happened from the time ye had left us. We believe we know who had our brothers killed. He's and Englishman who is going after young women with blond hair. He was the one who kill William's cousin. She was found with a baby girl on her. He cut her neck because she didn't give him a boy. There has been many girls all around that has been killed. They are finding the women with a baby girl on the mother's stomach. The towns that we have visit we had told many people about him.

"His name is Marcos Huascaran. Eleanor wrote me about him, but he use the name Albert Huascaran. At the party that her cousin gave he came as Albert. He also took one of the girls. There was no way to get out but by magic. Eleanor said that he had a young face. But he walked like an old man. When she looked at him his face change. Things have been happening to me, I've been having Eleanor's dreams. I've seen the man's face and what she was talking about. When his face change, his eyes are purer evil, and he was and old man."

Duncan was overwhelmed with all this information. Then Donald spoke. "When I was much younger there was a young man who had that name. It was said he took a young girl and raped her. She was found on the tenth month dead. Her mother was a witch who curst Marcos. She had found out who he was through his wife. For he was killing his wife's saying she died in childbirth."

As they listen Thomas wanted to know about the church yard. Also, about the story of the magic rose. He was getting inpatient to find out if their visions was true or not. Then Thomas spoke. "Duncan is there a church yard in Karnal with a fence in yard?"

William knew why Thomas was inpatient. He also wanted to go home. Duncan spoke, "Aye... there is one. That's where my father-in-law is buried. How did ye know about that."

Thomas had to take a breath. He had to close his eyes to slow down his thoughts. "Lizzy told us there is a woman with a map. She said that there are three magic roses that we will be needing. Have ye heard the story before? Ye been there long enough."

Duncan knew this was too much. "How is Thomas knowing all of this. Aye... there is an old woman at the pub who tells the story about three rose bushes. She tells the story at the full moon. That the next moon will be at the end of this month. I will take ye there for lunch. I know that there are men that watch the churchyard. One of the men digs the holes for father."

*   *   *

It took them two days to get to Karnal. As they rode in, they could see it was a small town, they saw the churchyard. Duncan took them to the pub to get lunch. They sat at the back looking over the people. Donald got beer for his boys. The food went down good with the ale. They had three days until the full moon. Duncan never asked the bartender if he heard about three bodies. Who had been buried about two years ago. He only came into the pub once for food and drink. It was late when he got into town. His plan was to look over the town and head out that next day.

Ronald had told him to end up at Karnal, now he knew why. It had to be Ronald who found the woman he married. How long was this all plan out he thought.

Donald went over to the bartender. He had asked the question about the three men. The bartender told Donald to come back on Friday.

Ye must speak to Mark he takes care of the churchyard. He also digs the graves for Father Sinclair. He could tell ye when and where the bodies are buried in the churchyard.

* * *

Not far out of town the men made camp. Thomas and William took out their whittling, that the two men was working on. Like Thomas William had let his horse breed with Catherin's horse. Her horse was the twin to Thomas's horse.

William knew he wasn't as good at whittling as Thomas. But he had to admit that Thomas was working at this longer than he. It would be a nice gift to give his wife. No one new that the two of them married at the castle. It was two days after the rainstorm.

Thomas didn't want to take any more chances on someone hearing them. "William let me see your work. You're doing good on this. May I show ye how to get this part. Mr. McDee showed me how to get this more like my horse. I wonder when they are going to come back. They told dad to come back on Friday. He forgot to said Friday night. Duncan went to check of his wife. Do ye know he hasn't told us much about her."

William tried what Thomas showed him. "Your right that works well. The letter I got from Catherin told me that man Eleanor talked about. She said that she saw the man walking over to her. I was so glad that Kain came and saved her."

Thomas put his whittling down. "I knew that he liked her, to Eleanor he was just a friend. He had to see if she was the one. It worked out for the two of them him and her cousin. Eleanor's friend fell in love with Kain. His mother went after her father. The two of them never thought they would find someone. Mikkel found a wife for himself and a mother for his sister's baby. Of all things it was Eleanor's friend. Who took to Mikkel? He found just what he needed; this young woman was hungry for love. Eleanor said when their mother came home with the baby and

Mikkel's parents. His parents had fallen in love with his wife. The baby fallen in love with her new mommy and daddy."

*　　*　　*

William had also put his whittling away for the night. That's when they saw Donald riding into camp. The two men got up they went over to talk with Donald. Thomas spoke. "What did he tell ye?"

Donald handed Thomas some deer meat and a bottle of Scotch. "He didn't tell me much about that day. All he said was to see father first. Come back here to the pub afterward. Bring the men that rides with ye. Tomorrow we are to see Father Sinclair."

Thomas felt a tap on his shoulder. When he turn Thomas saw Ronald. This was the first time his brother came to him. "Ye don't need to say anything. Father will ask ye some question's that only the three of ye will know. Don't worry about all of this. The three of ye have the answers. Thomas ye can stop worrying about seeing me. My spirit is here with ye, that is who I am now. I couldn't live without them. I'm happy for the three of ye. It will be good for mamma and dad to have little once around. I will see ye there. Don't say anything that ye saw me."

*　　*　　*

After they had the deer meat. The three of them got into the Scotch. Donald started to ask them about what they had seen. "Dad I've learned so much, I made this at the metal shop." Thomas took out a small knife that he made.

Donald took the knife and looked it over. "Ye did a good job my boy. It's the size of your hand."

Thomas was happy to hear that, in his saddle bags he took out three bundles. He had put one back then he and handed the two men what he made. "Here open them."

191

Both men did just that. Donald looked at the knife he made. "My boy ye did a good job. Thank ye for this gift."

William looked at his knife. "So that is why ye need these pouches for the knifes ye made."

Thomas was so please that they liked there knifes. "William made the cases for the knifes, I bought everything. The blacksmith liked the work I did, I worked on one as the other was heating up. The blacksmith who trained me saw that I had the gift of wheeling steal. A lot of times we went hunting for them. Mr. McDee had said something to the blacksmith in town. When he had a lot of work, he had asked Mr. McDee if he would lend me out for the day. It worked out at times when he had just enough work for William and Jimmy.

"We travel to many of the towns. When we were low on money, we found work. I like working with metal. Some of the towns we did some fishing on the boats."

William sat back for he knew Thomas was going to tell the story, that the captain had told them. Thomas show Donald how the captain looked. He had pick up a small piece of wood. Then he put it in his mouth as if it was a pipe. First, he gave us a lesson about the waters of Loch Ness.

"If ye fall into the water of Loch Ness, I tell ye this a man can lose his bearings. He may not be able to tell which way to the surface. Ye see young lad even though the water is so dark. Loch Ness is our pride for the greatest volume of freshwater in the British Isles. There is more freshwater here than in England and Wales put together. Even with their lakes and reservoirs it's not enough to match our waters."

After he got that lesson out of the way, he started to tell the story that came from the Irish Monk Saint Columba. While we was on the ship. The captain told us that Saint Columba was staying in the land of the Picts. He and his companions came across some people burying a man by the River Ness. Other people also told the same story word for word. The people explained that the man had been swimming the river. It was passed down that a "water beast" had attacked and mauled their friend's body. That the beast had dragged their friend under. They told Columba they tried to rescue him in their boat. They couldn't save him but were able only to drag up his corpse. When he heard of this, Columba stunned the Picts. He had sent his follower Luigne moccu Min to swim across the river. The beast came after him. Quickly Columba made the sign of the cross and commanded; "Go no further. Do not touch the man. Go back at once." The beast immediately halted as if it had been "pulled back with ropes." fled in terror. Both Columba's men and the pagan Picts praised God for the miracle. After that story William and I was extremely careful not to fall overboard."

Donald also knew of this story, but he laughed the way Thomas showed how the captain looked. "If he did that it must have been hard not to laugh. I have heard that story before. After we got done with that man. Duncan wanted me to meet his wife. I told him not tonight I like to hear about the boy's travels. After we met this other man. He went back to be with his wife. It's all most over ye have done will my boy's."

*   *   *

Thomas could see the sun setting behind the mountaintops. It was a rich color of red and orange tonight. The sunsets were beautiful to see every night. The next day would be a lot warmer than today. It had been a long year, the days are going by fast now. Before long they will be heading back home. In their travels William and he had seen so much poverty. He had learned that not everyone bathes. Some only bathe once a year in June. This was when they would get married or have a baby.

Thomas found it hard not to bathe often. As a child of ten he had always tried to get out of bathing. Until his brothers had enough with his stink. It was in the month of October when the weather was colder. He smiled as the memory came back to him. He had gone hunting with one of the clans. Thomas was able to hunt small game that year. He also had to clean all that he killed. Even at ten he was a decent shot with a bow. When he got home after that long hunt.

His mother told him. "Get outside! Ye stink! Go and bathe before ye come back inside."

He remembered telling his mother that he was too busy to bathe right now. That was a big mistake on his part. For his father heard what he had said and sent his brothers after him. "Ronald, Michael I need ye to assist your brother down to the pond."

It was Ronald that hogtied him. He was the biggest of the three boys. Then Michael grabbed his feet the two of them through Thomas over his horse. They had brought him down to the pond. This river ran into and through his land. Then their brothers took his hands and legs. They carried him to the deep part of the river and threw him into the water.

He remembered coming up sputtering. When he was back on his feet, an able to head into shore. Ronald had thrown some soap at him. This was the soap his mother made. "Dad said to wash…! Ye can't get out until ye are done."

After he washed every part of his body. He remembered that he went after his two brothers. That day all three of them had a bath. Thomas laughed to himself of this memory. He had thought that growing up his life was so much different from what he had seen. The families that they stayed with. He now understood why his family fought so hard to keep their land.

The landlords discovered their land was worth more to others. Like a group of people for deer hunting it brought more money to them. Another way to use the land was raising livestock. The landlords could charge much more than using the land for crops. They had taken so much from these people. It had come down to more money for the Lords. That's why they took the land just to rent it out for more money. Thomas now understood what Ronald told him. He was the kind of man that had to learn by doing or to see what his brother was talking about.

*   *   *

William and Donald had gone to bed. Thomas thought about the times before he left the Highlands. With his arms crossed he closed his eyes and thought of Eleanor. In all his travels she was never far from his mind. Some of the places he had gone there was so many beautiful young women. He remembered she is telling him not to think of her when he was kissing another. He had to play the game to look for a wife. These young women could never hold a candle to his wife. Eleanor's hair was so silky and her skin so soft. He remembers when he kiss the lassies. There kisses never had the same a feck on him, it was just a kiss. Even when he deepen the kiss, he knew that he didn't make a mistake.

Now he thought about when his father came out to the pond. Why does his father always have to be right? When it's my turn to become a father. Will I have the right question and answers for his own children? Thank goodness…! His father had the right question to ask me. When he said have ye kissed Eleanor. Who knew she could light his body on fire? Even now thinking of her his body ached for her touch. Could this be love or lust? How does a man know the difference? I love being with Eleanor. We enjoy working with together, we never fought, well, it wasn't really a fight. After he read that title he found himself in her room. Her body was naked. After that I wanted to marry her for she was bonded to him as he was bonded to her. That night I could keep my hands off her. I even roped William into also. So, the two of us married.

Thomas found that he hunger to be with his wife. Tonight, the moon was out it was directly overhead. Friday will be the full moon. He felt strange as he closed his eyes. His thoughts was asking how he could feel cool air. His body felt as light enough to float. When he opened his eyes, he found himself flying over the land.

CHAPTER TWELVE

The line was golden

THOMAS LOOKED IN back, he saw a golden line that was attach to him. He had heard of this the line is his orra, now realizing he had left his body. How in hell did he do that. All he knew he was heading to the castle where Eleanor was. What was happening to him. Then he saw his mother's roses, he went down to cut two roses. One he will keep with him the other he gave to his wife. Thomas then went to his old room. There he saw his wife, she was so beautiful as she slept. He wonder if she could hear him. Could he touch her or make love to her. Why not didn't he cut these roses. Not thinking he went inside the castle.

Thomas called to Eleanor, he saw when her eyes flooder opened. "Honey don't ask me why I'm here. For all I know is that I need ye now. Take me inside ye so we can be one together." He remember seeing her set up and pulled off his old shirt. She didn't question it, did she think it was a dream. Were we in a dream together. Right now, he didn't care her hand was wrap around his heat. All he knew he wanted her any way he could have her. The two of them went down on the bed, he didn't remember taking off his clothes. All he knew he had felt her warm breast against his chest. He knew her hand guided his heat between her legs. Quickly he pushed inside her, at last he was home with the one he loved.

Thomas couldn't get enough of her as he moved inside her. He felt the moment she came. "Honey is it safe to give ye my seed."

He looked into her eyes when she said. "Aye… make me come again. I want to feel ye move inside me. Will ye come with me, I need this too."

Thomas's tounge made love to her mouth. She had lifted her legs and push on his bottom so he could go deeper inside her. Now they came together. His lips kissed her face all over until he was back at her lips. They kissed and touched each other. How wonderful it felt to be one with his wife. When he came, he open his eyes. He wanted to look into Eleanor's eyes that wasn't what he found.

Thomas looked around he was back at camp. His body told him that he had been with his wife. When he touch himself, he was wet the hole length of his heat. There wasn't any other woman around him. He knew he had come, quickly he got up and went to the water. His seed wasn't on his kilt. What he found on his heat was liquid. Thomas took a finger and ran it down his heat. He knew that sweet smell, it came from having hot sex with his wife. The last test was to taste it. He may have been away from Eleanor for a while. Damn it he knew what his wife sweetness tasted like. Then he remember the roses that he picked.

Now he could hear Eleanor's voice. "Thomas I'm scared were ye here with me tonight."

Before he answered. He quickly opened his sporran. What he found was the rose he had cut off his mother's rose bush. "Honey do ye have a rose on your nightstand."

Eleanor lit the candle and found the white rose that Thomas left her. "Aye… Honey I wish ye could have stayed with me. Do ye know that Grana said that I should start taking what she made me. That ye were going to visit with me. Honey that was two weeks ago."

Thomas washed himself. "That means she knows your married to me."

Eleanor had walked over to wash up. "Aye… She told me that I looked older now. Honey how soon will ye be heading back home. I had a dream that ye found are brothers. Ronald had come to ye, did that happen yet."

Thomas then looked at the water what he saw was the moon light. "Aye… that he did. It happen tonight. Uncle saw a man at the pub. We will be going to see Father in the morning. Ye know that Duncan is married."

Then he heard Eleanor laugh. "I knew she was because she asked for the same thing as I did."

Thomas could still feel himself inside his wife. "Do ye know I can still feel my heat moving inside ye."

Eleanor looked out the window she had to grab the windowsill. When she came again, she took hole of his heat. "Can ye feel me taking hold of ye."

What was happening to them. Here we can talk to each other. How can she feel his heat and be able to take hole of him. "Aye… I can feel it can ye feel me moving inside ye?"

Then she wanted to try something. "Aye… honey picture my mouth around your heat. Thomas went to lay down. Your tounge is in my heat. Now think of that and tell me afterward if ye drink my sweetness."

Eleanor went back to bed, now she felt his heat in her mouth. She could feel his tounge bringing her up again. She felt herself come as he came, she had tasted what was in her mouth. Thomas heard her say. "I've had enough for now. My love how are the two of us able to do this."

Then Thomas stop picturing drinking her sweetness. "I don't know. Somehow there is magic in the air. Has anyone heard from Michael yet."

Eleanor closed her eyes. "No not yet. I have a feeling once ye have the bodies. Someone will send word to him. Thomas, I have a feeling the two of ye will see Ronald more. Grana said something funny, not a ha-ha. She said that ye three brothers will fight evil. Michael and ye will fight a demon with the help of William and Donald. Ronald will fight Marcos in the heavens. It will only be after Marcos is dead."

Thomas looked at the moon. "Honey I must go to sleep. May be we can feel each other sleeping together. I don't know what is going to happen. I've heard that there is a magic rose that I must find. I had a dream that it has something to do with Fairy Magic. I'll tell ye all about it when I find them. I Love ye honey, good night my love."

*   *   *

In the morning Eleanor and Thomas felt that they had sex last night. They remembered the white rose one on the nightstand and the other in his sporran.

Eleanor picked up her rose. Her body told her that Thomas was here with her. Her mouth felt swollen, not only that. Her heat felt like the first time she made love with Thomas. She called to her man. Before she could ask the question. He answered her question. "Honey if ye have the white rose with ye. I made love to ye last night."

She had looked out her window and held the rose in her hand. "Aye… I'm holding it in my hand now. Can I tell your mother about this."

Thomas thought about it. "I believe ye should, in case of what Grana had made ye don't work. Wow! To have made a child with only my orra. Tell Grana also, I was with ye last night. I remember cutting two roses. I saw my orra, as I flew over the land last night. I headed to the castle and into my bedroom where ye laid. Honey I must go Duncan just rode in. I love ye my love.

*   *   *

Eleanor headed downstairs to help with the breakfast. Franceam was already cooking. "Good morning what may I help ye with."

Franceam turn and looked at Eleanor. "Ye can cut some bread for us."

When she turned, Franceam saw that there was something on her mind. She had seen a puzzle look on her face. That wasn't like Eleanor. "All right out with it. Start the conversation anywhere and stop chewing on your lip. When ye do that it tells me, something happen and ye don't know how to tell me."

Eleanor went into her arms. "Aye… last night Thomas came to me, it wasn't in a dream. Ever since Thomas started talking to me. I can hear him even though as far away that he is. Last night he came from where he was. He gave me a white rose. He came into the room by the window. All he said was "Honey I need ye.""

Franceam looked at her. "The two of ye made love together, are ye afraid to get pregnant. Because he's not home with ye."

Eleanor just looked at her. "Ye think that was all, right. He had left his body to come to me. It was after Ronald came to him. He told him that Father will ask the three of them questions. He also said to him, don't worry about seeing me. For ye know I'm a spirit now. Thomas also said that Lizzy had a vision. She said there will be a story about magic roses, that the roses will save us. Lizzy even told him what town to head to. Thomas even told me that Duncan is married.

"Franceam talking with Thomas all these times he thinks Marcos has magic black magic. I believe Thomas when he said that Ronald will fight Marcos in the heavens. He also believes that Michael will be coming home. After he gets word that Thomas has the bodies. He believes that he will have his family with him."

Franceam took off the eggs and meat. "Wow! That was a lot of information to take in. Have ye got what Grana made for ye yet."

Eleanor had the plates and glasses. She set the table and came back to help with the food. "It's hard enough to be away from him. I know what happen to Ronald. It had scared Thomas to the point he didn't know what to do. So, I play the game that he asked me to do."

Franceam smiled at her daughter-in-law. "Ye are a good wife. Did ye know that my mother-in-law also had her husband came back to her. This was before the war was over. She told me that it was magic. He had left his body to be with her. She told me being scared ye find a way to be with the one ye love."

*　*　*

At the table Franceam told her husband what had happen to Eleanor. "I knew Thomas was a lot like his grandfather. When our son loves, it's with all his being."

Eleanor looked at Daniel. She remember that they were going to a pub. It would be from an old woman was going to tell a story about magic fairy roses. "Have ye heard this story the magic fairy rose."

Daniel looked at her. "Is that what Thomas told ye."

Eleanor looked up. She had taken a bite of her food. She had to think about it, did Thomas tell her or was it in that dream she had afterward. "No… I had a dream just afterward. Have ye heard of this story."

Daniel smiled at her. "There is a story about A Fairy Queen. My mother has the story book about her. Aye… I heard about these roses a long time ago. I believe Donald and I along with Theseus. We three were on are way home. We stop at a pub before we brought my brother home. There was a church that clean are brother and place him in a coffin for us. We needed a drink of Scotch, it was very late when we got in. Father told us to drink to my brother's memory. There was a woman my age. I was told she tells the story around the full moon. So, we three listened to the story. At the time I didn't need any roses. Thinking back, it would be our son who would know how to take care of them. These roses has strong fairy magic, I believe the four of them will need this magic to get home this time."

*　　*　　*

After they ate Eleanor helped Franceam to clean up. She wanted to find out more about this Fairy Queen. Thomas will need all the help he could get. Daniel had told her that the book could be in the study or in a trunk in the attic. She had asked if she could go looking for it. They both said aye… Eleanor went looking for this book. What she found was a notebook. The story was about a man who lost his wife in childbirth.

Eleanor didn't think it was about Ronald. This man had found three rose bushes. At first, she was puzzled about this story. So, his grandfather also heard this story along with Daniel. At the time, this storyteller was a young woman. What if she was the daughter who took over for her mother.

If it is the same woman, she would be older then Thomas's father. How far does this story go back to. She had said that the roses had fairy magic. This was told to her when her husband came home from the war.

Eleanor thought this must be Thomas's grandfather. All right she thought. I have one of the stories. I think if it would be all right with Daniel. I will finish the story she started. This must be the one he heard about. What happen to the man who brought the roses home. She kept looking for another book. Still nothing here in the study. It was time to head for the attic. With the book in hand, she went for a scarf to put her hair up. Eleanor put the book on the end table then she grabbed the candle. Now she headed up to the attic. When she got there, she found many trunks. Now witch one has the book. One by one she went through each of the trunks. At last, she found the right trunk. There was two story books one was about a young fairy and a young Wizard. What she saw that the first book was about a young girl. Who met this young boy that they played and help each other with their magic? The two of them grew up together. The other book was of two adults a Wizard and Fairy.

Fourteenth century

Eleanor had found another book. I am one of the daughters who keeps these roses alive. Throughout time, these roses has been taken to few places. I will tell ye about my father and the one he couldn't live without. Ye could thing back to many men-women that had that trouble. But this story is about my mother and father.

At the time this land belong to my great grandfather. A young man worked for my grandfather. His name was Logan, grandfather lived aways from the waterfall. He own a good amount of land in the lowlands of Scotland. He had one daughter her name was Mhairi. As he worked

Logan would watch her hand clothes out to dry. He would clean the vegetable garden for her father. Logan wanted to ask her father for her hand in marriage. At times she would go for a walk, and he followed.

One day she stop, and he didn't know what to do. "Do ye want something from me she had asked."

He was quiet man. "Aye…, I want to get to know ye. After we talk about things and ye know me better. I like to court ye, if ye agreed I like to marry ye."

She smiled at him. "All right we can talk and see where this my lead us."

It went like this. He work hard to get his chores done. At the same time, she had hers done. The two of them would walk and talk. One day a wild cat came at them, Logan had a big branch that he cut down for protection. He push her backwards and told her to run. Logan swung the branch, this cat didn't want to run. The next time he swung he would die.

Mhairi's father looked at him. "Why were the two of ye walking down this way."

Logan stood tall in front of him. "She likes to walk here. The two of us just talk about anything. I use to fallow her to make sure she was safe. One day she as want I want from her. I told her to get to know her. Then as ye if I could court her. Then I would ask ye for her hand in marriage."

He looked at the young man. "So how far are ye to ask to court my daughter."

Logan smiled. "I was going to ask ye if I could court her."

Her father can running to see if he need help. Logan was fine, the cat was too young to find food. He knew the man would kill him.

He looked at his daughter and she nodded her head. "All right ye may court her."

He had land of his own. It wasn't far from her home. "He had fixed his place up. On his land was a hill. One day he came to the top. When it was a few, moon. There was three rose bushes. He knew she loved roses, and he was making her and a rose garden.

Everything went just find. They were married and their first child was a girl. Time went on she had seven she. He need a son to keep the roses.

*　　*　　*

The other book was about the King and Queen. Their two children was part fairy and human, the King was a MacGregor.

*　　*　　*

Eleanor didn't know what happen to the roses. The story had just stop. Tonight, she will tell Thomas about what she had found. The book, ye have—cigam. That work is magic it's backwards. Did it just tell me that Thomas has fairy magic. If that is true, he will have the power of both grandparents. There was a smile part about Wendy's sister. She mated with a friend Jonathan friend Joseph Heart. What I have fairy magic also. She ran downstairs to her mother-in-law. Please look at this of what it says.

Franceam looked at this book. "So, the two men mated with fairies. That is why ye have strong gifts. My son is going to flip, that book he found is opening with little bit of information. Come to think about it there was always a Heart with a MacGregor.

After she read that more words came up. If they gave their powers to the roses and Thomas get the roses. Could he be able to have strong magic.

Kina was a young Fairy Princess, all her sisters were married to a Fairy King. His mother's parents had a Kingdom near the lowlands of Scotland. Once again, her mother told her to look for a man with whom she would rule. Kina grown up with Kenyon he had strong magic. Most of all away from Marcos. She never like him, he always tried to push himself on to the other fairies. It was a sad day when Kenyon and Kina left the kingdom. His mother had taken him and her to the Highlands to keep them safe. Marcos captured the Kingdom a long with the King and Queen. The door to the vortex had been hidden from in the fairy castle.

*   *   *

In this part it talked about Marcos. His mother was taken away from him. The woman that took care of him, was mean to him. She did things to him as little baby, if he cry she did other thing to him to make him stop. As the child grew, he stole things. If he didn't bring anything back he was whip.

The girls didn't like him, his eyes were evil. Some who pushed him over his limit he would play with their body. He did what that evil wife did to him. As he grew that woman made him to have sex with her. One day he killed that woman, she had disappear. Marcos didn't have anyone to tell him what to do. He know fifteen years old, he went after the ones that couldn't get with child. There was girls who was mean to him. Payback was sweet to him. He was ruff with their nipples. He did care if they haven't had sex before. The dark side came out in him. He rode them hard they didn't know who rape them. He left them, where he had taken them.

The girls that was nice to him. He gave them pleasure, Marcos was gentle to them. When he took them there was no pain. But a lot of pleasure, they didn't know who he was. But for five nights he drove them to cum each time. He had let them go and in their mind they didn't know what happen.

When the five women who could get with child. One by one he got the pregnant, in childbirth they died. The child live for two days. The evil came out in them quickly. They became the age of fifteen then they died. Five women and five children. Right then the whole story disappear.

CHAPTER THIRTEEN

Daydreaming

THOMAS WAS SETTING by the water. He was reminiscing one of their dates he had with Eleanor. After they ate, he was teasing her with the long grass stem by tickling. She would take it away from him one grass stem at a time. When she had put everything away, she had jumped on top of him. How he laughed as he took the grass from his shirt. Then he surveyed the damage. Thomas was looking at Eleanor. There was strong feelings that first day on his land. He went down and kissed her. Gently he let his fingers move over her hair.

Thomas smiled as he picked pieces of grass out. He was enjoying touching her long silky hair. His fingers ran through that long hair of hers. Now he was wondering what color her eyes were, he had to find out. His hand ran over her face. Slowly Eleanor turn her head tort him. She looked deep into his eyes, they were the color of the ocean. A beautiful bluish green. Thomas thought a man could drown in them and be happy doing so. He felt her eyes had power over him. He found those eyes were pulling him down toward her.

Eleanor knew just what she was doing. He remember she was watching all his movements. Even when he brushed over her cheeks and down to her lips. She had lay there very still letting him touch what he wanted. Why hadn't he noticed her full rosy- red lips? Her eyes had bewitched him. All he could do was stare at her perfectly shaped lips. He realized they were the shape of a heart. Her lips said her name. His fingertips were tracing those lips.

Thomas remembered his mind tried to warn him. "Don't forget what happened to your sister-in-law and her child. It's not your time they could come after Eleanor." He told himself "I no…I needed to just touch her. To see what it would be like if they married." Thomas found that he had started to call her honey. "Eleanor ye are a beautiful woman. A man could be lost in your beauty. There is a hunger in me to touch ye."

Her hand brought his head down to hers. Thomas knew then that he had to marry her now. He couldn't wait to get home to bed her for the first time. Now that he had crossed over, he couldn't keep his hands off her. He was so glad that his parents helped them to marry. After they had food and drink, and the two couples had dances they went up stares. In the back of the castle, he remembered that he scooped her up and stepped into their room as husband and wife.

She was do bold to touch him. She took care of his friend so he would have time to enjoy her.

Thomas followed his hand with his eyes. He traced the outline of her chin with his fingertips and went down her neck. He watched her eyes close when he ran his fingers over her breast. He knew they both needed this. My god her skin felt so soft to his touch. What else have I missed? It's time to find out as he moved his fingers over her cleavage. He knew he couldn't leave Eleanor with their child growing inside her. I was so grateful that mamma had gave Eleanor something to not get her with our baby.

Now he was dreaming. When we have a baby, he wanted to watch their child grow and move inside his mother stomach. He knew he would touch her stomach and talk to their child. He would laugh when their child would kick her.

His dream took him to where the two of them saw each other's body for the first time. Eleanor must have felt the war with in him.

"Honey I'm yours do what ye like to me." Her voice was so soft as her hand drew his eyes back to hers. She led his head down to her lips. Softly his lips brushed over hers. Her sweet scent drew him back to take more of her lips. His tongue brushed over hers until they parted. Their kisses ignited their passions as he held her in his arms. There was a hunger driving them to places they had never been. Thomas remember wanting to put his lips on her nipple. He knew when he came home, he would find a place to make love to his wife.

Remembering as his fingers felt the softness of her skin. At that time, he took off her clothes and she had taken his off. He notice as he sucked on her nipple. He felt her hands trying to push his hand closer to her heat. Her nails dug into his bottom. Thomas remembered hearing a moan escaped her lips. That had drove his hand to travel down her long leg. She was so soft when Thomas went down and then up her leg. He found warm mound of curly hair and moved through it. Moist lips surrounding a small piece of skin. When he found the opening, he took his tongue and made love to her mouth. At the same time, he push his finger inside her heat. Her hand held him there until the pleasure had stopped. He wished he were with her now.

It was funny when William came to get him. The time had come to go see Father. "Thomas, stop thinking of my sister and wake up. Donald and Duncan are ready to go were waiting on ye."

It took him a moment to realize what William had said. "Damn it all, how the hell do ye know I was thinking of my wife."

William laughed and looked down at his kilt. Then he pointed at what was standing straight up. "Thomas don't feel bad, I've been thinking of my wife. I know how ye feel, I feel the same way." Thomas tried not to turn red. He fought back with anger. "Damn it all, go away I will be right there." He closed his eyes. "William it's getting hard to stay here in the Lowlands. I want to be with Eleanor. There is a lot of things happening the past few months."

*   *   *

On Friday, the four of them went to see Father Sinclair. At the churchyard they had to ring the bell. A young boy came and opened the gate. The boy spoke, "Father Sinclair is waiting for ye. Please follow me." After the gate was close. He led them where to leave their horses.

Inside the young boy spoke. "Father Sinclair, these are the men that was asking about those men with no last names."

Donald shook Father's hand. "Father these are my boy's. Duncan Thomas and William."

Father led them to a place to set down. "So ye believe that these men are your brother's."

Thomas looked at Donald. He spoke, "Dad may I speak."

Donald nodded his head yes. "Father there is a few things I would like to know. Has anyone tried to get these bodies."

Father looked over at the four men. "Aye… At first there was many men trying. They couldn't answer the questions that was left for me to ask them."

Thomas thought about that. "Father who was the person that brought the bodies to ye."

*　*　*

Father was remembering that day. "A young man and woman had brought them to me. I thought that these men were part of their family. For the bodies was clean and wrapped up with loving care. Come to think about it ye are the first to ask about them. The young couple had a newborn baby boy with them. Child wasn't that old. At the gravesite, the father of the boy helped dig the holes. He said that his name was Michael. He came upon these men after the fighting was done. The men that wone the battle was burning the bodies. There was one man still alive, they were trying to burn him. Michael said that the man called Ronald still had some fight in him. He took out the man on his left. After Michael took out the man on his right. He took his bow and arrows and started to fire at the men. He said that one of the men must have been the boss that he hit. For everyone left had quickly disappear by magic. Michael had said that the one who gave him these questions. To tell me to ask these questions to anyone that came to claim these bodies. He said that their families will know the answers to these questions.

Ronald told Michael no last names. For his family will not give their last name ether. Michael said that Ronald wrote their first name with their own blood on each of their chests. His wife help her husband right up to the time she had gave birth to their son. The way he had prepared their bodies was the way a family member would have done."

*　　*　　*

Thomas stood up. Donald saw him square his shoulders. "Father could ye ask the questions now."

The priest saw that their helper was still in the room. "Aye…" Then he pointed to the boy. "It is time that ye go and help in the kitchen. This is not for your ears." They stayed very quiet until Father knew the boy was gone.

Father looked around at the men. "I have had to be careful. That young boy also works over at the pub. Michael said these men will stop at anything to get these bodies. In this time frame he was right about this.

"All right the first question was given by Ronald. In his family there is a young person who we call the keeper of the roses. Who is this person?"

Thomas knew that the questions was made up before the battle happen. This man would stop at nothing to end his family. "The answer is Thomas the keeper of the roses. He takes care of his mother's rose garden."

Father didn't let on if the question was right or not. "All right there is two more questions to be answered. At the end I will tell ye if they are right or not."

Father didn't smile or nod his head. "The next question was for three of ye. What happened to the men to give up on life? There are three answers to this question."

This was getting hard for Thomas. He had to close his eyes to bring back the memory. "The first part was why Ronald gave up on life. It was on the day his wife and only son died. When his wife's horse broke away and the wagon had flip over on top of her. She was in her fifth month. Ronald couldn't live without them. This man sat out to kill all the men that could bring in new life to the family name."

Father watched the faces of Thomas and William. He saw him bite his lip to not show any weakness. This has been hard on this family. He found that questions cut deep into this young men's heart.

William then answered. "Jonathan was going to lose his legs soon. He was going to be bedridden in two years. He couldn't let his son and wife watch him die a little at a time. His wife was still young she wanted to have more children. Before he left, he asked his best friend to take care of his wife and son. He knew in time she would turn to his friend. Now when they tell his story. Jonathan died in battle as a man not one that was bedridden."

Duncan had looked at his father. Donald nodded his head to go ahead. "Peter was also sick. As days goes by, he saw his twin falling in love for a young woman. Peter couldn't take a wife, he knew he could pass on what he had. He couldn't ask anyone to watch him die a little at a time. Peter knew what happen to Ronald's wife. They had set up to kill his wife and child. This evil man wanted this family men to all dies. Peter took the place of his cousin. He wanted what Jonathan wanted. To die in battle as a man. Peter was a strong fighter, there was just one thing that would take him down. His body would run out of strength to keep going. All three men would fight to the end of their strength."

Father looked at the four men. "One of my questions about Peter and Michael has been answered for me. When I went to bless the bodies, Peter looked like Michael. Peter is the cousin to Ronald and Michael. They are the brothers to Thomas. Donald Duncan and Peter are your son's. William ye are Jonathan's brother. Then again, the three of ye are brothers. Ronald was Duncan's best friend. As ye and Thomas and William are best friends. As many men who try to take this bodies from their holy resting place. They are desperate to wipe out anything that they have done. There is one thing that happen when I place the cross around Ronald's neck. His body for a moment glowed with heavenly light. When that happen, I was waiting for Ronald to speak to me.

"When I went to bless Peter. There was a sadness for this poor soul. This young man was tall with wide shoulders just like Michael. When I had pointed that out, Michael looked at me so I could see his eyes. They were a deep green. His hair was a reddish brown. The only difference was their beards. Michael's beard was redder than the beard on the one called Peter."

Donald stood up and looked at the priest. "Father ye know the stories of these men. Did we answer the questions right."

Father had gotten up from his seat. "My son ye are the true family members of these men."

Thomas took a deep breath and let it out. "Father may we go to the grave site now."

Father Sinclair nodded his head yes. "Duncan ye know the way. How is your wife today."

Duncan then realized he knew right where the bodies were. Even saying they're near his wife's father didn't hit him until now. "She is doing quite well, thank ye Father for asking."

*   *   *

The four men along with Father walked down to the graves. Each of the men walked to the head stone of their brothers. They found only their brothers first name on the stones. There was the month, day, and year of their deaths.

*   *   *

Thomas was looking at his brother's headstone. Right then he heard a voice say. "How could Michael do this to me." It was his own words coming back to haunt him. Thomas drop to his knees and in his mind, he cried out. "Michael forgive me. I thought I had the hold world on my shoulders. This is nothing compared to what ye had to do. In a vision he saw Michael trying to sleep. He saw Ronald made him leave them. Then he saw the fighting going on. "Michael ye couldn't fight beside Ronald. Like me we saw the fighting going on in our minds. Ye had to leave your wife to save their bodies. Ye were there to see them try to burn Ronald alive. Michael at least ye were there to say goodbye to him. I'm sorry to act so young at that time. Come home as soon as ye can. It will be my turn to fight these men. I will get these bodies home. We have too much to live for."

Thomas then took a deep breath. He had to blink his eyes clear of the tears. Then he stood up. Now to find out what name Michael used. "Father Sinclair what was Michael's last name?"

The priest saw the pain in Thomas's eyes. "It was Michael McGee. He was a kind man. He even helped Alexander to put the bodies in the holds. He had to make sure they were lay to rest the right way. Michael said to give the remains to only the ones that could answer every question."

Donald saw that Thomas had grown up even more this day. "Thank ye Father Sinclair. We will arrange to get a wagon for the journey home."

*　*　*

Before the four could leave. Father had something on his mind. "Donald are ye going to the Highlands."

The four men turn back to Father. They were going to head to their horses. "Aye… We do live in the Highlands. Why do ye ask this?"

Father looked to the heavens. He had said a quick prayer. "May I accompany ye on this trip. I have been here long enough. It is time for me to try to start a church in the Highlands."

Donald looked at his boys. "Father it will be dangers to ride with us. These men have orders to burn the bodies of are fallen brothers."

Before Father could answer Donald. Thomas spoke up in a whisper. "Dad may I have a word with ye and my brothers?"

Donald looked back at Father. "Father give me a min to speak to my boys. I will hear what the lad has to say. Then I will give ye my answer then. Also, we have no church like yours."

Thomas and the others walked away from Father. "Uncle what I have in mind, may help us to get the bodies into the Highlands. It will take two wagons. Duncan ye wife she is coming with us?"

Duncan looked at Thomas he didn't think ahead on this madder. "Aye… she is my wife. I will have to get a wagon for all her things."

Donald then spoke. "Out with it my boy. Ye have something in mind. Tell me what ye like to do? For ye are just like your father and Ronald. They always had a plan."

*　*　*

Thomas looked at everyone. "All right we need two wagons. One for our brothers and another for your wife's things. We all know that these men are going to come after these bodies. We need to get our brothers into the Highlands. What if we put the bodies in a false bottom under Duncan's wife's things? She will be with Father and ye Uncle. The three of us will have the coffins with us. Before ye say anything, I have another idea. I been able to talk with Eleanor. I will ask her to tell dad and her father to meet us. There are a lot of things happening to me. Just now I had seen ye at the ferry with the wagon. Dad and Theseus with one of your sons. I know Damian will want to go with us, he must stay with Duncan's wife. He will go back to the hunting cabin. I know that Eleanor will be with Gallivan at the hunting cabin. For this to work Father must not know about any of this. If they stop ye, Father can speak truthfully to them. We don't have to convince our people that his religion is better than ours. That will be Father Sinclair's job.

"It may work since the churchyard is safe behind these walls. No one can see when we will dig the bodies up. I see they have a lot of wood over there. We could use that wood. If Father comes with us. At the end of the wagon, Father could carry food and blankets along with anything to give our people. If we make each wagon wide and a bit longer. Then Duncan's wife can bring everything with her. We must all agree on this. What say ye..."

The three looked at each other. Then there was three nods of their heads. All three said aye…

Donald looked at Thomas. "Thomas how will we know if Eleanor got the message. Do ye think ye could get word to ye father?"

William then spoke. "Thomas and I have been together these two years. He knew about that man going after young women. Before Eleanor's letter had even reached us. He told me that day she has spoken to him in the night."

Donald looked at his nephew. "Thomas ye and Eleanor has been very close to each other. I know your father had done things like ye have. We will try this for now. I don't like the idea that ye three will have to fight by yourself."

Duncan spoke. "I don't like it either. We three have found are loves. We will do what we must to get our brothers home. It's going to be a long way to get to the ferry. Now we can tell Father about some of our plans."

*　*　*

The four men went over to speak with Father. Donald spoke. "Father we all agree that ye can come. I want ye to know it's up to ye to convince our people about your religion. Ye do know that it's going to be dangerous. These men don't want these bodies to go home. If they get the bodies, they will burn them. If ye do come. Duncan's wife will be with ye. If we make it, we will meet ye at the hunting cabin. If we're not there in two days. One of the horses if ye say take me to your home. It will do so. Duncan's wife can lead the way. She can ride Peter's horse now. Peter is my son."

Father had made the sign of the cross. "Do ye think there will be enough room on the wagon for things for your people."

Thomas spoke up. "Aye… we must make the wagon bigger for Duncan's wife things. The same with the wagon. That will be for the coffins, we will work on that first. We will have to get wood for the wagons."

Father then smiled. "Over there we have wood that ye can use. It will help ye some. That is for payment to take me with ye. Thank ye I will make sure to get things to bring with us."

*   *   *

It was at five o'clock when the men went to eat. As they went into the pub. They had found a table, one of the barmaids came to get their orders. "Four deer stakes and four ales. Whatever that goes with it ye can bring it to us."

Around six o'clock there was music. The men wanted to just relax for a while. Thomas could see that the air was filling up with smoke. Donald saw that two men were looking at them. One of them walked over to them. "Are ye MacKinnon the one I sent the note to?"

Donald looked at the man. The man's face looked of a hired killer, there was a cut on his cheek. Thomas had a bad feeling about this man. He gave his uncle one of these looks that was for danger. Donald nodded to Thomas. Then spoke. "Aye… tell me who ye are?"

The man was sizing the four of them up. "Rodney McNeill, tell me if ye talked to Father Sinclair yet."

Donald had looked at Thomas. He knew that he didn't like this man. "Aye… we did. Tell us how ye know of our brothers."

Rodney gave him a smile that had some teeth missing. "May I set down." Donald nodded his head. Rodney went to get another chair. Ones he was seated he spoke. "There was a note I was to deliver to the MacGregor. The only thing that saved me I was too late to deliver the note. I was able to see what happened to them."

Duncan also didn't like this man. "Rodney did ye know what was in the note. So ye hid like a coward and watch them cut our brother's down. Why didn't ye help them."

Rodney didn't like the questions or to be called a coward. It had shown in his face. Thomas was right in front of him he was watching his eyes. "Aye… I wasn't there to fight. I could hear the fighting going on. There was no moon out that night, it had been raining. The MacGregor had a small fire that night. I did see a man come up behind one of your kinsmen. He had stabbed your family member in the back. I heard a man laughing when that happen. That man was dress all in black, right down to his horse. I only saw the white of his teeth when he laughed.

"That man in black had sent three men into fight. The MacGregor's had taken those men down. When they thought that they had won. The boss sent three more men in. Two of the MacGregor's was taken down fast. They had run out of energy and was easy to take down."

Thomas watched the man's eyes. He could see that it made him mad when the last MacGregor was harder to take down. Ronald had fought until they ganged up on him. "The man in black had sent the back stabber in to take him down. He had smile with pleasure when his men stabbed your family member in the back. He didn't take him out he was still alive. That made the boss mad. He had told the last three men to build the fire bigger. Then through the bodies into the fire.

"It took time to get the wood to dry. There was a lot of smoke the wood was still too wet. The man in black had the young man start the fire. All he did was waved his hand and there was a big bomb fire. That young man must have had magic. Ones that was done the other men was putting their men on the fire. I could hear the man in black laughing.

I thought that man had black eyes. Until he laughed, I could swear his eyes change to fire."

Rodney eyes had showed to much pleasure as he talked. "There were nine men to your three family members. The boss enjoyed watching his men cutting down your family. He sent three men in waves."

In Thomas mind he heard his brother's voice. "Beware of Rodney, when ye fight him. He is the back stabber. He's here to hurt ye."

William kept and I on Thomas. If this man were one of them Thomas would know. Right then William saw Thomas's face change. He had cleared his throat and Donald looked up at him. He saw William's head nod toward Thomas. Donald had come to the same conclusion. There was too much pleasure in Rodney's voice, or he had anger when it didn't go his way. He knew soon Thomas will not take any more of his lies.

* * *

Rodney's eyes dance with pleasure as he talked about the boss's horse. "His horse was called Devils Maker, he has two defiant color eyes he also likes killing men."

The more this man talked the angrier Thomas got. Rodney's the one who takes care of the black horse. He even told them how the man in black came after their family members. Rodney kept talking. His eyes was in joying the pain he was giving. "There was three men that came in waves. He had eight men with him. Your family members killed three of the men."

This man kept going over parts of the story. He knew it was to give them pain. Thomas could see he didn't like that idea. "The boss had let them rest. This gave your kinsmen false hope. It let them believe that they had won. Then he had sent one man on each side of them. It had taken them by surprise. Two of them weren't that strong they had tired quickly. Those two were killed first. That left the MacGregor. He was a strong fighter. After your kinsmen were down or killed."

Thomas thought this man keeps repeating. He is enjoying the part how they killed them. "The MacGregor by himself killed four out of the nine men. With the bonfire going. The boss had the two men throw in their men who was dead first. They hadn't thrown in your kinsmen into the fire yet. The boss was angry that the MacGregor was still alive. I heard the man in black yell, throw the MacGregor into the fire. He would like to hear him scream."

Thomas's fist was balled up he wanted to get his hands around Rodney's neck. Then Rodney spoke. "Without any warning someone in the woods were shooting arrows. One man had an arrow in his heart. Another arrow shot the man who was going to pick up the MacGregor. I saw the MacGregor take his knife and killed the man on his left. Then another arrow hit the man in black. The young man with him, wave his hand all the men that was left were gone.

Thomas saw Rodney's face change from joy to anger. This man was cold hearted. He was bringing bad news to people he never met. His eyes showed to much enjoyment with the bad news. Rodney was no actor. Then his eyes change when his men were getting killed. That had told Thomas Rodney must be the man in black's right-hand man. The young man must take care of the man in black, he has the magic. Thomas knew all those men who fought his brother was evil. They had followed Rodney, his brother had told him that Rodney was a back stabber. Then Thomas asked, "Did the arrow missed your heart? Were ye the one that the arrow went into your arm."

Rodney then spoke. "Yes it…"

Thomas hands wanted to kill this man. "I knew ye weren't there to help the one who brought the men to Father Sinclair."

Thomas couldn't take it anymore, he had jumped to his feet and bellowed. "I had enough with ye lying about taking a note to the Mac-Gregor. Ye were the one who stabbed two of our brothers in the back. Ye took and arrow in the arm. Ye said so. Besides ye know the man in black's horse's name, if ye wasn't one of his right-hand men. I watched your face and eye's. Ye weren't there to give the MacGregor a note, ye were there to kill him. Ye have too much pleasure telling this story."

Donald knew that Thomas was right. He had to stop him and yelled. "Enough…, Thomas. Go and get yourself a Scotch and be quick about it."

He had seen William grabbed Rodney's arm. For he had gone for his knife. Thomas didn't see Rodney's hand. He had bowed his head to his uncle and stormed over to the bar. Rodney was going to stab him in the back. It had been too much for Thomas to bear. William had his best friend and brother-in-law's back. Ones Thomas was gone Donald took out his dirk. He told his boys to follow his brother to the bar. William made shore that Rodney couldn't use that hand for a while.

*   *   *

At the bar Thomas raise his hand to the old woman who was help-ing the bartender. He had called for two fingers of Scotch. The storyteller walked over with a full bottle of Scotch to pour him two fingers. Thomas grabbed the Scotch and downed it in one gulp. The old woman watch him grabbed hold of the bar as the Scotch burned its way down his throat. He slammed his glass down and told her to fill it again. Duncan and William came over to him putting a hand on each of his shoulders. It was Duncan who thrown some coins on the bar for the bottle of Scotch. He asked the storyteller for three more glasses. She was nearby and lis-tening to what the boys were talking about. When she had looked into Thomas's eyes, she saw the magic in him. He was the one that would take the magic roses to the Highlands. This young man had some magic from the Fairy and Wizard. It was said that over two hundred years the magic will come to the one in need.

*   *   *

Thomas looked at his friends his brothers. "That man was lying about him delivering a note. He was there in the fight, Ronald told me he stab our brother. I'm sorry I just couldn't take anymore. His eyes was enjoying telling us the details to much."

William knew his friend could tell what kind of person they were. He would look into the man's eyes and almost see into his very soul. Didn't his own sister have that power also. William didn't know he also had that power. "Aye… ye saw the evil in him. I heard the pleasure in his voice. Right now, let's salute our brothers."

Thomas missed his brother Ronald. He now knows that Michael is alive. Now that they have found their bodies. The battle to get them home will start. With his Scotch in hand. Thomas stepped back and raised his glass. The two men touch Thomas glass and spoke. "To our fallen brothers may they rest in peace!"

All three of them held their glasses up high and spoke. "Hear—hear… to our brothers. May they rest in peace."

The three men downed the Scotch and slammed their glasses onto the bar. Duncan grabbed the bottle and the glasses. As they walked closer to their table. They knew Donald was giving Rodney an ear full. "Ye participated in killing those men. When the time comes, I will kill ye myself for doing what ye did. Ye have mess with the wrong family. The evil in ye has shown through. Leave now before my boys come back. I will thank ye for telling us where our family members were buried. Be gone Satan for your time will come. We will send ye back to hell."

Before the men got to the table the storyteller came over to Thomas. "Would ye… like to hear the story of the Magic Roses?"

Thomas looked at her she had kind eyes. Did she have magic in them. Why would he think that. "Aye… we would love to hear that story. Could ye bring us four pints of ale please. Also, something to eat."

Thomas went to get some money out for her. "When we bring everything to ye. Ye can pay the other barmaid. We will be right there."

*   *   *

In the Highlands Eleanor with all the midwives were having a meeting at the castle. Grana was telling them what she had heard. "A young woman was taken. They found her ten in half months later. One of my friends who knows about black magic has sent word to me. She was asked to look over the body of the young woman. What she had found there was a small mark burn into her neck. It was the mark of the devil. This man had taken and slit her neck.

"The mark meant that he drank her blood. She also said there was some of her hair was cut. My friend said there is only one reason her hair was taken. If she is right. This is a spell for the man to come back from the dead. He must be and older man to want a younger body. The body must be someone he knows. He will keep that young man close to him.

"My friend had checked the body to see if there was more to these killings. There was a child with the woman. The woman was the baby's mother. They found the child on the mother's stomach. She was asked to check the child if the baby was evil. My friend said she had taken a small cross and dip it in holy water. Then place it on the baby's skin. If the baby were evil the cross would burn into the skin. The reason for so many women killed. These women can't give him a son. My friend said there must have been a spell place on him. I have sent word to all the towns about this. I have told if there is any devil's mark on the woman's body. To take a small cross and dip it in holy water. Then place it on that mark.

"I have sent word for any young woman should wear a cross around their neck. My friend had check on Bridget's cousin, she had looked at the mother and child. There was no devil's mark on her body. The way she was killed her neck was cut like the other's. The child was not evil. Now that he is coming closer to the Highland's. I have asked the blacksmith to make as many crosses as possible to give any young woman one.

*　*　*

Eleanor had a bad feeling, that this man has more on his plate. Could he also be involved with what happen to her brother, Peter, and Ronald. I need to find out more about this black magic. Didn't she have to find a spell to help Thomas. She also must ask Grana if she knows about the Magic Roses. Why do I feel everything going on has something to do with my man? Tonight, I must see if Thomas and I can talk again. What if he leave his body again. I don't want his ora too brake.

*   *   *

Duncan set down the glass and poured his father two fingers of Scotch. Donald took the glass and down it. He didn't show that it burn going down.

Thomas knew that a lot more had happen here. He sat down and looked at his uncle. "Dad I'm sorry for that outburst." Every time they were with Donald Thomas had to play the game. "I couldn't stand the way he was talking. He was the one doing some killing of his own. We need that information."

Donald saw that Thomas eyes was trying to water. He poured Thomas another drink of Scotch. "Drink up, ye need a little more of this."

Thomas took it and down it. "Ye are right thank ye. A now we know who was shooting those arrows. Ronald had it plan out for the four men. We also know there is a child. I believe that he will be notified that we have the bodies.

Then Thomas remembered he had asked the storyteller to tell him about the Magic Roses. "Dad that storyteller is still here, after how many years. I hope it will be all right. I can't wait until I hear the story that the three of ye heard here of the Magic Roses.

Donald smiled and saw that two bar maidens had more drinks and food coming toward them. "So ye found her. Good more food we will be needing this."

*   *   *

Thomas saw that Donald was going to pay for it. "Dad it's on me." He had paid the one bar maiden for the drinks and food.

Then the storyteller sat down with the group. "Hello Donald. It is good to see ye again. It's too bad Daniel and Theseus couldn't come with ye. But then again maybe they did." She had pointed to William and spoke. "Ye looked like Theseus son." At that time, the music was loud they could only hear each other's voice.

Donald smile it was good to see her again. The last time they were here. Didn't she say that Daniel was a distant cousin. "Hello Meghalaya. Aye… It has been a long time. So ye are still working here. Last time ye said Daniel was a distant cousin of yours."

*   *   *

Meghalaya laughed at the look that Thomas had given. Thomas saw that time has been hard for her. She had some teeth missing. What his uncle had said took the three young men by surprise. Then she pointed to Duncan. Ye must be Donald's son. Ye do look like him when he was younger. This young man must be Daniel's son. If I didn't know that he is more my age, I would have called ye Daniel. Ye four men has had a bad day. That Rodney be careful around him. He is a very bad man. I had heard that he took out my friend and cousin Ronald. I knew ye lived in the Highlands I didn't know where. I knew something was going on, I know that Donald Daniel and Theseus was close. I believe their children would come looking for them. Enough of that my boy could ye tell me your name."

*   *   *

Thomas looked at Donald, he nodded his head yes. He knew she was safe to talk to. "It's Thomas and Daniel is my father; Ronald is my brother. These young men are also my brother's, their families are all close to each other."

She then looked at William. "Aye… This one mean's more to ye then Donald's son. Ronald and Duncan was close to each other, ye and him grew up together. Ye had Thomas back, I saw ye grab Rodney's hand. That man would have killed Thomas the moment he had turn his back. William made sure he didn't have the chance. My boy what is your name."

William was watching Thomas, he saw the grateful look in his eyes. "I'm called William, aye… Thomas and I have gone through a lot together. Ye are right about us being close to each other. Ye know a lot about our three families. Why do it has something to do about the Magic Roses? From the time we came to the Lowland of Scotland, things have been happening to Thomas. I've been feeling that there has been a lot of magic around the Lowlands. Could ye tell us how the Magic Roses is connected too ye. How is it that ye are somewhat of Thomas's cousin. Could ye tell us what that means."

Meghalaya laughed, she looked at the two men. "Do ye two have sisters?" Both men looked at each other. Thomas nodded yes. She then said. "That's why the two of ye have magic now. Thomas's sister has strong magic, but she hasn't been using it.

"I knew Donald and his friends had magic. Ye two young men married each other sisters didn't ye. Thomas ye have been talking to her, ye even went to see her."

*　*　*

Thomas's mouth had drop open. "How do ye know all of this, I haven't said anything about it. It was the other night I was thinking about Eleanor. Then I found myself flying-through the air, a golden line was to my body and me. I remember picking two white roses from my mother's favorite rose bush." Thomas took out the rose from his sporran.

That had gotten Donald's attention. "Wow… I believe ye Thomas. Then it will work what ye have planned."

Thomas heard Eleanor in his mind. "Thomas what is going on with ye. Honey we got to talk I found out that ye have blood from a Fairy and Wizard."

Thomas eyes went wide. "What… How could I have blood from a Fairy and Wizard?" Quickly he told Eleanor to talk with his father and her father. "Honey tell dad and your dad to get ready to ride. We need help. These men are not going to let us bring the bodies home. I will talk to ye tonight Love ye."

Eleanor took a breath then spoke. "Ye are saying this book is true. Honey ye do know I'm going with them."

Thomas had to close his eyes. "Aye… it's true. What can I say, ye can come, only to the hunting cabin? I'm not going to fight with ye on this. Make sure that Duncan's brother's is with ye. I love ye." Then he heard I will.

Thomas looked at Meghalaya. "I have Fairy and Wizard magic in my blood. There is a story that Eleanor found is that true?"

Meghalaya laughed again. "When she feel something is wrong or ye are upset or angry, she calls to ye."

Thomas smiled and spoke. "Aye… she does, and so do I."

CHAPTER FOURTEEN

The talk with Meghalaya

MEGHALAYA SMILE BACK at Thomas. "Every two hundred years the Magic Roses is sent back to the once that has the magic. Ye will be needing this magic, the man in black has black magic now. He got it when he was almost killed by Michael that night. Ye two boys have gifts that let ye do things that no one else can do. It is time to tell ye about the roses.

"Also, about what happen to my Grate grandfather. Your brother told me that your father had started bringing a rose bush home with him. Then when ye boys grew up ye also brought a rose bush home. Thomas ye are the youngest son."

He watched her closely. Then their eyes met, he had seen the twinkle in her eyes. Could that be what she saw, in his own eyes. She had the magic also in her, then he saw what she really looked like. All these years she was under cover. Then Thomas spoke. "Ye are a beautiful woman, all this time ye have been under cover."

She was so please what Ronald had told her about his two brothers. "Ronald is right ye do know how to see into someone's very soul. Your two brothers when ye love someone it's forever. Ronald and my great grandfather, the two men loved their wife. One thing the rose will stay with your family if ye have a son. My great grandfather didn't have a son he had daughters. I'm the last daughter with him and my great grandmother's blood. The magic will be reborn when ye take the roses with ye.

"What I have seen, ye will have peace for a while. Only after Marcos is sent to hell, until two hundred years later. This evil man will be sent back for your children's, children he will go after Tom and Ellen. There will be a time that your sons will choose a wife that come from this man. They will want to take him down for good.

"Ye may be wondering why there is no roses. It is because of these Magic Roses… once they are gone. We will have our roses come back. The only place that has roses is in Aberdeen right now. I hear that they are along the side of the road heading into the city."

"Thomas, I saw why Ronald left, he had a vision that he must take all these evil men to be judged. Make the vest for all ye, the rose petals has strong magic. Duncan's wife has made nine vests, she had a vision about this. One is for Michael and his son the other is for Ronald and your father's."

William saw Duncan's mouth drop. Meghalaya laughed, Duncan's spoke. "How did ye know this? That it was my wife Briana who made these vest."

Meghalaya smile at Duncan, the rose stem has powers to see in the past and future. Ye are also my cousin through Thomas's mother.

*　　*　　*

"Thomas, I have some petals here with me. Place some on Eleanor's hair ye have with ye. William ye do the same. Tonight, think of your wife and ye will be able to go to them. Only after ye place some petals on yourself. Now if ye burn a stem ye can see what ever ye like. Thomas thank ye for thinking about me. I have more petals for myself and stems at my home."

He looked at her. "Ye can read my mind?"

She nodded her head yes. "Now to tell ye about your weapons. If ye place petals on them it will make the weapons stronger. For the vests, ye place petals on your vest so nothing will go through. Ye must place one on Ronald and his weapons and anyone who fights with ye.

*   *   *

"I will tell ye this that ye and William will fight the demon that has magic. Michael with Donald will back ye up, but it will be Michael and ye. Your two skills that ye have will take him down. Ye will fight him in the Highlands. Ye must take these men down here in the Lowlands. If ye don't ye will not win. There are two young man who is trap. One has a locket around his neck. Marcos will try to take his body for himself. He then will send his soul to his master. The other young man is trap inside his body with the demon. Ronald's been talking with the boy. They don't know about him. I see in your eyes that this is a lot to take in. William ye wife has strong magic and so do ye. Ye can have what Thomas and Eleanor has, ye love your wife very much."

William looked at her. "Her name is Catherine, thank ye for telling me that."

Meghalaya smiled at William. "Donald ye know that ye have magic with in ye. Thomas also has magic. A Heart has been around the families of MacGregor, let him know there is a demon inside her.

Now when ye put on the vest and ye best friends do the same. Ye will have the ability to fight these younger men. Your strength will match the one ye fight. One thing at the full moon lay everything outside. This is to charge the petals so that everything can be still used. If ye don't the petals will come off."

Thomas couldn't believe what was happening. Then she took out a piece of deerskin. The deerskin looked to have been used a lot. It had been in her family for a long time. The map had held treasure to get our brother's home. Also, to save us from being killed. Then he had a question. "Meghalaya if I wave my hands to get the bodies home. Ye are saying the men will come to the Highlands to fight with Marcos. Even with are magic, we will lose. Why do this is true."

She looked at Thomas. "Aye… That way would be easy, it will backfire on ye."

∗　∗　∗

I must tell ye what the rose petals can do and can't do. These rose petals can't bring back your loved ones from the dead. There will be times were ye can see spirits and talk to them. I know ye have talk to Ronald. The rose petals can bring things closer to ye. These roses can't help ye to have a son. With your marriage the rose can't help ye, that is up to ye. What ye put into it ye will get back, ye must work on that yourself. Ye can't kill a person with the wave of your hand. If a demon die's and ye get to place a cross on them. Put a rose petal on the cross to stop anyone from taking it off. Demons have the power to come back from the dead. This man who will become a demon will have black magic to prevent a cross to be place on him.

"If the Lord wants ye to fight ye must. Ye can't change things, it will just come back some other place. When ye fight ye can be hurt, where the petals are not. Ye must be careful in this fight. Remember your adrenalin will be strong. Ye may not be able to tell ye are hurt."

∗　∗　∗

"If ye look at the back of the map it says the year is 15th century. My great grandfather was working around here. There was a young woman that had caught his eye. He wanted some land to raze horses on. My great grandmother her father had only one daughter.

"He had asked her father if he could court her. They had fallen in love with each other. Her father wanted to keep her close to him. For he was all by himself, he had given them some land two miles down the road. My grandfather had some money to build them a house. One day after working on their home. He sat near a stream to clean up before going down to her father's place.

"It was late, and the moon had come out, he turn to go get his horse. There on top of the hill was three rose bushes, he had never seen them before. Then he remember the story his parents told him. There was magic roses some where's near England. They had said these roses will appear to the one who carries the Fairy and Wizards blood in them. If it is the time of the full moon, the roses will show themselves if he is nearby. My Grandfather had started toured the hill, once he was on top the roses had disappeared. When he went up the hill, he had seen a good size stone. It didn't madder what was on top of the roses.

"He looked around and remember that he had clean this hill up? This was so his love and him could set at night, to look at the moon and stars high in the heavens. When he got to the stone there was words on it. It told him to takeoff this stone. Once the stone was off, he found a tablet and many things under the tablet. Grandfather had taken everything out that he saw. On the other side of the tablet, it told him to feed the roses and give it lots of water. Then it told him to come back at the full moon and give it more water. What he found out the next day when the sun was out the roses was invisible. Just before the moon came out, him and his wife to be came back to feed the roses more water."

Thomas watched the storyteller closely. Meghalaya had stopped to take a drink of her ale. He had some food and took a drink. She then went on with her story.

"After they gave more water, he had gotten a fire going. His love had gone and sat on his lap. The moon was for lovers, and he kissed is love deeply. Grandfather felt the magic in the air, he had placed all the things under the tablet on the ground. When he looked up the roses started to show themselves to them. Once the moonlight hit the tablet words appeared, his love was able to read what was on the tablet. After the roses was fed and water the moonlight will make them grow. Remember they haven't had any water for a long time. As they grow keep pouring the water until ye see the rose buds. On the tablet it told him that only your mate can choose the one rose bush. Once she had found the one rose bush. Plant the other two away from the one. It is as ye have married and built your own home. So must the rose bush make his on home. Make a new tablet by placing it on top of the old one. Then use your magic to make a copy. Place it over the hole for someone with ye blood line to find them.

Duncan then asked the question about the two rose bushes. "Why would the other two not stay with the one?"

Meghalaya smiled at him then spoke, "tell me would ye want your mother to live with ye. When the two of ye are getting to know your wife. Like most parents they try to protect their child until they marry. This rose bush must have roses of his own. Make a rose garden for your wife. Then place it near the rose bush your wife likes best. Treat this rose bush as if ye bringing it to be married to one of your wife's roses?"

Thomas look at Donald and smiled. Meghalaya had seen the look between them. Then she asked. "Ye have a story about your mothers roses."

Thomas laughed and had a big smile on his face. "Aye… The rose I would put with this magic rose bush. Had brought my mother and father together. Her garden has grown through the years. My brothers used to bring her one every time they went away."

*   *   *

Suddenly pain of losing his brother hit him. Thomas's face changed. His thoughts went to why they were here tonight. William had placed a hand on his brother-in-law and best friend shoulder. "Ye must understand for two years, we been looking for our three brothers. Most of all we have been growing up. We didn't see much of Duncan that was all right. He didn't know he had found our brothers. Most of all he found himself a wife. Thomas and I have been friends for as far back as children. We work and learn a lot about Scotland. When we go home, we will start our family of our own."

Thomas was having trouble with his feelings, he had closed his eyes. This time he heard his brother when he opened his eyes, he had seen him. Not knowing he had the pouch of rose petals in his hand. "Thomas ye are going to be all right, the pain will past for all ye. Michael will be home when ye get home. Now the two of ye will need each other. I will see ye soon, once ye are done here go see your wife. I love ye little brother, I will always be watching over ye. Until we meet again. Thank ye Meghalaya it's time to let them go."

Meghalaya nodded her head; she had seen Ronald also. "It's hard to lose someone ye love with all your being. Grandfather loved his wife like your brother had loved his soulmate. My Grandmother knew the roses would leave, she had given him all girls. She was up in age but still wanted to try for a son. Her body was too old to carry another child. The child was a son, but he was too young to live. My Grandfather lost them both, as time went by, he started to drink. His children saw what he was turning into. "At last, his wife came to him she told him, enough it's time to let go of me." He just didn't know how. After his oldest married he asked his sister to take the last two daughters. He had told the oldest this story to take care of the roses until the next ones come for them. What my grandfather did was go off to war since the drink wasn't fast enough for him. What better way to die but in battle?"

Three young men bowed their heads. Donald spoke. "Meghalaya is this all of the story, my boys had enough with sadness."

Thomas looked at Meghalaya. Then spoke. "Ye have seen a lot of what happen. These stems showed ye things that I must find out myself. Ye knew my brother came here. Tell me how the rose will know who will be taking care of them?"

* * *

Meghalaya took a deep breath. "When ye go to take these roses home with ye. One of these times ye will get picked on your finger. It may take some of the blood, it will happen to ye love also. That is how she will find the one. Meghalaya why is it the back of this map has the date of April 30, 1420. Today is April 30, 1720, did ye know that I was coming to see ye?"

* * *

Meghalaya smiled at Thomas. "Ronald was on his way to the meeting he stopped here for lunch. I had come in to eat before I had to work, I sat down with your brother to eat with him. Ronald had a bad feeling something was happening. That's when I gave him a rose stem. He burned it in the candle on the table, he saw Marian and the man who cut the line to the buggy. Then he saw the buggy hit the rock and flip over. The man who brought her home was also in on it. He was cold hearted and enjoying seeing her in pain. Then he knew it was time to bring her home. That man knew there was no way to save her.

* * *

"It was hard for Ronald to see what had happen to his wife. The man that brought her home Ronald saw ye listening, ye had looked into his eyes. He saw the anger in your eyes. He knew ye didn't believe that man who brought Marian home. Michael shared your feelings he knew they had planned all of this. To try to stop ye from changing Scotland, Ronald took some of the petals with him. On the way home he saw the man who cut the line. The higher killer was waiting to tell him what had happen. Ronald saw the laughter dancing in his eyes. He was close to the killer and had his dirk in hand. He had told the man, ye were the one who cut the line to the buggy. Before the man got his knife Ronald killed him.

"I had watched it in the fire what Ronald had done, he was riding hard now to get home to Marian. That's when he caught up with Michael. Before Michael could tell him, Ronald told him who done it, and that man is dead. Then he took out some rose petals and asked him to put it on his wife's hair. Ronald told Michael now ye will hear the once ye love. He had told him the man that found her was in on it. He had followed the buggy until the horse had brook away from the buggy. I saw the man watch her crying for help. He stayed there until he knew she wouldn't make it.

"Michael said he can't be far, I will take care of him ye to keep heading home. Meghalaya had burned another stem then thought of Michael. He had caught up with the man and rode close to him. Michael told him ye watched Marian bleed out, until she would die from lack of blood. Michael took his dirk and stab him where he would bleed out. The man fell to the grown, he was in a place where no one would see him for days. Then road hard to catch Ronald, all he did was nodded his head. Ronald knew that evil man was dead, those men was out of the way.

"Before Ronald went to battle, the three men came here for their last meal. Together we burned a stem and saw when ye would be here. Your brother's loved ye three. The letters will be in their sporran, William ye will have three letters. One to ye and your sister. Another one for your father and mother. The last to his wife."

Meghalaya watched Thomas and William. They had drunk a little of their ale. They knew the letters will be hard to read. Thomas knew these roses could tell them a lot. The stem could tell us who is in with Rodney and where they are.

$*\quad*\quad*$

He was looking at Meghalaya. "I was wondering if one of my children is not sure who is his love. Could he find out if she is the one."

Meghalaya smiled but took a drink of her ale. She shook her head yes. "Thomas when ye are home ye can find out even then. Remember your love will have to do as ye did. Take off the stone do as the tablet says. Everything under the tablet is yours. Turn the soil and feed the roses. Give it a lot of water for it hasn't had water for a long time. Everything ye done she must do to find the right rose bush. Ones ye find the rose bush plant it together. When the rose bush blooms, then kneel in front of it and think of her. If the rose drops in your hand. Ye must breathe in the scent of the rose. For her to have the magic she must breathe in the scent the same with ye. The longer ye are out the stronger your love is."

Thomas eyes went wide. "Meghalaya what are ye saying. Do ye mean I will pass out ones I breathe in the scent."

She all most laughed. "Aye… That goes for both of ye. So be close to her when she breathes in the scent. Now remember the petals can stop a knife from killing ye. Put a lot on both sides of your vest.

*   *   *

"There will be many pouches one for the petals one for the stems and another for money. Place three rose petals inside the money pouch. When that is done all ye need to do is think of how much money ye need. The pouch will give ye just what ye ask for. There is a big one for the tablet. Thomas ones ye have the magic roses leave some other bags with your magic. Make sure ye cover the hole and put the stone over the spot. For there may be another person, who has the blood line they may come and take the roses."

*   *   *

Thomas was thinking what else does she know. "Meghalaya what else do ye know about William and me?"

236

Over the brim of the cup of ale, she looked at Thomas. Then took a drink of her ale. "So ye like to see what I know about the two of ye. How about the time ye saw your wife from the hill? Ye knew the buggy and they were inside. Ye both called to them and talked to them. How about the time the two of ye saved this young lass from an icy grave? The man who is taking these young women knew she saw him. This evil man try to kill her. He had used a spell to put everyone to sleep. Eleanor gave ye a spell to wake them up. Ye was talking with her when this evil man casted the spell. How about a young woman was scared she tried to make ye marry her? The young man didn't know what to do. Ye had brought him to stand by her father. That his father had beaten him and through him out. Her father looked at the young man. The young man was a man that work hard. Ye were there to see them marry.

*   *   *

William looked at Thomas. In a soft voice he spoke. "Thomas, may I have a word with ye at the bar."

Meghalaya smiled at William; she knew it was getting to much for him to understand. "William take one of the stems and burn one. Think of Catherine, only ye will see her."

William looked at Thomas. Donald then spoke. "William try it. I know ye would love to see her right now."

He took the stem and thought of Catherine. He saw her top was off, she was washing up. He smiled knowing she was his. In his mind he then spoke to her. "My love I wish I were there with ye. I would love to make love to ye now."

He saw it had scared her, she had grabbed something to cover herself with. "Who is in my room? Show yourself right now."

Thomas saw William's eyes go wide. He didn't know what William saw. "William tell my sister who ye are. Tell her something only she knows."

William watch her trying to find out who was watching her. "Catherine it is your husband, William. Please honey don't be scared. Talk to me in your mind."

He saw her slowly relax. "How can ye see me?"

Thomas knew he wanted to be with her now. "Tell her ye will see her tonight. Also, to tell your dad ye need his help, to get ready to ride then to fight. For there not going to let these bodies go home without a fight."

* * *

William looked at Thomas and nodded yes. He smiled knowing he will be with her tonight.

Thomas went to stand up when he was hit hard with a vision. It felt as if someone hit him in the mouth. It had slam him back into his chair. William grab the chair preventing him from falling backwards. Duncan helped by slowing his fall to the chair. In Thomas mind's eye, he saw Eleanor riding hard with their father's and cousins. In her eyes he saw fear, then he heard her speak. "Thomas stay with me. Honey don't die. I need ye, please I don't want to live without ye."

That look on her face, was the look of his brother when he lost his wife. Then he saw Duncan, one of the men had thrown a knife at him. That man saw that the knife wasn't going through to the skin. He had thrown the knife up higher to his neck. Thomas saw himself jump up to catch the knife in his chest. Now he knew why he had that vision. Without the vests and rose petals on it, that knife would go into his chest. All it did was bounce off the vest and slid into his arm. Thomas saw that he took the knife and send it back to the man that threw it. Now he knew what Meghalaya mint about being careful. She had seen the knife go into his arm. How many men would understand that they was being protected?

When his eyes opened, he saw everyone was looking at him. Meghalaya smiled at him she knew he would have that vision. She had poured him some Scotch and hand it to him.

It was Donald who spoke. "So, my boy what did ye see?"

Both Duncan and William still had their hand on Thomas shoulder. William spoke. "Ye better tell me what happen for ye are as white as a ghost."

Thomas grabbed the Scotch and tossed it back then closed his eyes. When he tried to speak, he found his voice was shaky, clearing his throat. "What can I say, it's hard to see someone coming after ye. Most of all to see the one ye love begging for ye to not die. As she rode hard to try to get to me. These men are higher killers, they know how a man will fight. Duncan we must make ye something to go around the back of your neck. One of the men found out that their knife wouldn't go through to the skin. They will have six men with them, these men will do what they had done to our brother's. They will make us fight until they will win. Eleanor been having those dreams, it's been scaring her that we might be killed. Tonight, William and I will talk to our father's.

"Before I left, I showed Eleanor how to protect herself. After that bear had attack her, she had asked me for a knife. The roses wanted to make sure I go after them. This is the only way we will survive this fight. We need our fathers to be able to win. This time the tables will be turn. We must make sure there is no other cuts on us after the fight is done."

*　　*　　*

Then Duncan looked at his father. "Dad tonight ye are coming home with me. Briana wants to meet ye. Dad she believe ye are going to be a grandfather."

Donald smiled at last he thought. "Will now I'm going to be a grandfather. How wonderful, there's going to be a little one in are home.

I wish Peter could have seen your child. Thomas why did ye say we must check are self for cuts. Why did ye say that we have to make Duncan something for the back of his neck."

Thomas looked at Duncan. "Now I understand the hole vision. Like I had said without the vests and rose petals a long with are fathers. Everyone will die but Duncan, I had jump up and took the dirk in my chest. I did that so ye could raise your child with your wife."

*   *   *

Meghalaya looked at the three men then at Donald. "Donald will ye tell your friends, and your wife's. That ye done a good job with their son's. They are strong and thoughtful, it will be good to have these evil men gone from this earth. The man in black is the same man who is taking these young women. Thomas and William go after these Magic Roses, tomorrow once ye get back here.

"Ye will need these rose petals to save your wife. While ye are building the wagon ye will have a vision. For your wife was heading to Grana's place. The man in black had taken Duncan's brother's wife to be. Take this cross and place petals on it. With your magic make the cross into a knife to throw at the man in black. The cross will go into his skin and threw his veins, it will make him suffer. I have place holy water on the cross it will burn him. Every time he tries to touch a woman, it will make his loins hurt. This man will be killed by his own men. Ask Father for many crosses. Remember once this man dies, he will be able to come back from the dead, for he is a demon. The men ye are going up against in the Highlands will be demons. Once ye kill them place a cross on them and rose petals so no one can take it off them. Have Father bless the bodies.

"After the man in black is dead, he will try to take your wife Thomas. Your wife will not take what he is trying to do. Tell your wife to place rose petals under her fingernails when she feels he is near. Make her risk bans and place rose petals on it. He will try to take her ora to make her do what he wants her to do. When she scratch him in the face that mark will stay on him even as a ghost. When he comes back in the future it will be there also.

*   *   *

"Thomas when ye go for the rose bushes. Ye must make sure to cover the hole back up before ye leave. After ye take the three rose bushes there will be three more to take their place. This will give the town their roses back. Make a tablet with your magic. On that new tablet place rose petals on it. Then put the old and new tablet together. The rose petals will place the words on the new tablet. Then my son can take these roses. One other thing my grandmother before she died. She saw a lad who took the three roses to the new world. This was to be in the future.

*   *   *

Meghalaya looked at Thomas and then at the others. "From the time my young's grandson turned your age. I'm hoping the next full moon the new roses will go with him. Ye are taking them to the Highlands. He will be taking these roses to Italy where my oldest is now living. There are things happening that he will need help with."

Then Thomas looked at everyone. "The Fairy and Wizard blood is going all over the world. I hope these roses will go where everyone will need help. This man in black must be taken down. Were ever these roses go may there be someone with are blood able to help take evil down."

*   *   *

"I know ye are worried about getting the bodies home. Place these roses with the bodies in the bottom of the special wagon. These roses will help keep the bodies safe. Evil will not be able to touch the wagon or anything on top."

*　*　*

William looked at Thomas. "Now that we know that we are married. There is one thing the two of us must promise each other. To never hurt the ones, we love. To always keep them safe to the best of our ability."

Duncan looked at Thomas. "Thomas ye risk your life for me. But why would ye do that?"

Thomas took a deep breath. "Duncan ye are telling me if it was ye. Would ye do the same for me?"

Duncan thought about it. "Aye... Ye are my brother and friend. I must look after ye until Michael gets home. Besides Ronald never thought of himself and you're the same way. Now we know what will happen, we must make sure it don't happen when we fight these men."

*　*　*

Meghalaya looked at them. "At last, the roses will be used again. Take the map for I know where the roses will be. I've made a map for my son. We all have two paths we can take, always believe in yourself. When ye love... Love with all your heart. Stand up for what ye believe in... stay true to yourself. These are word's my family, live by. I pray ye will have many sons. Long life to ye and yours... I pray ye will be able to take down that man. Remember ye can see what happens in the future. It's not put in stone for the Lord can change it if he see fit. Thomas looked at her and gave her a big smile. He went over to her and gave her a hug. "Thank ye for being here for my brother. Thank ye for keeping the roses safe. I'm glad that ye could tell us this story. May your son's have sons of their own. Take care Meghalaya and Thank ye again. Goodbye my cousin we will meet again.

The plan to get the roses

THE FOUR MEN went to leave the table. They thought that they felt a big pop. Now the music is even louder than before. The smoke was thick, and they all started to cough. Thomas looked back at Meghalaya. She smiled at him and nodded her head. She knew what he thought. With the map in hand, they made their way to the door. It was late when the four of them walked out of the pub. At the door, Thomas and William breathe in the cool night air. It had cleared the scent of smoke from his lungs. What they had drunk of Scotch and ale hit them. The two men thought that they were fox but not this much. What they had drunk made everything look like it was spinning. With their back up against the wall. He thought he was fox before. Now he knew he was out right drunk. For two years he thought he could manage drinking. When Donald and Duncan turned to look at the boys. Thomas saw them laughing at them. William was having the same trouble as Thomas was. The old men watched the two of them. They were trying their best to walk straight. Now they were struggling not to fall flat on their face. They found it hard to walk down the street to the inn.

Thomas couldn't think why he was so drunk. He knew he was fox but not like this. "All right ye two. Why did the alcohol hit me this hard?

I've drunk before and it wasn't this bad." The two young men staggered through the doors of the inn.

Duncan smile at his friends. "It's because of the fresh air. Ye should have eaten more food." Then he turn to his father. "Dad I would like for ye to come home with me. Briana asked me to bring ye home. Let Thomas and William get their rooms here and ye come with me. Thomas and William, I will get your horses bedded down for the night." Duncan looked at his friends his little brothers. "Will that be all right with ye two?"

He rubbed his eyes then shook his head. He went over to Duncan then spoke. "Take them with ye. I have a feeling we won't need them until where at the place of the roses. We will talk in my room."

*　　*　　*

Thomas and William nodded their heads. "That's fine with us. I don't think I could stay on my horse tonight. Could ye come up to my room before ye leave? There is a list of things we will need."

Thomas got the key to their room; they didn't need two rooms. They were going home for a bit. Upstairs they went to William and Thomas room. There he gave Duncan his list. The men talked about the wagons. "I believe we will need two more horses. I know our brother's horses will pull the wagon. They know their master is gone, the words to tell them is take us home.

"I had made a list out of what we will need for the coffins and wagon. After ye get the wood from the church yard. Then ye can go and get the rest of the wood." Thomas knew what he needed for the roses. For him that was going to be the easy part. In a low voice he said. "We will need a place to work on the wagon. I don't want to build the coffins near the church yard. It won't work if were too close."

Duncan whispered. "Aye… my lovely new wife lives out of town. There is a barn that we could work in. I'll tell her we will be coming out there tomorrow. I've been thinking Father Sinclair could take her things on the one wagon. It would be good cover for the bodies. Do ye think we should tell Father Sinclair about that wagon?"

Thomas gave Duncan a unpleased look. "Duncan what are ye thinking about? Didn't I tell ye we can't tell Father what we are up to. He is a holy man, they are not ones to lie. Even to save their life, we must keep him in the dark. This way he can tell the truth that there is no bodies in the bottom of the wagon."

Duncan nodded his head yes. "Thomas ye remine me of Ronald. I sure miss him. Dad." The three men looked around for him. Duncan spoke, I must also be fox to not see when he left us."

*　　*　　*

Donald had gone to get some coffee for the boys and himself. He had nock on his boy's door. The three men had just realized that he was gone. When they open the door there stood Donald with coffee and a bit of food. Thomas looked at the coffee and food. "Thank goodness this is just what we need right now. William get off the bed and come and get the coffee and food. That's if ye are going to see Catherine."

William jump to his feet. "Food that is just what I need. Now for the coffee to wash the food down."

Thomas's mine was clear once he came into this room. The fog that was over his eyes also cleared. Now he can walk right. Duncan then spoke. "Dad I want ye and Father Sinclair to take Briana to the crossing. If Thomas and William do their part. Ye will meet up with their father's."

Thomas rubbed his eyes. He knew his uncle wouldn't like that plan. So, he tried to change the subject. "Duncan stop making plans. Tell us how long ye been married?"

Donald was shaking his head no. "Ye hold on right there. I'm going with ye. Ye don't know how many men will be coming after ye. Ye will need all the hands ye can get."

Thomas looked at the two of them. "No, ye two stop this now. If I'm right, there will be six men. Before we do anything let me see if William and I can go back home." Thomas took out some petals that Meghalaya had gave him. He placed three rose petals on William. He gave him three stems. So that his parents could throw one into the fire if they had a question. The way Meghalaya was talking they can do a lot. When I had my vision, without the rose petals on us. Duncan ye were the only one left. With the roses I saw dads' friends with us, we will talk more later." Thomas pointed to the walls and then to his ears. "We make are plans out of town."

All three men nodded their heads. Donald smiled. "All right my boy, if ye find out I should go with them I will."

Thomas looked at his uncle. "Dad I have a feeling ye would like to see your wife after ye meet Briana. Here is three rose petals to place on what ye carry for your wife. This way ye can talk to her. Then he place three on Donald sporran. I think it would be best if ye could talk to our father's. I have a feeling ye may be fighting with your best friends. I'm going to give these rose petals and stems a workout. Until then we will do what we must. Here Duncan three petals to put on what ye carry for your wife. See if ye can talk to her."

*　　*　　*

Donald looked at his son. "How long have ye, been married. Tell me where ye met Briana."

Duncan looked at Thomas and William. "I had been mapping out the towns. Ronald had told me the places he wanted Thomas and William to see. I enjoyed the places ye took the three of us in the Highlands. I haven't seen those places before. Michael told me the town to end up at. He had said to take this one road heading back from the scouting trip. The sky was getting black. I knew this one road there was no place to get any cover. This storm was going to be a bad one, I decided to go straight. Not too far down the road was a farmhouse, it was the only farm for a couple of miles. There was a young woman coming out of the barn. With the storm behind me and her beautiful face drawing me to her. I rode up to her quickly for I felt a couple of drops of rain. She was the most beautiful woman I have seen. When I got off my horse and walked up to her. I had asked her if I could bed down my horse and myself in your barn until the storm passed.

"There was something about her that drew me in. Even a way from her I could see her face it seem to glow. I've met many women they didn't have that effect on me. Dad can a person fall in love the moment their eyes meet. Those eyes drew me in they were the greenest of emeralds. I found that her eyes had bewitched me. She was a kind person she told me that I could stay in the house with her and her father. These days her father hasn't been feeling well. That they haven't had much company.

"When I walked into the barn, I couldn't believe what I was seeing. There in the first stall was Peter's horse, I didn't think of this before. Who else could of know her but Ronald? Michael told me to go the other way, Ronald had set me up. There was Ronald and Jonathan's horses were also there. She even helped me get my horse bedded down for the night. She had taken me in to meet her father. He was a kind man and told me the story about the horses. I told him what my name was, his name was Codey and his daughter's name was Briana.

"As I ate, he said that a man called Michael McGee. He had given us money to keep them fed for two years. That Michael had said if she need help to get on one of the horses. Tell them to take me to your home.

"When Kenyon was talking, he would start coughing. He had gotten worse, and the color of his skin wasn't that healthy looking. I had two weeks left before I had to leave. Briana and I was getting closer when I kissed her, I knew she was the one. I had asked her father for her hand in marriage. I stayed with them until her father had passed. I had helped her to clean him and get him ready to be bury. I didn't think of it until now, her father is right next to are brothers. Wow! When they say love is blind, they were right. I didn't feel right staying with her without her father not there. In the house she wanted me to make love to her. I knew once I started, I wouldn't stop. The two of us had Father Sinclair married us the next day after we had buried her father.

"Now I understand what Ronald was saying. Before he had left the Highlands, he told me that the three of us will finely find the ones that we will marry. That their love for us will make us hole."

Duncan looked at his father and smiled. "We'll be leaving soon, I must tell ye this first. Briana can ride Peter's horse, she has a new whistle and a new name for her horse. She calls her Flower. The first time Peter's horse saw Briana's flower garden. She went right over to her garden and ate a few blooms. Thomas and William when ye get back. I know where the roses are, ye go ahead and get what ye must get done. We'll meet ye at the spot where the roses are to be."

*   *   *

With two cups of coffee and a little bit of food, the four men was ready to get started in what they must do. Thomas looked at William and spoke, "William ye have all the things ye need to get home. Call to Catherine and ask her where she is right now."

William had seen Thomas do this a lot with his sister. He took a deep breath and closed his eyes and called to his wife. "Catherine where are ye my love."

In his mind he heard her say. "All of us are at the castle. We had a meeting us women about this man taking young women."

William then had to find out if the men were there also. "Where is my father?"

It took a bit for her to tell him. "There in the den right now. Honey are ye coming to see me tonight?"

William told her after we talk to our father's. He had thanked his wife and turn to Thomas and spoke. "Everyone is there at the castle. Our fathers are in the den."

Thomas looked at Donald. "What would ye, want me to tell our father's?"

Donald looked at his son. He wanted to meet his wife. "Tell my old friends get ready to ride we fight in four days' time."

*   *   *

Duncan looked to Thomas and William. "I'm sorry that I didn't take ye to those other places. If only I paid attention when we put her father next to her mother. I don't know why I didn't put it together until now."

Donald smiled at his young men. He saw Thomas yon. "My boys it wasn't your time to go back home."

Duncan looked at his brothers. Aye…, we weren't ready to go back. Ye could say, I needed to keep my bride to myself for a while. The three of us had to get stronger and older."

Duncan laugh at his brothers. "One thing I like to know. Are the two of ye mad at me?"

Thomas gave a little laugh and punch him in the arm. "So that is why ye found us places where we could work. Ye made sure that the people we stay with could teach us about Scotland. Some of the jobs we could use back home. William and I enjoyed looking around those three months. If I didn't have to do these things I would be with my wife."

William yon and rubbed his eyes. "Ye were right Thomas that it was a woman who caught his eye."

Duncan just looked at Thomas, here before him was now a man. "How did ye know that?"

Thomas was now setting on his bed. He then said. "When ye came back ye looked different. Ye were happy and putting on weight. When I got married, I was able to make love to Eleanor. Her cooking was wonderful, I to was putting on weight. That was the good thing, I had kept some of my weight."

*　　*　　*

Donald looked at Thomas and William. They had a hard day, the coffee and food had helped them a bit. Before the four of them get too sleepy. They need to let William and Thomas get going. He looked at his son. "What are we waiting for? I'd like to meet my daughter-in-law. The coffee and food has helped, but it won't last for much longer."

Thomas and William said their goodbyes. Then Thomas spoke. "All right clear your mind. Think of the den and were ye like to land. I think the best place will be in front of the door."

*　　*　　*

While they held on to the map, the two men thought of their fathers at the castle in the den. In a blink of an eye the two men appeared in a dark room with their father's voice. The only light they had was coming from a wall, the light looked to be eye holes. With great care they went toward the light. Thomas ran into a table he heard something dropped. He felt around and found a candle, he got his flint out and lit it. Then he saw a book, the words on it was the second book of the Magic Roses.

William went to the eye holds and peered into them. He could see their fathers in the den, then he went back to Thomas. "I don't know what is going on. The voices was of our fathers, it seems like where in a secret room behind the bookcase. What are ye looking at?"

Thomas then held up a book. "This is the next book for the Magic Roses. Eleanor said that the story of the Fairy and Wizard had just stopped."

*　　*　　*

With the candled in hand, he looked around the room. Then he saw a hallway and the two men went down it. Thomas was trying to think where he was. "William, I believe where on the other side of my room. Why would there be stares to my room?"

Then the hallway went down under his sister's room. "Hold the candle for me, I believe there is a map inside this book."

Thomas took out the map so the two of them could look at it, the map had shown another stairway. Then there was another door, and they went inside. This room had bottles of different chemicals. Thomas spoke, "My great grandfather was a Wizard, Eleanor has been looking into ways to stop the man in black. Her and Grana would love to look this room over."

Then William spoke up. "Thomas there is more books here." He took one down and saw it was a book of spells. "Wow, I don't think we should tell many people about this place."

Thomas then had a vision. He saw his great grandmother with her husband. Then he heard them speaking. "Dear I have placed a spell on this room. The next person to bring the roses here to the Highlands will have the power to open this door."

Thomas saw her showing him the two people who will come into this room first. He saw William and himself. "Dear these two men and their sisters will have strong magic. The one wife her magic will match his. As ye can see they are here. The two men that ye see here are young. They will protect each other with their life. He has rose petals with him. If he takes two petals it will lock the door so no-one can get into this room. In less they have the magic of the roses with them. It is sad that the young men will have to fight to get their brother's home. Already they have travel here by the magic rose petals. The map that was given to them has brought them here to this room. These three families has been close for many of years. The evil one who we have stopped is now back. The oldest gave his life to help the youngest son to find these roses. He has a strong plan, the old woman will help his wife with a spell she may need. This woman is her grandmother. Go my great grandson and rest with your wife. Place two rose petals on the door. May the Lord be with ye always. Beware of the darkness for evil will be there."

William saw that he was having another vision. "Thomas come out of this vision and tell me what happen."

He looked at William. "They saw us here, I must put two rose petals on the door. Come on we must call to our wives, uncle is here." When they step out of the room, they heard laughter. "His father said congratulations."

The men went and called to their wife. There was two petals place on the door. Then both men went up the stairs. There in his room was a big bed. Then William came down from Catherine's room. "Thomas there is a big bed in her room."

*   *   *

Then the men saw their wife. Quickly the two women ran up the stairs. Both men picked up their wife and kissed them. They brought them to their bed and close the door. Thomas took a petal and place it on his finger. It turned into a ring. He wave his hand, and their clothes was gone. Before she knew what was happening, she was one with him. Eleanor didn't think she moved with him. He had taken her up so many times until she felt him come with her.

Thomas got up to wash himself then came back to clean her. He had taken out a petal and place it on her finger. There appeared a ring like his. "I could have done that for ye. What is this."

Thomas enjoyed cleaning his wife. "Ye have one just like mine."

He looked at his wife. "Ye can do it the next time. Come here and lay on my shoulder. It's been quite a day, we will talk tomorrow." He had felt her hand move over his body. When her hand stopped the two of them were asleep.

Like clockwork Eleanor was up just as the sun came up. She couldn't believe he was here with her. Now she wonder if she could wake his friend up. With loving care, she straddled him. When she took his friend and laid him under her. She started to move, before long she was one with her man. Thomas's friend enjoyed her pussy to the point she came. Eleanor's eyes were closed when she felt to strong hands pull her to his mouth. Now she was under him, and he took over. He made love to her and enjoyed each time he made her come. The last time she came he had joined her. Eleanor spoke, "Good morning my love. Did ye like the way I woke ye up."

Thomas turn her over, she had sat up. "Aye… and good morning to ye." How he loved her as his hand moved over her body. He brought her breast to his mouth.

Eleanor felt the pull from her heat. She could feel his friend move. Her hands was on his chest as he brought her up. Thomas sat her back up when he came. "Are ye still on what Grana gave ye. If not, we could have made us our child."

Her eyes were dreamy as she gaze into his. "Honey do ye want a child now."

How could he answer her. What if he don't come back. Eleanor wouldn't have him or a child from him. "I don't know if I want one now. Then again to see our child grow inside ye. To feel our baby, move and react to my touch. All I know is I'm torn from both ways. I want more of this, to be able to see your love in your eyes for me. To know ye carry my seed inside ye right now."

Eleanor looked at him. Something had happened, then she knew. He's here because they need help from their father's. "Honey I'm on what Grana gave me. Remember your seed stays inside me for three days. If the Lord wants me to have a child I will."

Then there was a knock at the door. "Eleanor are ye a wake."

Thomas knew that was his mother. "Aye… I'm a wake. I will come down right away to help with the food."

Then Thomas spoke. "Good morning mamma."

Franceam smiled and spoke. "Good morning son, when ye two are ready come on down."

Eleanor started to get off him when he turned her over to her back. "All right mamma, we will be right there. Honey do ye know I could have ye again. Before we leave here, I will do just that."

She looked at her man, "Aye… I know ye could and will."

*   *   *

Without saying a word, the two of them was dress. Eleanor had a new dress on, she had given a little squeal and did a little dance. There was also a cross around her neck with her locket. Then he pulled her into him for a kiss. "Ye are my mate I'm told that ye will have the powers I have." With a wave of his hand, the book he had found had appeared. Thomas took out the map that was in it and showed it to Eleanor.

She took it and looked at it. "Thomas where did ye find this?"

He pointed to the map, near the two eye holes. He gave her a smile then went to the closet to open the door to the stairway. There she saw stairs going down. Thomas wave his hand, now he was holding a candle that was lit. The book Eleanor had she put it with the other books in a drawer. Thomas went over to the dresser and wave his hand. He had taken a copy of the books. Then he place a petal on the drawer. "Honey now that I have place a rose petal on this drawer no one can take these books. Ye can get the books anytime ye like. Ye have the magic with ye now. Would ye, like to see what is down there?"

Eleanor was looking at the map. It shows that there are two stairways. It's like it goes into your sister's room. Thomas took out another two petals and placed it on the closet near the floor. Then he led the way down to the other stairway. "William are ye a wake?"

To Thomas he said, "Go away." Before William could say anything else. Thomas waved his hand, and they were dress. Catherine had a new dress on. He had heard a squeal of pleasure, the two of them was up and dress. Thomas spoke. "Are ye coming or are ye going downstairs by yourself to face your mother?"

William looked at Thomas. "I will be happy once where home. Then I can sleep or make love to my wife without being interrupted. Where coming. Thank ye for bringing the new dress that I had bought Catherine to her. I didn't think to bring it along with me. We are going to show the girls what we found."

Thomas nodded and waved his hand for another lit candle. Then he place two petals on the bottom of the closet. Around his sister's neck was a cross. "Come on we have to get to the table for breakfast."

Thomas gave William a look, "I need to show the girls this room first."

Eleanor was looking over the books on the shelf. "Thomas, can I take this book? It has some of the spells I think we will need."

Thomas went over to her and took the book. He looked at some of the spells. William and Catherine was also looking at some of the books. "Eleanor look at this one it has more things to heel our people."

She took the book and showed it to Thomas. "Can I have these two books. I like to show them to Grana."

He nodded his head yes. "Honey ye can use these books here in the castle. As ye can see there is a lot of things on these shelfs. Do not take anything out of the castle. If ye need anything from these books. Take a copy of what ye need."

In the candlelight she saw a spell to keep out evil spirits. "I really need to show Grana these two books."

Thomas nodded yes. "Remember do not take the books out of the castle. Keep them locked up in here or the drawer. Ye can copy a page like this. Honey try this think of where ye like to keep these books. Then place them there by waving your hand like this. Come on we must get to the dining room table."

William and Catherine was looking out the two eye holes. "There is no-one there in the den."

Thomas was looking for a way to open this door. When Eleanor spoke. "Try waving your hand."

Then the door open to them. He had place two petals on the door. "Catherine ye have the magic in ye. William and ye can talk to each other now. So, use your powers more. Come on let's get some food. William and I must talk with are fathers. I must get going I must feed the roses before the full moon tonight."

As they close the doorway. Thomas thought to ask Eleanor if she has made any new plant food up. She had heard his thoughts. "Aye… that I have done. Before ye go I will get ye some."

At the table everyone looked up when the two couples came down the hallway. William's mother stood up. "What's going on. How did the five of ye get here."

Then her husband told her to "Set down."

The two young women went to get their husband some food. While the young men sat near their father's. Thomas spoke, "Did ye get to talk about are plans to get our brother's home uncle?"

Donald looked at Thomas. "Aye… That I did. We still have more planning to do before we go back."

Thomas notices that they need more chairs and another leaf to the table. With a wave of his hand, they had more room for his wife and sister. Daniel spoke. "The stories Eleanor has told us is true."

Thomas pulled out Eleanor's chair as William did the same for Catherine. Eleanor spoke. "Aye… last night Thomas found the other book."

Then Bridget then saw Thomas kiss Eleanor. "Just a moment Thomas. It's not right to take kisses from my daughter. That is for when ye are married to her. William that goes for ye too."

Thomas looked at his mother-in-law. Then he looked at William and just smiled. "What I'm going to tell ye. Ye will not be able to say anything to anyone else. Everyone knows but ye, before I tell ye. I must make sure no-one else will be told. If ye go and tell someone that William and I are married to Eleanor and Catherine. If ye try to say anything ye will lose your voice. Ye can't right that we are married." Then Thomas waved his hand, and it was done.

She looked at Thomas. She couldn't believe he could put a spell on her. "How will ye do that. I have my voice. So ye are married, when did ye get married. How long have ye, been married."

Then Eleanor looked at her mother. "Mamma don't push your luck. Just be happy about all of this. Then she looked at Daniel. I have the rest of the story of the Magic Roses. Grana there is some other ways to make medicine. I can't take the books out of the castle."

Grana looked at Thomas. "That will be fine with me. Before I leave ye can show me these books."

Eleanor had finished her food. Then she wave her hand, and the next book appeared. This is the part where she came out to see if he was there.

Eleanor's father looked at his daughter. "Daughter when did ye get magic."

She smile at her father. "I'm Thomas's mate, through him I have some magic."

Her mother couldn't believe what she heard. "What are ye talking about, ye are not married to him not yet."

Franceam looked at Bridget. "Enough of this, my son said the four of them are married. Ye weren't told, because ye can't keep a secret. Why are ye trying to make trouble. Grana did ye put a cross on Bridget."

Then Grana turn to Bridget. "Where's the cross I gave ye."

She looked at Grana. "What cross are ye talking about."

Something was wrong with Bridget. Thomas got up from the table and went over to his mother-in-law. Then he wave his hand, a cross appeared. He waved his hand again. There was a bowl of holy water and Thomas dip the cross into the holy water. Bridget wanted to run. Thomas place a bubble around her so what was in her couldn't get out. "Grana I don't know the spell to use for casting out evil spirits."

Grana had looked at her daughter. How long has this been going on she wondered. She had spoken the spell then she place the cross around her neck. They all watched as it burn her skin. There was a scream, but it wasn't from her. The demon came out of her body quickly, the mark was on him. Thomas spoke. "How long have ye, been inside her. What does Marcus know."

The demon pulled at the chain. "Not long only off and on. He don't know much." Then Grana spoke more words, and the demon was gone. Grana then spoke, "How do ye feel daughter."

Bridget looked at her mother. "I feel like the hold world is off my shoulders. What happen to me?"

Then Eleanor looked at her mother. "Mamma evil was using ye. To find out about the MacGregor's." She now waved her hand, this time the cross won't come off around her neck.

*　　*　　*

Now that was done, and everything was put away. Eleanor then started the story.

It starts where Kina had come out from the waterfall. She had seen Kenyon laying on the ground. He knew she was near him now. When he opened his eyes, he saw the fear that was in her eyes.

*　　*　　*

Thomas looked at his wife. "I guess you're coming with me. Get what ye need for the roses. We must talk with our fathers. We have a lot to do before we can face those men."

Then Donald looked over at Thomas. "How about ye take Eleanor and set up the roses for tonight. Ye are getting use to your magic. There is something more to that story. We need vest with half sleeves to put the rose petals on."

Then Eleanor went over to her husband. "I have a feeling we are going to fix all the roses. Does that mean I get to see the valley of the Fairy's?"

He then kissed his wife. "Honey I wasn't going to bring ye to the roses. That book change my mind. What ye said about the roses has me worried. The roses came from the valley of the fairies. All right we will set up the roses. Then we can go to the waterfall to see if we can get into the land of the Fairy's. We go while we wait for the roses to show themselves. Then we can look around the waterfall. I've been wondering if there is a way into the valley of the Fairy's.

Eleanor smiled at her man. "Let me get what I need first. I need to give more of my plant food to the roses here. She had everything she needed in the sack she carried."

* * *

While he waited the men went to the den. Thomas told them what he had in mind. Then there was a knock at the door. Thomas when over and opened it. "Are ye ready to go? I have everything here with me." She had her pale and the sack with everything she would need.

Thomas looked at everything she had with her. A thought came to him. "Honey did something happen to the roses here."

She looked at Thomas. "Aye… while I was gone, we all most lost them all. Grana and I had to come up with something to bring them back."

Then Daniel took over the conversation. "Eleanor ye did nothing to make these roses sick. I had heard that many flowers got hit."

Then Eleanor had a thought. "What if Marcos remembers about the three rose bushes the King made. What if he knew that he had to kill the magic roses? If all the roses have been hit. Remember the book said, we must go to the land of the Fairy's to heel them there also. Thomas, we need to go now. If I'm right before these roses come back. I must protect them first. Then we need to get into the land of the Fairy's."

* * *

Thomas pulled Eleanor close to him, his arm was around her waist. Then a thought came to him. "Uncle will ye get Duncan and his wife.

Ye need to be there around when the moon will be coming up. Have him bring food and drink in a wagon with everything else we will need. William when ye go to the farm could ye bring my horse and yours. Then he made a copy of the map he place petals on it. Eleanor will be with me. I guess Catherin can come along with ye. She can check on Duncan's wife. Eleanor will be with me tonight."

No…" is all William said.

Then William looked at Thomas. "Our women will only be with us for that night. We can't keep using magic for everything."

Eleanor was now looking at him. Her husband can read me to well she thought. "Thomas, I found this in the lab with this note."

Then Thomas took the small bag and looked inside. There was more petals inside the bag. "To my children-children. My brother Kenyon told me to leave ye this bag of magic rose petals. Kina said the once that must fight Marcos again will need this. She also said that his mate will be able to heal the roses. Good luck and God speed."

Thomas looked at everyone. "Will now here is a few more rose petals to keep on ye. This will help ye to get to the Lowlands. We will have a lot to do before sunset. Bring food and drink. The snow is not gone yet. Dress warm for the women. Honey we can't go under the water not yet. What we can do is see if we can go to the land of the Fairy's."

*　*　*

After saying goodbye to everyone. Eleanor and Thomas left the Highlands. They landed on top of the hill. The map said once on top take fifteen steps south and five steps west. Then he had to dig down till he felt a tablet. Thomas didn't remember seeing these instructions on the map before. Eleanor helped her man to clear the snow away. Under the snow was rich dirt. He, place the dirt a side until he could find the tablet. Quickly he dug down and ran into it. Thomas removed all the dirt from the tablet and pulled it up. He had to brush it off there was words carved into the tablet. Under the tablet are three magical fairy rose bushes. These roses are the color of cherry red. Thomas placed the tablet a side. He removed more dirt. Then he found a small wooden box.

When he open it there inside the box was another deerskin with writing on it. "To the next keeper of the roses. This tablet protects these roses. Remember to take it with ye. Young lad I'm glad ye came after these roses. My wife had seen ye in the fire. She said these roses will protect ye and your family. When ye are home, have your mate find the one rose bush. She must do as ye have done. Place it near the rose bush that is your favorite. Ye will have to make a new map ones the other two roses have been separated from the one. These fairy roses their magic is very strong. When ye place the petals on ye they can keep ye safe. At the next full moon ye must place everything in the moonlight. Remember the moonlight feeds the petals so the magic can work.

*　　*　　*

Eleanor had the mixture ready for when Thomas brought the water up on the hill. After climbing the hill, he gave her the water. She then pour the mixture, with a stick he stirred it into the water. Thomas covered the hole up, then he poured the water over it. The water went very quickly into the ground. He went down and got more water. The dirt was dry again, he remember what she had told him. That the roses haven't had water in a long time. No, he thought he wasn't going down the hill again. With a waved of his hand the pale was filled up with water. Ones again it drank the water down, this time the dirt stayed moist. Thomas didn't want to leave the tablet here. In the box was more bags. With a wave of his hand the tablet went smaller. Eleanor had everything ready to go. Thomas touched her face then drew her head to him. He kissed her deeply before they left the hill.

CHAPTER SIXTEEN

Saving all the roses

A T THE WATERFALL he felt the pull to make love to her. Is this what his family felt for their mate. If he wanted to see if there was a way into the Land of the Fairy's, they better get going. "Honey ye better let me make the pale smaller for ye to put in your pocket."

Thomas then looked for a way to go under the waterfall. Then he saw a path it looked to have been use a lot even now. With her hand in his, they made their way to the back of the waterfall. Thomas then saw the vortex. "Shall we go say hello to my cousins."

Walking closer to him. She kissed her man. he had his arm around her waist. The two of them stepped into the vortex. They were pulled into a valley they never seen before. As they walked, they saw many children playing. This land was full of beautiful flowers. A child ran up to them. "Hello, my name is Salena. Could ye tell me your names."

The two of them looked at each other. "Ye not afraid of us."

Then many children came over to them. "Should we be afraid of ye."

Thomas laughed and Eleanor jabbed him in his side. "My husband is enjoying being here. I'm called Eleanor and this is Thomas MacGregor."

The children looked at each other then ran as fast as they could to the castle. Salena smiled at them. "Come with me. My father and mother will be glad to see ye."

As they walked down the path Eleanor saw the roses. She went up to the roses, quickly she took out the pale. She wave her hand, and the pale got bigger. "Honey could ye help me clean them. I see his magic reach even here."

Salena then asked. "Whose magic are ye talking about."

Eleanor worked as she told the story. "At first I thought it was Albert Huascaran. My dreams have told me it was Marcos who I saw. I don't know where Albert comes into the picture yet."

Eleanor then asked them for water. The two of them worked until the roses were all clean. One of the girls watched them do everything. Then Eleanor took what she had to feed the roses. Ones the water was mixed up she started to pour it over the soil. Quickly the roses drank in the water. Before their eyes, the roses started to bloom. Eleanor place everything back into the pale. "Honey will ye make me a big beryl of water. I will place the last of what I have here into it."

*   *   *

Thomas did as she asked. Then he saw the King and Queen standing near the children. Quickly Eleanor mixed it all up. "There this will keep those things away from the roses."

Thomas went over to her. "Ye did well my love. Now it's time to meet my cousins." When she had turn, she thought it was Thomas's brother. She all most asked when did Michael get here. He had the look of Thomas his hair was light brown with red highlights. Eleanor curtsy as Thomas bowed to his cousin. "Ye look just like my brother Michael your-highness. My wife and I have come for the roses outside the water-fall. Something pulled us here. When Eleanor saw the roses, she went right to work."

The King and Queen smiled at them. "Come now and ye can wash up. It's time for us to eat. Will ye dine with us. I can see your wife has many questions for us."

They had shown them a place where they could change into the close laid out for them. Eleanor never saw a beautiful dress like this before. Thomas had a new kilt on and his family seal that was pin to a cape. At the large table there was all kinds of food. After they had enough food. The King asked how did ye find this place? Thomas told him. "It was my wife who found the first book. Her brother found the last book in the lab in my father's castle. The book had a bit of the story. It had stopped and told us to come to the waterfall."

Then the King asked how she knew it was Marcos magic that was killing the roses. Eleanor then spoke. "On my sixteenth birthday my mother took us to the Lowlands of Scotland. I met Albert. There was something different about him. I could feel the evil with in him. Albert face changed to and old man's face then back to Albert. Reading the book, I found out that Marcos would come back. My cousin was killed by him. Her little girl was still alive. It had said he wouldn't have any sons."

Then Thomas took over speaking. "We knew of the roses through a cousin. I found out that a man wanted to wipcout the MacGregor name. My uncle told us about this man. He's been killing a lot of men. Now he rapes women with blond hair trying to get a son. If she gives a little girl, he kills the mother."

Eleanor picked up the story from there. "As we rode home, I saw many roses slowly dying. When we got back to the Highlands the roses was also dying. Grana was staying at the castle; she was working to try to stop the roses from dying. His mother and Grana and I we work hard to save them. When Thomas came home, he had rose petals that had magic. My brother found the next book about Thomas grate grandfather and the fairy queen. What led me to think about the rose bushes. Marcos knew about them back when. Marcos would know about these rose petals through the people who was under his command. He didn't want the men of the MacGregor to get their magic back."

Thomas took over for he had the next part of the roses. "Marcos thought he had the last of the MacGregor's. My cousin Peter took my brother Michael's place. Peter was dying and so was Eleanor's older brother. Ronald lost everything his wife and son. Marcos sent in three higher killers at a time. Michael had seen what they were about to do to Ronald.

"In the Highlands, my brother is called Hock. He can see without much light. He took those men down with his bow and arrows. They call me Eagle eyes, I can hit anything from far away with a dirk. Marcos don't know about me yet. If my brother's and I were together those higher killers wouldn't win. Peter was also good with a sword, he would run out of energy fast. The petals show my family what the man in black had done. Now that he almost died, he has his black magic back. He also has a demon with him helping him. The only way they took Ronald down. Someone had to go behind him and stab him in the back. I know who that man is. My uncle told him, if he finds out that he was the one to stab his family in the back. He will die by my uncle's hands. It didn't kill my brother, Michael saved Ronald from being burn alive. Ronald asked Michael to go after those killers."

Thomas took a drink of his Scotch. Eleanor then asked about Riemann did he married Malina."

The King smiled at him. "Aye… that he did. Thomas ye look just like Riemann. There looks seem to go down through the family."

Thomas smile back at the King. "Ye look like my brother Michael. Soon we will be going to get the bodies of our brothers. William will be meeting us at the hill where the roses are. We have started the process for the roses."

Eleanor looked at her husband. "My love can we look around before we must get back to the roses. I told Catherin to check over Duncan's wife. It's too bad that there wasn't a closer way to get to the Highlands. There are five heelers and midwifes. Thomas's sister and I we are heelers. His mother and mind are getting too old to ride all over."

Then the King said we have a way to come and see ye. In the bottom of the castle there is a door. If ye open it there will be a vortex that will bring ye here. If you're not one that has the magic roses on ye. The door goes to just a room. We have the same in the bottom of the castle also. Only the ones that has the magic rose petals on them can come here."

*   *   *

Off in the distance they saw William. He went down the hill to give him a hand with the wood. "Hey Thomas did ye find out anything about Riemann. Did he marry Malina."

Thomas had picked up some of the wood. "Aye… he had married Malina. Marcos knows about the roses. We got to see the valley of the Fairies. Marcos tried to take down the magic roses. Even in the land of the Fairy's their roses was also dying. Eleanor had given them the stuff that her and Grana made. Beside trying to take down my family. He wanted the magic roses out of the way."

On top of the hill William saw his sister. "Hi sis what did ye think of the land of the Fairies?"

She when and gave her brother a hug. "The land was beautiful, when this is over with, I like to go back there."

Thomas brought the last of the wood up. William looked at the wood. "Do ye think this will be enough wood for a while?"

Then Thomas wave his hand and got a big log. Then he cut that big log in half. He had place smaller pieces of wood to go around that log. "I think that should do it."

William took a box out that he had found. Eleanor had picked it up to look at it. "What is this box for? It looks like the one Thomas had found with the tablet."

He looked back to what Eleanor was talking about. "I found it on the ground. It looked to be left there for some reason."

Thomas smiled. "Good I don't have to leave the one I found behind. I have a use for it."

Then William looked around. "I see some rocks to put around the firepit. How about ye give me a hand. Then I'm going hunting."

With and arm full of rocks the two men headed up to the top. "Thomas is the roses all set?"

Dropping his load, he said. "Aye… take a look of what I have found in this hole." Thomas showed William everything. "I want ye to take a minute to read this. In the story it said Marcos's magic had turn to black magic. When he came back here, he had no magic. I believe that night when Michael came for the bodies. He found that they were trying to burn Ronald alive. Remember what we saw in the fire. Michael's arrows must have hit him. I thought I saw the man in black fall forward. The one that takes care of him took him away. Marcos has his black magic back. William do ye think ye were followed here."

He handed everything back to Thomas. "No once I was out of sight, I use the magic to take me here. I'll see ye before sundown. That's when everyone is to be here."

Thomas yell down to William. "Make sure ye save the deerskin at least a piece of it."

William had made a sled for the deer. He just got onto his horse and looked back at Thomas. Then headed out.

Eleanor and Thomas had time on their hands. Thomas had put a shield around the hill so no one would see them. Then he laid a blanket down for them. We have time for each other. Would ye, like to make love with me."

Eleanor giggle as he took her to the blanket. After they made love, she started to tell Thomas about the meeting they had. "Honey Grana been really upset about these women. Her friend told her he's been using black magic on the bodies after he kills them. I know how to clean the spirit and remove the black magic from the body. Another woman came home with a child on her stomach. This woman was like the others. There was signs of black magic use on the woman, her hair was also cut. This man been going from town to town. When I get back, I must get some of the things I may need from Grana. Your magic is getting stronger. I'm glad that the King gave me that beautiful dress. I had sent it home, I like to take Catherine to the land of the Fairy's. Your mother would like to go. We could check out the Fairies.

Then Eleanor stopped talking. She was getting a vision of when Thomas brings the bodies to the farm. Thomas notice that her eyes was looking funny. He held her close to him. Then she started to speak. "Don't look at the bodies at the church yard. When ye look at your brother at the farm. Call to his spirit, ye must place on his body a vest like yours. On each of the vest place their names on it. Thomas Ronald has plan to take on Marcos in the spirit world. Petals must go on all your weapons even Ronald's weapons. Place a cross on all their shields even Ronald's. Ye must ask father for holy water. I know that Ronald wants to take him to the valley of the dead. Marcos could destroy the Highlands if we let him. Ye and my brother with Michael and Donald. Ye will have to place a bubble around the land they will be fighting at. With Albert there is three demons the strongest demon will be with Albert. Albert is being used, the black magic he had done was for the locket around Albert's neck. A man will tell ye all about it at the pub."

Eleanor fell limp into his arms. Thomas laid her down on the blanket. "Honey are ye all right my love."

He clean them both and got them dress. He didn't like her being dragged into this. The plan to keep her safe just went out the window. Now what Meghalaya told him that Marcos was coming after her. I will get her the things she will need. When she woke up Thomas had made her some wristbands. They had rose petals on it. "Honey here is some petals for your nails. Meghalaya said if ye since Marcos put this on your nails. She told us that even as a spirit ye can mark him for live."

* * *

William had just got back with the deer meat. He had it all wrapped up for them. When he came up the hill, he wasn't sure that anyone was there. Then he saw his sister sleeping. "Thomas is my sister all right."

He looked at his wife. "Aye… She is now. Just a while ago she had a vision. It left her tired, so I let her sleep."

Then William spoke. "How about we get some food in her. When the stakes are done, we can get her up. Now tell me what the vision was all about."

Thomas gave him a rundown what she told him. Then they got Eleanor up, he had gotten some Scotch from the castle and gave his sister some. "Sis drink this it will help to clear the cobwebs away."

They had cut six more for later. It was around sundown. Donald Duncan and Briana with Catherine came to the small campground. They brought food and drink to keep them warm. It was sunset and the moon was slowly rising in the sky.

As the note had said the snow was melting. Thomas touch where the moon was hitting. He found the ground was warm to the touch. There before him three small plants appeared. When Thomas add watered the plants grew taller. There were many leaves unfolding at ones. Quickly small buds was growing between the leaves. Thomas gave the roses more water. He watched the plants drink the water as fast as he could pour it. Three more inches when the water ran out. Thomas went down the hill to the stream where he filled the bucket. When he came back, he added the bucket of water slowly to the plants.

* * *

He felt there was something evil was around. Could it be Marcos that found out what we are about to do. Then a cloud passed in front of the moon. Right then the moon light was snuffed out. Everyone had watched the three rose bushes closely. They saw the rose bushes had just stopped growing. All chances of survival were gone. He could feel something crawling over his body. His head was starting to hurt, he could feel his mine panicking. This wasn't like him to lose hope like this. There was a battle going on in his mind.

The cloud will past he thought. Then he heard a voice saying. "The cloud will not pass. Ye will not be able to take these roses home with ye. All ye will die."

Then he saw the vision again. He couldn't bear to see Eleanor riding hard to get to him. Thomas then saw her face when she found him. Then he heard her scream. Fear tried to take over all his reasoning.

He then knew that evil was with them. Thomas cried out… "Be gone Satan get out of my mind leave us. In Jesus name I pray. Ye will not stop us, our brothers will go home. The men ye send will die not us."

Thomas looked to the heavens. The voice was gone, and the cloud had moved away. Everyone knew that evil was trying to mess with Thomas. Donald watch Thomas as he battle evil in his mind. He had also said a prayer. His nephew has grown even more. Something has happened since he gone after these roses. He notice his willpower is stronger.

Thomas felt better about himself. He thought if he could fight a bear and win. Then he can fight evil with the help of these roses. Meghalaya told him Eleanor will see him alive. Then Eleanor put her arms around her man. "Are ye all right my love."

* * *

He pulled her onto his lap and buried his face into her nick. "Aye… let me just hold ye until I can steady myself. He knows where here at the roses. There must be someone in the land of the Fairies telling him about the roses. Evil want Thomas to believe he can't control his power. He is afraid that he may lose again. I will make sure that he does, I can do anything if I set my mind to it. I must believe in myself and my ability. He kissed Eleanor deeply. Thank ye honey for being here." Thomas looked up when he heard a squeal of delight.

It was coming from his sister and Briana. "The roses are opening they're beautiful. Thomas ye did it."

Meghalaya was right they will be all right. As he looked upon this rich color of cherry red blossoms. Evil will not win, these roses will keep us safe. Those men who kill for money will meet their maker. Thomas took a deep cleansing breath. He had a feeling that many times evil will try to rock his world. Briana had handed him a glass of Scotch. Thomas lift his glass, "to our women who puts up with us. To my great grandfather, who saw away to give are magic back to us when we need it the most. To our brothers who fought evil first. Those men will meet their maker. Now to us who will send evil back to hell." A cry went out into the night. Here… here!

Thomas then called to the King of the Fairies. "Hear me my King, someone in the valley been telling Marcos about the roses. Be aware of this. He was here trying to stop the roses from appearing."

Then he heard a voice call back. "I understand I will keep an eye out for the roses here. Thank ye for telling me."

It was time to prepare their clothes. "All right Duncan said that Briana has vest for us. I'm so glad we have women who knows when us men, need things to keep us safe. These rose petals have strong magic. What I have found out my great grandfather, along with his wife and brother gave the roses their magic.

"There is a man who fought the twins in the valley of the dead. He was called Marcuse back in the 12th century. Now his name is Marcos he has three demons with him. We will take these men down it wound be easy. These men have killed for a living, so they know all kinds of fighting.

"Our vest is our defense for staying alive. Make sure that ye put enough petals, on both side of the vest. I want ye to assess your vest out, ye must believe in these petals. Don't take off your vests, we will be fighting two battles. There will be a brake in between fights. The last battle will be with my two brothers. Ronald will fight Marcos in the spirit world. What I have seen after burning a stem. I saw one of his men will kill him, only after this will happen. When Michael comes home, we will have our brothers with us. I know it will take Michael's and my skills to take down that powerful demon. This demon has black magic.

"Marcos, ones he is dead he will become a demon. He believes he will be coming back. Albert is his ticket back from the dead. Right now, he is fighting for his life as the locket goes into his chest.

Duncan looked at him. "Thomas how do ye know all of this?"

He had passed the roses to everyone as the roses opened. "As ye know Eleanor and I have been having visions. That is where my information has been coming from.

Tonight, we will put petals on everything, we will fight with and wear. The vest Briana had made us. We will have to place the petals on the vest front and back." Then Thomas waved his hand and there was half sleeves. "Make sure to place petals on that sleeve also. If they realize that their dirk are not going through, they will go after any skin they see." Thomas then realize that everyone must have the caller also.

"Once again, Thomas waved his hand, then they had callers. "We will also have our coats on, so they won't know of are vest. I had that vision in the pub. One of the men will figure out that the dirks don't go through. If there is any skin showing he will throw the dirk, there. Don't forget to place your name in the vest. Now that we have are vest, I see that Briana has made a little one. Michael has a son he will need a vest and Ronald will also need one. All right as I cut the roses off ye can take them and put them on your vest. Both sides Then tryout your vest with your dirk, for it to work ye must believe in them. One all the petals are on make sure they fit ye. I can do some adjusting for ye. They will be going for are heats. I think clips will help to keep the vest close. Briana could ye tell us when ye had the idea to make these vest."

*　*　*

Duncan was so please with his wife as she told her story. "One night I had a dream, I saw these roses bloom in the moon light. Then there was a battle going on and my husband was in it. It had shown me that six men need to have a vest. I saw a young man putting something on this vest, I felt the magic with in it. I didn't know the man who was in my dream. I remember seeing this man putting rose petals on these vests. Then he took his dirk to the deerskin. All I knew it was very important that I make them. For I had this dream many times. Duncan had brought me many deer's homes when he went away. I started to make the vest, it keep me busy while he was away. Now that I have met ye Thomas, for it was your face I saw. Ye were putting these rose petals on the vest."

Thomas had given Briana a big smile. "Thank ye Briana with your help we will survive this battle. These two years the three of us have grown. Duncan, William, and I knew ye found your true love. Ye was happy and ye had filled out more. She is like your mother, Briana has the gift of sight. I have found that the women we have married has these gifts. Her dreams told her to make these vest. With the rose petals on them we will have a suit of armor. Now for all ye women place petals on a sweater. I want all our women to have these petals on something they wear."

All the women smile and took off their sweater. Then Thomas said we will have to do our weapons next. It's going to be along night.

Thomas looked at the women and smiled. "We must have these rose petals on us. If these roses, make it hard to hurt us. I feel we should put it on are weapons. Before we leave, I like for father to bless us and are weapons. Evil has magic, I will use everything I can to save us and our brothers. When we are done with are vest, I'm going to see what happen to our brothers. If ye like to try this yourself I will give ye the rose stem. Uncle, do ye have enough money to get what else we may need."

Donald looked over to Thomas. "If I were home, I would say aye. We still must get another wagon."

Then Thomas place rose petals inside the black pouch. Then after a few minutes he pulled out some money. "Here uncle get what ye need. Bridget anything ye need for the trip go and buy it."

Donald looked at the money he had given him. "Thomas where did ye get this money."

He held up the black pouch and spoke. "I got them from this pouch. It was one of the things that was under this tablet. When we get home, I will pay all our taxes."

Donald closed his eyes he knew now that Rodney was doing some killing that night. "These things that has been going on. It's been hard to take. There has been a lot of bad things happening. Right now, a lot of good is happening. I know that I must wait until my brothers are with me. A long time ago we fought together. Here we will fight again together." Duncan also gave his word. Everyone heard Donald say. "Rodney ye have three days to live. I will be coming for ye then." Bridget had the bottle ready to pour the men more Scotch. Both men down the Scotch it had help to kill the pain of what they saw. The three women sat next to their man. They had seen what their mate saw. Eleanor and Catherine buried their face into their man's neck.

*　*　*

It was time to take the roses with them. When the last rose bush was up. At the bottom of the hole was another deerskin. "The magic comes from the Queen of the Fairies her mate was the King who was a wizard. These roses were made by him. The power from these roses will help him find his true love. It can give ye strong magic through your gifts that ye already have. Don't forget to place three-hole roses in this hole. Keep what ye have found. Put in the hole different things that ye have found. When ye need the writing, on the next skin or tablet. Place rose petals on the blank skin then put the two skins together. Do this to everything ye found. Once everything is in the hole place the tablet on top. Then cover the hole. Good luck."

Back at Bridget's home Thomas and William took their wife home. They found their self in the girl's room in the Highlands.

Back in their room Thomas slowly took her clothes off her. He ran his hand over her body. "Ye must be sore there. Honey I have had ye three times today. Your body feel so good to me. We don't have to make love. I don't need much, just let me hold ye that will be enough for me."

Eleanor brought him down to her mouth. She couldn't get enough of him. "Husband, are ye telling me that your sore there? Don't worry about me, my heat wants ye again. It will be good for us to make love again, to wash away all what we have seen today. Just so we can relax and go to sleep. Honey It's been hard to sleep at night I know when we make love. Everything we saw will be washed away.

Now he wave his hand, and his clothes was on the floor. Thomas pulled the covers back and his mouth went for her breast. Eleanor felt her heat crying to be with him. He was between her legs his heat moving over her lips. "I was thinking of ye. Thomas, I want to have ye again." He had found she was ready for him. His wife was so wet, he slipped inside her. His lips laid kisses over her face and neck.

As he drove her higher until she came. "Thomas, I can feel ye need more of me. It's as if ye like to go deeper inside me. My love take what ye need from me. I know ye need this."

He had gotten up and pulled her to the floor. He placed her on her knees and hands. "Honey this way I can go deep inside ye. Ye are right about this, I just don't want to hurt ye doing this. I can go deeper in ye. Thomas pushed her arm down and drove them over the edge. He pulled her to him. "My love how do ye feel now." Thomas moved his hand over her body. "Ye feel so good to me. How did ye know I need ye in that way."

The two of them went and cleaned up. "Thomas what we had seen I knew it had made ye angry, as if ye were going to kill those men. Ye needed to pour out the tension into something beautiful. What better way to do that is to make love to me? I need it also all I could do was cry. I have done enough of that."

The two of them went quiet. There was someone coming up the stairs. Quickly they put clothes on. "Eleanor is Thomas with ye."

They both knew what they wanted to know. "Aye, we will be right down. Thomas has something for his father."

It was time to give his father the vest. William took Catherin to his home. After they made love, he would give his father the vest.

Honey make sure ye ware the sweater, don't forget to use the spell to keep out evil.

Thomas had touched her face. "I didn't even tell ye that I needed ye. Ye always know what I need before I do. Aye… That I did. Honey it cut deep into my soul. To see what they tried to do to them. Ye were right I wanted to kill those men. I wish we could just go to sleep together right now. I haven't had much sleep."

*　　*　　*

Thomas pulled Eleanor to him. "I'm glad I had court ye before I left the Highlands. From that day on your body always calls to me. Honey I'm glad that ye are mine." He kissed her and took her hand. With the vest in hand, they went downstairs. Franceam stood up tears was running down her cheeks. "So ye were able to get those vests with the petals on them."

Thomas pulled his mother into him. "Aye, we even seen the King and Queen of the Fairies. Marcos was trying to kill all the roses as I thought. Here is petals to put on your weapons, Eleanor knows how to do it. In four day's ye must be riding toward us. If all goes well, we can trap them between us. Just like they did to our brothers."

He didn't have time to tell all that he knew. He had also showed the deerskin to them. Then he took out his dirk and the vest he had for his father. Thomas told his father to try to put a hole into it. Daniel took the map and tried to do just that. "Son, does the vest have the rose petals on it also?"

Thomas handed his father his vest. "Go ahead and see what happens. Ye see dad what they had done to are brothers. They took nine men to fight in three waves at a time. This time there will be six men to come after us. Dad we need ye and Theseus. If Eleanor is coming with ye. I like for Duncan's brothers to be with her. I have a plan to get the body's home. There has been many men trying to get our brothers. Tomorrow we will get the first wagon ready to go and get them.

Thomas rub his eyes. "I know I need sleep. Dad, do ye carry momma's hair with ye."

Daniel got up and went after the piece of hair he carries everywhere with him. "I like for ye to put these rose petals on her hair. This will help to keep momma safe."

Franceam was watching her son. She knew Daniel's dream was to the point of anger. When he woke up, he would have killed that man if he were in the room. She had to see what happen for herself. "Thomas, ye know I need to see what happen to my son and nephew."

Eleanor looked at Thomas. "My love I saw some of it, I need to be strong and see it all this time.

Thomas down his Scotch. Then he poured more Scotch in his glass. He looked at his father for some help. He heard his father's voice. "Son if ye can do it. At least she will see Michael holding his brother."

Then Thomas picked up his chair and brought it over to the fireplace. His father did the same. "Honey will ye come here and sit on my lap?" Eleanor nodded her head and went over to her husband. His father and mother did the same. Then he took out two stems to give one to each woman. Then he said. "Think of what ye want to see then throw the stem into the fire." Thomas and his father had on their vest. When the women threw the stem into the fire. Both men saw what the women saw. Tears rolled down the women's cheeks. The men held onto their loved ones. Thomas knew both women if they had something in their hand, they would have ended that man's life. When the vision was over Eleanor turn into his arms. Tears flowed down his back.

Thomas saw his mother's hand straight out. Now his mother's lips were moving. She had put a curse on Rodney. "Michael is alive. At least Ronald wasn't alone when he died. Daniel ye must go and help our son. These men love to kill. Only the strongest can take them down. Ye must all come back to us. Thomas can William go to your sister?"

He was rubbing Eleanor's back. She had held onto him for dear life. Her head was on his shoulder. "William and Catherine is there with his father and mother. Dad, do ye remember this man in black. Uncle said that there was a man back in your time."

Daniel had picked up his chair. As both women went after their drinks. "There was one. I saw that man dress all in black. He was built the same way in the fire."

Eleanor had drunk the rest of her drink. "Daniel was there anything about women coming up missing. Then later she came back dead with a baby on her."

Daniel took some of his drink then said. "Duke Marcos Huascaran was thought to be the man in black. About women coming up missing I don't believe there was. One thing I do remember. Each time his wife had a child. If it was a girl, the child was found dead. I believe after his wife died in childbirth. He remarried number two wife also gave him nothing but girls."

Thomas was having a hard time staying awake. He went over to his father and mother. "Dad I will see ye in three days' time. Mamma I will see ye after this is all done. I will make sure dad will let ye know were all right. "We will also have a priest with us. He kept are brothers safe, he like to start a church in the Highlands. Father Sinclair, uncle, and Briana will be in the first wagon. They will have the bodies of our brothers. I was told that the magic roses will keep my brothers safe. This part that Meghalaya told us. After Eleanor finds the one rose bush, I will take the other two to my land. She had told us also many years from now. These two rose bushes will become three again. Those three will go to the new world. I will place our brothers into the bottom of the wagon. At each of their feet one rose bush will be there. The tablet will also be with them.

"We will place Briana's things on top. When those men ask about the wagon. Father can say there is no bodies under this wagon. He will not know about what we are up to. The three of us will have the coffins with us. I will call to Eleanor to tell her when the first wagon leaves. Ye and Theseus must be on the other side of Lock Ness. Honey I want ye at the hunting cabin. Please do this for me. Ye can make sure that dad has things to treat cuts and other things. Will ye do this for me."

Eleanor had tears in her eyes. "I will do as my husband says. I will clean the cabin and get food ready for ye all. Honey, please come back to me alive."

Thomas kissed his mother and hug them both. He took Eleanor's hand and went up the stairs to their room. With the door close he lay down with his wife. Eleanor held onto Thomas, she watched him sleep. When she knew he was asleep she kissed him goodbye? Then she heard Uncle Donald's voice. She looked up and saw her brother and Catherine. The women were in the barn with their husband. They heard someone was coming up the ladder. Then Donald saw the women with their sweaters on. "Uncle Donald Thomas father knows about everything." Donald looked at Catherine. She nodded her head yes. The trap is in motion Donald thought. The women gave their husband one last kiss to wake them. When their eyes opened the women was gone.

*   *   *

Eleanor had to go to Grana's place. She knew that she would need more of that ointment to help with the heeling. She had gotten dress and made shore she had her sweater on. Thomas was very clear that trouble was near town. Then she got a vision of the face of Albert and those evil eyes of his. With her sweater on this time the eyes changed. There was fear in them, she could hear a weak voice pleading for help. Eleanor saw a man on the ground fighting with a locket. She could see it was going into his chest. Why is this being shown to her now. What if it's the next part of what is to come.

Then she saw a young woman with the man in black on top of her. Eleanor saw the forest that she must ride through to get to town. Soon the sun would be coming up.

Outside Eleanor saw the ranch hand that helps the MacGregor's. He had seen her coming down the hill. The horse she been using was with him. Once she got there her horse would be ready for her. She wonder if she was to meet up with that man in black. Would she be able to help that woman? Time will tell. Mick helped her on her horse. Once she was on Lady, she thank him for his help. Then she rode through the darkness. It took her down the path where she would live with Thomas. She kept riding pass her home. About three miles down the path she came to Michael's home. It led to a hill where she could see everything. Eleanor had reached the top of the hill when the sun was coming up. She remembered what Thomas told her. This was the first time she was able to sit and enjoy the wonder of the sunrising. It was as Thomas said the sun looked to be chasing the darkness back. On top of the hill, she could see for miles. Eleanor was able to see where the darkness could hide anything evil. There was so many places they could hide in the blackest spots of the night. Thomas was right about the wonder of the time between night and day. She hoped to be able to sit with her man to enjoy the bright colors of the sky. As they watch the sunrising and enjoy the twilight together. The beauty of night and day was a wonder. She closed her eyes and call to her man. "Honey I have my sweater on. I love ye. I'm enjoying the time of twilight."

Thomas had stopped what he was doing. "Be careful from here out. Call to me if ye need me. I love ye too." He looked up at William and spoke. "It started she is on her way to town. William I'm afraid for her."

He looked up at his best friend. He understood what he was going through. Eleanor was his wife they have just started their lives together. "Thomas there is nothing ye can do right now. We need this done now. All I can say be ready to help her when she needs ye."

Eleanor sat just enjoying the battle of night and day. There was rich reds, yellows and orange as the sun came up. The darkness still fought to control the earth. Twilight will come at night and in the morning. Does good and evil do the same? Is this what her husband meant? Eleanor stayed where she was, until there were enough light for her to see by. While she rode, she saw small animals looking for shelter. She knew that other animals hunt the smaller animals during daylight. This was her first-time riding at twilight. She could see the mountain tops. Higher up there was still snow. The days were getting warmer, and the trees were budding. Beautiful flowers was pushing up through the patch of snow. Spring was slowly coming to the land. Soon the snow would linger no more. Until then the roads she traveled would still have mud and ice on them. It was a good thing Lady enjoy going through the snow or mud. She didn't even slow down when she hit a little bit of ice, she was also strong footed. After that time when she had jumped over that river. Thomas gave her Lady she was like Sunshine to ride. He knew she was a strong horse like his.

Eleanor headed down the hill. The path brought her closer to the forest. Beyond the forest lay the town where Grana lived. While she rode something was making her uneasy. The closer she got to the forest the stronger the feelings became. Then it hit her square in the chest knocking her breath out. The impact seem to slither through her body. It left her feeling cold right down to her bones.

Eleanor pulled her sweater around her, it gave her the warmth she needed. She wasn't the type of person afraid of things. The last time she felt this. She was at the party where her cousin had died. All this time she wonder if that Englishman had something to do with it. She had felt the evil within that man. This time what she felt is even stronger them before. Her vision had shown her evil has his pray with him. That's why it was much stronger. The fear she was feeling was coming from the woman he has. She wondered if he could since her coming. No, he wouldn't because he has her.

Eleanor knew that her husband would feel the fear she might have. She thought she must be strong for him. With the locket in hand, she felt the presence of her man. There was a calming feeling that move over her body. Thomas had put rose petals on her locket. In her mind's eye, she saw the man in black from her vision. This man loved to have power over women. Now she could see the face of his victim. He had something over her mouth. She knew this woman, by her reddish hair and bluest gray eyes she was the girlfriend of Damian.

I can't let this man have Rosemary. Damian has gone through enough he had lost his twin. Now if this man takes her, he will lose his love. Eleanor had to do something. This man had Rosemary's hands over her head. The man in black was having fun playing with her breast. My Lord he is doing things that my husband has done to me. No, she thought. The man in black is making love making dirty under his hands. I must do something right now. Eleanor felt if she didn't help Rosemary. She will end up like her cousin. How many women has he killed because they didn't give him a son? Don't he know the man picks the sex of the child.

What she had seen in the fire. The man in black thought his men could manage Thomas's group. What he didn't know is her husband had seen what he had done to his brothers. With the magic roses he will win the battle. Because their fathers will even the score. Now it's my time to fight this battle. Damian will have his love back. A thought came to Eleanor, did the man in black follow them here to the Highlands? I can't think about that now.

Eleanor had to take a deep breath, then she motion her horse to continue. The path she was on went deeper into the forest. There was a group of trees where she got off Lady. She walked softly through the trees trying not to make a sound. In front of her was a good-sized limb.

Eleanor knew she would need a weapon to fight with. Up a head she heard movement, she only saw was just a black spot. Slowly her eyes a adjust, now she saw the shape of a man. Around him was bits of snow. She moved in closer and saw an outline of four legs. He was on top of her his black cape hid them. Then she heard Rosemary scream. The man in black must have taken off her gag. He had a scarf over her mouth quickly he put it back.

Eleanor remember that voice from the party was an Englishman. The way he said young lass. When he came toward her his eyes were evil. That night she had dreamt of him, the next day another woman came up missing. A cold wind blew through the forest when he said. "My sweet don't worry young lass. You will come to enjoy my touch. The other women love the way I made love to them. I know all the ways to give you pleasure. All that I want from you is a son. After he is born, I will let you go. If you give me a girl, you will die. There-there don't worry the baby will be just fine. I will send you and the child back to your parents. Now we are going to have some fun. It's too bad you screamed. I would have kissed you. But at last, all I want right now is to see you climax. Will see how long it will take to get you ready for me. I don't want to hurt you, but if you keep pushing me I will. You will carry my child one way or another."

Eleanor thought she was going to be sick. Why did he have to make love making dirty? She could see Rosemary trying to fight his touch. There was enough noise to cover any sound Eleanor made. It had helped her to get in closer to them. He didn't notice her until it was too late. With all her strength she brought the limb down on his head. Quickly she work to push him off Rosemary. Eleanor went for the knife in her boot. It was good that Thomas had given her this knife. With the rope cut from Rosemary's wrists. The two of them turn to run. Just as Eleanor cleared his foot, she felt a hand grabbed her ankle.

Eleanor went down hard, her knife had drop from her hand. Quickly she grab the knife and ran it over his hand, she heard him scream in pain.

Rosemary went for the limb and hit him over the head. She used all the anger she had felt and hit him again. The two women ran for their life's, neither woman wanted to carry his child. Eleanor and Rosemary got on to Lady.

They had to make it to the bridge before he could get to them. Rosemary could feel him getting closer. She did a quick check to see how close he was to them. Eleanor felt her give Lady a kick in her side. Then she said. "Rosemary is he that close?" She looked for herself and found he was closing in too fast. Rosemary's fear was rubbing off on to her. In her mind she call to her man. "Thomas I'm sorry honey. I couldn't let the man in black have Rosemary. Where riding as fast as we can. The bridge is too far away from us. I would jump the river but it's too wide for us to make it. The town is too far for anyone to see us. Honey I need ye. Is there anything ye can do? Please help us."

*　*　*

Thomas and William was finishing the wagon inside the barn. The last part that needed their attention was the cover. This was the part that went over their brothers. They had to reed build the bottom of the wagon. Now it's wide enough to lay three men across. Briana had enough things to fill the hole wagon. She didn't have to leave anything behind.

The two men were talking about their barns. Thomas had said now we have just our homes to build. Both of our wife's paid to have the logs cut. Our fathers had enjoyed building the barns for us. He was smiling as he nail the last bord on to the wagon.

The vision hit him so hard that he drop the hammer. Thomas felt his wife's fear. What he had saw scared him. He had to push his fear away to be able to see the danger. In his mind's eye he saw the man in black. He was in the Highlands and going after his wife. Eleanor was riding hard to get away from him. Then he saw Rosemary behind Eleanor. Thomas's mind was racing, he had to focus to try to understand what he saw. The hammer he was holding drop from his hand. Now he held Eleanor's hair. He could hear the plead for help from his wife.

William went over quickly to his side. Thomas looked at his friend and spoke. "Eleanor and Rosemary is in trouble. The man in black is in the Highlands. He is closing in on them. We must stop him or make him turn around."

The End of this book

EPILOGUE

It looks grim for the two women. Will Thomas and William make it there in time. Will Marcos stand and fight or would he turn and run away. Fine out what happen to Eleanor and Rosemary. Will the two young men make it back to finish the wagon.

See if Thomas, William and Duncan be able to get the bodies of their brothers.

Can Briana and Father Sinclair be able to cross Loch Ness. See if Donald must fight Marcos's men, to let the first wagon cross into the Highlands.

Eleanor was to go with their fathers to the hunting cabin. Will she make it or did Marcos change it. Will their fathers be in time to catch the last ferry, to be able to fight with their son's.

What did Ronald mean when he said he will fight Marcos in the heavens.

DICTIONARY: GAELIC WORDS

Aye: -   a Scottish or northeastern English way of saying 'yes.' Scottish and Geordie people mostly say "Aye."

Biodag: -   Dirk, a knife, a dagger a Highland Weapons.

Dee: -   a Scot word for die.

Dirk: -   "Knife." The word Dirk is a Scottish word for a long dagger; sometimes a cut-down sword blade mounted on a dagger hilt, rather than a knife blade.

Ye: is for the word you.

History

Clan: Popular history has painted this to mean that every member of a clan was related to its chief of the clan. Only the higher echelons of the clan were related to the chief and his immediate family. The majority were simply ordinary men not necessarily related to the chief. Who looked to him as their leader and most importantly their father?

"Brosnachadh Bhruis:" Is a patriotic song of Scotland written in the Scots language.

Biodag or Dirk; was a long stabbing knife. Ideal for close-quarter fighting. After the 1745 uprising, many broadswords were cut down and made into dirks.

Broadsword: From the mid-16th century, basket hilt swords were in common use in Scotland. The idea of a basket to protect the hand first came to England and then Scotland from Scandinavian and German sword makers. By the mid-17th century, ribbon baskets were made in large quantities and by the turn of the 18th century, the Highland basket was reaching its full pattern.
Scottish slang for "do not." "Say sorry, you do nothing wrong.
Frog: When worn, the dirk (knife) normally hangs by a leather strap known as a "frog" from a dirk belt, which is a wide leather belt having a large, usually ornate, buckle that is worn around the waist with a kilt.
Sporran: A pouch of skin with the hair or fur on that is worn in front of the kilt.

The word "Aye" was also used in the navy, the response would be "Aye, Sir."